Zachary moved toward her, a wicked light in his eyes. Melanie backed away. All at once, he tackled her in the snow.

He laughed, stretching out over her. "Are you cold?"

"No—just let me up!" The weight of his body was doing strange things to Melanie's stomach.

"You know the price that has to be paid," he warned.

"All right, kiss me then and get it over with."

"Get it over with?" Zachary laughed. "Hmmm, wasn't it you I kissed last night? Wasn't it you who said it was very nice?"

"I didn't want to hurt your feelings." Melanie sniffed.

Zachary gazed down at her seductively. "We could go inside and find *lots* of ways for you to not hurt my feelings . . ."

DARK EYES

COLLEEN CORBET

AVON BOOKS ◆ NEW YORK

**To Adele Leone for believing.
And to Ellen Edwards for all your hard work.**

Thank you both.

DARK EYES is an original publication of Avon Books. This work has never before appeared in book form. This work is a novel. Any similarity to actual persons or events is purely coincidental.

AVON BOOKS
A division of
The Hearst Corporation
1350 Avenue of the Americas
New York, New York 10019

Copyright © 1995 by Patricia Pellicane
Published by arrangement with the author
Library of Congress Catalog Card Number: 94-96288
ISBN: 0-380-78026-7

First Avon Books Printing: April 1995

AVON TRADEMARK REG. U.S. PAT. OFF. AND IN OTHER COUNTRIES, MARCA REGISTRADA, HECHO EN U.S.A.

Printed in the U.S.A.

RA   10   9   8   7   6   5   4   3   2   1

Prologue

June, 1721
Virginia, the Colonies

"Help me, sir. Please," came the whispered voice of a child, crouched behind one of the many low crates that cluttered the docks and their alleyways. The words brought Zachary Pitt's footsteps to a wary halt.

He knew his way around ships and their ports of call. He knew waterfronts especially well, having as a boy in England prowled them himself. The youngest of the lot, it was his job to spot quick and easy marks. It wasn't beyond the realm of possibility that some street tough was now hoping to lure his remaining pound or so from his purse by using this child in much the same fashion that Zachary had once been used.

His eyes narrowed as he studied the vague outline of the small huddled form, half hidden in shadows, even as his gaze moved to the next crate and the next, wondering if behind them, other thieves were prepared to pounce. Zachary took a step back. "Show yourself," he ordered.

Melanie Townsend knew she had made a mistake. The man's voice held not a shred of pity or compassion. She could expect no help from this quarter.

She tried to make herself smaller. If she remained quiet, perhaps he would move on and forget the soft cry that had interrupted his walk. After he was gone, she might venture from her hiding place and find an unlocked door, a warm vestibule, an empty building. Someplace dry. A place that would protect her from the elements until morning fully arrived.

She shivered from the chilling wind and her wet clothes. Three hours ago she had been warm and dry. Melanie clamped her teeth together lest they chatter and the sound give away her position.

She'd had time to reconsider her actions. She should have waited of course. She and the rest of those poor, wretched souls. She would have been brought to the auction block on the morrow. She'd heard the guard say as much. Once there, she could have summoned the magistrate and insisted he rectify her untenable situation.

Melanie sighed as she mentally relived this night. Powers, her guard, had drunk himself into oblivion, as he had most every night since the ship had sailed from England. And Melanie had been unable to resist the simple temptation to relieve him of his keys. She could swim better than most, so to jump into the harbor had been no great feat. It was only after she climbed to the docks that she realized her mistake. It was night and she was soaking wet, in a strange land, without a shilling to her name and no idea where to find help. Lord, would there ever come a day when she'd think before acting?

The quiet stillness of predawn hours followed the man's command. He took another step back, "Show yourself or I'll call the constable," he said.

Yes, Melanie thought. A constable would know

what to do, where to bring her, how to right this terrible wrong. "Oh please, sir, I'd be so grateful if you would," she said.

Zachary Pitt frowned as a small, feminine figure emerged from behind the crate. His first impression had been wrong, he realized. This was no child, but a woman with curves as lush as any he'd ever seen. The fact that her dress was soaking wet and clinging to a very rounded form made that fact obvious. What was she doing here?

There could be only one answer. The woman was a prostitute looking for another customer before this night's end. He didn't know why she was wet, and he cared even less. What he did wonder was why one of her kind seemed delighted at the thought of contact with the law.

Zachary frowned again as she came more fully into the pre-morning light. If the woman was looking to make her quota tonight, she might have done a better job of seeing to her personal hygiene. Despite the lushness of her form, and the natural beauty of her face, Zachary had rarely seen a woman less likely to tempt a man to sin. Her hair was long, tangled, and blacker than pitch, with knots that suggested she'd gone days, perhaps longer, without seeing a brush. Her tresses lay wet and heavy against her head, thickly matted around her face and shoulders.

Her dress was filthy and torn from neck to breast, exposing a generous glimpse of white skin at her throat and chest and an undergarment as grimy as any he'd ever seen. Her features were good, better than good, in fact. Her face, washed clean, likely would be as clear as her dark eyes, but Zachary knew the eyes of a woman in her profession wouldn't stay clear for long. Like most of her kind, this one was destined to a bad end. In a few years she'd have the pox, and that beautiful skin and those lustrous black eyes would be naught but a memory.

"What do you want?" A foolish question to be sure, Zachary reasoned. He knew what this woman wanted, he just wasn't in the market for her services. He had a wife. Granted it stretched the imagination to call Margaret a wife. Still, the vows had been said and even if she were less than the most loving sort, the vows would hold him nonetheless.

Her nagging drove him from the house more often than not, especially since she'd gotten with child, a condition that caused her unhappiness in the extreme. Still, he hadn't as yet thought to turn to another. Perhaps he would if after the baby's arrival, things got no better between them, but surely he wouldn't seek out this one.

Zachary couldn't deny the fleeting thought that he might relieve himself of months of pent-up needs in a quick, impersonal taking right here. He couldn't be blamed after all, especially since his wife had refused him his own bed for nigh on seven months . . .

Melanie Townsend stood there trembling. Her arms wrapped around her small form, hugging her body against yet another chill. She studied the tall, dark man with the forbidden expression for a long time. He was dressed in high black boots, dark brown trousers, and a matching vest. His white shirt stood in sharp contrast to his deeply tanned skin. A dark tricorne hat sat upon his head. Beneath it, his hair was equally black, pulled back and tied neatly at the nape of his neck. Melanie thought he looked a decent sort, a merchant perhaps. She could only pray that he would listen.

The man obviously expected an answer to his question, and Melanie wondered how to begin her improbable tale. She shook her head. It was too complicated, especially if she included Waverly in her story. No, what she'd been through didn't matter right now. All this man must know was her desperate need for help. "If you could see your way clear to helping me, sir, I would be ever so grateful."

Zachary frowned. She didn't sound like a waterfront whore. She didn't act like one either, for he'd known them to be far more brazen. Oddly enough, she sounded like a lady of some means and education. He grinned at the thought, for no doubt she had picked up that cultured accent from her more gentlemanly clients. His blue eyes grew cold with derision. "I think not, mistress. I have a wife awaiting my return."

Melanie frowned at his odd reply. What did his waiting wife have to do with anything? She watched with some surprise as he turned from her, dismissing her as if she were but the lowest and most unimportant of creatures. "Wait! Please, you haven't heard . . ."

Zachary turned back, annoyed that she would persist, despite his disinterest. "I told you, I don't want your services."

"Services? What services?" Melanie didn't understand. Was it possible that although people in the colonies spoke the King's English, there were terms that only a native could understand?

Zachary was tired and when he grew tired, he tended to lose his patience. "Mistress"—he sighed the word, as if clinging to the last of his tolerance—"I think we both know what you want, and I'm telling you for the last time I'm not interested."

Melanie blinked in confusion at his obvious anger. She couldn't fathom what this man was about. She hardly had the patience, or the desire, to decipher the man's gibberish. But she tried again. "I'm asking for help, sir. Are you so dim-witted as to—"

"Dim-witted, am I?" His laughter was cruel. "Have you found it profitable to insult potential customers?"

She took a half-step back. "Excuse me?" Could it be she had made a serious error in bringing herself to this man's attention? Could he be more than simply dim-witted? Could he be insane?

"I haven't time for this, mistress," he insisted. "Kindly find yourself another."

Melanie might have done just that, had there been another. It took only the morning's silence and a quick glance to know the docks, buildings, and alleyways were empty.

Zachary watched her closely. He wondered what she'd say next. No doubt a suitable lie meant to entice him to do her bidding. But she was wasting her time.

"Let me start at the beginning," she pleaded.

Zachary grinned. She was about to tell him her story. Apparently he was to take pity on her and oblige by passing the last of his coin to her. He shook his head. "Mistress, I—"

"I am the Duchess of Elderbury."

Zachary's mouth split into a grin and then, despite his growing annoyance, he laughed aloud. He had expected a story, but he hadn't imagined she'd go so far. Still, despite her outrageous claim, he couldn't deny she intrigued him—and not only because of her beauty. There was something about her, a gentle quality oddly mixed with haughtiness that was not usually found among her kind. *Could it be . . . ?* He was thinking nonsense. She was a prostitute all right.

The woman was bold, he had to admit. Bold and more, if one took into account the tempting lushness of her form. Zachary felt his manhood's unwanted response and whispered a low curse. Damn, his body plainly ached for a woman, but he didn't want her kind.

"Duchess," he said with a dismissing nod, his mouth tight. "It's been a pleasure, I'm sure."

Melanie's eyes grew wide as she watched the man turn from her again, her hope growing dimmer with his every step. He couldn't simply walk away. What kind of a man would leave a woman in such urgent need? He was her only chance, perhaps her *last* chance. She walked toward him, and her desperation getting the better of her common sense, she suddenly raged, "Bloody ignorant beast! Witless oaf! Illiterate colonist! Do you realize what you're giving up? Can you not understand that I could make you rich?"

Furious, Zachary spun around, surprised to see that her hands were raised as if to strike him. He shoved her back, uncaring that her head hit the wall none too gently, and pinned her small frame between his body and the brick building. His lips were thin with anger as he grated out in contempt, "A duchess, is it? Well then, Duchess, you should have no problem understanding this." He gave her a little shake, as if to make sure he had her complete attention, but her dark eyes were already huge with anger and misgiving. "If you think to strike me, I'll knock you senseless. And I don't care if you're the bloody Queen of England."

Melanie took a deep breath. It wasn't beneath her to admit to a wrongdoing. But it went against the grain to do so now. This imbecile had the means but refused to help a fellow human being. She hated him and if her hands were free, she'd gladly hit him.

She raised her chin and returned with equal harshness, "I need your help."

"And you mean to beat it out of me?" Zachary laughed as he looked at her in a new light. In truth she was a spunky little thing. A bit free with her hands, perhaps, but he had to admire her spirit. Even now, trapped between his body and the wall at her back, and him the obvious stronger of the two, she showed not a glimmer of fear.

Her body was soft against his. Softer than he had dared to imagine. Zachary had no doubt that he could find pleasure here. Her body could make him forget his misery. Damn, it had been months since he'd last touched softness, either in body or soul.

The truth was, it wouldn't matter if he took this one. Margaret wouldn't care, even if he threw the truth of it in her face. Margaret didn't love him. No doubt she hadn't loved him from the first. So what in hell was the sense of denying himself a few minutes of pleasure?

He moved his hips forward, telling her that he had reconsidered her offer. His voice lowered to a teasing murmur. The woman had some obvious needs. All right. If it meant that much to her, he could comply. "I apologize, mistress. I wasn't aware you were in so great a need."

Melanie narrowed her gaze and watched him for a long moment, wondering whether to believe him. It suddenly occurred to her that she had little choice in the matter. The man had said he was sorry. She'd best leave it at that. "Your apology is accepted."

He grinned. "A question, mistress?"

"Sir?" she asked, tipping her head to one side.

"Does a duchess have the same equipment as most?"

"Excuse me?" What in the world was he talking about?

"Name your price."

Name your price? What did that mean? Was he perhaps in his own confusing way telling her that he'd be willing to help her after all, but for a price? Melanie thought that must be the case. "If you help me get back home, my father will give you a thousand pounds."

Zachary grinned in surprise at her answer, for it wasn't even close to what he had expected. "A thousand pounds, is it?" He chuckled softly, knowing she spoke in riddles. "Your father is a generous man."

Melanie blinked at the beautiful sight of his smile and wondered how she'd noticed such a thing. It wasn't like her to notice men. And then she frowned as she realized his tone of voice. Was that ridicule she heard? Surely not, and yet she couldn't put aside the unsettling feeling that he was making fun of her. "Will you do it?"

"Well now . . ." His voice dropped to a lower, even more husky tone, sending chills down Melanie's spine. "A thousand pounds sounds overly generous to me."

"Does it?" She swallowed, oddly breathless. Was she coming down with an ague? "Do you mean you'd do it for less?"

"Much less."

Melanie realized his breath smelled clean, and somehow inviting. She cleared her throat. "Sir, do you think we could continue this conversation while standing a bit further apart?"

Zachary laughed softly at her teasing and released her hands. Ah, if she were dressed properly, bathed and perfumed like the best of her kind, she would be absolutely irresistible. Her features were perfect. A small nose, wide mouth, full lips, and large dark eyes. The eyes gave him pause, for they seemed fathomless and pure. He shook aside the ridiculous notion. She had made a serious mistake in choosing her profession. A woman who looked this good, even without a farthing to her name, could have married well. Still, it was hardly his concern. And if she saw the need to play out her act of innocence, he supposed he could go along with it. "Of course. Do you think we're standing too close?"

Melanie frowned. He said the right words, yet continued to lean against her. Oddly enough, she somehow knew he posed no threat to her person. She couldn't have said why.

She bit her bottom lip, trying to think of a way to extract herself from his hold when he suddenly lowered his head and kissed her on the mouth. She was amazed. Shocked. What in the world was he doing? She pushed against his chest, but he didn't move away. His hips brushed against hers, pinning her more tightly to the wall. "What do you think you're doing?" she demanded, the instant he lifted his mouth from hers.

"I was thinking you should get out of these wet things. You're likely to catch your death."

"You were kissing me."

"Was I? You must be mistaken. I couldn't have kissed you. I don't even know your name."

"My name is Melanie and you most certainly did kiss me."

"The truth is, Melanie, I never kiss a lady without her permission, so you must be mistaken."

"Step away from me."

"Now?"

"Right now."

Apparently 'right now' did not mean the same thing in the colonies as it did at home, for the man stayed where he was. Melanie frowned, wondering why everything about this man caused her confusion.

"Why are you wet?" he asked.

"I jumped ship. Move."

"Where are we going? Do you have a room?"

"Have a room?" she repeated with yet another frown. "Did I not just tell you I jumped ship?"

Zachary grinned again. "So you did. I was just wondering what that means. Is it a new term?"

"I don't think so. Have you never heard it before?"

Zachary figured this conversation was getting them nowhere. Not having had the experience of most men, he didn't understand her innuendos and sly words. Besides, he'd had enough of talking. She had a sweet mouth, and he thought to taste it again.

After a few seconds of pleasurable kissing, the doxy wrenched herself from his arms and said, "Deny you kissed me that time. Go ahead and deny it."

She sounded breathless, but just a little annoyed, and Zachary wasn't sure why. "Is that what you want me to do?"

"Is something wrong with you?" she demanded, her voice rising.

"I don't think so."

"But you're not sure?"

"Fact is, Duchess, you have me a little confused. I don't understand exactly what you want."

"Firstly, sir, I want you to step away from me, right now." Of all the bloody bad luck. She'd escaped her prison aboard ship only to encounter an imbecile. Obviously this man was not about to help her.

"Why?"

Melanie stiffened at the sound of two men approaching. "She's got to be here somewhere," one of them said.

"She couldn't have gotten this far," said another. "Probably drowned, she did."

It took only a second for Melanie to realize the

men were looking for her, and that she was about to be recaptured. It took less than another second to realize the only way to avoid detection was to hide in her captor's arms. Her hands moved quickly around Zachary's neck and she pulled herself closer than ever, even as her mouth sought the warmth of his.

The gray morning light illuminated a man and woman in a heated embrace. Melanie squeezed her eyes closed, just as she had as a child, pretending if she could not see, she could not be seen. Her body grew stiff with fear as she prayed.

"Just a doxy," one of the men mumbled as they moved on to the next alley.

Zachary parted his lips and brushed his tongue over her mouth. Apparently she had given up her play at last and was content to get on with the business at hand. Considering the soft curves pressed against him, he wasn't the least bit sorry.

His hands were at her breasts, pulling aside the fabric that hid them from his touch, when she demanded, "What do you think you're doing?"

"What?" he returned a bit groggily, having succumbed to the promise of her eager kiss.

"Take your hands off me this instant!"

"What are you lookin' to do? Drive up the price?" Wasn't it just like a woman to pretend to give over all and then at the last second hold out for more. Apparently street whores were no different than their supposedly more genteel sisters.

"We've already settled on a price. Now do as I say."

"A thousand pounds?" His tone all astonishment. "Are you insane? There's not a woman in the world worth that much."

"I told you . . ." Melanie's eyes widened in obvious fear. "Oh my God, they're coming back," she said as she lunged into his arms again and proceeded to kiss him with all the fervor of a woman in the depths of passion.

A second later Melanie was torn from Zachary's arms. The evil John Powers laughed at her look of shock. "Come on, Duchess, that's a good girl."

"Don't let them take me!" she implored.

"What the bloody hell is going on?" Zachary shouted.

Powers laughed. "Sorry, mate, but if you be wantin' a go at this one, she'll be on the auction block in the morning."

"Please," Melanie called as she was dragged back. "Get word to my father. Tell him where I am."

"No need to pay her any mind. She's been saying that since we left London."

"Mr. Stone," she almost screeched as she was dragged to the end of the alley. "Mr. Harry Stone of Wedgewood House, London. Please!"

Zachary could hear her calling out long after she disappeared from sight. He didn't want to believe it. He couldn't believe it. She wasn't a duchess. It wasn't possible. And yet there was something about her that left him doubting his own common sense. Could it be that she was exactly whom she claimed? Had he done the woman a grave injustice?

Zachary thought the matter over for another minute and then shrugged aside his doubts. He had to get home. Margaret was close to her time. Even now she might need him. The truth was, if the impossible were true and the woman was indeed a duchess, all would be found out soon enough.

Still, it was another three hours before he left the city.

Chapter 1

August, 1721

A boy lay dead at her hands and Melanie wondered if the horror of what she'd done would linger in her memory forever.

She walked on, pushing aside thick branches, forcing one foot and then another to carry her as far from the murder scene as possible. In a daze, she felt her emotions roil—euphoria because she was free at last; fear of the unknown that lay beyond every hill and turn of the path; eerie shadows and strange sounds; being alone, lost in an endless forest.

Would they find her, despite her efforts? Did they hang women in the colonies?

There were moments when Melanie wondered if she truly cared. It was so hard to concentrate, so hard to worry about what she'd done when fever raged inside her. She was ill, more ill than she could remember. There wasn't a part of her that didn't hurt. Her head ached, and chills sent her body into uncontrollable tremors that left her exhausted.

She'd lost count of the days. It didn't matter. She had to keep moving, as far from Joshua's dead body as possible.

Half delirious, she walked past two Indian braves.

14

Oddly enough, she saw them long before they noticed her. They were staring to her right, perhaps watching an animal, when one of the men turned at the sound of a broken twig. Both stared as if amazed as she merely glanced in their direction and without a shred of fear, or a word spoken between them, walked on by.

Melanie wasn't sure if they were friendly or not. She thought to ask for help but decided the wisest course of action was to resist the temptation. Later she regretted that decision.

What could they do to her, after all? What could they have done that Waverly, her husband back in England, hadn't done; that Blanche Moody, the woman who had bought her indentured servitude, hadn't done; that Joshua, Mrs. Moody's 16-year-old son, hadn't tried? What further harm could they have inflicted that the raw elements had not inflicted? She stumbled forward, tripping over rocks and the uneven ground, her exhausted body trembling with fever, coughs, hunger, and most of all thirst.

She should have asked for help. Anything would have been better than this fear, this loneliness, this helplessness.

She took one step and then another. She couldn't stop, couldn't allow herself even a moment to rest. If she stopped, if she dared to lie down, she might never get up again.

At least she had thought to take Joshua's boots. The horse had gone lame three days into her journey, and she had been forced to leave it behind and walk. But every step became untold agony as the loosely fitted leather rubbed again and again over blisters that had finally broken and then begun to bleed.

Twice she'd tried to walk without the boots and twice sharp rocks had cut into the soles of her feet.

Wearing the boots was torture, but not wearing them was worse.

Melanie's stomach rumbled. She tried to ignore it, tried not to think of food. Three days back she'd stolen an apple pie left cooling on the window ledge of a crude farmhouse. She'd tried to eat it slowly, but it had lasted only two days. Since then she'd found nothing and knew it might be days before she ate again.

The sky was growing dark. Melanie frowned at the gray clouds that dipped menacingly close to the earth. Another storm was coming. She sighed. Fool that she was, she'd left the saddle blanket with the disabled horse. She had nothing but Joshua's jacket to help ward off the elements and if the distant thunder meant a storm like the last one, the jacket wouldn't be of use for long.

A fat raindrop slapped against her burning cheek, and Melanie quickly searched out the thickest limb she could find and sat beneath it. The limb, though heavy with leaves, offered scant protection.

That night was the most miserable of her life. Melanie sat huddled in a tight ball, trying to protect herself from the downpour. Amid her shivers and soft moans came tears of self-pity. She would die here, she knew.

Her father back in England must have known of her kidnapping mere hours after she'd been taken. He must have worried, but eventually he'd have believed that she was dead, never imagining she'd been brought by ship to the colonies and sold into indentured servitude.

She shivered again, but not from the cold seeping through her clothes. She was lost in a more recent memory, of the afternoon just past. She remembered the taste of Joshua's mouth, of his rough and hurting hands, of the atrocity of his naked skinny body, of his knowing smile . . .

Her own coughing awakened Melanie. Her headache was worse, her fever higher. It was still raining, but daylight shone through the thick foliage.

She considered her predicament. She could either remain here and die, or come to her feet and walk. She might die in any case, but she wasn't the sort to give up. No matter how ill she felt, she wasn't ever going to give up.

Zachary Pitt fired his rifle and sighed with relief as the giant bear groaned out a last mournful sigh and lumbered back into the forest to die.

Zachary himself was near death, suffering deep gashes on his chest and belly, and an arm that had nearly been torn off. He hadn't the strength to come to his feet and wondered how he'd make it back to the cabin.

The bear had come upon him in the barn, as he milked one of his two cows. His dog Rusty had growled out a warning, but the sound had come only seconds before the bear's attack. Now, the cow was dead and Zachary close to it. Thank God, he'd thought to take his rifle with him.

He needed to rest for a minute, only he couldn't. Baby Caroline was inside the house alone. She needed him. She'd be afraid when she awoke from her nap to find no one to care for her.

Zachary struggled to his feet. Using his rifle as a crutch he made his way slowly, painfully to the cabin. He was losing blood at an alarming rate. It came steadily from his chest wound and poured from his dangling arm. The first thing he had to do was stop the bleeding. He couldn't allow himself to die. Caroline had no one else but him.

Melanie stood on a ridge and saw a house in the clearing below. Was it her imagination? Could it be she'd wanted so badly to find food and shelter that she had willed the sight to appear before her? She hadn't eaten in more than five days, hadn't drunk in more than two. Surely the lack of nourishment had done something to her mind, for this wasn't the usual small settlement scattered here and there among the otherwise empty colonies. This was a farmhouse in a clearing, in the midst of endless forest.

She stumbled down the small rise toward the welcoming sight before her. Chickens pecked at the ground in the front yard, while a dog lay listlessly upon the wooden porch, his eyes wide as he watched her approach. He barked a soft sound in greeting, but made no attempt to rise. There was a pump in the front yard. Melanie ran toward it and sighed with relief as it produced clean, sweet water after only two tries.

On her knees, she nearly drowned herself in her greed. Choking and gasping, she pumped the handle again and again. Her head was wet, her shoulders and bodice as well. She didn't care. The cool water felt wonderful against her hot skin, and tasted even better. She couldn't get enough.

Vaguely she realized the dog was at her side, drinking steadily from the puddle she'd created, the chickens as well. She frowned. How long had they been without water?

No sooner had she filled her stomach to overflowing than it suddenly and quite unexpectedly emptied itself. Weak and gasping for breath, Melanie sat by the pump, leaning against the thick pipe, the dog at her side, the chickens fighting among one another for still more water.

Tears trickled down her cheeks as she willed herself to go slower this time. She'd take only a few sips, she promised herself. A few sips and then she'd wait before taking more.

It took almost a half hour before she finally eased her thirst. It was only then that she realized no one had come to the door of the house.

The place was obviously deserted, but not permanently or the dog and the chickens would have left with the owner. Perhaps the owner had gone away for a time. Would he mind if she went inside? Would he care if she found something to eat and then laid down for a bit?

Melanie was beyond a concern for etiquette. If the owner of the little house came back while she was still here, she'd face his wrath then. She hadn't the strength to worry about it now.

She pushed back her wet hair and came to her feet. She was weak, but the water had gone far toward reviving her. Now all she needed was food and some protection from the elements. It was going to rain yet again.

"Are you hungry?" she asked the dog as they headed for the house.

Inside it was dark and quiet. She found a table and two chairs just beyond the door. A fireplace, blackened and cold, lined the wall to her left. Before it stood two padded rocking chairs and a small table. To her right stood, of all things, a harpsichord. Melanie hardly had time to wonder at finding such a musical instrument in the wilderness, for her gaze was drawn to the back of the cabin where a drawn curtain suggested a bed for her aching bones.

She wrinkled her nose at the smell of decay. A

black pot hung over a dead fire, filled with rotting food. She'd put the pot outside and make a fire later. First she had to eat something.

There was a loaf of stale bread in the larder, along with a good supply of smoked meat, butter, and two eggs. Melanie dropped a handful of meat to the floor and watched the dog finish it in a matter of seconds. The poor thing was starving. Melanie wondered at his owner. Had he become disabled? Was he even now lying dead in the woods? What else could explain the dog being left to fend for himself?

Melanie managed to eat only a small portion of the hard bread and meat.

There was a jug on the table. She reached for it, intending to moisten a throat gone dry from the bread. She downed two mouthfuls before she realized she wasn't drinking cider.

The whiskey spilled onto her dress as she tore the jug from her mouth and gasped. The gasp caused her to cough, long and hard.

She had barely brought the bout of coughing under control when she thought she heard a sound from beyond the curtain. She frowned and called out, "Who's there?" only to hear again the soft, almost undetected whimper.

Slowly she moved toward the curtain. Someone was behind it, to be sure. And from the sound of things, that someone was in bad shape.

Melanie's mouth dropped open at the sight of a baby hardly beyond its fourth or fifth month. A baby? Here? Alone? Melanie couldn't fathom the possibility and then she realized the baby wasn't alone. A darkly bearded man lay upon a bed along the opposite wall, not ten feet from the weakly whimpering child.

Melanie approached the bed. The man looked to be dead, or close to it. She touched his forehead. He was burning with fever. At least she thought he was. Melanie's own fever prevented her from knowing for sure.

She sighed in despair. Here she stood, almost as bad off as the man and the child. The baby breathed in hurtful sighs, obviously in the last stages of her life; it was up to Melanie to help. How in the world was she to manage such a chore?

She'd manage it, of course. She had no choice.

The man would have to wait, she thought. The baby was in most dire need right now. With fumbling fingers, since her experience with babies was limited, she finally managed to clean the baby—a girl—of her soiled clothes and bedding. Next she carefully spooned water into her sweet, tiny, almost lifeless mouth. Not to repeat her own mistake, Melanie made sure to wait before allowing the baby more.

It took hours, at least it felt like hours, before the baby had the strength to cry. Her eyes no longer stared sightlessly, but actually squeezed shut as tears sprang forth.

Melanie cuddled the baby against her, and the little girl soon fell asleep. With the baby safely back in her now clean bed, it was time to see to the man's care. But Melanie had no strength left. She dribbled a few spoonfuls of water into his mouth and placed a wet rag over his forehead, just before the last of her energy gave out. Pulling a quilt around her, she lay down on the floor beside his bed and slept.

A clap of thunder had startled the baby. Caroline was crying. Zachary fought his way up from the depths of illness and sleep. He tried to come to a sitting position. Damn, but he was sick. Sicker than he'd ever been. His entire body trembled. He'd never known such weakness.

He moaned at the pain in his chest and arm. The wounds were festering, and making him feverish. Idly he wondered if he was going to die. He wished he could pray. He wished he believed enough for prayers to make a difference.

Zachary struggled almost to a sitting position only to find himself falling back. He couldn't make it. He couldn't.

And then before his eyes a vision appeared. A woman rose from the floor, a demon come to claim his child. His body trembled. He had to stop her.

She stood and pushed back a mass of black hair. Did she wobble, or was that a trick of the light? Was she floating? God, yes she was. But demons could float, couldn't they?

Zachary cursed as she moved toward Caroline. His cry was ragged and raw, drawing on the last of his strength. "No! Don't touch her. Don't take her! She's mine!"

Melanie jumped and turned at the man's sudden roar, expecting to find him upon her, only to see he hadn't the strength to leave the bed. His eyes were open and filled with fear as well as fever. What was the matter with him? He looked terrified.

"Your baby is crying, sir," she said, the words husky from a painful throat.

Your baby's crying sir, your baby's crying sir, repeated again and again in his mind.

Zachary hallucinated wildly. She floated toward the ceiling and then back, as if trying to disguise what she really was. Only she couldn't disguise it. He knew. She leaned over him and laughed wildly and he knew. "Please, Jesus, please, don't," he begged as he sank further into delirium. He couldn't save his daughter.

Chapter 2

As soon as she was able, Melanie fed and watered the animals in the barn and the chickens that roamed the yard. In an apron, she gathered almost two dozen eggs. She couldn't do anything about the dead cow or the black cloud of flies that feasted upon its carcass. For the time being, it would stay where it had fallen.

The cabin was warm and cozy against the cold wet howling winds that battered both window and door. Melanie thought the little house a most cheerful haven as a fire brightened a floor and walls made of softly glowing pine planking.

She sat alone in the kitchen, having put the baby down for a nap, sipping at a cup of coffee and feeling ever so much better. It had taken days, but her fever was gone at last and thanks to the meat she'd found in the smoke house, her strength was fast returning. A pot of thick stew bubbled fragrantly over the fire, and two loaves of bread baked in the brick oven.

Until she'd been sold into indentured service, Melanie had had no knowledge whatsoever of cooking. At home, all had been done by servants. She had never found it necessary to boil water for tea. Now in the aromatic kitchen she smiled at her handiwork. It seemed her experience with the Moodys had not been for naught. At least she could keep herself alive with a reasonably well-cooked meal.

The baby was better as well, thanks to milk from the remaining cow in the barn. Melanie wasn't sure how she had accomplished it, considering the cow seemed to have some aversion to being touched, at least by her, but the moment she was able she had milked that ornery cow and fed the baby. She felt real pride at the accomplishment.

Her thoughts and gaze drifted toward the man, who was still terribly ill with fever. Despite the beard that disguised the lower half of his face, she had recognized him as the man who had dared to kiss her on the waterfront, the same man who had obviously ignored her plea to send word to her father. Fool.

As Mr. Moody had driven away from the auction, after having bought her services, Melanie had inquired both of the man who had bought her dear friend Ellen's service and of the dark silent man who was following them. According to Mr. Moody, Ellen was in safe hands, for her new master, Mr. Martin, was a respectable sort who had long sought a companion for his ailing mother. The response to her questions about Mr. Zachary Pitt was less satisfying. According to Mr. Moody, Mr. Pitt was a quiet man, but a decent sort whose wife was expecting their first child. *A decent sort?* Did a decent man kiss a total stranger while a wife, heavy with child, waited at home? Melanie thought it highly unlikely.

Twice during the months she'd spent with the Moodys, she'd had disturbing dreams that centered around this man and his kiss. Had she unconsciously set out to find him? Melanie sighed at the nonsensical thought. *No.* Coming across Mr. Zachary Pitt had been an accident of fate. She'd known he lived some days west and south of the Moody's farm, but she had not given him a moment's thought as she made good her escape. The truth was, she hadn't been at all sure of her direction and had only wanted to go home.

She sighed as she finished her coffee, came to her feet, and moved toward her patient. As she placed a cool cloth over the man's feverish brow, she wondered what it was about her story that made it so unbelievable. She'd begged and pleaded with so many people, including this man, and yet not one of them had seen fit to explore the possibility that she might be telling the truth. Melanie shrugged aside her thoughts. It no longer mattered who believed her. Once this man was well again, she would be leaving.

Melanie was struck with the distinct possibility that he might not get well. She hoped that wouldn't be the case. Granted, she did not like this man. He had a vulgar mouth. Thanks to his delirious ramblings, she had no doubt of that. Still, she'd be sorry to see him die.

Should that happen, the baby would be left in her care. Lord, how was she to manage that? She couldn't, nay wouldn't, stay here indefinitely. Granted there were supplies aplenty and food that could last for months, but what of her intention to return to England? How would she manage it with a tiny little girl in tow? Melanie knew she had no choice but to make sure this man lived.

Melanie frowned as she studied the man's sleeping form. If he made it, he would no doubt send her on her way. Still, he was bound to be grateful. Perhaps he would reward her efforts with the use of his horse and directions that would lead her to safety.

Her spirits brightened at the thought. She'd post a letter to her father then. He would come for her soon after and the hardships she had suffered these last six need a woman, especially not the nagging sort, and he knew of no other. He had Caroline. His daughter made life worth living. She alone gave reason to his life. Her happy gurgles were a balm to his soul.

During the day he brought Caroline into the field with him and delighted in the fact that she was growing as brown as a berry. The future was bright as long as he had her. It was too late if Margaret had changed her mind, if she thought to leave her lover that the man was probably still in the throes of delirium.

"Caroline, of course. I'll kill you if you try to take her." He raised his uninjured arm, his fingers closing painfully over her wrist, almost crushing the delicate bones.

Gently Melanie pried his fingers from her. "I won't take her," she assured him as she continued replacing cool rags for heated ones and applying still another poultice to his wounds.

"Why did you come back then? Did your lover tire of your nagging?"

Melanie frowned, wondering who the man thought he was talking to. Both he and Mr. Moody had mentioned a wife. Could he have mistaken her for his wife? And where was the woman? Had she died, perhaps in childbirth? Or more likely, considering the man's ramblings, had she left him for another? If that were the case, Melanie couldn't find it in her to blame the poor woman. After all, she had firsthand knowledge of the man's abundant lack of charm, never mind his tendency to dally with women.

Still, none of it was her concern. Her only goal was to get this man well again. "Rest easy, sir. Your wounds won't heal if you don't rest."

"I'll get better. I promise you that. And when I do, you'd better not be here."

Melanie sighed. Lord, had he the ability to speak kindly, even once?

As he had since the first day she'd come here, Mr. Pitt rambled on, occasionally adding a curse as he suffered through some distant, obviously upsetting memory. Still, he stirred not a shred of fear in her heart. He might be a disagreeable sort, but he posed no threat to her person and Melanie somehow knew he never would.

The warm bread poultices were doing their job. The wounds had eased in their draining and the puckered red skin at the edges of those wounds had turned a healthy pink. His fever was lower. Perhaps Mr. Pitt would make it after all.

Melanie laughed as the baby gurgled sweetly in response to her gentle words.

"What are you doing here?"

Melanie turned toward the sound. He was awake again, and no doubt still convinced she was someone else. Soon the small cabin would be filled with his curses, his rages, his warnings that she should take herself from his sight. "I'm caring for you and your baby, sir."

Melanie checked his wounds. They were better. Much better. She thought she might remove the poultices tomorrow. She replaced the bread and covered him with a blanket again as she asked, "Would you like some broth?"

His blue eyes narrowed. "Why?"

"Why? Because you need nourishment. How else can you—?"

"I mean, why are you here? I saw you on the waterfront months ago. You said you were a duchess, but I watched Ebenizer Moody buy your papers the next day. So why are you here now?"

Melanie knew she couldn't tell him the truth. If she admitted to having run away, he would surely force her to return to the Moodys. And once returned, she might very well hang for murder, long before word could reach her father. Joshua's death had not been her fault—at least not directly her fault—but who would believe her, an indentured servant? From the beginning no one had believed her, not even this man. Lord, she should have prepared a lie. She should have had a story ready.

"Mr. Moody received word," she began, "about my father. He wrote to say he was on his way."

Zachary frowned. If that were true, why wasn't she right now sitting in the Moody's kitchen awaiting her father's arrival? Zachary knew the truth of it. She wasn't a duchess after all. If she had been, she wouldn't be in his home, looking guilty. For a time there she'd had him thinking that maybe, just maybe, there was some truth to her claim. He put aside his disgust, knowing he'd been swayed by a pretty face. "And have you changed your mind then?" he asked. "About going home? Are you running from him?"

"No, well the truth is, I was so anxious to see my father that I borrowed one of the Moodys' horses, hoping to meet him on the way. I got lost."

Zachary thought that was the worst lie he'd ever heard, and he'd heard plenty. He scowled his disgust. "The first thing one should do when lying is to tell a believable tale. The next is to sound as if you believe it yourself."

Melanie clamped her lips together. The truth was, she'd never felt compelled to lie before and had obviously done a poor job of it. She shrugged aside the thought, knowing it didn't matter what he believed. All she needed was a horse and directions to the nearest town. No, not the nearest, she thought. That would be a mistake. The Moodys would have alerted the authorities and the law might be waiting for her there.

Her heart sank at the thought. If that were the case, the authorities would be looking for her everywhere. Which meant she'd never be safe no matter where she went.

There was only one way out. She had to get word to her father. He alone could save her. And in the meantime she must stay here. Here, where she was safe.

She spooned warmed broth to his mouth. Between mouthfuls, Zachary said, "So you ran, did you?"

Melanie kept her gaze on the spoon.

"You might as well admit to it. I know you are lying."

"You don't know that," she returned stubbornly, daring to raise her gaze to his. "You think I am lying, but you are wrong."

Zachary nodded, unwilling at the moment to pressure her further. He was too weak, too tired, and too damn sick. He'd take care of the matter later. Later when he was well again. And the moment he was, this woman would go back where she belonged.

Zachary listened to the sounds of water splashing, soft laughter, and the occasional shriek of a happy baby from beyond the curtain that separated his bed from the kitchen. He was supposed to be asleep. He had been asleep, but how the hell could a man sleep with that infernal noise?

"What the bloody hell are you doing?" he demanded angrily.

A moment later water splashed again and this time Zachary had no doubt as to what he heard. She was coming from the tub. There could be no other cause for the sound.

Zachary felt his heart pound suddenly, painfully in his chest. He might still be weak, but the thought of her standing naked on the other side of the curtain caused his body to surge with instant energy. The fact was, he'd been too long without a woman. Far too long, if he was thinking of this woman along those lines.

For days now he'd been watching her move around his home, caring for his baby, for himself. For days he'd thought he should thank her for her labors, but he knew he would not. She was here because she had nowhere else to go. She was here because she had run away. She only cared for him and his baby because she needed a place to hide.

Zachary wasn't a man given much to conversation. He rarely spoke unless something needed to be said. And it seemed the longer he waited, the harder talking became.

He wished she'd leave. God, he wished he was well enough so he might see the last of her. The woman, no matter her labors, her smiles, her agreeable demeanor, annoyed him to no end. He didn't know why or how a simple elegant turn of her head, or movement of a hand, could anger him. Perhaps she reminded him of Margaret. All he knew was that just watching her often caused him to grind his teeth.

There was something about her, something sophisticated and cultured. She didn't belong in his home, for her refined manner and speech only made more glaring his own homespun ways, his rough nature.

Without realizing he was doing it, despite the effort it required, Zachary rose from bed and shuffled past the curtain, then leaned heavily against the kitchen wall. Melanie was completely clothed, standing at his kitchen table. On the table stood a pot of water large enough to hold Caroline, a number of towels, plus a tiny clean dress and bunting. Melanie was just now drying the baby.

Zachary couldn't account for his crushing disappointment. He hadn't actually thought to find her naked, had he? "Why didn't you answer me?"

"Stop shouting," Melanie said. "You made the baby jump."

"Well, she's my baby, so I reckon . . ."

Melanie brought the baby tightly against her, in what Zachary thought to be a ridiculously protective fashion. Who the hell was she protecting her from? Him? "She's yours so you have every right to abuse her? Is that it?"

Zachary told himself he was still annoyed, but he couldn't help the pleasure he felt at the way she hugged Caroline to her breast. "You're talking like a fool."

"Sit down before you fall down."

Zachary sat, not because he was told to sit, but because he wanted to sit. "Why didn't you answer me?"

"Because I thought you were yelling in your sleep again."

"Yelling in my sleep? When have I done that?"

"All right, mumbling loudly then, and you've been doing it since I came here."

Zachary supposed she was right. She'd come while a fever had raged in him, and fever often loosened a man's tongue. "What did I say?"

"Nothing that made sense."

He nodded even as he wondered if he believed her. "Have you got anything to eat?"

Melanie nodded. "Let me put her in bed, and I'll get you something."

"No. I want to hold her." It had been far too long since he'd known the joy.

Melanie shook her head. "You're too weak."

"Woman, the child belongs to me and I'll hold her if I say I will."

Melanie said nothing. Zachary watched her mouth tighten as she fought against the need to answer him in kind. A moment later, apparently once again in control, she lay the baby in his good arm. Zachary grinned, feeling he had come out the winner in some sort of mental battle for control. Melanie ignored both him and his smile.

After placing a bowl of stew before him, she silently stepped outside, leaving him with the impossible chore of eating and holding the baby at the same time. Impossible because she had neglected to bring a spoon along with the bowl; and even if she had, his left arm was next to useless and he couldn't have held a spoon.

Zachary was just stubborn enough not to call her back and ask for help.

Melanie paced the wooden porch for close to a quarter of an hour, walking off her annoyance with brisk, angry steps. Finally she bent down and petted the dog, who seemed always to want attention. "Poor thing," she said, "I'm leaving here soon, but you'll be stuck with him."

This wasn't going to be easy. The man was unbelievably disagreeable. It had been hard enough contending with him in his delirium. Now that his fever was gone, or at least almost gone, and his strength fast returning to normal, Melanie wondered how she would endure his presence.

She'd manage of course. Somehow she'd find the strength, until her father came for her.

If it weren't for her, he might be dead, and his baby would be for sure. And not once had he said thank you. Not once had he murmured "please," smiled, or in any way conveyed a pleasantry. Did he believe it was his right that she should administer to him?

She might be a runaway indentured servant, but did that make her less than human? At home she'd never thought to so abuse a servant. Surely in return for all she had done, she had a right to expect a little kindness.

It was about time Mr. Zachary Pitt knew what she expected.

Melanie opened the door, intending to tell the man exactly what she thought of his crude and abominably rude behavior. But her words were instantly lost at the sight before her.

Mr. Pitt sat where she had left him, his meal untouched, the baby still in his arm, his face gray with exhaustion, his mouth pinched with pain. She shouldn't have left him. Lord, she'd known, despite his insistence, that he wasn't strong enough.

The man was purely cantankerous, but Melanie realized then that his ill-humor stemmed mostly from his illness. No man enjoyed being so obviously weak, so helpless.

She said nothing as she took the baby from him and put her to bed. A moment later, again at his side, she said, "Hold on to me and I'll help you back to bed."

Zachary put his good arm around her waist. He wasn't going to make it. She'd never be able to hold his weight, even if by some miracle he managed to get to his feet. "I can't do it."

"You can." She reached an arm around his back, another around his chest just below his injury. "Just hold on."

"Never knew a woman who wasn't a damn fool," he murmured, his mouth coming close to her ear as he brought himself to his feet at last.

"You haven't known many then, have you, Mr. Pitt?"

"I reckon knowing one is trouble enough."

Melanie grunted as he leaned a good part of his

weight upon her. "Trouble comes to trouble, I've always thought."

Zachary grinned at her remark and wondered how she managed to say such biting words in the sweetest tone. "Meaning?" he asked.

"Meaning, Mr. Pitt," she said, grunting again as she took a step back and her knees trembling against the weight pressed upon her shoulders, "we . . . often . . . reap what we sow."

"Do we?" he asked as he watched her struggle, wondering if they were going to make it to the bed. Wondering what would happen to his wounds if he fell on his face, or more likely fell on her. And then he suddenly couldn't keep his mind from the thought of falling on her. Would her body be as soft as he remembered? "What did you do?"

"Me?" Surprised at his question, Melanie raised her gaze to his. It was probably a mistake, since they were standing so close. She felt her heart skip a beat and the ability to breathe suddenly left her. Their gazes clashed and clung. Melanie had the distinct feeling that she was being drawn to him. That her body was growing softer, that her breasts tingled where they touched his chest.

It took a long moment before she shook away such nonsense and forced her gaze to his throat. She swallowed, even as she wondered what in the world that long, silent moment had been about. "I didn't do anything that I know of. Why?" she said.

"Nothing?" he asked in disbelief. "Then how did a duchess end up an indentured servant?"

"There were circumstances beyond my control."

"Amazing, isn't it, how one can twist the words of the Bible to suit?"

"I take it you have no use for the Good Book?"

"Why would you think that?"

"I'm sure I couldn't say. Of course it couldn't be the scathing way you referred to it just now, could it?" she asked, her voice dripping sarcasm.

Zachary laughed, for the first time in months. "It looks like you've found me out, Duchess. I ain't much of a believer."

"Which of course means you don't believe in saying 'thank you,' or 'please' either."

Zachary shrugged as he finally reached the bed and sat. He was exhausted and wanted more than anything to lie down. Still, he found himself continuing the conversation. "I figure a person does what he has to do. And doing what you have to do doesn't justify a thank you."

"You're wrong about that. I didn't have to take care of you, Mr. Pitt."

"I think you did."

Melanie stiffened. The man was impossible. "Do you?"

"If I had died, you would have been left to care for Caroline."

The accusation touched just enough upon the truth to bring color to Melanie's cheeks. She dismissed a surge of guilt. The thought might have come to her in the beginning, but that wasn't the reason why she had stayed. There was no way she could leave a fellow human being, no matter how disagreeable, to die. "You're being ridiculous. Had I wanted to leave, I would have taken one of your horses and done so."

Zachary wasn't about to believe that this woman had acted out of the goodness of her heart. As far as he knew, women didn't have any goodness in their hearts. "Then why didn't you leave?" he asked.

"You needed my help."

"And you didn't need a place to stay and some food?" he retorted.

"I could have taken what I needed and left days ago."

"Then why didn't you?"

"I've already answered that question."

"So why not tell the truth this time? Did you think to take her place?"

Melanie frowned. "Whose place?"

"My wife's."

Her look of astonishment told him he was far off the mark. "Good Lord, Mr. Pitt, does your mind always fail you so miserably?"

Zachary grinned. "All right, so maybe you hadn't thought of it before, but you'll be thinkin' on it now."

"Only if my thoughts become as demented as yours. And I assure you that could never happen."

Zachary couldn't resist the temptation to tease her. Maybe it was because she looked so pretty with her dark eyes flashing and her cheeks flushed with anger. Zachary wasn't sure why. All he knew was that he was enjoying himself for the first time in months.

"How much longer will you stay?"

"Until you are well, I expect." Melanie didn't mention the rest: Until he was well enough to send for her father. Until her father came for her.

Zachary wanted to say that she could leave now, but he managed to keep his mouth shut. He knew he wasn't ready to care for Caroline. But he would be in a few days. In the meantime, why should she sleep before the fire each night when there was plenty of room in his bed?

"The bed is a lot softer than the floor."

"I'm sure," she returned, dismissing the odd look in his eyes. Of course he didn't mean what she thought he meant. He had made it perfectly clear that she was not welcomed in his home. Besides, it was more than obvious that the man disliked her, and her him for that matter. Surely he didn't imagine she would be willing . . .

"But you prefer the hard floor?" he asked.

"Are you saying you'd be willing to give up your bed?" she countered.

"Actually, I was thinking maybe we could share it."

"The bed? Are you delirious again?" She reached a hand to his forehead, believing delirium the only excuse for such talk, and then frowned when she found him cool to the touch.

Zachary smiled. "It was only a thought. After all, you might be here for some time. And since we're adults . . . we are adults, aren't we?"

Melanie glared at him. The look caused him to smile again. "Well, then, what harm would it do if we sought comfort in each other?"

The man could hardly hold his head up, never mind walk on his own, and yet here he was contemplating the most deplorable thoughts. What in the world was wrong with the male species? "I'll be leaving soon," she said. Perhaps sooner than she'd expected, she mused.

"The snows come early in the mountains. I might not be able to get you out in time."

"But we're not in the mountains."

"No? What do you think those hills outside are?"

Melanie felt flabbergasted. How could she be in the mountains? How could she have walked here and never known it?

Because she'd been desperately ill at the time, she thought. Because she'd forced herself to go on, step by agonizing step, ignoring the slaps of low hanging branches, inclement weather, and scurrying animals. She'd propelled herself forward, never noticing her surroundings until she'd stumbled down the last rise and come upon this little house. No wonder the nights had been so incredibly cold.

"When? When will the snow start?" she asked.

Zachary shrugged. He was too weak to get her out now and by the time he was strong enough, it would be too late. He could tell her to take his horse, but there was no telling when or if he'd ever get the horse back and he needed it for spring planting. No, even though he didn't much want her here, she'd be staying for a bit. "Who can say? Any day probably," he answered.

"We won't be snowed in," she said, the words a fierce plea that he should give her the answer she longed to hear. Zachary did not respond, and Melanie knew his silence meant the worse. "I can't stay here." She almost moaned the words, while sending the four walls a look of desperation. "I have to send word to my father."

"I'll do it, the next time I go for supplies."

"Why? You didn't do it the last time."

"I didn't believe you then." Zachary thought the wisest course of action was not to mention the fact that he didn't believe her still.

Chapter 3

~ⱺ∞ⱺ~

Melanie sat on the edge of his bed and lowered the quilt to his waist. She said nothing as she set about cleaning his wounds with a rag dipped in a pan of warm sudsy water. She washed both arms and chest, smiling a bit as she realized his wounds were almost completely healed. Today the bandages could be left off, for the gash in his chest and arm had finally closed, leaving only a puckered pink line that would grow into a long white scar.

From beneath half-closed lids, Zachary watched her ministrations. His chest and arm had been badly mangled, but the sight of the ugly scar sent no shivers of revulsion through her. In truth she looked upon his disfigurement with a gentle smile.

Zachary wondered how that could be. Surely a lady—and he had no doubt now that this woman, if not a duchess, was indeed the lady she appeared to be—could not be accustomed to such administrations. How then had she come to care for his with such ease. Where had she found the courage to ignore the sight and smell of his festering wounds?

"Have you studied medicine?" he asked.

Melanie's gaze moved to his dark blue eyes as a smile curved her pretty lips. "I'll take that as a compliment, if you don't mind."

40

"I didn't mean . . ."

"I'm sure you did not, Mr. Pitt." She sighed as she leaned back, finished with her work. She brought the quilt back into place. "It seems fair to say that you never mean to compliment anyone."

Zachary brought his good hand to his cheeks and rubbed the thick growth with annoyance. "Get my razor, will you? I can't stand this beard any longer."

"Why not wait another day or so? Until you're stronger."

Zachary frowned. He hated to be reminded of how weak he was, of how much he needed her help. "How much strength does it take for a man to shave?"

"None, if I collect the bowl, water, soap, razor, and towels."

"I'll do it myself," he said, making as if to rise from the bed.

Melanie pushed him back against the pillows. "I'll do it."

"I wouldn't want to put you out." His voice dripped sarcasm.

"I'm sure you wouldn't, Mr. Pitt," Melanie returned in much the same fashion.

Moments later she deposited the needed supplies at his side. Zachary, in a half-reclining position, wet his beard and then managed to bring the soap into a lather. He rubbed it over his cheeks. Next he took the straight edged razor. It took less than one swipe to realize the damn woman was right. He was too weak. He'd done next to nothing and yet his hand, the only hand he could use, trembled as if palsied. He was exhausted.

Melanie knew that to take the razor from his shaking hand would only bring on another bout of angry resistance. It was clear the man couldn't manage, although stubborn to the core, he'd never admit as much. No, she'd have to take another route or see his bed soaked with water from the teetering bowl. She had worked hard enough these last few weeks. She had no need to add to her labors. "I've never shaved a man before."

Zachary refused to think on the reason behind her words. It was an opening. One he couldn't resist. "Would you like to try?"

Melanie smiled. Lord, he was easy enough to control, once one understood how to go about it.

She sat, warning, "I might cut you."

At the moment Zachary didn't care if she sliced his throat. His beard was itching like hell, and he couldn't manage the chore under his own steam. There was no other way. "You won't, if you're careful."

Melanie brought the razor to his beard. "Easy," he said as he felt the pressure of the blade against his skin.

Her movements were clumsy at first, but she soon got the hang of it. She moved the razor over his cheek and then washed the soapy remains in the bowl. Engrossed in her chore, she forgot her usual distant manner and moved closer. Without thinking she touched him intimately, never knowing the effect of her touch. First her free hand rested upon his chest, supporting her weight. Next, her chest almost touched his as she leaned closer to maneuver the blade around his mouth and nose. Their mouths inches apart, Melanie seemed not to notice as she concentrated on her chore. Zachary only wished he could have been as unobservant.

It had been a mistake. He should have waited. He never should have let her do this. It had been a long time since a woman had touched him, willingly touched him. Far too long. And he was looking for trouble if he thought anything could come of it.

From beneath half-closed eyes, he watched as she bit her lip in concentration. A warm gust of her breath hit his mouth as she smoothed his beard from one cheek. He smelled her clean scent and despite his weakness, ached to bring his mouth to hers. The truth was, other things ached as well, but he would have been satisfied for the moment with a simple kiss.

It took some time, but Melanie finally wiped away the last of the soap, rinsed, and then rubbed his face dry. She leaned back and admired her handiwork, only to hear his gruff, "Now I have to recover from the loss of blood as well as my wounds."

Melanie's eyes sparkled with pleasure. She hadn't expected a thank you and was certainly not doomed to disappointment. She grinned at his sour look and then pressed the linen cloth to a cut on his cheek, and another at his throat.

Too bad the glaring look in his eyes did not in the least lessen the man's good looks. Melanie felt a jolt of surprise at the thought. Surely it meant nothing to her if the man was handsome or ugly. His disposition was deplorable and that was all that counted. "I told you I never did this before and I only cut you twice."

Zachary watched in silence as she gathered the things and then left him to lie there, aching for her touch again. Hours passed before he could relax enough to finally sleep.

It was time to harvest the crop, past time actually, and there was no way Zachary could do it alone. He had not regained his full strength, and his left arm dangled nearly uselessly at his side. How in the world was he to gather his crops in time for the arrival of Mr. Holbrook, the man who owned this land, rented it out to Zachary, and accepted a portion of the crop in payment as rent. The man would be here in two or three weeks at the latest, and if he didn't have the crops ready for market, Zachary would lose everything.

He'd have to ask for Melanie's help. She was a small woman, petite and slender. He held out little hope that she could do much. Still, what choice did he have? Without her help he'd lose more than his crop. He'd have to dip into his savings to pay the rent and another year would pass before he had enough to buy his own place.

At Caroline's stirring, Melanie pushed aside the curtain that separated the kitchen from the back room. Her gaze widened when she found Zachary sitting in bed, his feet over the edge. "What are you doing?" she asked.

"I have to get up. There's work that needs doin'."

"Work?" Then realizing his meaning, she said, "Don't worry about the animals. I've been feeding them."

"Field work," Zachary said as he pushed himself from the bed with his good arm.

"And how do you expect to work when you can hardly stand?" she asked, watching him stagger trying to gain his balance.

"I'll work." He seemed not to notice that he stood before her dressed only in his long johns. Melanie wished she hadn't noticed as well. She quickly turned away. "Where are my clothes?" he asked.

Without looking in his direction again, Melanie took his trousers and shirt from a hook and flung them upon the bed. She had Caroline in her arms and was walking toward the kitchen as she said, "I repaired them as best I could."

Zachary mumbled a sound. Melanie took the sound for appreciation of her efforts. It was the best she could expect, she supposed, from a man who had never once said "thank you."

Zachary was dressed and standing before the fire sipping at a cup of coffee before he spoke again. "I've only got one arm that works." There was a long pause before he added, "Do you think you could work with me?"

"Me?"

"Of course, you. Did you think I was talking to Caroline?"

"Mr. Pitt, it's been my experience that when one needs a favor, one asks for it in a polite fashion."

"I'm not asking for a favor. I'm offering you work for pay. I'll give you a fourth of the profits." Giving up a fourth would cut deep into his revenue, but Zachary felt he had no choice. He wouldn't beg for a favor. He'd never owed a man or a woman in his life and he wasn't about to start now.

"I don't need your money."

"It doesn't matter if you need it or not. You'll take it."

Melanie smiled as she shook her head. Lord, but this man was stubborn. "I don't know how." The closest Melanie had ever come to harvesting a crop had been to cut roses from her garden.

"I'll show you."

She nodded in agreement and then remembered the baby. "What about Caroline? Who will care for her if—?"

"There's a basket out back. We'll take her with us."

They began immediately after the morning meal. It was backbreaking work that involved kneeling in the dirt, digging potatoes from the ground, and gathering them into a sack. Zachary dragged each sack to his wagon, but it took both of them to lift the fifty-odd pounds over the edge of the wagon to fall inside. It was slow going and Melanie's every muscle ached.

"Why don't we take a few pounds at a time to the wagon and fill the sacks there?" she asked, gasping as they deposited another sack upon the wagon's bed. Her legs were shaking from exertion and she had to hold the wagon for support.

"Because it takes too long that way."

"Perhaps, but neither of us would have to lift."

"We would when we store the bags in the barn. Not counting the few I'll keep in the root cellar."

"Oh Lord." Melanie sighed.

Zachary ignored her sighs, her grunts, the way she arched her back, twisting and turning in an attempt to relieve the ache. At least he tried to ignore it. But the fact was, there probably wasn't a man alive who could ignore the way she arched her body and moaned. The woman was slender, but full in all the right places, and arching her back like that—well, it caused a man to think thoughts he had no business thinking.

Her skin was damp and beneath her straw hat dark ringlets had escaped their pins and clung to her cheeks and neck. Her hands were grimy with dirt. She had obviously twice forgotten their state as she brushed aside a tickling hair, for mud streaked her nose and cheek.

She was sweaty, dirty, completely dishevelled and Zachary thought she couldn't have looked more appealing had she tried. For hours now, he hadn't been able to stop thinking about her. The way she looked, the soft moans that could have been mistaken for pleasure had they been engaged in another, far more enjoyable pastime.

"Stop doing that," he snapped. He shuddered as he watched her breasts press forward, almost bursting through the bodice of her dress.

Melanie gave a slight jump at his sharp command. "What? Stop doing what?"

"Stop stretching like that."

She shot him a scowling glance and returned to the business of digging. Completely misunderstanding his concern, she said, "I'm bound to be half crippled after today in any case, Mr. Pitt. I doubt if a stretch or two will do further harm to my aching back."

"I'll rub the ache out later."

Melanie glanced again at him. She said nothing. She didn't have to, for her look said it all. Zachary figured if she were dying there was no way she was going to let him touch her, so he might as well take the notion from his mind right now. Trouble was, once he'd said the words, he couldn't think about anything *except* touching her. His body trembled with the need to rub his hands over her back, to smooth away the stiffness and pain, while his own pain increased tenfold.

It would take three more days before the potato crop was packed and ready in the barn. After that they had to pick corn and then bind hay into stalks. Melanie didn't want to think about the vegetables. She could only wonder if she had the strength to finish, for she'd never known exhaustion such as this.

After the first day of labor, she had entered the little house and washed the grime from her hands and face. "I'm sorry," she'd said, almost asleep on her feet, her gaze on Caroline slumbering in the basket, "but I can't . . . "

"Don't worry about it. I'll take care of Caroline."

A moment later she'd settled herself on a mat before the fire. She was asleep before Zachary could

ing meal.

For two weeks, from the moment the sun came over the horizon until it fell to the west, they worked. Although she always wore her hat, Melanie's fair skin changed from creamy white to pink and then to a gentle tan.

As the days passed, Melanie was surprised to realize she wasn't nearly as tired at the end of each day. Upon awakening, while Mr. Pitt clumsily saw to his daughter's needs—for he'd yet to regain the full use of his arm—she would put together a pot of stew. She allowed it to cook during the day just out of the fire's direct flame. Usually she even had the strength to eat once they returned at night.

She was growing stronger, and despite her labors, felt very well indeed. By now she was able to lift heavy bags of corn and, taking her cue from Mr. Pitt, managed to bring the wagon to the barn and unload it without his help.

Mr. Holbrook would be arriving with his huge wagon soon, to take the harvest to market. Melanie was determined to stay inside while he was there. If she was wanted by the authorities, and she had no doubt that she was, no one must know she was here. Zachary had promised that as soon as he was able, in a few days in fact, he's go into the city and post her for his own use. Melanie smiled as she cuddled the baby to her breast and watched him work from the front porch. In less than a week he would post her letter. A few months from now, she'd be home.

Zachary entered the warm, fragrant house with a gust of cold air, his hat and shoulders covered with snow. Rusty gave a low growl and whined, as if complaining of the chill's discomfort. A moment later he was back asleep before the fire.

Zachary shook his hat and coat free of snow and hung them on a hook behind the door. He poured a cup of steaming coffee, using his good hand. Melanie almost smiled as he refrained from wiping his mouth on his sleeve, as was his usual habit, but reached instead for the napkins folded upon the mantel. She imagined the man would deny it to his dying day, but apparently her gentle reminders of what constituted good manners were having some effect on him. The truth was, his table etiquette was greatly improved. No longer did the man grunt as he downed mouthfuls of food, and occasionally he even responded to her conversation with a question or two. Most especially he listened when she talked about Caroline. There could be no doubt that he loved his daughter beyond life.

Melanie held the baby close against her and sighed at the melting snow Mr. Pitt had tracked in. It had been snowing for days. Weeks. Idly she wondered if it might never end.

His promise to post her letter had been delayed due to the weather. Melanie sighed her disappointment upon seeing the first large flake. The crop had had to be harvested first, and then suddenly it was too late.

Once he was able, Mr. Pitt dug a path through the

snow to the privy and barn, creating a tunnel whose walls were taller than she was. Outside white snow piled up, all that was visible as far as the eye could see, as each day brought added accumulation.

Months of isolation lay ahead of them. Melanie wondered if she were up to the task. The hard work, the loneliness. She didn't miss the pampering of servants back home so much as she did the small luxuries. A confection now and then, a cake, festive parties, the company of friends, her sister, an occasional glass of sherry.

She might have sunk into melancholy, but fretting over what could not be helped was not her way. Granted there would be a long delay to her departure now that the snows had come, but spring would eventually arrive. Her father would be contacted. By this time next year, she'd be home, surrounded by her loved ones, preparing for a round of holiday parties with her family and friends.

She smiled at the thought.

Her smile brought a growl of disapproval from her host. What the hell did she have to smile about? What was it that always brought her good cheer? "One would imagine you happy to be here, Duchess, what with the way you smile and all."

"I *am* happy, Mr. Pitt."

Melanie spoke the truth when she said those words. She was a woman of high-spirits, and there was much to enjoy in life, despite the fact that her goal had been postponed. For one thing, she loved this baby and the small cozy house. She didn't mind the hard work. She didn't even mind this man's company—or wouldn't have minded if he could have just once put aside his grumpy, often sarcastic and usually downright unfriendly ways.

She sighed at the ridicule in his tone as he said the

word *duchess* and then wondered at the sigh, for he rarely spoke except in ridicule. Surely she should be used to it by now. Had she any sense at all, she would have ignored him, for no amount of kindness could bring this man from his self-imposed misery. Still, Melanie couldn't resist the need to comment, "No one would accuse you of so unsavory an emotion as happiness, I'm sure."

"You're mistaken if you think I'm not happy, Duchess."

"Considering your usual snarls, I doubt, Mr. Pitt, that you know the meaning of the word."

"Why? Because I'm not constantly grinning like some poor dim-wit?"

"Constantly? Please let us not ask for miracles. How about starting with one?"

Zachary grunted as he refilled his coffee cup. The truth of the matter was he didn't dare speak or act except with sarcasm and bitterness. They were his only weapons. Without them he might strike up some sort of relationship with Melanie, and he couldn't allow that. No, he couldn't ever allow himself that luxury.

What he had to do, what he forced himself to do, was to remember exactly how far out of reach she was. And when he forced himself to remember, Margaret always came to mind. Margaret had had fancy ways about her, too and had soon grown tired of being a farmer's wife. This woman had even fancier ways, and he'd be a fool to forget the glaring differences between them.

Despite her fancy ways, this lady wasn't anything like his wife. Margaret had complained all the time.

If Melanie wasn't smiling, she was humming. If she wasn't humming, she was laughing. The woman annoyed him to no end. "And of course you, the

Duchess of Merriment, could show me how to smile, couldn't you?" he said, to goad her.

"It's very simple really. All you do is this." With one finger Melanie curved her lips, first one side and then the other, into a smile and then giggled softly at yet another scowl directed her way. "It is disappointing, I must say, to find your companion scowling all day."

"Perhaps you could think of something to make me smile, then." He shrugged, as if his words meant nothing, but his gaze lingered on her face for a long moment before dropping to her breasts. Melanie knew what he was hinting. This wasn't the first time he had looked at her that way. He wanted her in his bed. But he could want from now until forever, for Melanie had no intention of going there.

Yes, the man was attractive. Despite his cantankerous ways, he was more than attractive in fact. But Melanie felt not the least bit tempted. Without the blessing of wedding vows, what he had in mind was a sin and besides, she'd had quite enough of marriage and men to last her, thank you.

She knew the degradation of lying with a husband, of the hurt and soreness, of having your face pushed into a pillow as your husband mounted you. She wasn't looking forward to suffering pain like that again. She vowed she never would, even if it meant giving up the chance to hold her own baby in her arms. All she could hope was that Mr. Pitt kept his desires under control until she left.

"Sure you aren't interested in wiling away the hours in more pleasant pursuits?" he asked softly.

Melanie tore her gaze from the man and concentrated her interest on the baby in her arms. "I think not, Mr. Pitt. I've found one cannot depend on others to bring about happiness. I've learned you must first find happiness in your own heart."

"Assuming, of course, that I have one."

Melanie smiled and Zachary felt something stir in his chest. He wondered how long he'd be able to force his anger at those smiles. Force it or leave himself open and vulnerable to something he couldn't, wouldn't name. She wasn't important to him, he vowed. She wasn't. It was just that she was here, and damnation a man needed a woman. It was natural and right and could have been so simple. He put his cup down and reached out to the fire's warmth as Melanie put the baby down for her nap.

She chuckled as she moved away from the crib. "I love the way she smiles when she sleeps. They say babies see angels. I wonder . . . "

He turned from the fire with a frown. "You don't believe that, do you?"

"It's a nice thought, don't you think?" Melanie asked as she sat again in the rocker and reached for her needlepoint. She'd found the frame, material, and colorful thread in a trunk at the foot of the bed, having searched through it looking for a possible change of clothes. In addition, her search had turned up a bolt of India calico, thank the Good Lord. With Mr. Pitt's permission she had made a skirt and simple blouse. For the last few weeks now, once her chores were finished for the day, she had busied herself with the needlepoint, slowly creating a picture of brilliant flowers. Melanie thought her creation would look pretty indeed, once it was hung on the wall by the fireplace.

"There are no such things as angels," he said.

"Many people believe . . . "

"Fairy tales."

Melanie looked up from her sewing and watched

him for a long moment before she asked, "What do you believe in, Mr. Pitt?"

"Not in angels, that's for bloody sure."

"What then?"

"In myself. In my baby. In what I can see and touch."

"That limits you some, does it not?"

"How so?"

"Well, you can't pray to yourself or your baby when you need help, can you?"

"When I need help? You mean like harvesting my crop, or shoeing one of my horses?"

"I mean like when you were ill."

Zachary's warm chuckle touched deep in Melanie's heart. It wasn't the first time she'd felt the fluttering and wondered how his chuckles managed to bring about the response. "Do you think you were the answer to my prayers?" he asked.

"No, but I do think that God managed to get me here because you and Caroline were in need."

Zachary grinned at the notion. "And of course your running away had nothing to do with it."

"It had everything to do with it. Had I waited longer, or perhaps never run away at all, both you and Caroline might have died." Melanie, not being a woman who lied regularly, had already forgotten her original story and didn't even realize she'd just admitted the truth.

Zachary thought it best not to remind her. "So you figure God told you when and where to run?"

"I do."

"Pretty smart of him, don't you think?"

Melanie frowned. "Is it me or God you're ridiculing, Mr. Pitt?"

"Neither, Duchess. Just having a bit of fun."

"I take it then that you don't believe in God?"

Zachary smiled again, in a manner that set Melanie's teeth on edge. Still she forced aside her annoyance. She wouldn't allow anger to ruin this chance to converse with someone other than the baby and the dog.

"I've already told you, I think, who I believe in," he said.

"So you have. But suppose you are wrong and there is a God. Suppose once you die you find that out for a fact. What will you say then?"

"I'll say, 'What did you think you were doing making me suffer like I did?'"

"And I expect, he will say, 'Son, I loved you but like a willful child, you brought about your own suffering.'"

Zachary laughed without a shred of humor. "You think he'd say that, do you?"

"I do."

"Well then I'd have to say, 'you have a mighty poor way of showing love'. And just how do you figure I caused myself to suffer?" he asked in scathing ridicule. "Did I ask my wife to be unfaithful and run off with Anthony, my neighbor's son? Did I call the bear to rip me apart and leave my arm almost useless? Did I bring a beautiful woman into my home so I could know torture every goddamn day and night?"

Melanie ignored the last of his words and concentrated instead on the first. "Were you faithful, Mr. Pitt? Did you deserve faithfulness in a wife?"

"As a matter of fact I was, Duchess. And I haven't touched another woman since Margaret."

"I take it you don't count those you meet on docks as women, then."

She referred, of course, to their first meeting, to the

fact that he had suspected her of being a prostitute, and had acted accordingly.

"Well, the fact is, Duchess, you were just too temptin' for a mere mortal man to resist." He chuckled, remembering the condition of her hair and dress at the time.

"Indeed," Melanie said with some disgust.

"And since my wife refused to let me in her bed, I thought maybe just once in my miserable existence, I could find softness somewhere."

Melanie's eyes widened at his admission. "She wouldn't?" There was a long moment of silence during which he neither confirmed nor denied his statement, and Melanie knew he spoke the truth. She hadn't imagined a wife could do that. She hadn't imagined anything but complete and absolute submission. "Why did she reject you? Were you cruel? Did you abuse her?"

Zachary frowned. "No, I wasn't cruel or abusive, unless you counted the fact that I wanted to be a farmer and she wanted the excitement of living in the city."

"But weren't you a farmer from the first?"

"I was."

"And she married you knowing that?"

"She did."

"I don't understand."

"That makes two of us, I expect."

Minutes ticked by as Melanie considered his words. His sincerity was obvious, as was his annoy-

She ignored his mockery. "Why didn't she take the baby?"

"Because I would have killed her if she had tried."

Melanie released a long sigh, her doubts stronger than ever. "Oh, such tender words from a man who claims he did not abuse his wife. I think you probably put the poor woman in fear for her life."

Zachary laughed. Melanie wondered if he knew how handsome he looked when he laughed and why that fact should cause her heart to leap and bang against her chest. "Do you think so?" he said. Melanie only shot him a stony glare as a response. He chuckled again. "Truth is, Duchess, she was a hell of a lot less annoying than you are and I haven't put you in fear of your life."

"I'm not your wife, Mr. Pitt."

"No, you're my savior, aren't you?" He smiled almost tenderly, and suddenly Melanie wasn't at all sure of her ability to speak. "I assure you, Duchess, I did not put her out. She left the baby because she didn't want her, hadn't wanted her from the minute she was conceived."

"Now I know that's not true, Mr. Pitt. All mothers love their babies. How could they not? None would willingly leave her child."

"Then I suppose she wasn't much of a mother, just like she wasn't much of a wife."

He said the words softly, calmly, and with a touch of remorse, leaving Melanie without a doubt that he spoke the truth. She couldn't fathom a woman who would leave her child, and yet his wife had left Caroline. That he'd been hurt by her departure was obvious, however he tried to hide it.

"Did you love her deeply?"

"I cared for her. At least I did at first." He hesitated and then added, "Love her deeply? No, I expect I did not. The truth is, Duchess, I doubt there is a woman worthy of a man's love."

Melanie heard the condemnation of her whole sex in that single comment. "Do you think all women are alike, Mr. Pitt?"

He shrugged. "More or less."

"Are all men?"

Men are a different breed, I think. They don't look for much out of life."

"No? What do they look for, exactly?"

"A warm meal, a warmer bed, children to love who will care for them when they are old."

Melanie ignored the reference to bed. "And does a woman not want the same?"

"Do you?"

"Most women do, I think."

"Do you?" he asked again.

"Well, Mr. Pitt, the fact is, I've had myself a husband, so I know firsthand the dubious thrill of a warm bed," she said. "It's not an experience I want to repeat. And without a husband, I won't be having any children." She shrugged, as if the matter were unimportant, but her eyes told a different story. Zachary thought he'd never seen eyes so suddenly and terribly sad.

"What happened to him?"

"Nothing, I expect. He lives in England, in the—"

"Are you divorced?"

She shook her head. "There will be an annulment."

"What did he do to you?"

"I don't know what you mean."

"In bed. What did he do to make you shiver at the very thought of being intimate with a man?"

"I don't think my private life is any of your concern."

"Nothing I've said so far was yours either," he reminded her.

Melanie knew the truth of that and thought perhaps she owed him the same in return. But she couldn't bring herself to speak of her marriage. Some things were just too painful, too personal, too private. Again she shook her head. "I don't want to discuss it."

"You might feel better if you talked about it."

"Are you hungry?" She put aside her sewing and rose from the rocker. "Dinner should be ready soon."

"Did he hurt you?"

She moved toward the brick oven. And using her apron bunched with her skirt to protect her hand, she opened the metal door. The aroma of baked chicken filled the room. "At least I think it will be. Do you think an hour is long enough to bake a chicken? Mrs. Moody only made stew, soup, meat pies, and an occasional roast, but I thought, besides burning it, what can one do to a chicken?"

"Did he hit you?"

"And I've made up a batch of biscuits. I know you like those."

"He did, didn't he?"

Melanie closed the oven and moved toward the larder. To reach it she had to pass him. He caught her wrist. Holding her at his side, he said, "Tell me."

Melanie stood stiffly beside his chair, refusing to bring her gaze to his, locking it instead upon the larder. "I hope we didn't use all the butter this morning."

"Melanie, tell me."

His use of her Christian name, which he never used, made her heart thud and her voice tremble. "It takes so long to make butter," she said, her eyes filling with tears.

"Melanie." His voice softened as he realized her distress. He came to his feet and turned her to face him.

"I really don't like churning it." She took a deep unsteady breath, and then quite unexpectantly a sob tore through her chest. He pulled her into his arms. Her face buried in his shoulder, her words muffled, she said, "It hurts my arms."

They stood there for a long moment before she spoke again. She turned her face so that her cheek rested on his chest. She couldn't look at him. "I never loved him, but I thought I would someday."

Zachary said nothing. A marriage of convenience. Why the hell did that make him feel so good?

"Father was thrilled because I would be a duchess. I thought we should get along nicely. He was very kind to me before the wedding."

"But not afterward?"

"Oh yes, then too."

"But not in bed?"

Melanie shuddered as she remembered the hurt, the silence, the degrading act, done without so much as a whisper of tenderness. She remembered the horror of that first night, the pain of the three that had followed.

"After the wedding night he came to my room once a month, for three months. He didn't say, but I assume he wanted a child, an heir."

They didn't share a room. Zachary had to force back the need to squeeze her hard against him. It was totally unreasonable that this little piece of news should make him want to laugh out loud. "And you wanted no children?"

"I won't subject myself to that again."

"He was rough?"

Melanie did not reply. She might feel nothing for

Waverly Townsend, but she couldn't state out loud the things he had done. The horror of being mounted from behind as if they were animals didn't bear repeating.

"What did you do?"

"I left him." Melanie knew she would have continued to endure the marriage had she not found him in bed with Duncan. But she didn't say as much.

"Melanie, all men are not rough. Most men would cherish a woman like you. They'd treat her gently, I swear."

She stepped suddenly from his arms. He spoke of men, not of himself. But Melanie knew he had just promised something. And she couldn't bear to think that they might one day share that unmentionable intimacy. It couldn't happen. It wouldn't.

"I won't sleep with you."

"I could teach you . . . "

"I don't want to learn. I won't."

"Are you afraid of me?"

"No."

He watched her for a long moment before he nodded and said, "Good. And the next time we need butter, I'll make it."

Melanie could only blink in surprise as she watched him turn from her, walk to the shelves over the sink, and take down two plates to set the table.

Chapter 4

London, England

Melanie's father, Mr. Harry Stone of Wedgewood House in the heart of London, waited
months in vain for the arrival of a ransom note. A
thorough search had been made, but his daughter's
body had never been found, which allowed him to
hope that she was still alive. Still, months went by
without a word, and he was fast losing his certainty
that he'd see his daughter again. Working at his
desk in the library, he picked up an envelope with
a return address that read: *Virginia, the America colonies.*

A moment later, as his dark eyes scanned the note,
he gave a mighty roar of joy. A roar so loud that
Bessie, the upstairs maid, was startled and knocked
over a crystal vase, and the downstairs maid who
had been dusting the shelves of his library tottered
dangerously off balance upon her stool.

Mr. Stone came from around his desk, his handsome face a picture of ecstasy, his teeth flashing in a
wide grin. He grabbed the still wobbling maid from
her stool and swung her in a complete circle, hugging her tightly against him in his exuberance before
setting the young girl upon her feet again. "She's

62

alive, Ellie!" He did a little dance while holding the girl's hands in his. "My little girl is alive!"

Ellie had lived in this house since she was an infant, her mother being the cook, her father the gardener, but even she forgot for a moment all class distinctions and hugged her handsome master in return. She backed suddenly away, her fingers coming to her mouth, her eyes wide as she realized what she had done. It wasn't until Mr. Stone grinned again that she smiled with heartfelt happiness. "Oh, sir, I'm so glad."

"I must go to her. Tell Mr. Hays to start packing. Tell Johnny to saddle my horse immediately." Almost to himself he added, "I must book passage on the first ship leaving for the colonies."

Mr. Stone ran into the hall and gathered his hat, scarf, and cape. Too excited to wait for a horse to be brought around front, he practically ran through the kitchens to the stables out back. Melanie's sister Susan would have to be told, but he dared not send a message, not with her expecting a baby any day. No, he'd have to tell his youngest daughter the news in person, his son-in-law William in attendance. "I'll be at Susan's for the afternoon."

"Yes, sir," Ellie returned as she followed him into the busy kitchen, her gray eyes wide with happiness. The mistress hadn't died after all. It was a miracle. Miss Melanie was alive.

The large house was abuzz with excitement for the next three days. There was much to be done. Mr. Stone's solicitor was sent for, as was his man of business, for Mr. Stone was a man of many holdings and much had to be put to rights before he left the country for such an extended time.

Trunks were packed. One for him and one for Miss Melanie, lest she be in need. And she more than likely was in need, since her belongings had been found the morning after her disappearance, still tied to the coach, the poor driver lying dead in the street. Nothing had been taken. Nothing except her jewelry box.

Harry Stone knew now that his daughter had been sold into indentured service. The note from Ellen, her dear friend and servant, had been brief and to the point. It simply said that they had both been kidnapped and taken to Virginia, that Melanie was working on a farm belonging to a Mr. Ebenizer Moody.

Harry needed no further information, knowing he'd learn the particulars soon enough. Eventually he'd know as well who was behind his daughter's kidnapping. He wouldn't rest until he did.

A note was immediately dispatched to Melanie's husband, Waverly Townsend, the Duke of Elderbury, but the duke was out of the country on business. Mr. Stone chose not to wait for his return.

Of a sudden, Mr. Stone found himself in somewhat of a dilemma. His one daughter was no doubt in need of his immediate attendance, while the other was at any moment set to have her first child. He was loath to leave Susan, though he knew her to be in safe hands. Her husband would be at her side, along with Doctor Wilbur who had been brought up from London some three days ago.

Susan nicely solved his problem for him. Being the obliging girl she'd always been, she produced for him a very lively grandson two days before Mr. Stone was set to board the *Charity*.

The *Charity*'s destination was Virginia by way of Jamaica. He might have booked passage on another ship whose route was more direct, but that would have meant another week's wait. And Mr. Stone was of a mind to set out forthwith.

Three days after Mr. Stone's departure for the colonies, the carriage of Waverly Townsend, the Fourth Duke of Elderbury, rolled to a stop at his mansion's steps. Waverly had just returned from the Continent, where he'd gone to visit his longtime friend the Duke of Kensington. Townsend's business of buying a chateau and accompanying winery had been quickly resolved, and the two men had set out to experience a week of debauchery that could know scant comparison. There had been women in attendance, and using their bodies had been pleasurable in the extreme, but what had most intrigued both men were the boys. There had been dozens of them, each well trained in the art of pleasuring a man. Night after night the duke and his friends had fallen into bed exhausted beyond belief.

Had the duke's party lasted a month longer, Waverly could not have found fault. As it was, his friend had had business to attend to in Italy and Townsend had returned home.

Duncan Hall rose to his feet from the drawing room settee as Townsend entered the house and handed his greatcoat, hat, and cane to a servant. The men exchanged tender smiles and then passionate greetings once the drawing room doors were closed behind them. The servants were well aware of the relationship between them, but the two men never flaunted their passion. "Pour me a drink, will you dear?" Townsend said as he sat, breathing a sigh of relief to be home in his comfortable surroundings at last. "Have I missed anything?"

"Nothing," Duncan said. "This place is as quiet as a tomb with you gone. How was the trip?"

"Tiring. The weather was wretched on the journey back."

"And your business? Did you buy the chateau and winery?"

"I did. It's a beautiful place. We'll go for a visit soon." Townsend sighed again. "David supplied delightful entertainment during my stay. Perhaps he'll do so again on my next trip." He took a sip of brandy and glanced at his desk. "Any correspondence?"

"Nothing that won't wait until tomorrow," Duncan said as he sat down and placed his hand on his lover's thigh. "Stone's man came by and left a note."

"Again? It's been over six months. When the bloody hell is he going to give up?"

Duncan shrugged. "I have a surprise for you upstairs."

Waverly smiled as the hand on his thigh crept slowly upward. "What kind of surprise?"

"A boy. He's very good."

Townsend was aware that his lover had kept himself entertained during his absence. The knowledge did not upset him. He was anything but possessive. "We shouldn't keep the lad waiting then . . . "

It wasn't until late the next afternoon that Townsend came downstairs again. Dressed for business, he went directly to his desk. A half hour later he finally opened Mr. Stone's note. His face went white with shock.

"What do you mean she isn't dead?" Duncan couldn't comprehend the possibility. He came naked from the bed and stood before a pitcher of water, splashing his face and head, trying to shake off the effects of last night's overindulgence. Townsend had been tired from his trip and hadn't lasted nearly as long as usual, while he himself had been content to continue with the boy. He hadn't gotten to sleep until a few hours ago. "Someone is probably playing the man for a fool."

"Her companion wrote on the Duchess's behalf from the colonies. The fact is, the bastards you hired to abduct and kill her did only half the job. The women were taken to Southampton and forced onto a ship bound for Virginia, where they were sold into indentured service. Stone is on his way to the colonies even as we speak."

Duncan blinked as the truth finally sank in and asked softly, "What are we going to do?"

"First, I want to find the two men responsible for this disaster, the villains you hired. Then, I don't know." He walked to a small table and helped himself to a drink. He rarely drank so soon after rising, but he figured he'd never needed a drink more than he did now. "I'll have to think about it."

"How long ago did he leave?"

"Four days ago, according to this note."

"We could follow and finish her off before . . . "

"No." Townsend shook his head. As his shock began to fade, he began to think more clearly. "I can't chance that. If she saw me with you, like I think she did, she might . . . She cannot ever know I was behind the abduction." He knew the consequences should his wife suspect the truth. He shuddered at the thought that his personal affairs might become public knowledge. Of course many of the aristocracy indulged in sodomy, but to be publicly accused would mean social ruin. Worst of all, Stone would make sure Townsend couldn't touch his wife's money. As her husband it would all come to him the moment she was officially declared dead. He might be a duke, but thanks to his father's bad investments, he didn't have nearly half enough income to live as a duke deserved.

"We could send someone to finish the task," Townsend mused. "It's best, I think, if I'm not nearby when my dear wife meets her end."

This time Duncan contacted and interviewed someone he could truly trust. A small amount of money exchanged hands. And this time, Townsend insisted on proof of a job well done before he would part with the rest of the promised reward.

He handed the killer a knife, a little trinket he'd once picked up in Algiers. The knife had an intricately carved handle. Very pretty, he'd thought, even if the jewels had long since been removed. Once, Melanie had mentioned she thought it a particularly gruesome piece. Townsend thought it a delicious twist of fate that she'd be done in by the very knife she had so disliked.

"She has a freckle on the side of her neck. In the shape of a star. Of course, I'll need to see it before I give you the rest of the money."

Townsend began to relax as his newest employee set off for London and the next ship bound for the colonies, with orders to kill Melanie Townsend and her father, if killing the man proved necessary.

Soon he would be a widower in truth. It didn't matter if Stone got to her first. Either way, Waverly could count on a job well done, for this time he'd hired a professional.

They had been trapped inside for more than two weeks and amazingly enough Mr. Pitt's company no longer caused Melanie to gnash her teeth. Yes, they occasionally argued and Mr. Pitt was frequently, especially upon awakening, his usual grumpy self. Still something was happening between them. A camaraderie of sorts was growing where there had been annoyance before. She couldn't say why or how, but their relationship was becoming oddly light of spirit, with a touch of breathless excitement, and Melanie could only marvel that they could honestly say they were becoming comfortable in each other's company.

Caroline was napping. Melanie had taken a pot of apples from the root cellar beneath the kitchen floorboards and was now peeling and cutting each piece of fruit before placing it back into the pot. She planned to make an apple pie, if Mr. Pitt could keep his hands to himself. When he reached for the fifth slice of apple she smacked his fingers.

Zachary pulled back his hand and laughed, for he couldn't remember the last time a lady had seen fit to chastise him in such a manner. "I see your hand is gaining some strength," she said. "Keep it out of my pot."

Zachary leaned a hip on the edge of the table and grinned. "Gaining strength? It's more like a useless stump. And what difference does it make if I eat them raw or cooked?"

"It would make no difference at all if you were doing the peeling."

A moment of silence went by before he said with exaggerated nonchalance, "Rusty wants a piece of apple."

Melanie was aware of his tricks and didn't believe him for a minute. "Rusty is a dog. Dogs don't eat apples."

"My dog does."

She sighed as she cut another apple into pieces and left them on the table. "Here."

"Is that all?"

"You mean he wants more than that?"

"Rusty is hungry."

fireplace, not at all
ual place. "Rusty is

in that case, I'll eat

ile curving her lips
e last of the apple.
alm."

gaze fell upon his
hand might get bet-

p appendage. "It

k a ball of yarn and

But it's not just my

things. Something

aking up," he said,

ugh she'd prepared
"Good God, are you

d and the man lean-
her or she'll get a

ed, obviously trying

fore you got here.
?"

ip of clean bunting,
," she said, never

thinking to refuse the soiled bunting he handed her in return. It took her a few minutes to wash away the mess, soap and rinse the fabric, and hang it up to dry. When she returned to the bed, Zachary had wrapped the baby in the bunting. Melanie looked at the poorly done job and then at the baby's father. "She won't stay still," he complained.

Melanie unwrapped her and did it again.

The chessboard stood between them. "Use your bad hand."

Zachary glared at her but did as he was told.

A few minutes later Melanie leaned back with a sigh and fought the need to grin at his oh-so-cocky expression. "I know you cheated."

Shock at her accusation and then a playful warning entered his eyes. "One should be careful of accusing a man of cheating, Duchess. There's no tellin' what might come of it." He knocked the tobacco from his cold pipe. She noticed he used his weak hand to refill it.

"The only thing that might come of it is for you to admit the truth."

"How could I have cheated? You watched my every move."

"It was a ridiculous wager. I don't know how you ever convinced me to agree to it."

"But you did agree. And it's time to pay your debt."

Melanie came to her feet and moved toward the curtained off area. "Where are you going?" he asked.

"To pay my debt, of course."

His eyes widened with surprise, his heart pounded with anticipation as he dropped his pipe to a dish and followed her to his bed. He hadn't expected this.

The wager had been a kiss. He hadn't thought she'd be half so willing to give over more.

He should have known better.

He stood just inside the curtain and narrowing his gaze, watched as she leaned over the crib and kissed Caroline. Her dark eyes flashed with laughter and a smug smile curved her lips as she returned to the table and began placing the chess pieces back in their box.

Zachary followed and sat down opposite her. "What was that?"

She blinked, her expression all innocence. Zachary might have thought her adorable, had he not just lost out on a kiss. "The wager was for a kiss, was it not? So I kissed Caroline."

"Duchess, you know the kiss was supposed to be for me."

"For you?" she said, feigning surprise. "You never said I was to kiss you, only that should I lose, you'd expect a kiss."

"And you accuse *me* of cheating?"

Melanie chuckled softly. "Shall we play again?"

"To what purpose? To see you avoid paying another debt?"

Feeling sure of herself, Melanie only grinned. "Well then, what do you want to play?" Immediately she realized her mistake.

"There is a game," he said slowly, "I think you might enjoy."

His tone left her without a doubt as to his meaning. Melanie pretended to misunderstand. "Cards? I don't think so. In truth, it's late. I should go to bed."

Zachary chuckled, knowing full well she knew he didn't mean cards. "We could play in bed. In fact, I'm sure we would be more comfortable there."

"Comfortable perhaps, but it would be terribly difficult to deal from our respective beds, don't you think?"

Zachary laughed. "I wasn't thinking of cards, actually. I was thinking of the games men and women play."

"Oh well, I expect that lets me out, then. I'm only twelve."

If she was twelve, he was the Queen of France. "In this case, I think twelve-year-olds are old enough."

"Well, the truth is I'm *almost* twelve."

Zachary grinned and leaned forward. "Pay your last wager and be done with it."

"Just one kiss?"

Zachary bit his bottom lip, trying to gain control of his now constant desire to laugh. "Just one."

Melanie came to her feet and smoothed her already smooth shirt. She touched her mobcap in a nervous gesture and took a deep breath. "All right. I'm ready."

Zachary sat there watching her. "For what?"

"For the kiss, of course."

"Unless your lips are a sight more flexible than they appear and can reach me from there, I don't see how you can manage it."

She blinked her surprise, only then realizing the man appeared not the least willing to move. "Do you mean *I* should kiss *you?*"

"That was the wager, was it not?"

"But I thought ... " She shook her head. "Ladies don't kiss men."

"Why not?"

"I don't know. They just don't."

"Married women kiss their husbands. You must know how."

She shook her head. "I don ... " Melanie caught herself too late.

Zachary felt his heart thump in his chest. She'd never kissed her husband? Did that mean he'd never kissed her as well? Was the man insane not to have enjoyed this woman? "Well, that puts us in a bit of a bind, wouldn't you say? How do you expect to pay your debt then?"

"Well, actually, I thought you would ... ah ... I thought ..." Lord, why had she ever agreed to the wager? It had been foolhardy and ridiculous even to consider such a thing. Of course, it was all her own fault. If she hadn't been cocky and arrogant, believing a colonist and a farmer could never match her in chess, a game she'd played since childhood, she'd never be in this predicament. No, that wasn't entirely true. He had boasted that he could beat her in less than five moves. She'd had no choice but to prove that he could not. The problem was, the man was an excellent chess player.

"You want me to kiss you? Is that it?" he asked.

Melanie could only nod. She felt intensely relieved as he put down his pipe, pushed back his chair, and stood. But her relief soon turned to trepidation as he moved toward her. Lord, he was big. Why would a man so big have built a home so small? Melanie felt her heart tremble and forced out, "On second thought, I imagine I could make an exception this one time."

Zachary grinned. "Good. Go ahead then."

She placed her hands on his upper arms for balance as she leaned forward and standing on her toes, pressed a small, chaste kiss to his jaw. She took a step back, obviously proud of her accomplishment, also obviously relieved that she was done with the chore.

"Duchess, I want you to remember this, for future reference," Zachary said as he closed his good arm around her waist and pulled her toward him. She gasped at the feel of him against her, but he seemed not to notice, speaking to her as if their present positions were but an everyday occurrence. "First of all, a kiss isn't a kiss unless it's on the lips."

"But . . ."

"And second, a kiss isn't worth anything unless you put some feeling into it."

"Mr. Pitt, I don't think . . ."

"That's exactly the right position for your lips," he said as his mouth brushed hers, so lightly that Melanie thought for a moment she must have imagined its touch. "Say 'I' again."

Melanie couldn't bring herself to obey. He was asking too much. She firmly closed her mouth.

She'd known his scent, of course. How could she not, living in such close quarters? But she'd never expected that the closer she came the better that scent would become. She took a deep breath, feeling dizzy as it entered her lungs, her mind, filling her to overflowing, leaving her with a vague need for more.

His lips closed over her mouth, pressing firmly against hers and moving, always moving, gently trying to bring her lips apart. "Melanie, feeling, remember?" he said against her mouth and she suddenly forgot why she was fighting him. Forgot entirely that ladies did not kiss men, forgot that allowing this intimacy was dangerous indeed.

She leaned into his body, unable to do less, and concentrated on the wonderful things he was doing to her mouth. How had he known, when she had never imagined anything could feel so good?

She felt her lips give up their struggle to remain closed, felt his tongue rub silkily over them. She tried to pull back, shocked that he should actually touch her with his tongue, but he allowed her no quarter.

His hand was on her head, holding her mouth in place.

And then his tongue was there again, only this time her softened lips permitted him the scandalous pleasure of dipping into her mouth. He ran his tongue inside her lips, over her teeth and then like fire he seemed to consume all within, until Melanie couldn't tell where her mouth ended and his began.

He took her scent and taste into his own mouth, eating at her lips, absorbing what he could of her texture and then when she thought she couldn't take any more, when she'd surely faint if she wasn't allowed just the slightest breath, he slowly released her.

Her legs wobbled and she took a step back, holding a hand to the table lest she crumble at his feet. She was terribly out of breath and for some godforsaken reason, she couldn't stop babbling, "Well, yes." She cleared a husky throat. "That was very nice, wasn't it?"

Zachary smiled, her confusion evident. But what was even more indisputable was her enjoyment of his kiss. Her body had softened deliciously against his as she lost herself in the moment. Zachary could only imagine how lovely she'd be in his bed. He had every intention of sharing many more kisses with this woman. But not tonight. Tonight he'd leave her to think about what had happened between them. Tonight he'd leave her wanting more.

He leaned forward and gently touched his lips to her forehead. "Very nice indeed, Melanie. Good night."

She lay on her pallet for hours, thinking about that kiss. It had been wonderful, magical. Just about the most perfect experience of her life. She hadn't imagined a kiss could cause her body to tingle with something that closely resembled excitement, or an ache to grow in the depths of her stomach. She didn't understand the insane need to rise from the pallet and ask him for one more kiss. She wouldn't of course. Not ever. But the thought of kissing him again made her chest go fluttery, and spread tingles throughout her body. Lord, she was so confused. Never in her life had she known such feelings. Never had she even suspected their existence.

She couldn't wait for tomorrow. Would he kiss her again? Would it be too bold of her to suggest another game of chess tomorrow night? Would he make another wager?

Good God Almighty! What are you thinking? Of course he will not kiss you again. Of course you are not foolish enough to want more of his kisses.

The situation was impossible. She was a married woman, at least for the present. And Zachary Pitt was married as well. They had never discussed what he might do about his runaway wife. Would he divorce her? Would he . . . ?

He is a farmer, Melanie. He is a farmer while you are a duchess. Perhaps you won't always be a duchess, but you will always be so far out of his world, and he yours, you might as well be living on different continents. What in the world can you be thinking?

She slept at last.

It took Zachary a bit longer to master the feat. He wouldn't soon forget the feel of her mouth against his. He shuddered in his need. It was going to take time. She'd been abused by her husband and was terrified of making love with anyone. Yes, it was going to take a lot of time, but considering the snow, they had all the time they needed.

There was passion under her cool ladylike facade.

Passion that would blossom into fiery insistence if he could only go slowly.

He rolled to his stomach, ignoring the ache in his groin. He would go slowly. If it killed him, he would, but he'd have this woman. He'd have her again and again until they both knew nothing but the madness, the ecstasy found in each other.

The next morning, still hot with desire, Zachary watched from behind the curtain as Melanie entered the house, her cheeks high with color and a smile curving lips, the memory of which had kept him awake for most of the night. Inside the door she lifted the pail of water that had been brought in last night.

Zachary had business to attend to in the privy. Business that could be conducted nowhere else. Business that the sight of her only intensified.

He slipped into his coat, hoping she wouldn't notice his aroused state, made worse by her smile. Half turned from her lest she see too much, he said, "You shouldn't carry that. And what are you doing out without your coat?"

"It was only for a minute," she said.

"You could catch a chill."

"I just wanted a bit of fresh air. I'll put my coat on the next time."

Zachary said no more as he left the house. Moments later he breathed a sigh of relief as he leaned against the privy wall, wishing this exercise in futility would last him awhile. It wouldn't, of course, and he hadn't a notion how to manage, what with the snow keeping him inside for most of every day.

It had been easy to imagine her acquiescence last night, but in the bright light of day, it wasn't so simple. Melanie was an innocent, no matter that she'd been married, and no doubt she considered what he had in mind a sin. He breathed another sigh, knowing it wouldn't be the least bit easy getting her to see things his way. He hoped he had the patience to gently break down her resistance, and overcome the aversion she felt toward men, thanks to the bastard who had so mistreated her.

Zachary reentered the kitchen after seeing to the care and feeding of the animals. He placed a basket of eggs on the table and breathed in the delicious scents of coffee, frying bacon, and Melanie Townsend.

He smiled as she turned toward him and handed him a cup of freshly brewed coffee. "Thank you."

She blinked in confusion. "What? Did you say *thank you?*"

Zachary chuckled. "I slipped. Sorry."

Melanie breathed a dramatic sigh. "Thank goodness. I thought for a moment someone might have hit you over the head and taken your place."

Zachary grinned. "Someone who looks just like me? That would have been convenient."

"That would have been awful, you mean. The world can only take one Mr. Pitt at a time, I think."

Zachary smiled. "The coffee is delicious."

"Don't compliment me or I'll be convinced you're an imposter."

"I can compliment you because it only tastes this good since I showed you how to make it."

"That's better." She sighed in dramatic relief. "Sit down."

"I don't take orders from a woman, Duchess."

"Fine, stand there then."

"I think I'll sit down."

A moment of silence passed as they watched each other's eyes, delighting in what they saw, although Melanie's delight was more wary than his. And then they were laughing. Neither could say exactly why, but both supposed a general, but unspecified feeling of goodwill to be the culprit. The laughter dwindled down to radiant smiles.

He took a step toward her, his intention to kiss her forehead. He had just managed exactly that when he thought perhaps he might extend that kiss to other areas. But Caroline had other ideas. She let out a wail, and Melanie backed away, her eyes sparkling.

"The baby is awake."

Zachary watched her disappear behind the curtain. And then he realized his condition. Wonderful, just wonderful. He'd already made a trip to the privy, and now he found himself in exactly the same condition after spending a mere five minutes in her company.

Later that day Zachary was lying on a blanket spread over the floor, Caroline sitting on his chest. The baby shrieked as he threw her into the air and caught her deftly. Melanie thought the baby's giggles sounded lovely. "I think you're right about using my hand. It feels stronger already," he commented.

"It might take some time."

Zachary grinned as he tossed Caroline again into the air.

Melanie smiled as the baby gave another shriek. She was just putting a loaf of bread aside to rise when she heard, "What? What was that? You want her to come down here and play as well? I think you should ask her then, don't you?"

Melanie glanced at Zachary and his wicked smile. She knew very well what might happen if she joined in the fun, but she knew as well, thanks to Caroline's presence, that all would remain innocent. Still, she hesitated. Things might remain innocent for the time being, but what would happen once Caroline was put to bed?

"Caroline wants you to come over here," Zachary said.

"Why?"

"She thinks you're lonely all by yourself."

"I'm not lonely, Caroline, but thank you for the invitation."

"What?" Zachary said again, his head dipping toward the baby, pretending to listen. "Oh. She says I'm too rough and she needs a more gentle touch."

"Touch her more gently then."

"No, she's not. I know she's not afraid." Zachary was talking to the baby again. A moment later he directed his words toward Melanie. "She says you're afraid, but I told her you weren't."

Melanie smiled as she poured flour upon the table.

"Was I right?"

"You were."

"I thought so. It's almost time for her nap, isn't it?"

"Not for another hour or so."

"All right, let's go then," Zachary said as he rolled to his feet, bringing the baby with him.

"Where are you going?"

"Outside. Caroline needs exercise."

Melanie laughed at the nonsensical thought that a baby might need exercise.

Zachary felt an almost overpowering need to hear her laugh again, and to hear it in his bed.

"Come outside with us," he invited as he bundled the baby into a blanket and a quilt.

"What about the bread?"

"You can leave it for awhile, can't you?"

"I suppose." Melanie wiped her hands free of the flour and slid her arms into her jacket. Zachary wrapped his scarf around her head and tied it under her chin.

"Thank you," she said and then backed away as he leaned forward. She had no doubt that he wanted to kiss her again and thought she should put a stop to this now, before things got out of control.

"What's the matter?" he asked.

"I don't think you should kiss me."

He nodded and opened the door. Taking the baby in his arms, he walked outside. They moved down the path toward the barn, the snow crunching under their feet, the cold air bringing color to their cheeks. They walked in silence for a long moment before he asked, "Why?"

There was no use claiming ignorance. Melanie knew what he was asking and knew as well that disaster lay within sight, should she allow this teasing. It was lovely being teased, but teasing wasn't all this man had in mind. She sighed, knowing she had to state her misgivings aloud. "Kissing is bound to give you the wrong impression," she said.

"What kind of an impression?"

"That I might be willing to join you in bed. You should know, I won't ever be willing."

"Do you like kissing?"

Melanie shrugged. "It's all right, I suppose."

Zachary turned to her, his eyes wide with disbelief and filled with laughter. After the kiss they had shared last night, there wasn't a doubt in his mind as to the depth of her liking. Melanie laughed. "All right, it's better than all right."

"And if I kept on kissing you, you still wouldn't be tempted to join me in bed?"

"Not at all."

"Then what's the problem?"

"What do you mean?"

"I mean, if you won't be tempted, then why shouldn't we kiss? We both like kissing well enough."

"Shouldn't the question be, if I won't be tempted why bother to kiss?"

Zachary chuckled. "I think you are tempted. I think you are afraid that my kisses might cause you to change your mind."

"You're wrong about that."

"I don't think so. I think you're afraid."

"If you're trying to trick me into kissing, it won't work."

"If you weren't afraid, you'd kiss me quickly enough. I think you want my body."

"You're ridiculous."

Zachary laughed. "Think so? Show me I'm wrong then," he dared.

"I know what you're doing, and it's not going to work."

"Do you think I won't be able to control myself, is that it? Do you think your kisses will get me so fired up that I'll take you against your will?"

"Well, no, but kissing is bound to lead to trouble."

"You're a beautiful lady, Duchess, but you're not that beautiful."

Melanie frowned. "Thank you, I think."

Zachary laughed as he left her side. A moment later a snow ball smacked against the top of her head.

Melanie turned with a vengeful light dawning in her eyes. "That wasn't very smart. I have two hands and can—"

"But I'm holding a baby," he said, knowing the baby would protect him from her retaliation.

"Put her inside."

"I don't think so." Even as he said the words, he

had the audacity to bend to the ground and take yet another handful of snow.

"Zachary," Melanie said as she brushed snow from her chest, "I don't think this is the least bit amusing. Put her to bed."

"No." He threw another snowball.

"Let me hold her then."

He chuckled and threw another.

Melanie ducked. The snowball went sailing over her head. "You'll drop her." He was holding the baby in his weak arm.

"No, I won't."

Melanie filled her hands with snow. "Don't throw it. You might hit her," he warned.

"Turn around."

"And make myself your target?" he asked, as if the thought were absurd.

"Why not? I'm yours."

She wasn't yet, but she was going to be, he vowed. He moved toward her, a wicked light in his eyes. Melanie backed away. What happened next caught her by surprise. All at once he had tackled her to the ground, and yet he hadn't grabbed her at all. She was lying flat on her back, while he, still holding Caroline, leaned over her, most of his weight supported by his good arm.

"How did you do that?" she asked, gasping for breath.

"What?"

"Fall on me and make it look like you didn't mean to do it."

Zachary laughed and leaned a bit more of his weight upon her. "Are you cold?"

"No, let me up." The weight of his body was doing strange things to her stomach. If she wasn't certain that it was impossible, she would have thought that she liked the sensation of his body against hers.

"You know the price that has to be paid."

"You're becoming obsessed with kisses."

"Only because you're so stingy."

"All right, kiss me then and get it over with."

"Get it over with?"

He laughed and Melanie felt alarmed as his warm breath brushed against her face. A man shouldn't smell so good, she thought.

"Odd, wasn't that you I kissed last night?" he asked. "Wasn't it you who said, 'Well, yes, that was very nice, wasn't it'?"

"I didn't want to hurt your feelings."

"You're very kind."

"I try to be."

"We could go inside and you could really try not to hurt my feelings."

"I don't think so."

Zachary laughed as he rolled to his knees and gained his footing. He extended a hand and brought Melanie easily to her feet. "You look very pretty all covered with snow."

"Thank you," she said as she brushed away what she could of the cold, melting flakes. "I'd better check the bread."

"The next time we do this, I'll leave Caroline in her bed."

"I should warn you that I'm very good at throwing snow balls."

Zachary grinned in disbelief.

Melanie felt forced to point out, "When I was a child, we spent many holidays with my father's sister and her husband in Switzerland. In order to survive my cousin's attacks, I became quite good at defending myself."

Zachary's smile grew a bit forced. "Have you traveled much?"

She shrugged at the question. "Everyone I knew visited the Continent sooner or later."

The fact was, Zachary had been born in England and had never once visited the Continent. Raised in the streets of London, he hadn't even known anyone who had traveled so far just for a holiday. What the hell did he think he was doing, becoming involved with a woman like her? Granted, for the moment they were on an equal footing, but that wouldn't last. The moment she got word to her father, she'd be leaving for England and the luxuries that awaited her there. For the servants, the mansion, the easy life spent among Britain's aristocracy. He'd be a damn fool to think she might give all that up for him.

Zachary steeled his heart against the nonsensical thought that she could be happy with him. The truth was, he didn't want her to give those luxuries up. He didn't want her period. At least not on a permanent basis. All he wanted was to enjoy her body. Nothing else entered into it. Nothing else ever could.

"Everyone with money visited the Continent, you mean," he said.

Melanie glanced up in response to Zachary's words. "What's the matter?"

"Nothing," he said as he entered the cabin and brought Caroline to her bed.

Melanie returned to making bread, while Zachary sat by the fire, staring morosely into the flames. He'd be happy to see her go. He would. Granted, he'd feel some loneliness afterward, but only because he was getting used to the woman. Soon his life would return to the way it had been. And that was fine with him.

He'd work his farm and enjoy his little girl, asking

nothing more out of life but to see her grow into a fine young woman. Nothing else mattered. Nothing.

Later, when the bread was done, Melanie took it from the oven and admired her handwork. She was getting better at it. Her first attempts at baking bread had been sadly disappointing. She had either added too much salt or too much yeast and each time the bread had been almost inedible. If these loaves tasted half as good as they smelled and looked, she and Zachary were in for a treat.

Melanie placed the loaves on the table and returned to the fire to stir the stew. She bent at the waist, holding her long skirt away from the fire, never realizing she was exposing a slender ankle to his view. Zachary cursed.

"What?" she asked, glancing up. "What's the matter?"

"I told you before, nothing."

She frowned, not having the least idea of the man's thoughts. "You just cursed. That must have meant something."

"I'm tired of sitting around here, is all. I'm tired of the snow."

"While I, on the other hand, love it, I'm sure," she returned snidely. "I can't think of a more pleasurable way to spend the day than cleaning, cooking, baking bread, sweeping floors, doing laundry. But the best part is watching wet clothes freeze harder than wood. And all in such lovely company."

"No one is making you do it. And if you don't like my company, leave."

Melanie had no idea why the man had just turned nasty, but his attitude was infectious. She couldn't stop the mean words that sprung from her lips. "Yes, lovely company and logical words to boot. You wouldn't mind telling me how I might manage to leave, would you?"

"How did you get here?"

"I walked and nearly died doing it."

"Seems to me, if you walked in, you can walk out."

"If you want me gone so badly, loan me your horse."

"I need my horse."

"You won't plant again until spring. I'll make sure the animal is back by then."

"You can't make sure of a bloody thing. You don't even know where you're going."

"I know the way I came." She didn't know, she'd been terribly ill at the time, but she wouldn't give him the satisfaction of hearing her say it.

"Suppose you're taken by Indians? Do you think they'll give me back my horse?"

Melanie couldn't help but notice where his concerns lay. He hadn't mentioned what the Indians might do to her, only that he'd lose his horse.

"I won't be taken. They didn't bother me before."

"Before?"

"I saw two braves a few days before finding your house."

Zachary looked shaken at the thought. "And they didn't . . . ?"

"What?"

"Hurt you?"

"I'm here, aren't I? Of course they didn't hurt me. As a matter of fact they didn't say anything. I just walked right past them."

Zachary was astonished. Didn't she know the danger she'd been in? Didn't she have any idea what two Indian braves could have done to her? The woman was a fool. "You've got to be the most foolish woman."

"While you, of course, are brilliant."

"I know enough to keep the bloody hell away from Indians, especially those I don't know."

"Where I come from there are no Indians. Where I come from a man treats a lady with kindness. Where I . . ."

Zachary came to his feet and reached for his coat. He needed a little peace and quiet, something he hadn't enjoyed since her arrival. "If I wanted a nagging wife, I would have gone after Margaret."

"Only I'm not your wife, Mr. Pitt, and I thank God I won't ever be."

"If I believed in God, Duchess, I'd thank him for that myself." And then, forgetting that Caroline was asleep, he stepped outside and slammed the door.

Chapter 5

~~~~~~~⚬⚬⚬~~~~~~~

Zachary could no longer control his shivers. He'd never known cold such as this. It penetrated to the marrow of his bones. Outside for hours, standing, walking, he'd checked the animals in the barn at least a dozen times. Damn, but the next time he went to town, he was going to order a stove big enough to warm the entire barn.

Zachary reconsidered. The next time he went to town he'd bring Melanie with him and return home without her. There'd be no need then for a stove in his barn. He'd have his home to himself with no bloody aggravating woman to bring constant misery down upon his head. He'd had enough of women, thank you.

They were only good for one purpose anyway. He'd use them for that purpose when he was in town and keep peace in his home.

The sun had gone down hours ago and if he didn't go inside soon, he'd probably die out here. Not that she would care. He'd never known a woman who was capable of caring.

Zachary headed for the house, his lips thin with anger as he imagined her heckling. He'd never hit a woman in his life, but he swore if she gave him cause he'd soon quiet the harpy.

90

Zachary entered his cozy home to find it filled with warm, tantalizing scents. A pot of stew hung near the fire, a pot of coffee as well, while a tempting tub of warm water stood close by.

When Zachary had left the house, Melanie had stared in surprise at the closed door until the sounds of Caroline's crying had brought her thoughts from the impossible man. It took a long time before she realized the problem here. Mr. Pitt was obviously annoyed at being forced to share his home. Well, if he preferred living alone, she had no right to insist otherwise. Still, there was little she could do about the situation now. She resolved to be kinder in the future, to keep her mean words to herself no matter how he provoked her. She'd make her stay here as pleasant as possible and if he still found fault with her, well she couldn't help that, could she?

She was dressing Caroline for bed when she heard him return to the house. A moment later she covered the baby with a warm quilt and left her snug in her bed, more than half asleep.

Zachary eyed the tub with longing, though there was no way he could use it. The truth was, he was so cold he'd never manage the chore of undressing. He couldn't feel his fingers, never mind get them to work.

Melanie brushed aside the curtain and entered the kitchen with a smile. "I thought I heard you come in." She touched the water and smiled again. "Bath's warm. I'm afraid there's only lye soap."

She said it nicely enough, but Zachary knew a complaint when he heard one. *Only lye soap.* No doubt she wanted soap with French perfume. Well, that was too damn bad, wasn't it? Out of pure orneriness, he almost growled, "I don't want a bath," but he forced back the words, saying nothing.

Melanie moved toward the fire and poured a cup of coffee. She set the cup near the tub and looked at him with some confusion, since he hadn't moved an inch since entering the house. "Are you all right?"

"I'm cold," he managed, though he was loath to admit it.

Melanie did not respond, at least not in words, and for that Zachary was grateful. Instead, she simply removed his hat and coat. Next his shirt joined his coat on the hook behind the door. "Can you manage the rest?"

"My boots," he said, never once looking her in the eye.

Melanie nodded as she walked toward his chair and waited.

He sat. A few minutes later his boots sat before the fire. Melanie pressed the warm cup of coffee into his frozen hands. "I'll leave you for a few minutes."

He watched her move beyond the curtain. It took some doing, but he finally managed to get the rest of his clothes off. He couldn't feel the water and only hoped it wasn't too hot, lest it permanently damage his more vulnerable parts.

He finished his coffee, wishing he could have more as his body slowly absorbed the water's warmth. And then, just as if she'd read his thoughts, Melanie was in the room asking, "Would you like more coffee?"

He nodded. She had to know he was freezing and still she hadn't said a word. He wasn't sure but what her silence didn't add to his aggravation.

She refilled his cup and handed it to him, careful to keep her eyes averted from the tub and his body. Then she picked up his clothes and laid them over the chair. "Are the animals all right?"

"They're fine."

Behind him she moved around the kitchen, wiping and polishing. "It's very cold out and I thought they might have been in trouble."

"No trouble. If they have enough to eat, they manage all right."

"I'm sorry, Mr. Pitt, to be so much bother to you. I promise the moment I can, I'll leave you in peace."

He did not reply.

"In the meantime, would you rather I spend my evenings with Caroline?"

"What does that mean?"

"Well, I could bring the rocker into the sleeping area, perhaps a candle as well, and stay there until you're ready for bed. Then you wouldn't feel forced to talk to me."

"I don't feel forced to talk to you."

"Well, I mean, you wouldn't be bothered by my being here so much."

"I'm not bothered." God, what a liar he was, he chided himself. The truth was, he'd never felt so bothered by a woman in his entire life.

"You're only being nice. I know—"

"I'm not the least bit nice, Duchess, so don't go letting your imagination run away with you."

A few minutes later, she asked, "Are you hungry?"

"Some," he said. "I want to get out now." He was as warm as this water was ever going to make him. What he needed now was to stand before the fire.

Melanie handed him a towel before moving behind the curtain again. She listened to water splashing and knew he was leaving the tub. Her heart pounded at the thought that he was standing there naked. She'd never seen a naked man until Joshua, who'd tried to rape her. Even her husband had come to her under the cover of darkness. Melanie felt her cheeks grow pink at the thought of a naked Zachary, for she couldn't stop wondering what he looked like. Would he be ugly? Were all men ugly? Somehow she didn't think so, but she couldn't say why.

She took a deep breath, forcing her hands to remain at her sides, wondering how so wicked a thought could have suddenly made itself known. She wanted to see Mr. Pitt. All of Mr. Pitt. Lord, what in the world possessed her even to imagine such a thing?

She took another deep breath and reentered the room. He stood before the fire, fully dressed, absorbing its warmth. Melanie breathed a sigh, certain it was a sigh of relief.

Dragging her thoughts from the man and the secrets of a body she had no business thinking about, Melanie placed a loaf of bread on a plate and cut it in half lengthwise. She scooped out the soft insides and filled the half loaf with stew. Again she refilled his cup.

"It's ready," she said.

Zachary nodded. A moment later he sat at the table and ate. And as he ate Zachary swore that the woman wouldn't again force him from his own house. In the future, when they disagreed on something, she would see and agree to his side of the matter and be done with it. He'd expect no less of a woman who was in effect living on his charity.

But they did not disagree. They never got a chance because they did not speak. Not that night, nor the night after, nor the night after that. And as each day and night passed in silence, Zachary grew more miserable, and more annoyed.

He entered his home on the evening of the fourth day of silence, having already seen to the animals in the barn. Caroline was sitting on a blanket in the middle of the room, clapping her hands—or trying to—while Melanie played the harpsichord. He'd heard her play before, but this time she was singing too. In French.

Idly he wondered how many other languages she spoke. Even as he wondered, he knew it didn't matter. Her knowing French made perfectly clear the difference between them. It emphasized the fact that he was an ignorant backwoods farmer and she was an educated lady. Damn, he'd never felt so inadequate, so beneath a woman. At every turn he came up against the knowledge that there wasn't a chance, not one bloody chance, that something could come of her staying here.

"What the hell are you singing?" Zachary found himself thundering.

Melanie's fingers froze on the keyboard as she raised dark eyes to him. "I'm singing for Caroline, Mr. Pitt. She seems to enjoy it."

"Singing in French?" he ridiculed. "She can hardly understand a few words of English."

"Every lady should know French. Eventually, if she hears it often enough, it will come easily to her."

"The point is, Caroline won't be growing up to be a lady, so there's no point in learning French, is there?"

"Don't you want what's best for your daughter?"

"That's exactly why she'll never learn it. Caroline will become a farmer's wife some day. Will she have cause to teach her chickens French?"

Without another word Melanie rose from the harpsichord, vowing to be careful in the future to play only when Zachary was not about.

Zachary wanted to smash the thing. It had been Margaret's, of course. Her father had given it to her on their wedding day. He wished to hell his wife had taken it with her when she left.

* * *

The silence continued between them, one day following another and then another. Zachary stood all
the strain he could, before he finally exploded one
evening. "What the bloody hell is the matter with
you?"

Melanie, sitting opposite him in the rocker, jumped
at the sudden sound and pricked her finger with the
needle she'd been using. "Ow!" she said as she put
the finger into her mouth and sucked at the injury.
Zachary watched the movement and wondered how
the hell he could be jealous of a finger. The bother-
some woman had him so upset, he was thinking all
kinds of nonsense. The fact was, she was making him
lose his mind.

"Why are you yelling?" she asked.

"I'm not yelling," Zachary said through clenched
teeth.

"It sounds like yelling to me."

"That's because it's so quiet in here, I can hear
your damn heart beating."

"You cannot, and kindly watch your language."

Zachary grinned, feeling as if he'd just emerged
from solitary confinement. Her sharp retorts were a
pleasure. He didn't mind that she was her usual up-
pity self. He didn't mind that she was glaring at him.
He loved it and didn't have the slightest idea why
that should be.

"I told you once before that I wasn't kind, so don't
expect it of me," he said. "Why haven't you been
talking to me?"

"Because I know my presence annoys you. I
thought if I were quiet—"

"I never said your presence annoys me."

"But it does."

Zachary took a deep breath and narrowed his gaze

in warning. "What annoys me, Duchess, is you telling me what I think."

"Well since you never speak your mind, what choice have I but to guess what you're thinking?"

Zachary grinned at her quick comeback. At the moment he couldn't think of anything more pleasant than to spend an evening sparring with this woman. All right, perhaps he could think of one or two things, but for the moment he was more than satisfied as things stood. "Aren't you afraid you might take sick?" he asked.

"No, I haven't thought..." Her words drifted to silence as she frowned. "Why would I suddenly grow ill?"

"Well, people who hold back their annoyances usually do."

She shot him a wry glance from beneath thick lashes. "I imagine then that you'll stay healthy for some time to come, Mr. Pitt."

Zachary wondered how she managed to say such sharp words so gently. "You called me Zachary the other day. Why are you calling me Mr. Pitt now?"

"I never called you Zachary," she coolly denied.

"Yes, you did. When I hit you with a snowball, you said, 'Zachary, this isn't the least bit amusing.'" He spoke in a voice pitched several octaves above his own, his accent suddenly elegant, in an apparent attempt to mimic her.

"Is that supposed to sound like me?"

He shrugged, unable to hide a smile. "Don't you think so?"

"No, I don't." Melanie returned to her sewing. "And it wasn't amusing. Imagine a grown man hiding behind a baby."

"I thought it was very smart of me, actually."

Melanie glanced toward him, certain she'd never

seen his eyes so full of laughter. "Very cowardly, I'd say."

"You wanted to hold her," he reminded her.

Melanie refused to give him the satisfaction of agreeing. She kept her gaze on her task.

"Does that mean women are allowed to be cowardly, but men are not?"

"This conversation is ridiculous."

"Do you always say that when you're trying to wheedle out of something?"

"What?"

"*Ridiculous*. You said it the other day when we were talking about kissing."

Melanie chuckled. There was no sense denying it. The man had found her out. She often said the word when she felt out of her depth. But rather than admit to her failing, she changed the subject. "What were you like when you were a boy?"

"You don't want to know that." Nervously he crossed his legs and then uncrossed them.

"Why not?"

"Because I came from the streets, is why. Because a lady shouldn't know some things."

"Did you?" she asked, with a touch of amazement. Having been sheltered from life's adversities, until her abduction six months or more ago, Melanie thought his admission fascinating. "How interesting. What streets?"

"London."

"London?" she repeated with a soft smile. "Were we neighbors then?"

"I doubt it. You said your father lives in Wedgewood House. That's on Sutton, isn't it?"

"You know the place?" she asked, her excitement obvious. "Have you been there?"

"The only reason I would have gone to a big fancy house like that would have been to rob it."

Melanie gasped. She touched a hand to her chest and leaned back in the rocker. "We're you a thief then?"

"I might have been, had I stayed. I left England before you were born."

She looked at him for a long moment, studying his face as if searching for a clue to his age. He was older than she, but she thought not that much older. Hard labor had kept his body fit, while the sun had brought squint lines to the corners of his eyes and deepened the lines that bracketed his mouth. She reasoned he was somewhere between twenty-five and thirty. If that were the case, he would have had to be a baby when he left. "You're not so much older than me."

"I'm thirty-two."

"I'm twenty-two. How old were you when you left?"

"Nine." Zachary chuckled at her look of disappointment. "We never would have met, in any case."

"We might have," she said, and then wondered why it seemed so important that they should have.

Zachary shrugged. "If I worked for your father, you mean?"

Melanie considered the glaring differences in their backgrounds unimportant. In this country, and especially in her present circumstances, class distinction didn't matter. She suddenly wanted very much to know this man, to know everything about him. "You don't sound like you came from London's streets. How did you learn to speak so well?"

"I was sold into indentured service to a Mrs. Morrison. In the evenings she sometimes conducted classes for her sons and myself in how to read, write, speak correctly and act like a gentleman. She seemed to think the last most important."

Melanie sighed. "Perhaps she did a good job of teaching you to read, then."

Meaning, of course, that his actions were far from those of a gentleman. Zachary chuckled and shook his head. "Numbers. I'm best at numbers."

"I've seen you read the Bible."

He shrugged. "A few words. I'm not very good at it."

"I could help you. You probably only need to practice."

Zachary didn't reply. It was enough that he'd admitted to his ignorance. He'd never allow her firsthand knowledge of his inadequacies.

"Why were you sent here?" she asked.

"I stole a loaf of bread. Turned out the old man could run a sight faster than I thought. I was caught and sentenced to seven years in the Colonies."

"Good God, you were just a boy! How could they give you seven years for stealing a loaf of bread? Lord," she breathed softly, wondering at the harshness directed at a young boy and at the many others who had suffered under her country's ruthless dictates, herself included. "What about your mother? Wasn't she—"

"I had no mother." At least none that Zachary was willing to tell her about. It was his mother who, while entertaining her gentleman friends, had sent him out of the shack they lived in. His mother who had told him not to come back until later, much later. He'd been only a child then. A hungry boy who had thought to ease his hunger with a loaf of bread.

As far as he knew, his mother had never learned where he had gone, or what had become of him.

Zachary wondered if she had ever noticed his absence, or cared.

"What happened to her?"

"I don't know. She died, I think."

Melanie frowned at the vague reply. "You think she died? You don't know for sure?"

"Well, she wasn't around much."

Her frown deepened. "I don't understand. She was your mother, but she wasn't around?"

Zachary's mouth tightened as he blurted out, "All right, she was a prostitute. Are you happy now?"

Melanie's eyes widened with shock. "Good God! Are you serious?"

Profound disgust shone in his blue eyes. "Have you ever heard a man admit to such a thing before? Of course I'm serious."

"How did you survive?"

Zachary shrugged. "I managed. I had friends to keep me company. When my mother was busy with her customers, I often stayed with them."

"Had you no other relatives who could have taken you in?"

"There was only a baby brother. He lives two counties over now. Owns his own place."

Melanie's eyes darkened further still in empathy as she imagined a small boy's plight. She felt the need to touch him, to console him, to hold him gently against her, as if he were yet that young boy. She wanted to soothe the pain and fear he must have known. "I can't imagine how you must have suffered, alone on that ocean crossing. You must have been terrified."

"It was a long time ago. I hardly remember it." Zachary felt his stomach tighten at the lie, knowing he'd remember the crossing as long as he lived. To this day he couldn't look at a ship without breaking into a sweat, without remembering the horror.

"When I get home, I'm going to speak to Father about the injustice of indentured service. Indeed, the practice is in dire need of regulation. Children should never be sent away because of one mistake. Do you realize people are kidnapped right off the streets? I can't imagine to what purpose."

"Profit."

Her gaze narrowed in confusion. "How?"

"A ship's captain will pay a few shillings for each captive."

"Lord." Melanie breathed the word on a sigh and shook her head. "There's no telling how many innocent people have been forced to come here."

"Innocent like you?"

"You needn't say the word with derision, Mr. Pitt. I assure you I was innocent."

Zachary's eyes narrowed with interest. He knew she was a sexual innocent, but if he had anything to say about it, she wouldn't remain in that virtuous state for long. "Do you think all who come here are as pure in heart?"

Melanie wondered if he was ridiculing her again. "I think none are. Still, the punishment inflicted hardly satisfies. Not one among us aboard my ship was a hardened criminal, deserving of his fate."

"What can your father do about it?"

"I don't know, but Father is a man of some influence." She added in all confidence, "If anyone can do something, I'm sure he can."

Zachary couldn't remember exactly when he'd begun to believe her story. He only knew he did. It would be months yet before he could post a letter for her, and longer still before her father would arrive. He had maybe four months before she left. A lot of memories could be made in four months' time. And those memories would have to last a lifetime.

"How did you end up indentured?" he asked.

"I was kidnapped. My friend Ellen and I were on our way to my sister's home when our coach was stopped." Melanie shuddered as she remembered that awful night. "Our driver was killed, I think, and Ellen and I were taken to the docks. We stayed locked up in a warehouse for two weeks before we were forced aboard the ship that brought us here."

"And no one knows where you are?"

She shook her head. "My father probably thinks I'm dead."

"Who's Ellen?"

"She was my nurse when I was little. Now she's my friend."

Zachary nodded, his gaze moving toward the fire in the grate. *Her nurse.* How many people did he know who had their own nurse? Not one. Not even Margaret. Idly he wondered how rich she was. He could never compete, never keep her in the style to which she was accustomed.

His thoughts were interrupted by her question. "How did you manage to buy this farm?"

"I haven't. I sharecrop this piece of land. I figure in three years I'll have enough to buy my own place."

"Have you already found some land you want?"

"I have. There's some tidewater property a week's ride from here. A small plantation really, but Mr. Simmons and I have agreed on the price. He's an old man with no family so he wants to sell. I'm almost ready to buy."

"How did you come to this area?"

"After I completed my service, I worked for the Morrisons until I had saved enough money to start. Mr. Holbrook offered to sharecrop his land."

"What about your wife? How did you meet?"

"She was the daughter of the richest man in town. It was a mistake to marry her. She and I wanted different things in life."

"Were you happy? At least for a time?"

Zachary shrugged. "A man is bound for disappointment if he looks for happiness."

"Truly? I thought everyone wanted to be happy."

"Of course I want to be. I just don't expect it."

"You're a complicated man, I think."

"Am I? Why?"

"Because you don't think like most men I know."

"And you know how men think, do you?"

"After talking to you, I'm beginning to wonder. Perhaps I don't."

"How many do you know?"

"Men?" Melanie smiled. "My husband, my father, my uncle, my cousins. My brother-in-law and a few friends. Why?"

Zachary would have given much to know just how friendly those friends were, but he decided the question would reveal too much. He asked instead, "What were you like as a child?"

"Not so different from what I am now, I suppose. A bit less patient perhaps, a bit less—"

"No, I mean what did you look like?"

Melanie smiled at the memory of a little girl with scraped knees, broken dirty nails, and hair that was forever losing its ribbons. "Well, let's see. For one thing I was most always dirty, my clothes usually torn from climbing trees and playing in the woods."

"You liked the woods?" Zachary would have thought otherwise. He imagined her taking her lessons dressed in the purest white, never mussed, never a hair out of place. A delicate porcelain doll.

Melanie released a wicked laugh, never imagining

how it might affect the man sitting opposite her. "As a child I thought nothing could equal the excitement of climbing trees. I imagined the tree to be a mast and I the captain of a pirate ship." Melanie chuckled softly at the memory.

"A girl captain?"

"It was my imagination, Mr. Pitt. Surely I have the right."

Zachary grinned.

"Those were good days," she said upon reflection. "Until my cousin Richard and I built a fort and almost killed ourselves by bringing candles inside. The leaves soon caught fire, as did about ten acres of woodland. Poor father, I'll never forget the terrified look in his eyes. I'm afraid I caused him some unnecessary anxiety."

"I would have warmed your ass."

"And I would have deserved it, I'm sure."

"How did your mother respond?"

"Mother died when I was very little." Zachary looked as if he might say something, but Melanie added, "I don't remember her."

He nodded. "Caroline had better not try burning down this forest."

"Caroline will learn how to handle you, and you probably won't even realize it. Little girls often know how to convince their fathers to see things their way."

"Not this father." Zachary gave an adamant shake of his head. "I'll see through her tricks."

Melanie gave a knowing laugh, the sound low, sweet, and sensual. Zachary couldn't prevent his body's response. He crossed his leg again, hoping to hide what he could not control.

"I'd give much to be able to watch Caroline grow up," she said.

"You could."

Zachary wished he knew why he'd said that. He thought for a second he might have imagined that he wanted her to stay. He didn't. So why had he said it? He shrugged, unable to answer either his question or hers.

"You think I'll be here that long?" she asked.

"No."

"Oh, I see." Melanie breathed a sigh that Zachary took for relief. "I agree that Caroline is already practicing her wiles." Melanie smiled as her thoughts centered on the baby. "I see the way she smiles at you, and the way you smile in return. Already she is a charmer and you've fallen quite under her spell."

"How does she smile at me?"

"I don't know, but it's different from the way she smiles at me. You're so fortunate."

"Why?"

"Because you have her. I'm going to miss her terribly when I leave." Melanie continued sewing, even as her eyes misted at the thought of leaving the baby. "I never expected to love her, but it's so easy, isn't it?"

"There will be other babies."

Melanie only smiled, knowing that there wouldn't be, not for her. A moment later her smile grew suddenly brighter as a new thought took hold. "I don't have to have babies to love them, do I? Perhaps someday, I could . . ."

Zachary shook his head, realizing the direction of her thoughts, and cut her off. "A woman alone could never adopt a child. The law won't allow it."

Melanie smiled. "But I don't have to adopt them. Zachary, do you know how many babies are abandoned each year? Why couldn't I simply take them in?"

Zachary felt the air leave his lungs at her use of his Christian name.

"Well, not all the children, but a few," she went on. "Who would say, 'Madam, I prefer you left them on the street'?"

"Suppose you have one or two of your own one day. What would happen to the orphans then?"

"I won't be having my own. And even if I did, I'd already love the others, wouldn't I?" She flashed a radiant smile. "It would be too late to stop loving them."

Zachary felt something squeeze around his heart and realized it was too late for him as well. He might not fully understand his feelings, or how they had come about, but he never wanted her to leave. She had become important to him. It was almost as if he'd lived his life in darkness and she had brought to him a solitary beam of light. She was sweetness, the sun to his night, and had to be handled carefully lest the light go out. He knew a sense of protectiveness and suddenly wanted to shield her from life's hardships. At this moment he would have given all he owned to simply hold her in his arms and tell her as much.

It was impossible of course. Zachary wasn't the kind of man who could say beautiful words. He'd stumble and act the fool, while she'd smile sweetly because it wasn't in her to cause a man pain. Still, she'd refuse him. She'd refuse him because she didn't belong here. Because she'd never be happy in such simple circumstances and he had no right to ask it of her.

Zachary rose suddenly from his chair. "I'm going to make some coffee. Want a cup?"

Melanie nodded. "There's some in the sack. I ground extra this morning."

In taking the small sack from the shelf Zachary accidentally spilled half its contents upon the floor. He cursed.

Melanie was instantly at his side. "Don't move. The floor is clean. We can save most of it, I think."

He frowned as he watched her scoop the coffee back into its sack. "Does nothing ever upset you?" he asked.

Melanie laughed. "I would have been greatly upset if this had been tea."

"Would you?"

Kneeling on the floor, Melanie shot him a puzzled glance. "Do you think I never grow annoyed?" She laughed at the thought. "I assure you I do."

"When?"

"When you aggravate me, for one."

Zachary grinned. "Do I aggravate you often?"

"Often enough. At least you did at first."

She came to her feet and stood at his side. Glancing at the fireplace, she asked, "What did you do with the broom?"

"I left it outside." He'd shoveled the porch and steps free of snow again and had used the broom to dust away the last of it, lest the powdery remains turn to ice.

Melanie made as if to move toward the door, but his arm snaked around her waist and held her in place. "I'll sweep it later."

They weren't touching, except for his arm holding her loosely around the waist. She could have backed away. She could have created some distance between their bodies. But she didn't. And because she didn't Zachary gained the courage to bring her closer.

There was no teasing here, no smiles, no laughing banter. Nothing but building tension, and desire unlike anything he'd ever known. He felt her tremble and pressed his lips to the top of her head. He closed his eyes against the pleasure as she allowed him to cuddle her at last to his hard length. "Don't be afraid, Melanie. I swear I'd never hurt you."

"Zachary, please," she whispered. Her gaze clung to his chest, for she could not summon the courage to look into his eyes. She knew what he wanted, but she couldn't oblige. "I cannot."

Zachary swore that if he ever got the chance he would make her husband pay for what he'd done. "You're afraid, I know, but there's no need. I only want to kiss you."

Melanie raised huge dark eyes to his and saw only gentleness in their deep blue depths. This man would never hurt her. She knew it as surely as she knew her own name. And still she could not give what he wanted.

"Just a kiss, sweetheart," he whispered against her mouth.

And then his mouth was touching hers, as light as a warm summer breeze, more fragrant than heather, more gentle than a baby's smile. It held a promise of exquisite tenderness, and Melanie couldn't help but respond. Her heartbeat quickened, her lips parting against a probing tongue. She could relax, she knew. Despite the need she'd read in his eyes, despite his ragged breathing, if he said a kiss, he meant a kiss. She had nothing to fear in this man's arms.

Her own arms moved from her sides. Her fingers slid up and around his neck.

Zachary groaned as her mouth widened, accepting the thrusting heat of his invasive tongue. She was more than delicious, she was perfection, and Zachary felt himself drowning in her taste, her texture, her scent.

Again and again his tongue dipped into her honeyed depths, until he knew nothing but this luscious woman and the need to have her.

"I'm dizzy," she murmured as his mouth left hers for a moment to discover the silkiness of her neck, the lovely shape of her ear.

"You're supposed to be."

He hadn't shaved since morning and his cheeks were covered with stubble. Melanie thought the scratch of his skin oddly pleasing. "Are you dizzy as well?"

Zachary smiled. His arm released her for a moment as he removed her mobcap and worked the pins from her hair. One by one he placed them on the table and then, unable to resist, he ran both hands through the black silk and breathed in its scent. His hand was almost fully healed, thanks to her encouragement and time's healing. He was thankful that he could use it to touch her. A moment later he admitted, "Yes, I am dizzy. We'd better sit before I fall."

He took her hand in his as they moved together toward the fire and their respective chairs. Only Zachary wasn't about to let her go just yet. It took only the slightest tug to bring her into his lap.

Melanie made a sound of surprise. "Do you think we should do this?"

"I can't think of anything else."

Melanie sat stiffly, obviously uneasy.

"Have you never sat on a man's lap before?"

"My father's, when I was a child."

Zachary smiled. "How does it feel?"

She looked everywhere but at him. "Well, you're not very cushiony."

"Lean against me."

"I don't think I should."

"Have you a freckle here?" Zachary touched the back of her neck.

"I don't know. Do I?"

His mouth found the tiny mark quite irresistible. He felt her soften a bit and heard a low, sweet sound of pleasure escape her throat.

Melanie couldn't believe the sensation. She'd never imagined it could feel so good, his lips so soft and his beard so rough. Her eyelids fluttered closed as her head tipped to allow him easier access.

"There's another here," he said and proceeded to kiss and love that spot as well. Zachary pushed aside her hair, tangling his fingers in the lush black silk, as his mouth lingered deliciously just below her ear. And then with the slightest tug he forced her head back just a bit as his mouth moved to her neck, and then her jaw, cheek, and eyes.

And then his mouth was on hers again, less gentle now, but Melanie didn't mind. She turned so she might more fully face him, her hands moving to his neck, his hair, dislodging the tie that held the long dark strands from his face.

"You feel good," she breathed on a sigh, moving her hands through his hair, as his kisses left her deliciously weak and pliant.

"Maybe, but not better than you," he murmured against her throat.

Her fichu fell to the floor. Melanie didn't mind, for it enabled his mouth to reach all of her neck and part of her shoulder. Lord, but she would have had to be a fool to have minded that.

And then the ties that held her bodice together were open and her chemise lowered, baring her shoulders to the heat of his mouth. Melanie shivered as his lips brushed over her skin, shivered again as his teeth nibbled, as his tongue soothed. How had she failed to realize the sensitivity of a shoulder?

She moaned and moved against him, like a cat instinctively seeking pleasure. And Zachary allowed her all the pleasure she could stand. Allowed it until her body trembled and ached for more.

He pulled back for just a second, but before Melanie could open her eyes, his mouth was on hers again, bringing her deeper, deeper into the magic.

She felt his fingers move from her jaw to her throat to her chest, but knew no fear. He was going to touch her, and she wanted his touch. Her back arched in breathless anticipation as his hand lowered and she moaned her delight and shivered as his hand closed over her breast at last.

He touched her as if memorizing the feel, the weight, the softness. Melanie moaned again as he cupped that softness and rubbed it into the palm of his hand.

Her arms moved around his neck as she lost the last of her equilibrium, pressing their mouths closer, unbearably closer. Hunger was there, burning, urging her on, causing the ache in her belly to grow beyond measure. Her tongue fought a loving duel with his.

All at once she realized he had removed his shirt. Melanie set about to explore this treasure with absolute fascination. She'd never touched a man before, not as she longed to touch him. Yes, she'd seen his chest many times as she'd administered to his wounds, but she hadn't let herself investigate the mat of black hair curling at its center, warm and inviting. Her mouth brushed softly over his collarbone as her fingers dared a delicious exploration.

Zachary moaned at her touch and Melanie grew braver, following with her tongue the scar that ran down one side of his chest.

"Stop, sweetheart. Stop just for a minute."

Melanie never heard the softly spoken plea over the pounding in her ears. And then she was in his arms with his arms pressing her tightly against him. "Give me a minute, sweetheart. Don't move, just for a minute."

A moment later, in a voice that was still breathless, Melanie said, "You said a kiss, Zachary. Only a kiss."

"Weren't we kissing?"

"We were doing much more than kissing, I think."

"Were we? How come I didn't notice then?"

Melanie pulled back enough to look into his laughing eyes. "Tell me you didn't notice that the two of us are half naked."

"Are we? Let me see," he teased as he tried to look down, only to find her pressing more tightly against him. Damn, the next time he managed to get her into this position, he was going to keep his eyes open every step of the way.

"How did you get my chemise down to my waist?" she demanded.

"I didn't do it. Caroline must have done it."

"Odd, but I wouldn't have thought Caroline to be the least bit interested."

"She's a very inquisitive child."

"Something like her father?"

"A lot like her father, I expect."

"How am I going to move? I don't trust you to keep your eyes closed."

"That's very wise of you."

"Meaning you wouldn't?"

"Not a chance."

"Are you a gentleman or not?"

"Foolish question."

"Zachary," she said in warning.

"Yes, Melanie."

"You're a beast."

"I know." He chuckled as he buried his face in the

warmth of her neck. A moment of silence went by before he said, "I have the answer to your problem."

"You're going to disappear?"

Zachary chuckled. "Stay where you are. I promise, I don't mind."

"Amazing." She said the word with a touch of sarcasm. "And you thought that solution up all by yourself, did you?"

"Truthfully, I'm not usually so brilliant. It was the feel of you against me that brought the thought to mind."

"What about Caroline? What if she starts to cry?"

"We could both get up and get her."

"And you'll hold her behind my back?"

Zachary laughed at the thought. "Move back a little. I want to see you."

"No." Her hold tightened around his neck.

"I can feel you. What difference does it make if I can see you?"

"It makes a difference."

"I'll find you tea tomorrow," he said in a voice meant to coax.

"You can't bribe me. I don't want tea that badly."

"I'm getting tired."

"Good. After you fall asleep, I can move."

Melanie giggled at his sudden and unexpected snore. She looked up to see his eyes closed and a smile curving his lips. And then his hands moved to her sides and smoothed gently over the plumped out softness of her. "Stop that!" she protested.

"I'm sleeping. I don't know what I'm doing."

"You talk very well for a man asleep."

"I can do a lot of things well in my sleep."

"No doubt." She pushed his hands away, only to find them returning to caress her again.

"The next time you want a kiss . . . Zachary, I said stop that!"

His hands were between their bodies now, cupping what she wouldn't allow him to see. "Stop what?"

"Touching me," she said, but her voice was hardly as strong as it had been.

"Are you sure you want me to stop?"

"Oh Lord," she moaned as he found the sensitive tips and with finger and thumb began to coax them into tight buds of pleasure.

"Does that feel good?"

"No," she groaned as the ache began again deep inside her.

"Move back a little. I need to see you."

This time Melanie didn't refuse his request.

Zachary had seen his share of women. He knew the female form and had imagined what Melanie would look like. But even at its best, his imagination hadn't prepared him for the sight of her body, her breasts, full and white, with soft pink nipples, darkening now as she succumbed to her desire. "Beautiful," he said as his head dipped toward the generous curves.

His hands, gently cupping her, pressed her softness together as his mouth drifted back and forth over the sensitive, ever-hardening tips.

Melanie took a deeply shaken breath as her eyes closed and her head fell back. It was unbearably lovely. She'd never imagined . . .

"Do you like this?" he asked, never taking his mouth from her.

Melanie only managed to groan out a weak, "Yes."

"We're going to make love, Melanie."

"I know." If he could give her such pleasure, she could allow him the rest. It didn't matter. It would be over within seconds, at any rate, and she could bear the position, the pain.

"But not yet. We have some exploring to do first," he promised.

"Tonight?"

"No. Not tonight. Tonight and from now on, I'm going to just hold you next to me."

"When then?"

"When you tell me you want me."

"I might never say it."

"You will, sweetheart. I promise you will."

Chapter 6

Zachary slid her chemise back into place and then with a smile and a tap to her rear, said, "Get up. I want to go to bed."

Melanie hid her disappointment as she stood and turned away, adjusting the rest of her clothes, which had become twisted around her. For some reason she'd imagined he'd meant to hold her for longer than a few quick seconds. She frowned in confusion. Odd, but she wouldn't have thought that his holding her would have meant so much to her.

She bent to pick up her fichu as Zachary added another log to the fire. A moment later she was spreading her bedding upon the floor.

"What are you doing?"

"I'm going to bed, too."

"Melanie, I meant together. To go to bed with you."

"Oh. But you said we wouldn't . . ."

"I know what I said, and we won't." He took her hand and brought her to her feet. "I said I wanted to hold you tonight. Remember?"

Melanie said nothing as she allowed him to lead her toward his bed. She offered no resistance as he removed her dress and petticoat. She sat on the bed, ready to finish the chore, but Zachary reached under her chemise and slowly pulled her cotton stockings away. Melanie couldn't breathe by the time they joined her boots on the floor. Clothed only in her chemise and drawers, she moved to one side of the bed and watched him undress.

The curtain had been pulled back, as it was most nights, to allow the heat from the fireplace to enter the sleeping area. Zachary had not replaced his shirt. The sleeves of his long johns hung from his waist. The light of the fire caused his tanned skin to take on a bronzed glow. Melanie trembled with the need to touch him again. To know once more the silkiness of his skin, the roughness of his hair. Lord, what was happening to her?

Zachary watched her. He knew her thoughts as clearly as if she'd spoken them aloud. "You can touch me."

She shook her head and bit her lower lip. "I shouldn't."

Zachary took off his trousers and long johns. He feared the sight of his nakedness might shock her but figured she'd soon get used to him. And there was no time like the present to start.

A moment later he was beside her under the blankets. Their shoulders touched. She stiffened. "Are you comfortable?"

"Very."

He rolled to his side. "I want to hold you."

"Zachary, you haven't got any clothes on."

"It's more comfortable that way. You could take yours off, if you like."

"I'm fine as I am, thank you."

Zachary brought her close against him. His arm pillowed her head, his other arm lay over her waist. "Isn't that better?"

Melanie nodded.

"Did I shock you?"

"Mostly, you do nothing *but* shock me."

Zachary laughed. "I mean when I took my trousers off."

"A little."

"Have you never seen a naked man before, Melanie?"

"No one like you."

Zachary smiled at the compliment and then frowned as he realized the full meaning of her words. "You *have* seen naked men?" Foolishly he'd forgotten her husband. Had he come to her under the cover of darkness? "Your husband?" he asked.

"No." And then, almost as an afterthought, she said, "Well, yes, him too."

"You weren't thinking of your husband when you said yes, were you?"

"No."

"Would you like to tell me about it?"

She moved closer, pressing her face to his chest, "Zachary, I did something awful."

Zachary smiled into the darkness, unable to believe this woman was capable of doing anything awful. "How awful?"

"I killed a man. Well, not a man exactly, a boy."

Zachary was shocked. Still, he managed to keep the emotion to himself and asked, "Is that why you ran away?"

"No. That happened after I ran."

"Tell me."

Lying in the darkness with his arms around her, her body snuggled close to his warmth, she felt protected and safe and found it easy to tell her story.

"It all started when Mrs. Moody asked me to go to the Stillwell's for lard. She was making pies because her son Joshua was to become engaged that Sunday.

The boy was not yet ten and seven and yet, because I was an indentured servant, he believed he had every right to abuse me. I can only imagine that his overindulgent mother had a hand in causing his bad end.

"He was almost skeletal in appearance, his nose long, his eyes too close together, his complexion less than fair, his hair often greasy. He made my skin crawl, always grabbing me, pinching me. But it wouldn't have mattered had he been blessed with the most handsome face. I did not want his attentions and told him as much often enough.

"I was so excited when Mrs. Moody said I should go for the lard that I almost laughed aloud. I knew I'd escape then, or at least try.

"Mrs. Stillwell's farm was three miles away if I crossed the fields, six if I took the road. In either case I wouldn't be expected back for some time. Those few hours might be all I'd need to make good an escape.

"She told me not to dawdle with Patrick Stillwell. I assured her I would not."

"Who is Patrick Stillwell?"

"I don't know the man, but I saw him look at me in church."

"I can't imagine why," Zachary said as he tightened his hold. "Someone as ugly as you gaining a man's attention is surprising indeed."

"Stop teasing. Where was I?"

"She told you not to dawdle."

"Right. I left right away, with only my shawl. I didn't dare take anything else, or raise her suspicions. I didn't care if I had to walk to the Pacific Ocean, I was never going back."

He felt her slight tremble. "Did she abuse you?"

"She thought I was wicked, that I had purposely

set out to tempt her son, and she didn't hesitate to punish me."

"She was ugly, right?"

"Zachary, I wouldn't call anyone—"

"Enough said, go on."

"Stop interrupting me. You keep making me forget."

"You were walking."

"I was walking when I heard a horse behind me. It was Joshua. I don't know how he found me, but he did."

"He knew you were unprotected. He was looking for you."

There was a moment of silence while Melanie digested the thought. She finally went on. "Perhaps. Anyway, I ran into the forest to hide when I heard his horse, but he saw me run in and promised to tell the authorities if I didn't come out.

"I was afraid of him and the Indians whom some said roamed the woods. I didn't know what to do. I stood behind a tree. I could see him, but he couldn't see me." Melanie shivered. "He knew I was hiding there."

" 'You might as well come out,' " he said. 'I can get you back before Mother suspects you tried to run off. You won't get whipped then.' "

"I thought to run. If I turned and darted further into the woods, I thought maybe . . . but Joshua had seen me. There was no way that I could outrun his horse.

"Joshua had implied he would not tell. And I could only pray he would keep his word.

"A beating surely awaited me, and in the future Mrs. Moody would keep a closer watch. It might be months, or even years, before I found another chance to escape.

"I started back, trying to convince myself that there would be other chances to flee. I wouldn't give up until I made good my escape.

" 'You'll have to ride with me,' " Joshua said. 'Because we'll be late getting back otherwise. And you haven't the lard mother sent you for.'

"Joshua laughed when I told him I would hurry. 'It won't matter,' he said. 'You're going to be late.'

"I started to run. He rode past me and dismounted. He grabbed my arm and pulled me into the woods. I was frightened half out of my mind. He wouldn't let me go, no matter how I struggled.

"I told him he was a disgusting boy. I screamed for him to let me go!

"Joshua only laughed. He said no one would believe me. That I was an indentured servant and that was as good as a slave. That I belonged to him."

Melanie shuddered as she remembered the feel of his mouth, wet and cold, sickeningly slimy. "I knew he was going to hurt me badly. I had to find a way to beat him. He was stronger. I had only my wits."

"What did you do?"

"It took a minute or so, but I finally managed to put my panic aside. I pretended to like him and implied that I would show him the best way to please a lady. I let him kiss me and told him if I showed him the things I knew, all the girls would beg for his kisses."

Zachary chuckled.

"He asked me what kind of things I knew. I told him to take off his clothes. He did."

"Most eagerly, I'd wager."

"Are you going to let me tell this story?"

Silence.

"When he was naked, I took his clothes and pretending to make a bed for us, threw them into a creek."

"What creek?"

"The one we were standing next to. He hit me then; went a little crazy I think. He ran into the creek and tried to get his things, but most of them were already floating away.

"He was coming out again, screaming curses, telling me to get his clothes, when he fell. He got up, choking, splashing water. He was going to kill me; I knew it. He fell again. I waited for him to get up, but he never did.

"I sat there for a long time. Never before had I wished a fellow human being dead. Not my husband, despite his terrible secrets. Not Mrs. Moody, despite her abuse. But I wished it then. I almost prayed for it. It was a sin to wish him dead, but I didn't care.

"I took his boots, his coat, and his horse. The horse went lame a few days later."

Zachary waited a long moment before saying, "*You* didn't kill him, Melanie. It was an accident."

"I know I didn't actually kill him, but I was responsible for his death."

"*He* was responsible, Melanie. He was trying to rape you."

"It's too bad others won't think as you do. I'm sure his body has been found by now. The authorities are probably looking for me."

"Is that why you stayed in the house when Mr. Holbrook came?"

Melanie nodded.

"No one is going to blame you."

"They will. I only realized days later, but I left my shoes behind when I took his boots. They'll know I was there."

"Are you the only woman in the colonies who wears shoes?"

Melanie shot his shadowy form a glare. "Mrs. Moody will know they are mine."

Zachary smiled and hugged her more tightly against him. "She might suspect they are, but she can't know for sure."

"Would you mind if I stayed here until my father comes for me?"

"You can stay as long as you like." Zachary knew again the longing that it would be forever. He didn't want to think about her leaving. Not yet. Not when he was only now getting to know her.

Zachary awakened just before the sun came over the horizon. The house was quiet. Melanie lay in his arms, her rump pressed to his middle, and Caroline asleep in her bed. For just a moment he pretended it would always be like this. That everyday she'd be here. That they could be a family.

She stirred beside him. It was only then that he realized her chemise had been lowered and his hand was cupping her breast. Apparently he'd done it in his sleep. Zachary grinned, knowing that should she awaken, she'd blame him for this and for once he was completely innocent.

Gently he removed his hand and readjusted her chemise. Melanie slept on. With his arm at her waist holding her close against him, Zachary dozed again.

The next time he awakened his head was cushioned upon her breast. Her very naked breast. Zachary smiled, unable to imagine a more delightful way for a man to awaken.

Caroline was making sounds in her crib. She'd be fussing soon, hungry for food and attention. Melanie was awake as well, although she seemed to think it necessary to feign sleep. "Good morning," Zachary said, turning his face so his mouth could more fully enjoy her generous curves.

Melanie sucked in a startled breath as he plucked a nipple between his lips. It was probably best to ignore what he was doing, she thought, even as she wondered how she was to manage the feat. "How did you know I was awake?"

It was the racing of her heart and her quickened breath that had done it, but Zachary said, "You always hear Caroline before I do."

Zachary raised himself to his elbow and dropped a quick kiss to her lips as he moved her chemise back in place. A moment later he was standing naked beside the bed, stretching. Melanie knew she shouldn't look, but there was no way that she could stop. The man was beautiful.

Zachary laughed at her heated expression. He leaned down and gave her another quick kiss. "I told you once before that you wanted my body. I knew it."

Melanie tore her gaze away, came from the bed and began to dress. "You were wrong then, too."

Zachary chuckled, the sound warm and seductive. "Admit it, Melanie."

"I admit nothing."

"You were looking at me."

"And how could you expect otherwise, what with you prancing around like a peacock spreading its feathers."

Zachary only laughed again, then dressed and brought the smoldering fire to life. A moment later he went to the barn to feed the animals while Melanie saw to Caroline and prepared coffee and porridge for their morning meal.

He returned a half hour later with a bucket of milk and eggs.

Melanie spent the morning and part of the early afternoon doing chores. Caroline's clothes had to be washed, as did her one and only pair of stockings. Hung on chairs around the fire, they were soon dry. She thought she'd make a pie with another sack of apples in the root cellar. While she worked, Zachary fed and then played with his daughter.

Melanie watched the man and his baby and wondered at the simple pleasure the sight of them together brought to her heart. He looked so big sprawled across the floor while the baby climbed upon him. Melanie thought he had never appeared more gentle, and at the same time more masculine.

She had just put the pie in the oven when he came up behind her. His arm went around her waist, pulling her back against his chest. Melanie felt instantly alarmed. The position too closely reminded her of her husband and the brutality she'd suffered at his hands. She spun quickly from Zachary's hold. Facing him with a weak smile, she asked, "Would you like some coffee? I was about to make a pot."

Her attempts at light conversation didn't fool him. Zachary knew terror when he saw it, even if it had lasted only a second. "What's the matter?"

"Nothing. Why?" She touched her mobcap in a nervous gesture.

"Tell me, Melanie."

"I just don't like to be held like that."

"Why not?"

"I don't know. I just don't."

"Is it all right if I hold you like this?" he asked as he brought her close, their bodies facing each other.

Melanie pressed her face into his shoulder and took a deep breath. Calmness settled slowly over her.

God, he felt so good against her. At times like this she felt safe, truly safe, as if no one could ever hurt her again. Why couldn't it always be like this? Why did the act he had in mind have to be so painful, so awful? Why couldn't there be a better way?

Zachary felt her relax against him. "What happened to make you so afraid?"

She shrugged. "Do we have to talk about it?"

"No. We don't have to talk at all. Caroline is asleep. We could take a nap."

Melanie smiled at the word *nap*, for the way he said it in no way suggested sleeping. "You know, I was thinking this morning. The Bible says Eve tempted Adam, but I don't think that's true."

Zachary smiled. "Don't you? Why not?"

"Because men know exactly what they want. No doubt they always have. Eve didn't have to convince Adam. He probably did the convincing."

"You might be right about that. But how do you think such a mistake was made?"

"Because men wrote the Bible, and men never admit to a failing. It's easier to blame the woman. 'Oh dear, I couldn't help myself. She was just too tempting for a mere mortal man.'"

Zachary chuckled, recognizing her words as those he'd once said.

"That was probably why women were made to wear veils, so the poor man wouldn't be tempted." She made a *tsk*ing sound. "Wretched beasts all."

Zachary chuckled. "Except for me, of course."

"Of course," she returned a bit too quickly.

Zachary smiled and rocked her gently against him. He thought her reasoning might hold a measure of truth. Considering what he had in mind, it might hold a great deal of truth. "But you could never be tempted, could you, Melanie?"

Melanie wished she could remain forever in this
man's arms. She'd never known what true contentment was until he'd held her. She might have known
a slightly unsettled feeling, but it wasn't temptation,
she was sure. "I'm a woman," she said simply. "How
could I be tempted?"

"Are you?" Zachary asked, as if he'd only just realized the fact. Grinning, he stepped back and looked
her over. "Yes, I think you might be right. You're
wearing a dress, so you must be a woman, but I'd
have to see what's under it to be sure."

"You're being ridiculous again."

Zachary laughed. "Not now, of course, but eventually I will have to see."

"I don't want to talk about it." Melanie began to
clear away the leftover dough and apple peels.

Zachary was at her side. "Did he never once touch
you gently?"

"He never touched me at all, except when he . . . "
Her hands grew still as the memory, the nightmare,
took hold. She tried never to think of it. Why did he
insist that she should?

"I can't imagine a man not wanting to touch you,"
he said. "Were I your husband, I'd never stop."

"Zachary." She turned away as she spoke. "I know
I sort of implied that I would, but I can't do this. I
truly cannot."

"Leave that," he said as he took her hand and
brought her to his chair. Again he placed her upon
his lap. "I can't fight your ghosts, Melanie. You have
to tell me what he did."

"What do you mean? He did what every husband
does."

"I don't think so. I can't believe you would be so
frightened if what he did was normal. I know he

didn't kiss you and now you say he didn't touch you either. What the hell did he do?"

"Let me up," Melanie said, only to find his arms tightening around her.

"No. You're not leaving until you tell me."

"I can't ..."

Zachary pulled her closer, pressing her face into his neck, so she wouldn't have to watch him as she spoke. "Is this better? Can you tell me now?"

Long moments of silence stretched on, and Zachary was beginning to think she might never tell him, when he felt her take a deep breath and begin to speak. "The room was dark except for a small fire in the grate. I waited a long time. I knew he was supposed to come to me, but I thought perhaps he had fallen asleep. And then he was standing beside the bed. I was a little startled because I hadn't heard him come in. I wanted to say something, but I was very nervous.

"He didn't say anything. He just pulled the covers down and knelt on the bed. And then he reached under me and sort of flipped me over onto my stomach. His arm reached around my waist and he pulled me to my knees.

"My face was pressed into the bed, into the pillow actually. He pulled my gown up. He was behind me and then ... and then—" She took a small shaken breath. "I screamed into the pillow." She shuddered at the memory. Zachary ran his hand over her back and cuddled her closer.

"When he was finished, he pulled my gown into place again and left."

Zachary understood at last why she was so afraid, why standing behind her made her so uncomfortable, why the thought of making love so disgusted her. Obviously, having had no other experience, she thought the horror she had experienced was making love. "And was every time the same?" he asked.

"It was. Except I didn't scream those times. I knew what he was going to do. It hurt, but I could bear it."

Zachary knew an urge to kill the bastard. How the hell could a bridegroom so misuse his lady? His impulse was to curse the man and his mistreatment in the most vile words he knew. But curses weren't about to ease Melanie's fears. No, that would take time and trust. Long minutes ticked by before he dared to speak. "Melanie, that wasn't making love. That was unbelievable abuse."

Melanie frowned as she faced him at last. "How can a man abuse his own wife? He was just doing his husbandly duty."

"My ass. He was brutal, unnatural. Something must be wrong with him."

"I think something is. I saw him once with another man. They were . . ." She almost gasped, realizing too late what she'd said. She hadn't meant to ever tell another living soul.

There was a long moment of silence before he asked, "And that shocked you?"

"It disgusted me. I left him after that." She breathed a sigh and then, unable to stop now that she'd started, added, "I never thought a man could . . . could . . . I never thought . . . " Her words faltered to a close. She might have needed to talk about it, but the truth was, the subject was simply too much for her to comprehend.

"What were they doing?"

"I shouldn't talk about it. I didn't mean to tell you."

"Were they kissing?"

Silence.

"There are men who prefer other men, Melanie. I

suppose you know that now. No doubt your husband is one of them."

"Why?"

"I don't know, but some do."

"It's a sin. The Bible says so."

"The Bible says lots of things."

"You don't think it's wrong?"

"I don't know if it's wrong or not. I only know it's not for me. What's truly wrong is to bring another person to your bed when you're married." Zachary sighed. "What I want to know is, if the man preferred other men, why the hell did he marry you?"

Melanie shrugged. "My father arranged the union. He wanted me to be a duchess."

And her husband got something in return, Zachary thought. Money, no doubt. The truth of the matter was, despite his preferences, her husband could have easily treated her with kindness. Knowing she was an innocent, he could have been gentle. That he hadn't, made Zachary furious. He silently promised if he ever got the chance the man would know some pain of his own. "You wouldn't feel pain in my bed, Melanie."

She did not respond.

"Do you believe me?"

She lowered her gaze to his chest. "I don't know."

"You said he never kissed you, that he never touched you. Already it's not the same."

Melanie had to admit that much was true. Being with Zachary wasn't anything like being with Waverly. Still, there were obstacles that would always keep them apart. She pulled back, her gaze upon her hands twisted together in her lap. "Zachary, it's not right. We're both married."

"We *were* married. You're divorcing him, aren't you?"

"I'll get an annulment as soon as I return."

"Don't you believe I'm going to do the same?"

Melanie raised her gaze to his. Until now he hadn't spoken about his plans. "Will you?"

"I'd do it now, if I could."

"You no longer love her?"

Zachary smiled. "I told you once before that I never really loved her."

"Yes, you said women aren't worthy of a man's love."

"There might be some women who are."

Their gazes held for the longest moment. Melanie's heart swelled at the tenderness in his eyes. Did he mean that he loved her? She waited for him to go on, but Zachary said no more.

He couldn't bring himself to say it. If he declared his love, he'd also beg her to stay. And she couldn't stay. She didn't belong here. They had only now, only this short time. He wouldn't ask her for more.

Chapter 7

"**C**aroline is hot." The baby was whining pitifully, lying limply in Melanie's arms.

"What?" Zachary left his chair before the fire and joined her beside the baby's bed. "Let me see."

He pressed a hand to the child's forehead and found the skin beneath his hot and clammy. "She has a fever."

"Why?"

"I don't know. Don't babies get fevers?"

"I haven't been around babies much," Melanie answered. "I wish I knew."

"Well, babies aren't all that much different from grown-up people, are they? I reckon cool rags will take the fever down."

Melanie nodded in agreement. "And water. Lots of water."

An hour went by as both adults ministered to Caroline's needs. But the baby showed no improvement. In fact, her condition worsened. Another hour, and then another, passed and it didn't seem to matter how much water they forced down her throat, or how many wet towels they wrapped around her, her skin grew hotter than ever.

She cried constantly and refused to be parted from either Melanie or Zachary. They took turns holding

133

her, carrying her, bouncing her gently and patting her small bottom, anything that might bring her a measure of comfort.

It was three in the morning when Zachary took the baby in his arms again. "You look exhausted," he told Melanie. "Better get some rest. There's no tellin' how long this will go on."

Melanie sat down on the bed. And the next thing she knew an hour had gone by and Zachary was shaking her shoulder. "I think she's worse."

It took a second for her mind to clear and then only a glance at the baby to knew he was right. Caroline was worse. Obviously weakening, she no longer cried, but whimpered softly, eerily. Melanie thought she sounded just like she had that first day.

It couldn't be that she needed nourishment. Up until last night she'd had a healthy appetite. No, the fever was too high. It was draining the baby's strength. "Isn't there anything we can give her?" Melanie asked.

Zachary didn't want to admit that his daughter was gravely ill. But he couldn't deny the fear in Melanie's dark eyes. And seeing that fear increased his own. He had to do something. *But what?*

"Take off her clothes. We'll put her in a pot of cool water. If that doesn't work, I'll ride over to Gray Cloud. She'll have something. She always does."

Melanie was too busy preparing a cool bath to ask who Gray Cloud was. "I'll give her the bath. You ride over now."

Zachary pulled on his coat. "It might take a while. She lives a couple of miles from here and the snow is deep."

"It doesn't matter. Just hurry as best you can."

Within seconds he was gone. Melanie heard the thuds of his footsteps as he ran down the path toward the barn. Alone with a gravely ill baby, she could only pray for his speedy return.

It was almost dawn before he came back. Caroline was sleeping fitfully in Melanie's embrace. Melanie's arms ached, her back hurt. Tears of relief misted her eyes as Zachary threw the door open.

"I've got something. Gray Cloud said to boil these leaves. They will lower the fever. She said that babies often get high fevers. That Caroline might be cutting a new tooth."

Melanie smiled, relieved at the thought. "Is that all?" She turned her attention toward the baby as Zachary placed a spoonful of leaves into a cup of water. "Is that what this is all about? Are your gums hurting, sweetheart?"

An hour later, Zachary entered the house again after seeing to his horse. Melanie had finished feeding the baby the herbal tea and Caroline was sleeping. "I think she feels cooler."

Zachary might have reached forward to assure himself, but his hands were cold. He nodded and went to the fire instead.

He didn't say anything for the longest time. And then finally, he said, "I know . . . What I mean to say is . . . " He breathed a deep sigh. "I want to thank you."

"For what?" Melanie prompted, returning from having placed the baby in bed at last.

"For taking care of her like you did. If you weren't here, I would have had to bring her with me to Gray Cloud's. Caroline might have died."

"If it's only a tooth, she wouldn't have. And there's no need to thank me. I love her."

"But you never . . . I mean, where you come from, a servant would have . . . "

Melanie frowned. "Zachary, my father has servants, yes, but I'm still an ordinary woman who was raised to contribute to the household."

"But you're rich."

"So? Must money make me into a China doll?"

Zachary might have said yes, but he knew she'd disagree.

Zachary sat by the fire, watching the golden red flames and thinking of Melanie and the elegance of her manner that no rags could hide. She might think of herself as an ordinary woman, but she wasn't.

Caroline slept most of the day. Periodically either Melanie or Zachary checked on her. Her fever broke early that morning and she awakened that afternoon, tired but much her usual self.

The next day, the house smelled of baking biscuits when Zachary came in, his arms loaded with freshly chopped wood. Melanie knew he chopped it in the barn, where it was warmer and the wood was easier to work with. Still, he looked to be freezing. As soon as logs were stored he reached for the ever-present pot of coffee and poured himself a cup. Melanie was happy to see that his hand had gained almost all of its original strength.

He turned to see Melanie on the floor with the baby, a wide grin curving her lips. "You're never going to believe this," she said.

"What?"

"Just sit down and wait."

Zachary took off his coat and did as he was told. The room was silent except for Caroline's soft cooing. And then she suddenly rolled from her stomach to her back. She trembled and her mouth curved into a pout as Zachary exclaimed a bit too eagerly, with a loud slap of his hands. "That's wonderful! Caroline, you're getting so big!"

Melanie shushed him. "That's not all of it." Moments later they both watched the baby roll again, this time to her stomach.

"I can't believe it. How did she learn . . . ?"

"Just watch."

The baby was off the blanket now. She rolled again, each movement bringing her closer to the fire. Obviously the heat, color, and movement of the flames were too tempting to resist. "Tomorrow I'll gather rocks and make a low wall around the fireplace opening."

As the baby rolled once again, Rusty, who appeared to be asleep as usual at the hearth, opened one eye and came slowly to his feet. He seemed to eye the adults with disgust. Zachary watched closely as the dog approached the baby. He looked to be sniffing her, but a moment later Rusty found a piece of clothing that he could grasp with his teeth and began dragging the baby back to the center of the room. Then he returned to his bed and settled down for another nap.

"I can't believe it. Did you teach him to do that?" Zachary exclaimed.

Melanie laughed. She was still laughing when she rose to take the biscuits from the oven. Her mind on the baby and Rusty's masterful feat, she forgot to protect her hand from the hot oven handle.

She gave a startled cry of pain and released a string of curses. Loud and amazingly varied, they filled the cabin as she shook her hand, as if shaking it would somehow dislodge the discomfort. She cursed again.

"What else did you do back home, consort with sailors?" Zachary teased.

"Oh, be quiet!" she said.

Finally taking pity, Zachary hurried outside and returned with a pail of snow. He buried her hand in it.

"Oh," she moaned, wiping her eyes with her free hand.

"Is it better?"

"No. But it's not worse."

Zachary smiled. "I didn't know ladies could swear so colorfully."

"What you mean is, you didn't know *I* could." Despite the pain in her hand, Melanie was able to produce a small smile. "I was gently raised, but not in a convent. Besides, the men aboard ship were kind enough to expand my vocabulary. Lord, this really hurts." Melanie couldn't help the thought that if she wasn't here, she wouldn't have been burned. That if these god-awful snows hadn't come early, she might right now be back home, perhaps visiting with her friends or her sister. Finally, as the pain began to lessen, Melanie was able to push aside the longing to see her family again. She was a sensible woman who knew there was no sense wishing for what could not be.

"Leave your hand in the snow," Zachary advised. "When it starts to feel better, I'll put on some salve that Gray Cloud makes for me."

"Gray Cloud is an Indian, I take it."

Zachary nodded.

"When am I going to meet her?"

"Do you want to?"

"Of course."

"After the weather clears a bit then."

He prepared the rest of dinner that night and washed the dishes. He did the same the next night. Melanie's hand was better by then, but he thought it wouldn't hurt to keep it out of water one more day.

Caroline was in bed for the night and Melanie was sitting by the fire. Unable to sew or do needlepoint because of her injury, she felt bored. "Have you nothing to read?" she asked.

"Only the Bible." He nodded toward the fireplace mantel.

Melanie dusted off the leather jacket and took the book into her lap. She paged through it and stopped at the psalms. "Do you like the psalms?"

"I don't read much." The truth of the matter was, despite Mrs. Morrison's best efforts, he'd never fully mastered the feat. Zachary wasn't ashamed of the fact. Still he didn't brag on it either.

"They're quite lovely, you know. Shall I read to you?"

Zachary shrugged. "If you like."

Melanie read and Zachary listened, not so much to the words as to the sound of her voice. How would he manage when the nights were quiet again? he wondered.

When the kitchen had been put to order, Zachary sat opposite her and lit his pipe. Melanie accepted a drop or two from his jug. For medicinal purposes, he said, but she noticed the generous portion he allowed himself.

Zachary took a hefty swallow. Melanie sipped, screwing up her features at the taste. "This is probably the worst whiskey I've ever tasted."

"It's probably the worst anyone has ever tasted."

"Why do you drink it?"

"Because Holbrook makes it and it's either drink it or hurt the man's feelings. He brings a jug or two every time he comes."

Melanie shot him a look of disbelief. "And I suppose pouring it out has never occurred to you?"

Zachary grinned. "Nope. Can't say that it has. It's good for what ails you, Holbrook says."

"Then it's fortunate for me that my injury is small."

He liked her smile. Sometimes there was a devilish quality to it. When she smiled, really smiled, she no longer looked like a lady. For one thing, she had a front tooth that was crooked. Zachary had once thought that all great ladies had perfect teeth. Perfect everything, in fact. So her crooked tooth made her look sweeter, more human. It was probably the tooth that caused him to forget things he'd best remember. Or maybe it was the feel of that tooth against his tongue.

"I like your smile," he said.

"Thank you."

"What would you be doing now, if you were home?"

"Visiting friends probably. Maybe there would be a concert or a new play to see. During the holidays there would be balls, with beautiful ladies in even more beautiful gowns, trips north, and sleigh rides." Another smile curved her lips. "The houses are so pretty this time of year. Holly and pine decorate every mantel and fires burn in the grates. It's all very cheerful and lovely." She sighed at the memories, never realizing how quiet Zachary had grown.

Neither heard the horse approaching. Rusty growled seconds before someone knocked on the door. Melanie and Zachary both jumped in startlement. Melanie came instantly to her feet and headed for the curtained-off room. Suddenly she dashed back and snatched her dry stockings from the chair. A moment later she was sitting on Zachary's bed listening as he exchanged greetings with what she assumed was a neighbor.

"Armstrong!" Zachary exclaimed, surprised to see the father of the man Margaret had run off with. He closed the door against a gust of cold wind. "What are you doing out in this weather?"

Zebadiah Armstrong shook the snow from his hat. "Had to come. Had to let you know what happened."

"What is it?"

"Margaret is dead. She was killed."

Zachary said nothing for a long time, unable to believe the news. "How did it happen?"

"You got something warm to drink?"

Zachary nodded toward the table and chairs. "Sit," he said. "I'll get you some coffee." He then poured two cups and sat opposite his neighbor. "What happened?"

"Indians got them. After leaving here, she and Anthony rode south. Probably made it to the Carolinas before they were attacked. Margaret was killed." Zebadiah lowered his gaze and added, "You should know they didn't go easy on her. Anthony was left for dead."

"How do you know this?"

"A trapper found him." Zebadiah cradled the cup in his cold hands and took a long sip of the hot liquid. "Took care of him until he recovered from his wounds. He came back last week to see me and his ma."

"Where is he now?"

"He left again. I reckon he knew what you'd do to him otherwise."

Zachary shook his head. They had had this conversation before and Zachary had told Zebadiah then that his son should feel in no danger, that he didn't want revenge.

Zebadiah finished his coffee, pushed back his chair

and stood awkwardly. He pulled on his gloves again. "I thought you should know."

Zachary nodded as the man walked to the door and let himself out.

A moment later Melanie touched Zachary's shoulder. He sighed as he imagined the suffering Margaret must have endured. He might not have cared for her much, might have known peace and contentment in seeing her gone from his life, but he had never wished her ill. "You heard?"

"Who is Anthony?"

"Zebadiah's son. The man Margaret ran off with."

"I feel so sorry for her."

Zachary placed his hand over hers, his heart filled with pity.

Caroline began to cry and Melanie left him to go care for the baby.

They didn't speak about it again. Zachary didn't talk at all until later, as he held Melanie tightly against him in bed. Breathing in the scent of her hair, he said, "At least now I can tell Caroline that her mother died. Now she won't ever have to know that her mother cared so little for her that she up and left her."

"How did she leave? What did she do?"

"I came in from the fields one day to find her and the baby gone. She left Caroline with Zebadiah's family."

"Were you very angry?" Melanie asked softly.

"I was at first. But later I was more relieved than angry. Margaret wasn't happy. It makes for hard living when your woman isn't happy."

"But she knew you were saving for a future. She knew she wouldn't always live here. Why couldn't she wait?"

Melanie wrapped her arms around his waist and

despite his nakedness, molded herself against him. Not waiting for a response, she added, "What was the matter with her? How could she leave you? How could she leave her baby?"

And yet in a few months Melanie would do the very same thing, he thought. He was falling in love with her and even knowing he was bound to suffer terribly once she was gone, he couldn't seem to help himself. "I don't know. I wish I did." Zachary wished more than that. He wished he knew how to make things right between them. He wished he could keep her with him forever.

"It's so sad. Caroline will never . . . Will you marry again?"

"I don't think so."

"But Caroline needs a mother."

"Why? She has me."

"Every girl needs a mother."

"You didn't have one. You said she died when you were a child."

"I had Ellen. When I was a child she was always there to take care of me."

"A servant?"

"Ellen is more than a servant. When I was little I would climb in her bed when it stormed at night. She bandaged my scrapes and kissed away my tears. I loved her as much as I could any mother. Ellen was indentured to another family when we arrived in this country. I have to find her before I go back. I can't leave her here."

"Do you know where she is?"

"Mr. Moody said she was sold to a Mr. Martin. Do you know him?"

Zachary nodded. "His mother is sick, I think."

"I hope Ellen is all right."

Zachary almost asked then. He almost asked her to

other, to be his love. But he
matter what his wants, they
This place wasn't enough,
wasn't enough. A woman
making her life with an ig-

" he said at last, and after a
lanie was asleep.

Chapter 8

❦

Edward Stacey was a gambler and half owner of the London gambling den and whorehouse called "Fancy." A handsome man, he stood tall upon the gently swaying deck, his feet spread slightly for balance. His thoughts far from his present surroundings, he allowed his long tailed coat to part against the steady breeze. Unconsciously he fingered the gold chain secured to a button of his waistcoat. A moment later he retrieved a gold watch from a small pocket, opened it and shut it again before replacing it in his vest. He breathed a long sigh, wishing this journey was at an end. He'd planned on three weeks, but three had become five as a storm had driven them off course.

He had to get his hands on his old grandmother's money. She had more than she needed, after all, and wouldn't miss what he took. Edward shrugged. The fact was, he didn't much care if she missed it or not. There was no time to lose, not if he wanted to keep the law off his back and his ass out of prison.

His partner Jim Brown already suspected something was wrong with the books. It wouldn't take long before he found the discrepancies. He had to get the money and return to London before that hap-

145

pened. His blue eyes scanned the horizon as he waited impatiently for land to appear.

Later, in his cabin below deck, Edward sat on a narrow bed. He took a sip of brandy and smiled as he watched the lady standing before him slowly part the bodice of her dress to reveal milky white breasts. He'd known she was full-breasted. Along with her obvious interest in him, her full hourglass figure was why he'd chosen to bestow his attention in the first place. Still, he hadn't realized she was so well-endowed.

"Very nice," he said, his voice husky with growing need. He leaned against the cabin wall, his legs spread as an erection pressed uncomfortably against his trousers.

"Nice?" she asked, obviously expecting to hear a more generous compliment. "I imagine they're about as nice as what you've got growing in your trousers," she said in all confidence as she carelessly discarded her petticoat.

Edward grinned as his gaze took in the white skin, wide hips, flat belly, and black silk stockings she'd kept in place. He watched as she ran her hands seductively over her body, lifting heavy breasts for his pleasure. She smiled as he licked his lips. Edward cleared a husky throat. "You think you could do something about these trousers? They're getting awfully tight."

The Countess Linda Vatalti, more correctly known as Linda Farrell, came from London's mean streets. Her mother was a prostitute and Linda had once thought it more than likely that she'd also end up servicing blokes for a pittance in dirty alleys. She was thirteen when she saw a high-class whore step from a coach accompanied by a distinguished looking gentleman, and realized the monetary advantage of acting like a lady.

That very day she'd told her mother she wanted to work as a servant in a rich man's household. Her mother had laughed at the idea that her little girl would dirty her hands in some gent's kitchen when money could be gotten so much more easily by whoring. But Linda had ignored the jeering. She had a plan.

She started in the kitchen, but soon worked her way to the rooms upstairs. And while she served, she studied the rich. Studied them until she could walk and talk just like them. Studied them until even the elite couldn't distinguish her from one of their own.

Two years ago, Linda went to the Continent, had a baby, left him inside the first church she came across, and married an Italian Count. At least she'd secured the documents needed to prove that she had. A title was bound to get her most anything she wanted. The truth was, it didn't matter if one were truly titled. It only mattered that one could play the part. In the end a woman couldn't lose if she were smart.

She'd learned the truth of that when she was caught in bed with a wealthy woman's husband and, in retaliation, the fat matron accused Linda of stealing her jewels. Although in this case Linda hadn't taken anything, she was arrested, imprisoned, and made to stand trial. But she had always been lucky, and the moment she'd stepped into court, she'd realized just how extraordinarily lucky. She had once taken the magistrate as a lover. Henry visited her three times in her cell during the five-day trial. The verdict of not guilty was a foregone conclusion.

Were it not for her extreme talent in bed, she might now be heading for the colonies not as a lady of leisure, but as an indentured servant.

With a title, real or not, and her looks, she could have married most any man, but Linda wasn't the sort to marry. It wasn't her dream to cater to a man, not when there were so many who might cater to her instead. Marriage meant your husband owned you, and Linda would never be owned.

All she wanted was money. Soon she'd have enough. And with that money wisely invested, she could live as she pleased, enjoying any man who took her fancy.

Today she wanted Edward Stacey. She forgot her pretense of being a lady as her gaze settled upon his growing erection. She knelt between his legs, her mouth salivating as she imagined what lay in store for her.

Edward Stacey rarely allowed business to interfere with an opportunity to enjoy a particular lady and her favors. There was, after all, a time for business and a time for pleasure. And he was about to enjoy the latter.

Just off the island of Jamaica, Harry Stone paced the *Charity*'s deck impatiently. Three storms—good God it was like an omen. Was he not meant to find his daughter? The *Charity* had limped toward the island of Jamaica more than three weeks late. Yet another week had gone by while Mr. Stone anxiously waited for repairs to be made.

Would he ever get to Virginia? Would he ever find Melanie? He would, he vowed, with never failing determination. It didn't matter how many obstacles God threw in his path. He would find Melanie and bring her home where she belonged.

Melanie wouldn't have thought it possible, but she was becoming accustomed to Zachary Pitt's lack of modesty. Without a hint of embarrassment he stood naked before her every chance he got, acting as if nakedness were a common, everyday occurrence.

Preparing for bed, he dropped the last of his clothes into a pile on the floor. He knelt upon the mattress and grinned as Melanie, already under the blanket and on her side of the bed, feigned a sudden fascination with the pattern in the quilt. It was one thing, she supposed, to watch the man while he wasn't aware of it, but quite another to stare openly, especially when he was so close.

Zachary smiled at her shyness, unable to imagine a woman more desirable, more perfect.

Every day he had pushed her a little further. Slowly, very slowly he was sorry to admit, she was growing comfortable with his touch. She could laugh now at his playful gropings, wicked leers, and bawdy comments, and she almost always came willingly into his arms, eager for his kisses. Still, every night she dressed like a damn nun, covered from neck to foot in her chemise.

Maybe it was time to breech her last defense. "You know, I've been thinking," he said.

"Do you think you could think under the covers?"

Zachary grinned. "Why? Am I bothering you sitting here?"

"First of all, you're not sitting, you're kneeling and, yes, you are bothering me."

"Why?"

"Because you have no clothes on, of course."

"And that bothers you?" he asked in pretend amazement, for he knew very well that she was bothered. The only problem was, she wasn't being bothered in exactly the right way.

"It would bother anyone," she said.

"I don't think so. For instance, if you took off that chemise, I wouldn't be bothered at all."

Melanie shot him a wry look that clearly expressed her disbelief. "You might as well get the thought out of your mind. It's not about to happen."

"Perhaps it's not *about* to happen, but it *will* happen eventually."

"I don't think so."

Zachary decided he'd waited long enough. He had to take the next step in this seduction and soon. If he did not, they might go on like this forever—sharing a bed, sleeping in each other's arms like brother and sister. Well, *almost* like brother and sister.

Without another word, he snapped the quilt to the bottom of the bed.

Melanie gasped and stiffened with dread. Her voice was thin and high-pitched. "I'm not ready. Please."

"I'm not going to do anything you don't want me to do. I promise you that."

"Then bring the covers back."

Zachary chuckled. "If you say so, Duchess. But you don't mind if I get under them, do you?"

"I would be grateful, actually."

Melanie might have sighed with relief as the quilt was returned to its former position. Might have, if Zachary weren't at this very minute under it. Completely under it. "What are you doing?" she asked the huge mound in the middle of the bed.

"Nothing. Why? Do you want me to do something?"

"No."

"That's good, because I was just trying to get warm."

Beneath the covers, Zachary moved to the bottom of the bed.

"Where are you going?"

"Nowhere. Just trying to find a comfortable spot. There, I think I found it," he said as he positioned himself at her feet.

"Do you expect to sleep there?" she asked with just a touch of panic in her voice.

"I wasn't thinking of sleeping at the moment."

"You should. It's late." Her panic was increasing.

Zachary touched her foot. She jumped and pulled it away.

"Are your feet ticklish?"

"Yes, very."

"But not on the top, right?"

"Why?"

"Well, I was thinking you have very pretty feet and I should like very much to kiss them."

Melanie thought that had to be his oddest request yet. Whatever made the man think of such nonsense? Although she could never bring herself to do it, she might have suggested that there were other places where she would enjoy a kiss more. Places like her lips, her shoulders and neck, and maybe even her breasts.

Zachary had seemed particularly partial to kissing her breasts of late and had done so at just about every opportunity. Why, just this morning she'd been kneading dough for bread when he'd leaned against the table at her side and without so much as a *please* or *may I*, had opened the bodice of her dress and sampled quite nicely the soft flesh he found there.

By the time he had finished, and had gone off to play with Caroline on the floor, Melanie had had to sit for a bit before she had the strength to finish her chore.

She would have enjoyed another sampling ever so much more than foot kissing. Still, she dared say nothing, lest the man believe she liked his attention a bit too much.

His mouth touched her foot and she jumped again. "What's the matter?"

"I'm nervous."

He kissed her foot again. She didn't pull away this time. "Do you like that?"

"I suppose."

"When you don't like it, tell me and I'll stop."

He kissed her foot most thoroughly and when he was finished, he showed the other foot the same consideration. Next came her ankles. Melanie thought they were perhaps a bit too sensitive. Still, she didn't have to think on it for long because before she could make up her mind as to whether she liked it or not, Zachary was kissing her shin. First one and then the other.

"Do you like this?"

She wanted to tell him yes. She wanted to tell him that although she thought his actions strange, his touch, his kisses were producing some tantalizing effects, pleasure being the most prominent. And along with that pleasure Melanie was feeling decidedly breathless, even as a lethargy slowly invaded her entire body. She felt almost as if she were floating at sea, feeling only a lovely, quite delightful sensation. She might have said what was on her mind, had she *understood* what was on her mind. Instead she said, "I'll tell you when I don't like it."

Zachary laughed and decided the wisest course would be not to ask again. Instead, his mouth slid to her knee.

Somehow the fact that he hadn't moved her chemise up, but had merely joined her beneath it, his body lying upon her legs, felt unbelievably erotic to her. His hands touched her legs, holding one and then the other. And as his mouth made love to her, Melanie felt her heart thud painfully in her chest. She couldn't breathe, though there could be no medical explanation for such a phenomenon.

She wanted him to come closer. The thought should have shamed her, but it didn't.

His hands slid up her legs to her waist. His fingers grasped the waistband of her drawers, undid the tabs and gently began to pull them down. He pulled them to her ankles and cast them aside as his mouth further investigated the taste and texture of her knees.

She was naked beneath the chemise and Zachary had only to reach up a bit. The thought brought a rush of color to her cheeks, while her heart pounded furiously. "Zachary," she said softly.

After a few seconds he answered with, "What?"

"What are you doing?"

"Kissing you."

"Why did you take them off?" The fact that he had taken upon himself the intimacy of touching her underthings, had actually taken them off, and was now in the midst of kissing her leg, in no way permitted her to mention unmentionables.

"They were in the way."

Lord, that opened the mind to possibilities, didn't it? *In the way? Of what?* Did he intend to touch her there? Kiss her there? Surely not. Still, his mouth was now at her thigh and moving upward to places where only she had ever touched.

"Zachary," she said again.

"What sweetheart?" he murmured against her, unwilling to leave the thigh that his tongue and teeth were so thoroughly enjoying.

"Nothing," Melanie finally returned. She couldn't ask if he was about to touch her there. If she asked, he might think she wanted him to. She didn't, of course. It was impossible that she might.

Something was happening to her. It was fear of the unknown, she supposed, for her body had lost some of its lethargy and was growing decidedly tense, more tense than she could ever have imagined, in fact. The closer he came to the forbidden, the more anxious, more breathless she grew, and still she murmured not a sound of protest. Why would the words not come?

She tried to shake her head and clear her thoughts, but the shake occurred slowly and her thoughts never materialized.

She felt his hands move her legs apart and had no will either to ask what he was about or to stop this slow but purposeful invasion.

Her breathing became jerky and harshly labored, her body tight. Now she understood it wasn't tight with fear, for she wasn't the least bit afraid. It was something else. Something she couldn't name.

She moved impatiently. Her body pulsed, just inches from where his mouth now lingered. An inch more. Just an inch. Would he do it?

And then his mouth reached her at last and Melanie sucked in a lung full of air through her teeth as her body tightened and her head pushed back against the pillow.

"Zachary." She moaned his name.

"Sweetheart," he said, the word muffled against her flesh, and the loud humming in her ears, and the thundering of her heart made her unsure of what she had heard.

Zachary's hands reached for her hips and as he held her for his enjoyment, Melanie's eyes closed. She'd never known a man and woman could share such intimacies. She didn't know exactly what he was doing. She didn't care. All she knew was that nothing had ever felt so good.

His tongue moved over her and Melanie gasped again and again, until a low, aching moan was torn from her lips.

She never noticed that her hips moved forward and she wouldn't have been able to stop the motion if she had. Her body felt alive. Every nerve ending tingled. Yet still, she hungered for more.

Deep inside she ached. Melanie had felt that ache before. She felt it when he kissed her, and especially when he loved her breasts, but never had it come with such intensity.

Her body grew tight, straining toward an elusive culmination. She stiffened. It was almost within her reach. Oh God, she needed it. She needed it so desperately.

She moaned again, trying to tell him something was wrong, that she was hurting, that he had to help. She was gasping now. She'd die if she didn't stop. If he couldn't stop the crushing need.

And then unexpectantly the tension reached a pinnacle and became an explosion of pleasure. Aching, delicious, incredible pleasure ripped through her in waves of mindless ecstasy.

Zachary felt the contracting surges of pleasure as her body opened and closed against his lips. And he knew that for the first time in her life Melanie had found release. He wished he could see her face and promised that next time he would. The next time he'd use his hands at the end so he could watch the pleasure as well as feel it.

He moaned his delight beneath the quilt, beneath her gown as her sweetness came. God, had a woman ever tasted so good?

Zachary continued to kiss her, to love her, until her

body grew heavy and pliant. It was only when he heard her soft sigh of contentment that he allowed himself one more delicious kiss and then slowly moved his mouth to her stomach, her waist and mid-riff, and then to the luscious softness of her breasts.

He lingered there for a long time, heavy against her body before he finally poked his head through the top of her chemise.

Zachary grinned at the narrowing of her eyes as she pretended to be annoyed. "I suppose you think I enjoyed that."

"Sweetheart, I promise you, the thought never crossed my mind."

"Good, because I wouldn't want you to think—"

He cut her words off with a long kiss that left behind the taste of herself. "I do my best never to try."

Zachary pulled back then, holding her face for his close inspection. Her eyes were soft, dark pools. He smiled and found his smile broadening as she answered with a smile of her own.

A moment later they were laughing for the pure joy of living, for loving, for this special moment of exquisite intimacy. He held her close as he rolled to his side, bringing her with him. There just might be a God after all, he thought, for nothing but God could have brought this perfect woman to him.

"I can see why you insist on wearing this. It's very soft, isn't it?" he said.

Melanie giggled and Zachary thought the sound was almost as delicious as the woman herself. "It's ridiculous that you should be in here with me."

"Why?"

"Well, for one thing we're squashed together."

"Are we?" He moved his body against hers again, delighting in the fact that she seemed to enjoy the feel of his body naked against hers. "I never noticed."

"And for another, *you're* not the least bit soft."

"Yeah, well, speaking of hard . . ."

"What?"

"I was just hoping you won't be too upset waking up next to a corpse."

"*What?*"

"The fact is, I'm probably going to die."

Melanie looked confused as she raised her head and leaned it upon her hand. "What are you talking about?"

"Well, the thing is, sweetheart. It's like this . . . Well, ah . . . "

Melanie had never seen this man at a loss for words. Never once had he shown even the slightest hesitation in stating his desires. Often, tonight for instance, he didn't state them at all, but merely acted on them. If she didn't know better she might have thought he was embarrassed.

Melanie imagined she knew the workings of his mind and what he hinted at. He was so wonderful. He had given her so much pleasure and had asked nothing for himself. She could not possibly deny his needs. "I wouldn't mind if we did it now, Zachary."

"No, I'm too far gone for that. You wouldn't find any pleasure in it at all. But you could do me a favor."

"What kind of favor?"

"Give me your hand and I'll show you."

And so Melanie learned the first step in pleasuring a man. And in learning to pleasure him, she found a degree of pleasure herself.

Zachary groaned as he buried his face in the warmth of her neck, his life-giving seed pouring from his trembling body. "Stop," he gasped, and then shuddered again. "That's enough, sweetheart."

A moment later he realized that Melanie was taking advantage of the situation to explore the rest of his body with a casual touch. He leaned back just a bit, allowing her hand to thoroughly discover what her gaze had only thus far seen.

"I can't begin to tell you how good that feels," he said.

She pulled her hand away. And Zachary realized too late that he should have kept his comment to himself.

Zachary brought them both to a kneeling position and pulled the chemise from their bodies. A moment later, with the material bunched in his hands, he wiped the perspiration from her body. Meticulously, lest one speck of skin remain damp, he rubbed her body until it glowed. By the time he was finished he was aroused again.

"I think I was dry ten minutes ago," she said as he continued to pay close attention to her breasts.

"Let me see," Zachary said as he suddenly kissed one breast and then the other. "You're right. They're dry."

Melanie could only smile, the fact of the matter being, they had now grown damp again from his open-mouthed kisses. She said nothing as she watched him dry himself.

Melanie noticed, of course, that she was kneeling opposite him, that neither was wearing clothes. And yet she felt perfectly at ease in her nakedness. No doubt the darkness of the room added to her lack of self-consciousness, for the only light came from the flickering flames of the fire. She brushed back a thick lock of hair as her gaze followed her chemise to the floor. She asked, "One question. What am I supposed to sleep in now?"

"My arms."

Melanie looked at him for a long moment before a soft smile curved her lips. She reached for his shoulders and, circling his neck, brought her body close to his, sighing her contentment.

Zachary brought his arms around her waist. "Would you like to sleep with me?"

"Do you think you can control yourself if I do?" She spoke against his skin, never realizing how she took advantage of her position and almost casually kissed him and ran her tongue and mouth over his neck.

"I'm afraid that's no longer the question."

She leaned back enough to look into his eyes and smiled at the twinkling mischief there. "No? What is the question?"

"The question is, can *you* control *your*self, now that you know about the pleasure?"

Melanie laughed and buried her face in the warmth of his throat. "I'll try."

They snuggled together under the covers, laughing and playing, as carefree as children. He reached for parts of her she thought he had no reason to casually stroke. She pushed his hands away, which simply made him reach again. He tickled her; she grabbed him. He shouted in surprise; she dissolved into a fit of laughter. "Be quiet. You'll wake up the baby," she admonished.

"Sorry. I just never expected you to grab me there."

Melanie laughed again, feeling more comfortable at his side as each moment passed.

"I promise I won't shout the next time," he said.

She said nothing.

"I mean if you touched me there again, you know. I wouldn't yell or anything."

Still nothing.

"I probably wouldn't even mind it. No, I can say with certainty, I wouldn't mind it at all."

"It couldn't be that you want me to touch you there, could it?" she asked.

"Well, I haven't given it much thought, actually."

"Why don't I believe you?"

"Because you think all I think about is touching you and you touching me."

"And I'm wrong?"

"Absolutely."

Melanie chuckled wickedly as she slid her body against his. "All right then, tell me one time when you're not thinking about it."

"One time?"

"One time."

"That's easy."

"Good, then tell me."

"One time when I'm not thinking of touching you," he said almost to himself. "One time," he mused again and then stated flatly, "I can't."

Melanie laughed again.

"You know, it might be better if I just lie like this," she said as she rolled to her back and placed her hands under her head.

"Why?"

"Because you might as well get it over with, so we both can get some sleep."

"You mean you want me to touch you?"

"I mean, I'm allowing you to touch me."

"Why?"

"Because it won't be quite so enjoyable when I don't object and you'll soon stop."

Zachary was instantly at her side, his hands moving freely over her lush, soft curves. He stroked, caressed, and loved her as he pleased. His lips were investigating her breasts quite thoroughly when he said, "You were wrong, you know. This is just as enjoyable."

And he continued to enjoy himself far into the evening.

She didn't mind at all.

Chapter 9

Melanie came slowly awake the next morning to a bed empty except for herself. She rolled to her side and blinked open one eye. It was early yet. Caroline wouldn't be awake for another hour at least. She sighed as she snuggled deeper beneath the covers.

Half asleep, she heard the cabin's door open and close. A moment later Zachary sat on the corner of the bed and removed his boots and trousers. He pulled back the quilt, not an easy chore since Melanie held the covers tightly around her. "Let me in, I'm freezing," he said.

Melanie gasped at the feel of his icy skin against hers. "Don't touch me." She tried to back away. "You're cold."

"I need you to warm me up," he said, ignoring her objection and pulling her close against him, rubbing his icy hands down her back. It did a wonderful job of bringing her instantly awake.

"Where were you?" she asked.

"Fighting Indians."

"Really? Why?"

"Because I had to protect you."

Melanie smiled as she rubbed her face against his hairy chest. "That was very brave of you."

"I thought so."

"How many of them were there?"

"One squaw."

Melanie chuckled. "You were protecting me from a squaw?"

"They're very brave and strong, you know."

"Are they? All of them?"

"I don't know that many."

Melanie came to her elbow.

"What are you doing?" he asked as he pulled her against him again.

"Are you serious?"

"Well, I wasn't fighting her, exactly. She came for some meat. She does that every so often."

"How did you know she was here? I didn't hear anything."

"I didn't hear her either. I never do. She shoved my shoulder."

Melanie stiffened. "She what?"

"Shoved my ... What's the matter?"

"She was here? In the house? She saw us sleeping together?"

"Well, unless she suddenly went blind, I suppose ... "

Melanie groaned and pushed herself away from him.

"What's the matter?"

"Nothing, it's just that ... What did you do after she shoved your shoulder?"

"I got up. Why?"

"You got up while she was still here?"

"Melanie what ... ?"

"She stayed here and watched you come from the bed naked?"

"Melanie, Indians see naked men all the time. It

doesn't mean anything. She probably didn't even look."

"She probably didn't look, but you're not sure?"

Zachary couldn't for the life of him imagine why Melanie was suddenly so upset. Apparently his vagueness had greatly upset her. "She didn't look."

"Get up."

"Why?" Zachary looked at the lady sharing his bed and could find not the slightest glimmer of last night's softness or passion in her eyes. Damn. He only wished he knew what he had done to get her all fired up.

"Because, I'm not sleeping with you. You're disgusting," she said.

They were almost the exact words Margaret had said to him the last time she'd shared his bed. And Zachary felt again the old pain of rejection. He hadn't been good enough for Margaret, and he certainly wasn't good enough for Melanie.

"So now I'm disgusting, am I?" he said. "You seemed to enjoy all the disgusting things I did to you last night."

Melanie knew that in a moment of confusion he should bring up the intimacy they had shared. *What did one thing have to do with the other?* "I didn't know last night."

"Didn't know what? What the hell is the matter with you?"

Caroline made a whimpering sound in response to his shouting. "Oh wonderful. Now you've woken up the baby," Melanie said.

Zachary cursed and rolled from the bed. A moment later he had his trousers in place and was heading for the fireplace, grumbling beneath his breath.

Melanie waited until his back was to her before she dared to scramble from the bed and drop the curtain back into place. She dressed hurriedly and went to see to the baby's needs.

By the time Melanie entered the warm kitchen, Zachary had gone out again. She made coffee, cooked, and ate breakfast before he came back.

When he did, she wouldn't look at him. Zachary sighed and said, "I think I know what's bothering you, and I won't let it happen again. If you don't want Indians in here, I'll tell Gray Cloud to stay outside the next time she visits."

"Would you mind very much making sense when you speak?"

"I won't let her in here again. All right?"

"You mean you'll bar your door?"

"Yeah."

"Why?"

"Because you don't like it."

"Exactly what do you think I don't like?"

"Indians."

"You know, Mr. Pitt, I didn't think anyone could be as dim-witted as you appear to be."

He ignored her sarcasm. At the moment it was more important to discover the source of their misunderstanding. "You don't hate Indians?"

"I don't know any Indians, so how could I possibly hate them? As a matter of fact, at the moment, the only person I dislike is you."

Zachary grinned as he reached for her. He knew for a fact she did not hate him. She might be a little upset at the moment, but if that was hate she showed him last night, then he didn't know up from down.

The baby was caught between them. "Let me go. Caroline will get crushed," Melanie complained.

As far as Zachary could see, Caroline was enjoying her close proximity to the adult faces, which she was exploring with a poking finger. He said, "I'll let you go as soon as you tell me what got that tick up your ass."

Melanie sighed. "Well, since you put it so politely," she said sarcastically, "I'll tell you. You stood naked before another woman."

Zachary frowned. "Gray Cloud is old."

"How old?"

"I don't know, probably somewhere around seventy."

"I don't believe you."

Zachary laughed and tightened his hold on her, careful not to hurt the baby. "The next time she comes, I'll introduce you."

"Oh, that should be cozy. Then we can both watch you standing there naked."

Zachary's gaze narrowed. "Are you jealous?"

"Are you ridiculous?"

He grinned. "There's that word again."

"Mr. Pitt, there is absolutely no reason for me to be jealous. The question is a matter of modesty, of which you have none, I'm sorry to say. People, at least civilized people, simply do not go around naked, especially when a member of the opposite sex is watching."

"She wasn't watching. She's old enough to be my grandmother. Maybe even my great grandmother."

"It's still disgusting."

Zachary nibbled on Caroline's exploring finger, causing the baby to gurgle happily. "What if I promised that from now on, the only woman who will see me naked is you? Would that bring peace to this house?" A moment of silence went by before he asked, "All right?"

"Are you hungry?"

Apparently it was all right. She might be too stubborn to say so, but Zachary knew it was. He sighed his relief. "Can I get a good morning kiss first?"

"Of course." Melanie handed him the baby, "Caroline, kiss your father good morning."

Zachary chuckled as he hugged his daughter against his chest, his gaze moving from his baby to the woman who was now busily at work in his kitchen. "Make it a good one, Caroline. Show her she's not the only lady around here who can kiss."

Zachary gave his daughter a loud smacking kiss and Melanie smiled as their gazes met. "Too bad," he said. "You lost out on a memorable moment."

Melanie chuckled and bent before the fire to ladle out a bowl of porridge.

"Don't worry, sweetheart, I'll get her later," he said to the baby, and smiled in response to Melanie's soft chuckle.

He watched her as he ate. She was holding Caroline, laughing as a chubby hand got caught in her hair and pulled her mobcap askew. Melanie managed to repair the damage and with a gentle smile asked, "Do you want a cap of your own, darling? I could make one for you."

Caroline burped loudly. "Oh dear," Melanie said in surprise, "you're becoming more like your father every day."

She shot Zachary an accusing look and laughed at his grin. "There is another possibility, of course," she said, addressing the baby again. "Your father might be a baby in disguise. I've heard tell most men are somewhat inclined to childish behavior."

"Oh, you've heard that as well," Melanie said, pretending to listen to the baby's response. She nodded. "It's common knowledge, after all."

Melanie gasped as she was suddenly lifted from the chair. A moment later the three of them lay upon

Zachary's rumpled sheets. "There, you see," Melanie said, as if his actions had proven her words. But she didn't get a chance to say more, what with Zachary's mouth pressing on her lips.

Zachary kissed her quite thoroughly before allowing her lips their freedom. He smiled in response to her sigh.

"That was very nice," she murmured.

"What was nice?"

"The kiss."

"Oh, did I kiss you? I thought I was kissing Caroline," Zachary said as he deposited a quick kiss to his daughter's tiny lips.

Melanie chuckled softly and then widened her eyes as he dared to run his hand over her breast. "Zachary, Caroline is—"

"Sticking her fingers in my ears," he finished for her. "Is it time for her nap yet?"

Apparently Caroline found it a bit unpleasant being squashed, even lightly, between two adults. What she wanted was to sit. She made her feelings known with some struggles and a good deal of whining. Caroline sat between them, her attention on Melanie's cap again.

"She likes that cap," Zachary observed.

"I know. Ow," Melanie said as the baby twisted her chubby fingers into her hair. "She won't like it half so much when she has to wear one all the time."

"Why do you wear it? I like your hair down. I like being able to touch it."

"Long hair does not fare well among the cooking flames," Melanie commented, reminding Zachary of the dangers to women in their very own homes. He cuddled both his ladies closer at the thought.

Caroline shot an unhappy look her father's way.

Melanie smiled.

"Would you like to go for a ride?" he asked.

"A ride?" Melanie said, brightening. "Where would we go?"

"Well, we'd have to be careful, especially with the snow so deep, but I thought maybe we could visit Gray Cloud."

"Oh, I'd love it." Except for hurried trips to the privy, she hadn't been outside in weeks.

Zachary felt a slight disappointment at Melanie's obvious delight. He hadn't imagined that she so wanted to leave his small house. But of course she would, he told himself, even as he swore he felt no discomfort in the thought. His home had become a prison to her the minute it had started to snow.

He said nothing as she came from the bed and began to gather milk and food as well as extra clothing to take along for Caroline. Holding the baby in his lap, he watched Melanie. Everything about her was elegant and refined, from the demure way she lowered her eyes, to her habit of tipping her head to one side while listening to him. Even the way she bit her bottom lip as she concentrated on a task intrigued and aroused him.

The problem was, she was so damn far above him that he didn't have a chance in hell of winning her for his own. He wished things were different, but they weren't. He was a farmer and she was a lady. He'd be smart to keep those facts in mind.

Zachary took the bundle Melanie had prepared to the barn. He saddled his horse and after a few trips to the smoke house, hung from the saddle a half carcass of smoked moose and a sack of potatoes. Then he brought the animal to the front door. Melanie, Caroline in her arms, was waiting with Rusty at her side at the end of the path he'd dug. Her eyes wid-

ened with surprise at the sight of the packed horse.
"Are we all supposed to fit on one horse?" she asked.

Zachary cursed silently. He never should have suggested an outing. Of course she would expect her
own mount, but all he could offer was one plodding
plow animal for the three of them to share.

"Is the snow too deep for a wagon?" she asked.

"Maybe we shouldn't go." Zachary couldn't face
her. "I shouldn't have . . . "

"Of course we should go. The horse can hold our
weight, can't he?"

"Melanie, I . . . "

"What? You're not going to take back your offer,
are you? Zachary, I really want to go. It's been weeks
since I've seen anything but four walls."

And four dreary walls at that, he reasoned. Only
she was too much of a lady to say as much. He nodded. "I'll give you a hand up."

A moment later Zachary held her before him,
while Melanie cuddled Caroline swathed in a small
blanket and placed inside the folds of a quilt against
her breast. The horse moved past snow covered
fields and into the forest that surrounded Zachary's
property, and Rusty darted to and fro, burying himself in the deep snow, then chasing a rabbit and a
squirrel, catching neither. As the horse moved along,
Melanie asked, "How big is your farm?"

"It ends about two or three miles into the woods
on all sides."

"But you don't farm all of it."

"No. It's too much for one man."

"You could hire someone."

"I could, but it probably wouldn't make much difference. I'd bring in more money, but I'd have to pay
out a salary. Besides, it's not easy to get someone to
live out here alone."

"Why not buy an indentured servant?"

Zachary smiled as he remembered the way she had looked standing on the auction block. He had stayed in town three hours longer that day, unable to resist, unable to stop himself from wondering if her story were true or not. He should have known it was.

She'd been dressed in clean though shabby clothes, but her manner and stance had elevated her above the others. How she had glared at every man there! The men had gazed at her with a lust that could almost be felt in the air. "I thought to buy you once," he said.

"Did you?" Melanie turned at the question. Her dark brown eyes grew warm with emotion and Zachary knew he'd be forever haunted by their memory. She seemed to look into his soul as she asked, "Why?"

Again he shrugged. "I don't know. You looked so cool and in control, standing on that ugly platform. You appeared unaffected by the gawking men, yet I knew you were afraid. You were so small and delicate. I watched until Moody made the last bid. I thought you'd be safe with his family."

"Why didn't you make a bid?"

"I had a wife."

"But you weren't bidding on a wife."

"I know, but Margaret and I were already having troubles. I thought it would only add to them if I brought someone like you into my house." Zachary didn't mention the fact that he wouldn't have been able to bid in any case, for he hadn't had more than a pound to his name, after having bought supplies.

"Someone like me?"

"Someone as beautiful as you."

Melanie rather liked the idea that he thought her beautiful. Many men had told her as much, although she couldn't see what there was to rave about. To her mind, her features were pleasant and even, her skin good, her hair pitch black, but she had seen others whom she thought were much more comely. For some unnamed reason she suddenly hoped Zachary would never see them. "I think you are a very good man," she said.

Zachary stared in surprise. "I told you before I'm not—"

"I know what you said. You said you're not kind so I should not allow my imagination to run away with me." Melanie chuckled at the thought and looked at him with gentleness and something else, something that left his heart knocking against his ribs and his breathing almost nonexistent. "Do you think kindness is a failing?"

"No." Zachary couldn't say more. He was lucky indeed to manage even that.

Melanie smiled and leaned comfortably against him. "I didn't say you were kind—although I think you are, even if you insist on denying it. I said you were good. Shall I tell you why?"

Zachary did not respond. He couldn't have if his life depended on it. Melanie went on as if he had given permission to proceed.

"Well, for one thing you were considerate of your wife. She didn't deserve it, I think, and still you were."

"And . . ." he prompted. Now that she'd started, he couldn't bear to have her stop. He wanted to know all that was in her heart.

"You're a good father to Caroline. You never lose your temper, even when she's fretting impossibly."

"I wasn't very good to you."

"Well, not in the beginning, but you soon forgot to be nasty."

Zachary watched her for a long moment before saying, "I hated being sick. I'm afraid I blamed you. Why didn't you take my horse and leave?"

"You were very ill. Someone had to care for Caroline."

"Why didn't you leave when I got better?"

"I don't know. I could have, I suppose."

"You could have easily. I was weak for a long time. I couldn't have stopped you. Had you fallen under my charm by then?"

"Charm? Actually, Mr. Pitt, I haven't as yet seen this mysterious attribute to which you elude."

Zachary laughed and hugged her tighter against him, planting a light kiss on her cheek. She didn't know why she had stayed, and Zachary didn't know why he hadn't ordered her from his house. Perhaps it was meant that they be together.

Damn. He was nothing less than a fool if he allowed himself to believe that. Still, for the time being she was here. He'd be even more the fool if he used this time to lament the fates. She would never truly be his, he knew that, but for now, there was today. He couldn't ask for more.

"I can be very charming, I'll have you know."

"Yes, like yesterday, when you dropped that piece of wood on your toe. I was charmed beyond belief by your lively vocabulary."

Zachary chuckled, remembering the incident and his curses. "I was in pain. That didn't count. Unless the words you used when you burned your hand count."

"All right, what about the day before yesterday and Caroline's soiled clothes?"

"What about them?"

"You said she smelled like a dead raccoon."

"Well, she did. What has that to do with charm?"

Melanie laughed and then forgetting herself completely, turned more fully and kissed him on the mouth. Zachary felt the air leave his lungs. She'd never kissed him before, at least not without cajoling. He couldn't believe she had kissed him now of her own accord, and he wished she'd do it again. But Melanie seemed very well satisfied with that one delicious, if meager, demonstration.

They were heading into the mountains. The path led almost directly up. Melanie held the baby in one hand and the saddle's pommel in the other, her eyes widening with apprehension as the ground dropped away behind them. "Does Gray Cloud live far away?"

"Just over this ridge."

The horse struggled forward, slipping now and then in the heavy snow. "Let me down. I'll walk. It would be easier if—"

"Don't worry. I'll get you there."

"Zachary, we're slipping backward."

Zachary let out a stream of oaths, swearing he'd have the mangy beast for dinner tomorrow night if he didn't keep going. Suddenly the horse gained the crest.

Below them, surrounded by a thick forest of snow-covered trees, were two large clearings. One stood empty. In the closer of the two were a few dozen small, neat wooden houses, looking cozy and warm as wisps of gray smoke escaped their chimneys, disappearing into the frosty winter air.

Even from the hill's crest, Melanie recognized it as an Indian settlement. Although she couldn't distinguish men from women at this distance, they all wore thick knee-length coats made of skins or furs, and buckskin leggings and fur boots.

Melanie had been aware that Indians lived close

by, but she hadn't expected so many, or that the Indians lived in houses that were just like those of whites. She had anticipated dwellings that were far more primitive.

Sensing her surprise, Zachary explained that the Cherokee were the most advanced of the Five Civilized Tribes. They had a representative government and had adopted the white man's housing. All had been baptized as Christian's although some of them, like those living in this valley, liberally mixed the white man's religion with their former spiritual practices.

They held to their old customs on matters of courtship, marriage, belief in evil and good spirits, and in the mystical properties of tobacco, and of course ceremonies, such as that of The Green Corn. But the men dressed like Zachary, and the women, except for the leggings and fur boots, wore dresses much like Melanie's own.

Zachary explained that the Cherokee had embraced European agricultural methods as well. Come spring, in the second clearing, they would plant corn, squash, tobacco, beans, and pumpkins.

It wasn't until they got closer that Melanie saw that something was seriously wrong. Apparently the village had withstood some violence within the last few hours. Four bodies lay still in the snow. Beside them blood puddled frozen and crimson upon the white ground. Three of the houses at the far end of the settlement had been reduced to little more than rubble and ash. Before one blackened silhouette stood a woman wailing and tearing at her hair. Near the other two burned buildings stood two dazed and grieving families. A baby cried and was put to a mother's nipple. Three small, obviously frightened children whimpered, hanging on to their mother's skirts, while a few men stood suddenly alert at their approach.

To Melanie's relief the men relaxed as they came closer. Zachary muttered a curse seconds before he pulled the horse to a stop. "What happened?" Melanie asked Zachary, as he said something to one of the men in the Cherokee language.

A man responded in the same tongue and Zachary nodded, repeating the response in English for Melanie. "There was a raid early this morning. Shawnee, by the looks of them." He nodded toward the end of the village and the still screaming woman. "Her family died in the fire."

A shiver of fear raced up Melanie's spine. She'd felt so safe with Zachary. How could she have forgotten the many stories of violent Indians raiding for forage?

Her gaze moved to Zachary. Anticipating her question he answered, "I keep the smokehouse unlocked. They take what they want. Mostly they don't bother me."

"Mostly?" she croaked, shaken.

Zachary didn't answer her, for others had come to welcome the visitors. In a blur of dark, smiling faces, and foreign words mixed liberally with English, Melanie felt totally out of her element.

Moments later, she was ushered into a small house, one not unlike Zachary's. Inside it was more cozy than one might expect. The floors were covered with animal skins and furs, as were two of the walls. As in Zachary's home, a fireplace took up much of one wall. On the opposite wall were four shelves filled with large, beautifully decorated pottery bowls. Hanging from wooden pegs were painted pouches of all sizes, some decorated with feathers, a few pipes and two gruesome looking masks. An eagle feather cloak, no doubt used for exotic ceremonies, hung nearby. A small table, a chair, and a bed comprised the furnishings.

An old woman sat on a fur rug before the fireplace, smoking a pipe. Melanie was surprised when the woman said to Zachary, in perfect English, "It took you long enough to bring her."

"Don't nag at me, Gray Cloud. I told you I would and I did. I've got potatoes outside and a half side of moose."

The old woman's face broke into a hundred wrinkles as her mouth stretched into a toothless grin. "Potatoes. Good. Get them while your woman sits with this old wise one."

Without asking, Gray Cloud raised her hands and Zachary took Caroline from Melanie and deposited the baby into her arms.

"Old wise one, my ass," Zachary grumbled, too loudly for Melanie's liking. And then Zachary, as calm as you please, left her alone with Gray Cloud.

Chapter 10

❩⸢⸣❪

As soon as the door closed behind Zachary, Gray Cloud cackled like an evil old witch. Melanie told herself not to think nonsense. Zachary wouldn't have left her with Gray Cloud if she would have been in any danger. Still Melanie didn't relax until the woman's dark, leathery skin crinkled again into a hundred wrinkles, and a twinkle of laughter gleamed in eyes as black as pitch.

Rusty, the lazy, useless creature, had entered the house with them. Melanie rolled her eyes toward the heavens as he made himself comfortable before the hearth. Apparently the dog sensed no danger here. Melanie thought to take her cue from him, considering she hadn't anyone else to take it from, thanks to Zachary, who had left her without so much as an introduction. She opened her coat, removed Zachary's scarf from her head, and sat at the old woman's side.

Engrossed in studying the baby, the woman didn't look her way again and Melanie felt decidedly uneasy as she searched for something to break the uncomfortable silence. Apparently it was only Melanie who felt the strain, for Gray Cloud chuckled as Caroline tasted one of the many colorful beads hanging from the old woman's neck. With gnarled, arthritic

178

hands she cuddled the baby close. "Your man is generous."

Melanie's first impulse was to enlighten the woman about her and Zachary's relationship, for she certainly was not Zachary's woman, nor he her man. But then she remembered that Gray Cloud had seen them sleeping together. She frowned.

Caroline whined, her arms outstretched. Her fascination with Gray Cloud's beads waning, she wanted the warmth and familiarity of the woman she knew as her mother. Gray Cloud handed the baby to Melanie's gentle care.

She puffed on her pipe and watched as Melanie soothed and comforted, until the heat of the fire made Caroline yawn sleepily. The baby soon dozed. "It's good, I think, that his first woman left. She didn't love this little one, or her man. What is your name?"

Melanie's eyes rounded in surprise at Gray Cloud's knowledge of Zachary's marital troubles. How had she learned of them? "Melanie," she replied. "Zachary doesn't talk about his wife much."

Gray Cloud nodded. "While he worked his fields, she left the little one alone to meet with another. One day she went away with him, but later he came back alone."

Melanie suspected that little went on anywhere in these mountains that wasn't reported back to the old woman.

"She died," Melanie explained.

Gray Cloud nodded, as if satisfied. "She was a foolish woman. Her man treated her well. A wise woman would be thankful for a good man."

Melanie assumed she meant that Zachary was good. If she ignored the rough edges of his character, which appeared lately to be growing smoother, she probably agreed. Still, she said nothing.

Apparently, in an effort to make her point, Gray Cloud said, "A white man lived among us once. He preached about God, and the white man's ways, but he was bad. We believed his words, for others had come before him and told the same stories. He gained our trust. And then hurt two young girls.

"The council met. It was decided that he must die. That nothing less could be done or the girls could never reclaim their honor.

"Zachary was a member of the council. He knows the white man's law, but he agreed.

"The night before the man's punishment, he escaped. My people hunted him down. William Wolf, the father of one of the girls, found him. The two fought at the edge of a cliff. Zachary found William later, clinging to the cliff edge by a root. Zachary saved his life."

Melanie assumed the preacher had not been quite so fortunate. She said nothing.

"In gratitude Zachary was offered all that William owned, even his eldest daughter Mary, but Zachary took only a horse. We forgot the white man's custom of taking only one woman at a time." Gray Cloud grinned. "It is our custom now."

Melanie was left to wonder how much influence Zachary had among these people. Having been welcomed only minutes ago by a dozen friendly smiles, she assumed that they were a gentle people. But had they adopted monogamy because of him? Had he changed an entire way of life by his example? The notion was staggering.

It was clear that Gray Cloud cared a great deal for Zachary. She praised him throughout the afternoon, as a mother might her son, telling how Zachary often

joined their hunts but kept only a small portion of
the kill for himself. How he shared his crops the year
theirs failed, how he had defended a young Cherokee boy who had been accused of stealing a horse
from a white farmer. As Gray Cloud spoke, she
smoked her pipe and prepared warmed cider and
cakes made of honey and sweet potatoes.

When Zachary entered the house hours later, he
was greeted by the delicious aromas of corn, squash,
and beaver stew bubbling over the fire. He placed
the sack of potatoes on his shoulder against one wall.
Melanie did not question his whereabouts but only
glanced in his direction, her smile radiating unusual
warmth.

Zachary's gaze narrowed, for he knew in an instant that the two women had been talking about
him. He glared at Gray Cloud. "Have you been filling her head with nonsense?"

"This woman does not talk nonsense."

"Don't believe her," he told Melanie. "She exagger-
ates."

Melanie looked up from washing out Caroline's
bunting and grinned. Zachary was uncomfortable,
more than uncomfortable if the sudden color flood-
ing his cheeks meant anything. He was actually
blushing. Melanie never would have thought it possible. She turned away, trying to hide her smile, only
to find that smile growing into laughter as he mumbled, "I'm not leaving you alone with her again."

"I take it her stories are true then?"

"What did she tell you?"

Melanie's answer was a vague, "Many things.
Where were you?"

"Talking to the men." Zachary didn't mention that
he had helped bury the bodies of those who had
burned in the fires, or that breaking through ground

frozen harder than rock had taken some doing. Neither did he reveal that the four Shawnee who had been killed in the attack had also been buried, without ceremony. Years ago their bodies might have been impaled and displayed at the entrance to the settlement, as a warning to others who might dare harm them. But these people had changed their ways since the white man had come. Granted, they could, when necessary, be as fierce as ever, but savagery no longer brought honor and tributes of praise.

During their meal, Melanie listened as Gray Cloud and Zachary spoke of the people in the settlement, in particular Martha White Feather, and what might become of her now that her family had died. "Her sister will take care of her," Gray Cloud said. "She suffers now, but after a time, she will marry again."

"Three men will guard the settlement at night," Zachary put in.

Gray Cloud nodded and began to explain, for Melanie's information, the source of the Cherokee's problem with this small band of Shawnee. "Black Bear saw Martha White Feather at the river two summers back. He went to her father and offered two dozen ponies for her. But her father said no, because Black Bear is not Christian and would have taken his daughter away.

"Black Bear then offered three dozen ponies, but still the answer was no. Black Bear is a chief. The refusal was a great insult. We've had trouble ever since then."

The story was interrupted when a woman came to Gray Cloud's house asking for a remedy for her husband, who suffered pain in his stomach. Gray Cloud took leaves from two of the pottery jars and mixed them together into a small sack. She directed the woman to boil the leaves to make tea, and promised her husband would be well by morning.

"Who taught you about medicine?" Melanie asked as Gray Cloud returned to the table.

"My father was a great man, a shaman. He had no son to whom he could pass on his knowledge. It was given to me."

After the dishes were washed and the kitchen put to rights, they sat before the fire. Caroline climbed happily over her father, gurgling her delight as she poked at his eyes and investigated his teeth. Gray Cloud began to speak. Her low voice grew whispery, as if she was imparting a great secret.

"It is said that man offended the animals by killing so many for food. In separate councils the bears, fish, deer, birds, and insects plotted their revenge. As punishment, diseases would visit their human enemy.

"But plants were our friends. Each gave us a cure. They said, 'I will help man when he calls me in his need.' Now we have the power to stop the evil," she finished proudly.

Melanie knew, of course, that the story was only a legend, no doubt passed down from generation to generation. The odd part was that here, in this tiny shadowy house, listening to an old woman as she smoked her aromatic pipe and told of ancient events, the stories sounded plausible. Melanie couldn't help asking, "But how do you know which medicine to give?"

The black eyes twinkled and Gray Cloud seemed well satisfied with the question, as if she'd been waiting for it. "The plants whisper their secrets," she returned simply, as if it were a common everyday occurrence.

It would have been impossible to miss Zachary's grunt and look of disbelief. It didn't seem to matter that he was a guest in this house and should show his host more courtesy by keeping his comment to himself. Zachary, it appeared, spoke his mind wherever he was. "Gray Cloud, why are you trying to make her believe you have supernatural powers?"

"I think she might," Melanie said softly, half believing the legend and Gray Cloud's abilities. In the light of the fire, the old woman certainly looked mysterious. Perhaps she *could* hear plants talking.

For Melanie's benefit he stated plainly, "Knowledge about the plants and herbs has been written down. For instance, to help lower a fever, she uses the ground-up bark of a white willow tree. Rhubarb brings on a sweat, squawroot flushes out impurities, mint cures upset stomachs, caffeine stimulates . . ."

Gray Cloud cut him off with another cackling laugh. Melanie smiled as the old woman poked Zachary's shoulder. "It was a good story. Allow this woman her secrets."

Zachary grunted again, obviously less than entertained.

Gray Cloud spoke to Melanie. "I told you he was a bad one. You should have consulted with this wise old woman before becoming his woman."

The fact of the matter was, Gray Cloud had told her quite the opposite. Melanie only smiled.

"One would imagine," Zachary commented, "that if she were truly wise, she would know when to mind her own business."

The two traded good-natured insults until Caroline fell asleep, and Melanie placed her upon a small mat of furs. Larger furs were then brought from a corner to accommodate the two adults. After a quick visit outside to the privy, Gray Cloud retired to her bed.

Considering the devastation that had occurred only this morning, Melanie was hardly thrilled to find the privy bordering the woods behind Gray Cloud's house. It was pitch dark and even though Zachary stood watch, his rifle in hand, she couldn't shake the thought that Indians prowled not a few feet from where they stood.

"Hurry up, I'm afraid," she said as he was about to enter the small building after she was finished.

"Take my gun," he said, handing her the heavy rifle while closing the door behind him.

Melanie grunted at the weight. "I hope you don't think I can protect you. I can hardly hold this thing."

"It's ready to fire," he called from inside. "Just pull the trigger if you see anything move."

"Anything move?" came her mocking reply. "Zachary, everything moves," Melanie said as she eyed the rustling, shadowy forms of swaying trees and bushes. "What shall I shoot first?"

Zachary reached for the gun. "Just don't shoot me," he said, already finished and standing beside her.

Melanie gratefully handed him the weapon. Moments later they were safely inside, snuggled under the furs. Zachary felt her shiver and cuddled her closer. "Cold?" he asked, his voice low so as not to disturb Gray Cloud, who was already snoring across the room.

"No."

"Afraid?"

"Not now." Her arm circled his waist. She squeezed closer. "You won't get killed, will you Zachary?"

"Black Bear isn't interested in me."

"So of course that means you can't get killed by mistake."

"I'll be careful. But I want your promise that you won't walk around the settlement alone."

"Gladly," she returned, still shivering.

They were silent for a long moment before Melanie asked, "Were you really offered Mary Wolf as a second wife?"

"Who the hell told you ... I hope you didn't believe ..." Zachary breathed a weary sigh. "What else did she tell you?"

"That it was the white man's custom to take only one woman at a time. That it's the Cherokee custom now, too."

"Meaning, what? That I was the cause of the change."

Melanie shrugged.

Zachary sighed. "Melanie, it's true that I was offered Mary, but these people have been Christians for a long time and changed their customs long before I got here. The fact is, I visited alone. They didn't know I was married."

Melanie chuckled. "Gray Cloud is very good at telling tales."

"Tales is a good word. Bull is probably better."

"But you did save William Wolf."

"I just happened across him. It could have been any of us."

"What is her plan, do you think? Why would she imply—"

"She has none," Zachary returned, not waiting for her to finish. "The woman just talks too much."

Melanie didn't miss the softness in his tone as he spoke about Gray Cloud. "You like her a lot, don't you?"

"Who? Gray Cloud?"

"Of course Gray Cloud. Who else do you like?"

Zachary chuckled and pressed his face against her hair. "Only you."

"I've heard tell that you're a hero among these

people. No doubt there is a maiden or two who might—"

"I'm not a hero, Melanie, just a simple man. Gray Cloud has been known to exaggerate on occasion."

"What about the boy you saved from the farmer?"

"That was just a misunderstanding. We found the horse."

Melanie didn't question him further. Obviously he wanted no praise and would only continue to insist he wasn't deserving. It could be that Gray Cloud was very good at telling a story while allowing the listener to come to his or her own conclusion. Still, the truth was, Zachary was greatly respected by all. She'd realized as much the moment they'd entered the village. And Gray Cloud treated him like a favorite son. No, Melanie reasoned, the stories were true. Zachary was simply too modest to accept the praise.

As the days followed, and their visit to the settlement lengthened, Melanie daily grew more convinced of the truth of her theory. Zachary's opinion was obviously respected by the men, for they consulted with him on various means to protect themselves from further raids. He helped to rebuild the three houses and promised to return after the weather broke to accompany them to town to buy rifles and ammunition. It seemed some folks did not take kindly to an Indian owning a gun, despite the fact that said Indian was equally as law-abiding as the most respected of the white community.

When it came time to hunt, Zachary was invited to go along. Melanie was surprised when whole deer skins, heads intact, were placed over the men, so the hunters might draw close enough to use their bows and arrows, without detection.

It was the women and their shy looks, whispers

and giggles that convinced Melanie that Zachary was held in high regard. One particular young woman, more brazen than most, managed to gain his attention at nearly every encounter. And today, Melanie thought, the woman had been most outrageous.

Later, that night, Zachary and Melanie were cuddled under the furs, talking quietly about the day's events. Melanie mentioned the girl. After having seen her fall from her horse with amazing accuracy into Zachary's arms, Melanie thought she'd just about had enough of her flirting. "Her mother slapped her for that and I can't say I'm sorry."

"She slapped her? For what? Falling?" Zachary asked.

Melanie wondered if he were truly as naive as he wanted her to believe. "For trying to get your attention. And for being a brazen hussy."

"Melanie, she can't be more than fourteen."

"She's old enough to take a husband."

"She's a baby," he returned, with little interest.

"If I remember correctly, you once said twelve was old enough."

Zachary laughed, remembering their teasing conversation from several days ago. He fumbled with the buttons of her bodice.

"Open this."

"It is open."

Zachary didn't comment as to why her bodice should be open. Every night he managed to undo buttons and pull aside her chemise while he was half asleep. Tonight he only smiled, delighted that she would have saved him the trouble. "I opened it so I wouldn't have to sew on another button," she explained. "Every night you manage to loosen at least one."

Zachary breathed a sound of pure pleasure as a

breast fell warm and soft into his hand. "That was wise of you."

"Mmm," she murmured, as he found the tip and brought it to hardness with his thumb and finger. "I thought so."

"I wish we were home."

"You say that every night."

"It was expected that we should stay on a while." Zachary rolled so that he lay half upon her. Pulling the furs over them, he sought out her softness with his mouth. After a lengthy sampling, he sighed, knowing he had only himself to blame for frustration that would not lessen until he brought this woman home. He rolled again to her side, bringing her close against him. His hand recaptured its prize. "We've stayed long enough, I think. Tomorrow I'll tell Gray Cloud we're leaving."

Zachary didn't miss the fact that Melanie snuggled closer and offered no objection to his plan.

Yes, he promised himself, by tomorrow afternoon, they'd be back home. And tomorrow night held many possibilities.

It was still dark when the sound of knocking brought everyone awake. A husband reported that his wife was suffering from fever and chills and a stomach that refused to settle. Gray Cloud had to help. The door hardly closed behind her when the thought crossed Zachary's mind that he might enjoy the privacy afforded him for the first time in five days. But just then, Caroline began to whine. She wasn't settled when another knock came and still another. By dawn's light, eleven people had been reported sick, all suffering the same symptoms. Zachary didn't mention returning home as he volunteered his help.

* * *

Six days passed before the first victims began to improve. By that time a dozen more had come down with the illness. Zachary administered to the men and began to wonder if every man in the village hadn't taken sick.

Under Gray Cloud's careful watch, he carried them one by one into the snow in an effort to lower their raging fever. Expectorants were liberally used in the hope of forcing the illness from weak bodies. And then soothing teas administered until much of the pain had eased.

James Running Fox, the chief of this band of Cherokee, was an old man. He'd awakened one of those days gravely ill and for most of the day had suffered terribly with fever. Twice Zachary had carried him into the snow, with no obvious results. Everyone thought the old man would surely die, since the fever ravaged the old and young with the greatest intensity, and three people had already succumbed.

But by some miracle, James Running Fox didn't die. Even now he lay ill and terribly weakened, but his fever had finally lessened and Gray Cloud had pronounced the worst of the illness past.

Zachary returned to the house late on the sixth day, his face gray with exhaustion. "Do you have any coffee?" he asked as he sat heavily at the small kitchen table.

Melanie placed a steaming cup before him, but he only stared at it, knowing it wasn't coffee he needed, but sleep. Days of it. "Are you all right?" he asked.

"I'm fine. Caroline is fine too," Melanie said. "If you don't rest, you'll have the fever next."

"I'll be all right." Zachary yawned and rose from the chair. "I just need a half hour. Wake me up if anyone calls for me."

Melanie promised herself that despite his wants,

she wouldn't awaken him. In the last week, he hadn't had more than four hours of sleep a night.

No one came to the door that night. Apparently there were no new outbreaks of the mysterious illness, and those who had suffered the worst were finally on their way to recovery.

It was almost midday before Zachary woke to Caroline's happy laughter, as Rusty tickled her neck with a cold nose. Zachary groaned wearily, feeling less than rested, his body aching. For just a moment he thought perhaps he had come down with the illness himself, but no. He might have slept for hours, but his body ached because he was still exhausted.

"I have coffee ready and warm corn porridge and honey, if you'd like."

Zachary looked around the room. "Where is Gray Cloud?"

"Looking in on her patients, I expect."

Zachary stretched and sat up. "Why didn't she wake me up?"

"No need. There have been no new cases, and the others appear much improved."

Zachary nodded and muttered a low and heartfelt, "Good."

After downing two cups of coffee, he went outside, used the privy, and returned moments later. He was starving. Still he eyed the steaming sweet porridge with something less than hunger. He didn't mind cornmeal. He enjoyed it, in fact, when made into small flat cakes. But he could barely get down the porridge. "What did we have for dinner last night?" he asked.

"Rabbit stew."

"Is there any left?"

"Hold Caroline and I'll get it."

As he ate Zachary watched Melanie carefully.

"What?" she asked finding his gaze upon her for the dozenth time. "I told you I was fine."

"I wonder why we didn't get sick."

Melanie shrugged. "I'm just glad we didn't."

"Do you think the four Shawnee were sick?"

"I don't know." Melanie shrugged. "Even if they were, how would it have mattered? They were killed and buried."

"Yes, but their clothing and blankets were distributed around the settlement."

Melanie imagined the illness could have been spread with the men's belonging and clothes. "Have you ever heard of the Black Plague?"

"No."

"It was a great sickness that came during the fourteenth century. A lot of people died. Some thought to stop the spread of the disease by burning the bodies, clothing and blankets. Anything the victim might have touched."

Zachary felt again the differences between them. She knew things about the world that he couldn't imagine. He felt a sense of hopeless inadequacy as he asked, "Did it work?"

Melanie shrugged again. "Who can say? Some think it did. Others say that the plague simply wore itself out. I imagine still others believe that God deemed that enough had died."

Later that same afternoon Zachary left the cabin to see for himself how the people were faring. Melanie, having withstood the confines of the little house for as long as she could, took Caroline outside for a breath of fresh air. The baby was wrapped tightly into a blanket and wrapped again inside the folds of a quilt. Melanie had fashioned a small hat that tied beneath the baby's chin. Within seconds Caroline's cheeks were a healthy shade of pink.

Melanie recognized a woman she had met, Elizabeth Running Deer, struggling with a large jug as she returned home from a visit with her mother. The woman had come to Gray Cloud on more than one occasion, first when her husband had taken ill and then when her baby had suffered the fever. Melanie smiled as Elizabeth approached. She asked if her family was feeling better.

Melanie never considered the picture she made. Since coming here she had abandoned her pins and mobcap for an easier-to-manage thick braid. In fact her hair was at least as long, black, and shiny as any woman's in the village. Today she wore her usual dress, but also had wrapped one of Gray Cloud's thick blankets around her coat.

Melanie knew some surprise at the woman's odd reaction to her question. The jug dropped from Elizabeth's hands as she suddenly froze in place.

Melanie looked at the fallen jug and the cider seeping into the snow and then back at the woman, whose mouth had opened in a soundless scream. "Are you all ri—?"

Melanie never finished her question, as something hard slammed into her back. A second later she was propelled into the air, the baby torn from her arms. She couldn't have said if the sudden force of movement had caused the fall or if the man now holding her high above the ground around the waist had ripped the baby from her arms. All she knew for sure was that Caroline fell to the ground, her screams of terror echoing through the village as she landed inches from the hooves of a racing horse.

Melanie couldn't manage a scream. She hung helplessly suspended in the air. Her eyes held Elizabeth's, silently pleading for help. She uttered not a sound. Not when in a blur, Zachary suddenly stepped from the building behind Elizabeth, drawn by his daughter's cries. Not when she was thrown belly down over the horse, which galloped away. Not even when the village grew distant and then disappeared behind the cover of thick forest.

All Melanie could hear was the thunder of her heart. The man above her said nothing, his hand pressing firmly against her back to keep her from falling. Snow kicked up into her face, but she was unaware of its stinging, unaware as well of her inability to breathe. Upon the thick snow the horse made hardly a sound. Only the rushing of cold air came to her ears as she forced a breath, forced her mind to clear, and searched for an answer.

She'd been kidnapped by an unknown assailant. And there could be but one answer for it. The authorities had finally found her. She'd pay now for what she'd done to Joshua. Even though she'd acted in self defense, she'd pay.

But would the authorities have come upon her in this fashion? Melanie couldn't fathom the possibility and yet could imagine no other explanation.

Black Bear had waited a long time for this woman. Many nights he had sat huddled just beyond the forest, waiting for his chance.

Three of his friends and his brother had died the last time he'd come for her. He would have attacked again, that very night, but the evil spirits had brought the weakness and the burning his brother had known the morning he died. It was the snake, he knew. The snake was Uktena and all five of them had seen it slither across their path just before attacking the village. Uktena always brought death. Only a sacred fire could ward off its evil. They might have stopped then and lit the fire, but a man from the settlement had called the alarm and it was too late to turn back.

He'd almost died that night, but the sacred fire had saved him. The evil one had gone away.

It had taken many days before Black Bear's strength had returned. He smiled, knowing the waiting was over at last; his heart pounded with the joy of it. This time her father could not refuse him. Not after tonight. Tonight he'd make her his woman. Should the old man not give his daughter then, she'd be held in disgrace and forced to take her own life.

She'd want him now, he knew. She'd offer no objection now that her husband was dead. Black Bear had thought he'd killed her baby along with her husband. All ties should be broken from the past. But somehow the child had escaped the flames.

It didn't matter. He had her now and soon she'd forget the baby. Soon her belly would swell again, this time with his seed.

Zachary knew a need to kill so strong it pushed aside all rational thought. He had saddled the wrong horse, but it didn't matter. Nothing mattered but that he reach Melanie before it was too late.

They were ten minutes behind them, no more. Three of the men from the settlement rode with him. Bill, John, and Thomas were all expert in riding and easily matched Zachary in their accuracy with a rifle. Zachary would reach her first, or die in the attempt.

Melanie realized by now that the man who had captured her was an Indian. Although she still hadn't managed to get a good look at him, because of her present position, she knew, for only Indians wore moccasins and buckskinned trousers. Melanie had no idea why she'd been taken. All she knew was that the horse seemed to race on forever. She grunted in pain. Lord, would he ever stop?

No sooner had the thought occurred than the man who held her down made a sound and the horse slowed. Still, the less-than-frantic pace hardly relieved her discomfort. The bouncing seemed to increase. She grunted again. Strong arms brought her to a sitting position. Sitting astride the horse before the man, Melanie finally managed a deep breath and expelled it with relief, along with the words, "I hope you realize you've made a serious mistake."

Black Bear stiffened with surprise. He didn't understand the white man's words and knew White Feather could speak them, but this wasn't White Feather. He knew the soft, musical sound of her voice; he had heard it so often in his thoughts, his dreams, that he could never forget, never mistake it for another.

He knew a sudden rage that his efforts had been for naught. And in that rage he struck out, placing fault where no fault stood.

For a second Melanie imagined the blow to her temple had come out of nowhere. She couldn't conceive that the Indian had struck her, couldn't imagine why he should. She moaned a low sound of pain, wobbled as the world began to swirl before her eyes, and then tumbled to the snow, dazed.

She didn't lie there for long. In a second he was upon her. Having jumped from the horse, almost directly atop her, he knocked the breath from her lungs. Apparently, and for some unknown reason, he'd taken offense. She must have done something, said something, for she couldn't imagine a man would kidnap her for the sole purpose of beating her. He hit her again. She heard and felt something snap in her jaw.

Melanie did not take kindly to being struck. She hadn't when Mrs. Moody had thought to impose such punishment and she didn't now. If she was about to die, she refused to leave this world with a cowardly whimper.

Knowing a taste of her own outrage, she didn't hesitate to hit back. She landed two stinging blows before the Indian realized what she was about.

Black Bear grew suddenly still, astonished that a woman had had the audacity to raise her hand against him. He pulled back. A moment later, admiring her bravery, he grinned. Of course she couldn't be allowed to think her blows would be tolerated. He hit her again just to make sure she understood that. He came to his feet and pulled her by the hair to stand before him.

Melanie couldn't see much purpose in standing, for the savage was sure to knock her down again. Still, with his fingers holding tightly to her hair, she had little choice but to obey.

Now that his surprise and rage had eased, Black Bear looked the woman over. A white woman. What had she been doing in the settlement? And then he realized the truth of it. She was a slave and he had raced his horse for half the afternoon for nothing. No one would come for a slave. No one would care that he had taken her.

She hadn't been the one he'd come for, but she was beautiful, perhaps even more beautiful than White Feather. Black Bear tore suddenly at her coat and blouse, ripping her chemise in his desire to see if she was worth his trouble. She was.

Black Bear decided his error had actually been a stroke of good luck. He would keep this one as his slave. White Feather would like that. Her work would be greatly lightened with the help of another.

If this slave was obedient and gave his wife no trouble, they might all three live in peace. If not, he'd get a good price for her. A beautiful woman always brought a good price. But he wouldn't think of selling her yet. He'd been a long time without a woman and if he couldn't have the one he wanted, he'd settle for a time for this one.

"Make camp," he said in words that sounded like little more than a grunt to Melanie's ears.

When she made no attempt to obey, he shoved her to the ground again. "Make camp," he repeated, standing over her, his features twisted into a menacing mask.

Melanie wished she could understand. At the moment he appeared on the verge of violence again and Melanie felt desperate, without a clue as to how to appease him. "I can't understand you. What do you want?"

He pulled her to her feet again, only to strike her once more. Melanie wondered how many more blows she could endure before she succumbed to the darkness that threatened to take her.

Black Bear knew she didn't understand. Still, to hit a woman brought a man no dishonor. Women were made for men to use and stupid women, especially white slaves, had to be beaten. It was the way of things. Still, to continue her punishment would bring him no closer to a warm fire. Black Bear decided he would gather the wood this time. The next time she'd know what was expected of her.

He tied her ankle to a tree, allowing her enough rope to move. When he returned with the wood, she'd make the fire.

Melanie watched him disappear into the forest. The moment she was able, she reached for the knot.

Her fingers shook in her terror that he would return before she was free.

She didn't have much of a chance to escape, but she had to try. She concentrated on the chore, but despite her struggles, the rope wouldn't budge an inch. Melanie felt a wave of panic. She had to unfasten the knot! And then she knew only crushing despair at the sound of crunching snow. He had returned and her chance was gone.

Twigs and larger branches, along with dried leaves, were dumped about ten feet from where she stood. Again the Indian said something. Melanie assumed he meant for her to make a fire. And how did he expect her to manage that?

She had never made a fire outside, without flint, and in two feet of snow.

She glanced at the Indian's stony expression. There was no doubt as to what he wanted.

Knowing she was in for another violent attack, she cleared snow from a small area and stacked the wood, leaving enough room for the fire to breathe. She paused then, not knowing what to do next. He hit her. But this time he didn't stop with one or two blows. This time he was on her again, pulling aside her coat, digging his fingers into her soft flesh.

Melanie was greatly tempted to allow her mind to slide away from this horror, to cocoon itself in delightful memories, to pretend she cuddled Caroline close and listened to the baby's sweet gurgles. But to allow that would mean this man could use her body without the slightest resistance. That she couldn't allow.

She gritted her teeth and fought back with every ounce of strength. She suffered greatly from the effort, for his blows only increased in both frequency and strength. Still she wouldn't give up. She'd never give up.

Lying full length upon her, he pinned her arms between their bodies, even as he tore again at her clothing. It was when he reached beneath her skirt that she got her chance. Her hand was momentarily freed and the knife that was tied to his thigh was instantly and tightly grasped in her palm.

She stabbed upward, realizing too late that had she reached around and attacked his back she might have had more success. The knife penetrated, but she knew almost instantly that the wound would not kill him. It wouldn't even stop him.

The Indian frowned, and an instant later he wrenched the knife from her hand and pressed it firmly to her throat as he looked more closely at the damage she'd done to his hip. His lips curled into a sneer, and a snarl of hatred slid through his teeth.

Melanie whispered a silent prayer that God would welcome her home.

Chapter 11

The snow was perfect. Just as it had offered no warning of the attack, it allowed not a sound as Zachary and the others hurried their horses along the trail.

Zachary felt only surprise as he broke out of thick forest and entered the small clearing. He hadn't expected to come upon them so suddenly.

The Indian above Melanie rolled to his feet and crouched, ready to attack. Melanie lay still upon the snow. Zachary caught the sight of blood, and thought it must be hers. She was dead, or very nearly so, because of this bastard and he was going to make sure the son of a bitch paid with his life.

The distance between him and the Indian disappeared in seconds. Nothing could stop Zachary from killing this man. Not God himself.

Long before the Indian had even the chance to glance at his rifle, Zachary's huge body was flying through the air. It slammed hard against him, knocking both men to the snow.

Melanie, stunned at first to see Zachary suddenly among them, scrambled to her feet. She watched, her eyes wide with building horror. She'd never seen anything so vicious and thought she couldn't have survived even one of the blows either man delivered.

And then they were suddenly apart. Bent slightly from the waist they faced each other. Silently they circled, gleaming knives in hand.

Melanie gasped as John Flying Hawk was the next to appear. Behind him Bill and Thomas Running Deer pulled up their horses in a cloud of snow.

To Melanie's dismay, none of the three appeared ready to interfere, for all sat as still as their horses, their eyes narrowed as they watched the unfolding scene. "Help him!" she called out, but no one moved.

All three men seemed to think it was Zachary's right to kill this villain, Melanie realized. If only she could reach the rifle, she'd stop the fight right now. The Indian had placed the weapon upon his blanket some fifteen feet from where she stood. The rope still tied to her ankle wouldn't allow her to reach it.

Zachary and the Indian continued to stalk each other, waiting for the opportunity to strike.

The Indian lunged first and Melanie screamed, certain that his knife had plunged deep into Zachary's chest. She breathed a sigh of relief to find he had twisted away in time. Next Zachary swung the knife. He too missed his target.

"Oh God, somebody please do something," she pleaded.

No one responded.

"Thomas, give me your knife," she demanded, but he either didn't hear or chose to ignore her. Fortunately his horse stood close. Without another word, Melanie took the knife tied at his thigh and cut herself free.

She ran for the rifle and with a sudden burst of strength, brought the heavy weapon to her shoulder. But she couldn't get a clear shot. Neither man stood still long enough. And then she realized she'd waited too long. Her stomach lurched sickeningly as the knife sank into Zachary's body and he fell back. A sneer twisted her lips as again she took aim.

But again, she never got the chance to fire, for Zachary was on the man once more and this time his knife went deep into the Indian's chest.

He lurched backward, surprise entering his eyes. His knees buckled, but quickly he regained his balance. Blood pumped from the wound, staining his shirt.

Vaguely, Zachary realized that Melanie was standing with apparent calm not five feet to his right, a rifle in her hands. She didn't seem to notice that her blouse was torn, that her coat lay open.

An instant later the Indian was holding Melanie against him, her back to his chest, his knife at her throat. "She's only a woman. A slave. Not worth dying over," the Indian said.

He couldn't be more wrong, Zachary thought. Melanie was worth dying for. She was worth his life and a hundred more.

Zachary steeled his voice, his expression, knowing he must not show a glimmer of fear, not if he intended to live. Not if he wanted Melanie to survive. "Kill her and you're dead. A slow, painful dead."

"I don't want her. I meant to take another."

Zachary nodded his understanding. So this was Black Bear, the brave who wanted Martha White Feather.

Black Bear pulled her backward, as if to hold her like a shield until the forest could grant him the safety he needed. The sudden tug caused the gun to slip from Melanie's hands. Still cocked, it dropped to the ground and fired.

The sound startled Black Bear into losing his hold. Melanie dove into the snow, leaving him without cover. In an instant a feather-decorated knife suddenly lodged itself just under Black Bear's nose. The man screamed, but the horrible gurgling sound was abruptly cut off as Zachary slashed the man's throat.

Blood was everywhere. Melanie crawled away from the horror of it, fighting the deep snow, as the Indian's fingers touched her coat. He never got a grip. He was dead before he hit the ground.

Zachary watched as Melanie gained her footing. She shivered and adjusted her coat. It was torn at her shoulder, but most of the buttons remained. Her hands moved with quick jerky motions, her face completely devoid of emotion. Her hands trembled slightly and blood splattered one side of her face.

She said nothing, not a word, and Zachary could only wonder why she didn't come to him, her face radiant with gratitude, her eyes filled with loving tears.

Standing there, Melanie wondered why he didn't come to her. Was he furious because she'd left Gray Cloud's house alone? She looked into his eyes. "Are you upset?" she asked, uncertain of the emotion she saw there.

"Not anymore." His gaze moved slowly over her, praying the blood he saw was not hers. "Are you hurt?"

"No."

That wasn't completely true, of course. Her abductor had hit her many times. Her nose was bleeding. Blotches of purple already circled her eyes and discolored her cheeks and jaw. Zachary couldn't help but notice her shiver. "Cold?"

She nodded. "A little." She took a deep, unsteady breath. "Caroline is all right." It wasn't a question, but a need for affirmation.

"Gray Cloud was holding her when I left."

Melanie smiled, but her smile crumbled and a lone

tear ran down her cheek. With an impatient wipe it was gone. "She loves those beads."

"I know."

"Did I ever tell you that when I was a child, my cousin Richard and I played pirates?"

Zachary nodded, his gaze narrowing as he wondered if she was becoming hysterical. He couldn't blame her if she were, for no one, man or woman, could have survived such an ordeal and not suffered for it. "You did."

"I thought I much preferred to be the rescuer."

Zachary frowned. What did that mean? Was she upset because he had saved her? "Have you changed your mind then?"

"No. It's just that I find it very hard to be the helpless lady."

"I can imagine you would."

"I didn't think you'd come."

"I'll always come."

Those three simple words said more than any vow of love. He'd always come, always be there to protect her. He loved her, she knew, even if he hadn't said the words.

"Could you hold me for a minute?"

Zachary hadn't been sure she'd wanted him to touch her. She'd seemed so calm, so completely in control, or perhaps holding to a thin thread of control, he couldn't tell which. Still, he'd fought back the wild urge to apologize for saving her. And now, at her gentle plea, he knew unbelievable relief along with a dizzying weakness. He smiled and took four steps to where he could lean against a tree; he was desperately in need of its support. She stood two feet away. "I imagine I can manage to hold you."

She was in his arms before the last word was spoken, her face pressed against his chest, her arms around his neck. Only now, safe in his arms at last, the danger behind her, did she allow the tears to come. She trembled uncontrollably, her voice breaking as she tried to say, "If you hadn't come, he would have killed me."

Zachary's arms tightened around her. He buried his face in her neck and shuddered at the thought. "It wasn't you he wanted. He might have used you, but he wouldn't have killed you."

"He would have. He was trying to . . . " The thought was too horrible to relate. She finished instead with, "I stabbed him and he was about to kill me when you came."

Zachary closed his eyes and breathed a long sigh of relief that he had managed to reach her in time.

"I couldn't understand. He kept yelling at me, hitting me." She couldn't stop shaking. "I was so scared." The words came on a sob, followed by another. "I was so scared."

Zachary ran his hand over the back of her head, pressing her harder to his chest. "I have you now." He hugged her against him; his heart was so filled with love that he didn't trust himself to say a word.

She was safe. Though she would never be his to keep, at least she was safe. She cried for a long time. Zachary knew she needed this release. He allowed time for tears, while rubbing his hands over her back in a soothing fashion.

When the tears began to ease and only an occasional hiccuping sob could be heard, Zachary said, "It's getting dark. Do you want to make camp here tonight?"

Melanie shuddered at the thought. "No. I want to go home. Is it too dark to go home?"

He could hardly speak. Home. She thought of his house as home. "No." His voice broke on the word, for never in his life had he known such sweet happiness.

He was about to pull his scarf from his neck to cover her ears when she suddenly gasped. "Zachary, I forgot about your side. You're covered with blood."

"It's nothing. He just caught a bit of flesh."

"Sit down and let me see."

"It's stopped bleeding. You can look at it when we get back."

Zachary didn't mention the wound he'd taken to his thigh, when the rifle dropped to the ground. He hadn't made a sound as the steel ball tore into his muscle. It was necessary then to portray not a shred of weakness. In truth, he'd been so concerned for Melanie he'd hardly felt the injury until now. And now he wouldn't mention it either.

Blood soaked his pant leg and had already puddled in his boot. He'd lost a lot, he knew, but he had withstood other injuries just as great. He'd be all right, he was sure, once Gray Cloud removed the ball.

Zachary helped Melanie straddle Black Bear's horse. It took a bit more effort for him to remount.

All three men saw his problem right off but said nothing. They knew Zachary would ask for help when help was needed.

The sun had almost set. The night air was frosty, an icy wind blowing against his skin. He was thankful for the cold. It eased the bleeding in his thigh and kept him awake.

It started to snow again. The tracks they'd followed were quickly covered over, but there was no need for concern. The men with him knew these mountains better than the lines on their mothers' faces. He followed as they chose a different, faster route back. It wasn't long before they mounted the hat are you

n her horse

me a hand

re you hurt
rtled cry of
orse, his fall

with them
im into the

aced on the
e men were
ids.
anie said as
arf.
e bowls of
ll three into
wl she took
o of hot wa-

felt relieved
arently suf-

s coat, shirt,
n she exam-
h, it looked
v this small
ary to faint.
saw his leg
oaked with

She gasped. He looked to have lost gallons. No wonder he'd fainted. No wonder his skin appeared so gray and felt clammy and cold to the touch. "He's been shot," she almost shouted, on the verge of panic, forgetting the sleeping child not six feet away.

Gray Cloud's dark eyes moved over the unconscious man. She pulled away his boots, Melanie his trousers. With no wasted motion, without even a flicker of hesitation, Gray Cloud cut away the leg of his blood-soaked long johns, just above his injury.

With the tip of a knife she investigated the wound. "The ball hit the bone," she said.

The ominous words brought terrifying thoughts to Melanie's mind. She couldn't bear the thought that he might lose his leg. How could a farmer work without two legs?

She nearly screamed that Gray Cloud must do something. That she should save this man and his leg. That she should call down the powers of heaven or hell, she didn't care which. Instead, she forced a calmness she was far from feeling. "Will he lose his leg?"

In her terror she heard a buzzing in her ears and wondered if she could hear Gray Cloud's response over the sound.

Gray Cloud shook her head. "Chips," she said as she brought small white fragments from the wound. "Just small chips," she repeated, the words soothing Melanie's panic, even as her stomach threatened to empty itself at the sickening sight. "The ball lies deep. It's good that he sleeps."

The blood wouldn't stop flowing. Melanie wondered how much more he could spare. She longed to tell Gray Cloud to hurry, but bit back the words, knowing the woman was working as fast as possible. And then, thank God, the ball was out. Somehow, someway the ball was finally out. But still, the bleeding refused to stop.

Gray Cloud poured powder into the wound and then stanched the gushing flow of blood with the red hot end of a fireplace poker.

Melanie shuddered at the gruesome sight and swallowed convulsively at the smell of burning flesh. She watched as Gray Cloud spread a paste of herbs into the wound and then covered the injury with a clean cloth. She wrapped Zachary in a heavy blanket.

Melanie cleaned the wound on his side and spread the same paste over it. Zachary had been right about this one. It had bled little and was already crusted over with dried blood. If he suffered no fever, he'd soon be well.

Her thoughts proved true. Apparently whatever Gray Cloud used worked wonders, for the skin around both wounds stayed a healthy pink. He slept day and night, thanks to Gray Cloud and a potion she administered whenever he stirred, and he suffered no fever.

Four mornings passed before Zachary awakened. Except for the throbbing soreness in his side and thigh, he felt quite himself. He had turned toward Melanie during the night and had snuggled his body behind hers.

She no longer feared the position. She'd awakened more times than she could remember to it of late and the fears and memories of her husband's abuse had long since slipped from her mind. Zachary's hand on her breast was also familiar to her by now. He sought out her softness despite his injury. Melanie smiled as she became aware of his touch and brought the hand that covered her breast to her lips. She kissed him. At the sound of his sharp intake of air she turned to face him. His eyes were closed. She smiled and whispered softly, lest Gray Cloud and Caroline awaken, "You needn't bother to pretend you are asleep."

"I must be asleep. You kissed my hand. That means I'm dreaming."

She kissed his mouth this time and Zachary forgot his discomfort in the feel of her soft, sweet lips. "You're not dreaming. How do you feel?" she asked.

"If you used your hands and mouth, you could tell me."

She gave his shoulder a little shove and repeated her question.

"Wonderful, if you don't count the ache in my side and the fire in my leg."

Melanie touched a hand to his forehead. "You're cool."

"I'm hot. We're too close to the fire." Zachary sighed. "Are we still at Gray Cloud's?"

Melanie smiled as she rested her chin upon her hand and looked down at him. "Yes."

"Damn." He opened his eyes. "Melanie," he gasped with shock. "Your face!"

"I know. It's a pretty sight, don't you think? I particularly like the green shade under my eyes."

"I should have—"

"You killed him. It was enough. Gray Cloud saved your life."

"Did she?" he asked. His gaze moved over her face, knowing her bruises were partly his fault. If only he had reached her sooner. "Did you help?"

Melanie smiled. "I was very brave. You would have been proud of me."

"Meaning you didn't faint?"

"Never even came close," she lied.

"Are you sure?"

"Well, it was a little chancy when she put the fireplace poker into the hole in your leg."

"God, I'm glad I wasn't awake for that."

"I thought the same thing."

"Did you?"

A tender look passed between them. It spoke of promises and vows and love. Words that couldn't be said aloud.

She touched his beard-roughened cheek and ran her fingers over the prominent bone to the hollow beneath. "You're a very handsome man."

"Thank you. Did you just realize that?"

"No." Melanie seemed unable to control her smile. "I've known it for some time."

"But you never said it before."

She adjusted her head to a more comfortable position, resting the side of her face against her raised hand. "I like looking at you."

"You have my permission to look for as long as you please."

"I don't need your permission for that."

"All right then, you have my permission to kiss me for as long as you please."

Melanie grinned. "That's very nice of you."

"I'm nice."

Melanie giggled since he nearly choked on the words. Greatly enjoying this tender moment of teasing, she thought to push him further. "So I can kiss you then? Anytime I like?"

"You don't even have to tell me when. Just do it."

"Thank you."

Melanie lowered her mouth to within inches of his. "Thank you for saving my life."

"Thank you for saving mine," he returned.

"Gray Cloud saved yours."

"I know, but I can't thank her the way I want to thank you."

Neither got the chance to thank the other since

they both heard the sounds of Gray Cloud getting out of her bed. In the silence of pre-morning, the old woman's joints cracked and she groaned as she came to her feet and stretched. More cracking.

She ignored them completely, acted as if two would-be lovers were not at this very minute lying before her fire snuggled in each other's arms and speaking sweet nonsense. They watched her slip her feet into moccasins and pull a blanket over her shoulders before leaving the house.

"We might have to wait until we get home before you can properly thank me," Zachary said.

Melanie, feeling very sure of herself, offered, "We have a few minutes, I think."

And Zachary put those minutes to the best use possible.

By the time Gray Cloud returned to the cabin, Zachary was in some distress and his disappointment at her untimely interruption couldn't have been more obvious. "Damn," he muttered into Melanie's neck, his hand under her chemise, enjoying her delicious, rounded curves.

"I have to get up. Caroline's about to start fussing."

He gave her one last hard kiss. "We're going home today."

"Can you ride?"

"I'll walk if I have to."

Keeping the blanket bundled around his waist to hide his erection, Zachary moved away from the fire, allowing the women to go about their chores, Gray Cloud to begin the morning meal, Melanie to clean and dress the baby.

As he watched Melanie care for his daughter, Zachary couldn't help imagining how good it would feel to have her care for him. He couldn't wait to get her back home.

There was a small box of tea on one of Gray Cloud's shelves. Melanie had enjoyed the brew more than once since coming here. The moment Melanie left the cabin for a quick trip to the privy, Zachary convinced Gray Cloud to part with the precious leaves with a promise to bring the old woman a case of the stuff the next time he went into town.

"One leg of my long johns is missing," Zachary said as he realized the loss just before sliding his legs into his buckskins. "Now I have nothing to keep me warm."

Gray Cloud handed him a cylinder of material, stiff with dried blood. Obviously, the missing leg. Melanie placed it among the rest of their things. "I'll clean it and sew it back on."

Zachary finished dressing and rested as Melanie gathered Caroline's things together. "I have Black Bear's horse. I'm leaving it with you," he told Gray Cloud.

She nodded, accepting the gift as just payment for her neighborly generosity and assistance.

It took the help of both women to get Zachary onto his horse. He should have known better. The distance to his cabin was hardly what one would call great. Still, forcing himself to ride so soon after twice being injured was a damn fool thing to do.

By the time he and Melanie reached his house, he was exhausted, covered with sweat, dizzy, and hardly able to sit on his horse. Now that it was too late he realized he should have stayed with Gray Cloud, at least until he was able to walk on his own.

Damn, but he was weaker than piss and had no business traveling. He was about as strong as a newborn babe. If they were to come under attack, perhaps by yet another hostile Indian, he wouldn't be able to do a damn thing to prevent Melanie from being carted off again.

His leg was killing him, his side as well, and the longer he remained on his horse, the more he was likely to hurt.

Zachary felt some relief as the horses came to a stop on the narrow path that led to his door. He looked at the long walkway and wondered how, and most importantly, if, he could manage the chore.

"Stay here," Melanie said as she started for the house, having already dismounted. "I'll put Caroline in bed and come back for you."

Zachary knew he had no choice but to obey. There was no way he could walk on his own. Probably not even with Melanie's help. *Damn.*

Melanie was back sooner than he expected. Without saying anything, she guided the horse down the narrow path, stopping at the first step to his cabin. "Slide off the horse, Zachary."

"I'll fall on you."

"It doesn't matter. You won't hurt me."

Zachary raised his good leg and slid his body over the animal's side, holding on to the horse as best he could to avoid falling on her. Her arm reached around his waist, his over her shoulder. He was far too heavy for her, but couldn't do a damn thing about it. "Wait. Maybe we could . . . "

Melanie's back was pressed to the hand railing that ran along both sides of the steps. "It's all right," she said, grunting with exertion. "Use your good leg and lean on me. Go slowly and take one step at a time."

She had left the cabin door ajar and Rusty stood in their way, barking and obviously happy to be home. The dog wasn't very big, but it took only one jump

both adults to the floor.
ie ordered.

ve no intention of sitting.
d wooden floor as he con-
vag his tail, nearly causing
asty fall.

the main room. Zachary
s he allowed Melanie to
d. Zachary, afraid of hurt-
work himself and in so
strength. He was sitting in
unable to remove his coat
g from crawling all over

e a fire and place a pot of
his side again she ordered
don't let me see you on
d. A moment later Rusty
at his favorite place before

sed. He's not used to see-

I'm going to kick his ass

chary asked as she pulled
for the fastenings on his
he could enjoy this more.
could remember her un-
uld think about was sleep-

t Rusty."

pulled away his shirt and
ht. Maybe I won't hit him
s . . . God, I can't believe

Melanie settled him beneath a thick quilt and hung his things on hooks along the wall.

"You've lost a good deal of blood, Zachary. You have no alternative but to rest some." She smiled as she added, "You'll be fine."

"Where are you going?"

"To bring the horse into the barn. I'll be back as soon as I can. Go to sleep."

"Make sure Rusty goes with you."

Melanie did not immediately return. Mr. Holbrook had promised to come daily to see to the care of the animals, but he hadn't done so in the last day or so. No doubt the added two inches of snow had kept him home.

While in the barn she milked that stupid cow. God, what was the matter with the bovine anyway? Why did she so dislike being touched? Who had ever heard of a cow not wanting to be milked?

Melanie breathed a sigh of relief as she finally finished the chore. She then fed and watered the horse, collected eggs, and saw to the feeding of the two cats that claimed silent ownership of the barn. Well, silent until Rusty entered their domicile. As the cats hissed their hatred, Rusty chased both into the rafters.

Zachary didn't sleep until Melanie returned to the house. "Bar the door," he told her.

Melanie nodded and did as he asked.

She was exhausted by the time she eased herself carefully into bed that night. Preparing meals, caring for a baby as well as an invalid, had taken their toll. She slept soundly.

The next morning, after again seeing to Caroline's needs, she left the child to play on a blanket stretched over the floor and set about nursing her sleeping patient.

Zachary awakened to her gentle ministrations. She

was cleaning the wound on his thigh, satisfied to see the skin surrounding it healthy and pink and the wound itself growing smaller every day.

The bullet had entered his thigh only a few inches from his hip and Melanie had placed linen toweling over his private parts. She was in the midst of securing a fresh bandage when she realized his body was responding. Her gaze moved quickly to Zachary's smiling, drug-glazed eyes. "Sorry," he murmured. But if his grin meant anything, he was not the least bit sorry. "There are some things a man can't control."

"I'm sure," Melanie returned as she quickly finished her chore. She breathed a sigh of relief as she whisked the toweling aside and at the very same instant covered his body with the quilt again. She was trembling, having mastered the insane need to lift the toweling and see for herself what was happening there.

Melanie knew enough about men, had seen enough in fact, to know what a man looked like when he was aroused. What she didn't know was what *this* man looked like. Granted she had seen him naked more than once, but she had tried not to look at that particular portion of his body. And even if she had looked, he'd never been fully aroused. Yes, she had felt his hardness pressing against her body, but she had never actually seen it.

The quilt lay tented over his middle. She couldn't do it. She didn't dare. Yes, she did. After all, his eyes were closed. Maybe he was asleep. Melanie watched him for a long minute, making sure. All she wanted was one quick look. It wasn't so much to ask, was it? She had no doubt that had he been awake he would have settled her curiosity without an instant's hesitation. Gently she raised one corner of the quilt, her gaze never leaving his face.

The quilt was almost high enough. In another second she'd look her full. She lowered her head and looked. She'd known he was big. Even if she hadn't already felt it, she would have known a big man was likely to be big all over. He was far bigger than Joshua, bigger even than she could recall her husband or his lover being.

Melanie glanced again at Zachary's face, only to find his eyes open and watching her. She gave a cry of alarm and dropped the quilt back into place. "I thought you were sleeping."

"Trying to take advantage of me?" he asked, closer to the truth than his drugged mind could appreciate.

"I . . . I was looking for the towel," she stammered, knowing the lie was ridiculous, since the towel was at that very moment in her hand.

"Don't let me stop you."

Melanie's cheeks were redder than cranberries as she hurried from his bed. Lord, she could never look at the man again. What in the world had ever possessed her?

It was three days before Zachary was able to stay awake for more than a few minutes at a time. Melanie fed him, washed him, and saw to his most private needs without the slightest hesitation, the temptation to look again firmly laid to rest.

This morning he had eaten heartily on his own and then napped until the midday meal, when the process had repeated itself.

Now, judging by the shaft of light coming from the cabin's only window, inching its way toward the fireplace, Zachary guessed it was late afternoon. The silence was broken only by the sounds of Melanie working in the kitchen. The curtain was partly closed and he couldn't see a thing, but she seemed to be preparing their evening meal.

He glanced toward his daughter's bed and found her asleep. Zachary wondered if she might not be a particularly good little girl and sleep for another hour or so, thereby enabling her father to occupy himself and his lady in a most delightful fashion.

His eyes closed, he released a soft moan of feigned pain, knowing it would summon Melanie to his side as no entreaty would. It did.

He watched from beneath dark lashes as she leaned over him, concern tightening her full lips. "Are you ill?" Her hand grazed his forehead and he heard a sigh of relief as she found his skin cool to the touch. He moaned again, hardly able to contain a smile.

Melanie wondered if he still suffered. After all, it had only been a few days. Surely his wounds were bound to give him trouble for a time. "I'll get the medicine," she whispered and an instant later, with a soft cry of alarm, found herself lying beside a suddenly wide awake Zachary. "What are you doing?"

"What medicine?" he asked, coming to his elbow so he might look down upon her, his free hand moving to the ties that secured her chemise.

Melanie pushed his hand away. "Zachary, let me up. You'll have a relapse if you don't rest."

"You didn't answer me. What medicine?" His hand had returned to the tie, his fingers grasping one end. Melanie pushed again and in so doing unwittingly aided him in his intent. The material parted. Zachary smiled.

"You'll come down with fever if you persist."

"Melanie," he said, still waiting for an answer.

"Gray Cloud gave me a bag of powder to make you sleep. I've been mixing it with your water."

Zachary realized then the cause of his unusual need for sleep. "No wonder I could hardly raise my head from my pillow."

She eyed the snowy white bandage that circled his hip. "You needed to sleep. Gray Cloud said—"

"I can think of something I need even more." He needn't have voiced his needs aloud. The look in his eyes and his free hand moving over her full breasts revealed his intention.

"You definitely don't need that."

Zachary chuckled. "Sweetheart, I was thinking I need a bath, but since your mind seems to be caught up in contemplations of another sort, I presume you feel inclined." He breathed a sigh, as if her desire might prove a bit taxing. "Well, I suppose I could oblige a lady's wants." His palm smoothed over her breast in a circling motion, teasing the tip into hardness.

"You beast." Melanie gasped softly at his inference, her cheeks flaming at his casual remark, flaming because he was closer to the truth than he could have realized. She couldn't stop her body's instant response to his touch. She couldn't stop thinking about the things they had done together days and days ago. It shouldn't be this easy. How had he broken down her natural resistance? Where was her modesty? How had he made her want his touch?

"Let me up."

Zachary laughed as he leaned his weight half over her, effectively keeping her in place. He couldn't help but notice it didn't take much effort on his part. That the woman was willing was a given. All he had to do was get her to admit it.

His lips and teeth sought out the warmth just behind and below her ear. He nibbled quite delightfully as he teased, "If you help me take a bath, I promise I'll see to your wants."

Melanie decided the best course was to ignore the last part of his comment. And she would have if his tongue hadn't dragged over her skin, causing her a distinct loss of breath. If his fingers weren't at this very moment seeking out an ever-hardening nipple. "You can't get your leg wet. It might fester."

"My leg is almost healed."

His mouth had drifted to her throat and was slowly working its way down her chest. With a tug he easily lowered her chemise and her dress along with it until her breasts were fully exposed to his view. Zachary smiled just before his mouth took complete advantage of the situation.

"You shouldn't be doing this." Her heart raced, her voice breathless, the softness of her tone belying her words. "You're too weak."

It had been days since he'd touched her, days since he'd sampled her softness, and there wasn't anything he needed more. Still he knew she was right. He wasn't nearly as strong as he would have liked. Suddenly he reversed their positions. Lying flat on his back again, he coaxed, "Lean over me, sweetheart. You're right. I am weak."

"Zachary, this is totally ridiculous," she said, her arms supporting her weight as her body was pulled forward and down, so he might fully enjoy the luscious softness hovering just above his mouth.

"Totally delightful, you mean," he said between delicious spine-tingling nibbles and open-mouthed kisses.

Modesty demanded that she deny the truth, no matter how lovely this felt. "Let me up and I'll heat the water."

"What water?" he asked as he pulled her dress from her arms down to her waist. Beneath her dress he fumbled a bit but finally managed to open the tabs of both her petticoat and drawers.

Oddly enough Melanie never thought to stop him.

"The water for your bath," she said, pulling away in a last attempt to ward him off, only to find his mouth following her move. He was sitting now, while Melanie knelt, leaning back a bit, his mouth still upon her breast.

"What bath?" he murmured against her skin. His hands around her waist untied her apron as well as her dress. The fabric began to slide down.

"Zachary, it's the middle of the day," she managed breathlessly, torn between desire and fear of the pain that would surely come. She hadn't forgotten the size of this man. She hadn't forgotten the pain she'd once known at her husband's hands.

"I don't think . . . "

Zachary's hands moved down her sides, pushing all the material to just below her thighs. For all intents and purposes, she was naked and Zachary took full advantage as his gaze and hands moved over her. "Close your eyes for a minute. Just close your eyes and let yourself feel."

Melanie did as he asked, helpless but to obey his every whispered demand, helpless but to lean into his kisses and to ache for even more. His mouth moved to her midriff, her belly. God, it was wonderful. How could anything be so wonderful?

Her hands reached for his shoulders, touching his neck, his hair, his back. He shivered and Melanie whimpered, a soft sound, knowing her touch had caused the trembling.

His hands were at her waist, guiding her back, pressing her gently to the mattress. Her clothing was flung away. He was above her and then his body was pressing hers deep, deep into the mattress.

"We're going to do this slowly. Very slowly," he murmured as his mouth brushed tantalizingly over hers, causing her lips to soften, to grow greedy for more. "I haven't a doubt that it will kill me, but you're going to remember this forever."

Propped on one arm, he held her gaze as his free hand moved down her body. His touch was so light, Melanie wondered for a moment if it weren't her imagination. She forced herself to watch and moaned at the sight of his dark hand moving over her skin. Lightly, ever so lightly, hardly touching, his hand moved over her breast, down her belly, brushing over her leg. And then her breathing shut down completely as his hand reversed course and began to move up. Her heart thundered in her chest. He was going to touch her there. God, how she wanted him to touch her there.

The last time he had touched her with his mouth, but this was no less erotic. It had been more than three weeks, but she hadn't been able to think of anything but the possibility of his touching her there again. True to his promise, he was slow. Melanie found herself oddly impatient as his hand inched its way up her thigh. She almost cried out for him to touch her. To please touch her.

And then he did, sliding his fingers against her, unerringly to the core of her passion, and she couldn't stop a low guttural moan of relief and pleasure, or the anxious movement of her hips.

"I know, sweetheart. I know. But it will be better, I promise, if we go slow."

"It can't be," she said honestly, her voice a breathless thread, hardly heard nor understood in a furor of pounding hearts and labored breathing. "Nothing could be better."

Beneath his moving finger he found her soft, warm, wet, ready for him. He couldn't resist. He wouldn't.

Gently he parted her thighs and rested a moment between them. With his hand still in place, his finger still moving, driving her mad with need, he entered her body, sliding deep, deeper into heaven.

So tight! God, she was so warm and so incredibly tight. He wasn't going to make it. Zachary shuddered, fighting back the need to move, to take her now, to end this pleasure with a mere half dozen powerful thrusts. "Melanie," he groaned, his mouth curving into a grimace as he forced aside his body's demands, "you can't imagine how this feels."

But she could imagine, for she also felt the pleasure. She hadn't realized coupling could be like this. That his entering her body would only strengthen the ache deep inside. That the ache threatened to drive her beyond madness. That her body would open like a flower to sunshine. That she had to have more, much more.

"Does it feel good?"

She felt herself being pulled from a tunnel of exquisite pleasure by his question. She frowned. "What?"

"I asked if this feels good?"

"Zachary, don't talk now. I can't think."

"Can't you?" He smiled above her, delighting in the fact. "If I stopped moving my finger, could you think then?"

It didn't seem to matter that she couldn't think. Her body was responding to the movement despite his questions, growing tighter, more needy. She was almost there, almost engulfed in the madness.

She could feel it coming, squeezing at her insides, and she knew there'd be no stopping the pleasure. It didn't matter what he said, what she said, it would come. It did. Waves of surging pleasure pulsed around his sex, squeezing at him until Zachary moaned and closed his eyes, his body stiff, struggling to keep the pleasure at bay.

Her body felt heavy again, heavy and lusciously free. He was teasing her into giving over all and she felt no will to resist. His mouth left hers to nibble at her throat and slide unerringly to a breast. It was then that her hand moved to where their bodies joined, her fingers circling his hardness.

Zachary stiffened at her touch. "Don't. Melanie, don't!"

An instant later her hands were pinned above her head, held in place by a hand trembling so hard Zachary wondered how he managed. "God, you almost did it."

"Did what?" she dared bravely, arching her back, taunting him to resist the offered prize.

Zachary released a low laugh. "No, you don't, lady. I'm not that easy."

"Yes, you are."

"Damn it, Melanie," he breathed on a groan as his body was drawn forward, his head dipping toward the irresistible treasure. "I wanted . . . I wanted . . . Oh God," he groaned as his hands gripped her hips and he began to move at last.

And then it was there again. It took only his movement to bring on a pleasure so sudden, so hard as to be almost pain, so demanding that she had no choice but to allow it, no choice but to revel in it, to lose her mind and her heart to this man forever. It was better than the last time, better than anything could be.

She cried out as the rapture tore at her body, convulsive waves of ecstasy that sucked him deeper into the insanity, but her cry was lost in his hot, luscious mouth.

And then she felt the shudder above her, in her, surrounding her. A trembling, vibrating groan escaped his throat as he clutched her desperately to him, thrusting forward with a cry, his arms tightening until he stole her breath, until she could only feel the pounding of two thundering hearts, until those hearts merged into one.

His body lay heavily upon hers, his scratchy cheek upon her breast. Long silent moments went by before she groaned beneath him, "Could that really have happened?"

"What happened?"

"I'm not sure, but something did. Are you certain you were feeling weak?" Melanie asked, not having entirely regained her ability to breathe.

Zachary grinned. In her arms he was weak to her temptation, strong in his need to love her. And he did love her, more than he'd ever loved another human being. It was going to kill him to let her go. *No! Don't think about that now. Don't think about the day she'll leave.* He glanced at her flushed features and murmured, "Absolutely. Why?"

"What do you suppose might happen when you're well again?"

Zachary's smiled grew into low wicked laughter. "I believe you're trying to tell me you liked that very much."

From his cocky smile Melanie realized she'd admitted far too much. "Actually I was trying to tell you that you're an arrogant beast."

Zachary laughed again and then, deciding it was time to find her softness again, he smoothed a finger over her nipple and said, "You were wonderful, you know."

"I was?"

He nodded. "The truth is, if being with you were any better, I'm not sure I could live through it."

Melanie blinked in amazement. "Are you teasing me?"

"I'm telling you the truth. You were better than all my dreams put together."

"You mean you've been dreaming about this?"

Zachary chuckled as he rolled to his side, taking her with him. He pressed his face into her hair. "Sweetheart, you'll never know."

Melanie lay gently against his chest as she savored the feel of his body against hers, of the pleasure he had brought her. She hadn't been able to resist him. She thought that odd, since she'd never before found it difficult to resist a man. An instant later she was besieged with guilt.

"What are you thinking?" he asked as he felt her slowly stiffen.

She didn't respond, but tried to back away. His arms tightened, bringing her back against him. "Tell me what you're thinking."

"I'm thinking we shouldn't have done this. Zachary, it was wrong. It was terribly wrong." *Tell me you'll make everything right. Tell me you want me to stay here forever. Tell me you love me. Tell me we will marry.*

"It's not wrong. We . . ." Zachary caught himself in time. He'd almost said the word *love*. He couldn't ever tell her that. "We care for each other, don't we?"

"Yes, but . . ."

"As long as we care, nothing we do together is wrong," he said firmly.

"It is when we're not married. It is when I am married to someone else." There, she'd left him the perfect opening. He had to ask her now. He would. She knew he would. But as the seconds ticked by, Melanie realized he would not. She felt an almost crushing disappointment, sorrow, and loss.

"You said you were getting an annulment, didn't you?" he asked.

"I don't have it yet."

"After your husband's abuse, do you imagine that you owe him loyalty?"

At that moment Melanie realized she hated Townsend for causing her pain when there should have been pleasure. There had been no need to make her suffer. No, she didn't owe him loyalty. She owed him nothing. Still . . .

There was a long moment of silence during which Melanie, straightening out her thoughts, decided a number of things. One was that she was in love with Zachary, but he did not love her in return. He'd had ample time and circumstance to state the fact if it were so. She sighed, supposing she'd just have to accept the truth of it. After all, a man couldn't help whom he loved, could he?

She pushed aside the depressing thought and considered his question instead. He was right. She owed her husband no loyalty and if she chose to indulge in the forbidden for this short time, it was no one's concern but her own and God's. There would come a time, she supposed, when she'd be called to answer for her sins. In the meantime, there was no way that she could undo what was already done and considering that she loved Zachary, there was no reason not to keep loving him until she was forced to leave his side.

She dismissed her long-held beliefs in right and wrong and refused to feel guilty. There would be time later to bemoan her actions. Time to wish for something that could never be. She wouldn't dwell on the impossible now. She'd take the pleasure this man offered. Take it as greedily as he gave it.

"You shouldn't have done this to me," she said. "It wasn't fair."

"What wasn't fair?"

"That you should make me want you."

Zachary breathed a sigh as he ran a hand over her hair and down her back, cuddling her even closer against him. She hadn't said she loved him, but he knew she did. He also knew their love could never be. No matter how much either of them might want or love, there was no way they could be together forever or marry. She did not fit into his life, nor he in hers. She was a woman of means, born to a wealth he could never hope to attain, while he was a farmer. It was impossible that they could ever have more than this short time together.

Melanie pulled back just a bit so she could see his face. "I think it was proximity that made you want me."

"Not true. I'm more discriminating than that. For instance, I wouldn't have wanted you if you were ugly."

"Beast," she said with a low, sultry laugh, and then moved back to her original position.

Zachary chuckled. "All right, perhaps I would have wanted you even if you were ugly. Come to think of it, I have a penchant for ugly women."

"Do you? Why?"

"Well, an ugly woman tends to be grateful for a man's attention, don't you think?"

"I think you are a cad."

"She'd be adoring and would allow me any and every liberty."

"You're disgusting."

"She wouldn't be likely to have a wandering eye, either."

"No, I think a wandering eye is more a man's specialty."

"Do you think so?"

"What I think is, I don't like men very much."

"You like me well enough."

"Only because you happen to be here."

"And available?"

"And very available," Melanie returned as her mouth explored his chest, finding it suddenly irresistible.

Zachary smiled. "I've been thinking."

"About what?"

"Well, since I'm here and available, do you think you might take advantage of me?"

"What, again?"

"I can feel my strength coming back, so you needn't be afraid of tiring me."

She pulled back and shook her head, even as a smile curved her mouth. "Caroline will be awake in a few minutes, and I left the bread to rise. It's probably all over the table by now."

"I'll let you look under the quilt again, if you stay." He said the words in a teasing, almost singsong fashion.

Melanie's cheeks grew warm with guilt. "What does that mean?"

"It means you were sneaking a peek while I was sleeping."

"I was not," she denied. She was never going to admit to such a thing. It didn't matter how true the accusation.

"I saw you."

"I was looking for the towel."

"You mean the one in your hand?"

"You were sleeping. You couldn't know."

"The truth is, I didn't know, not for sure at any rate, but I do now." Zachary laughed as her cheeks grew redder still. "Sweetheart, if you feel you must lie, you'd best try to control your blushes while you do it."

"I hate you."

Zachary laughed as she shoved him back, scrambled from the bed, and into her clothes again. They'd finish this tonight, he thought. He settled comfortably beneath the quilt as he watched her dress, a useless endeavor, he thought, since in a few hours she'd only have to take everything off again. Zachary sighed, his body sated for the moment, his heart filled to overflowing. Yes, they'd finish this and more tonight.

Chapter 12

Linda's lips curved as she realized Edward Stacey was at her side, leaning against the railing, his gaze on the distant horizon where the captain had said land would soon appear.

"Where have you been all day?" he asked.

"In my cabin. Have you missed me?"

"I knocked on your door. You didn't answer."

"Did you?" She turned just enough to allow him the view of a neckline that should have been two inches higher. It took the better part of a minute before Edward could tear his gaze away. When he did, he'd quite forgotten their conversation.

Linda, aware of the man's obvious desires, since he never bothered to disguise them, sought to intensify the need by batting her lashes flirtatiously, while a practiced but alluring smile curved her beautiful mouth.

"I'm sorry, darling. I suffered the most god-awful headache earlier and took one of my powders." Linda smiled again, with every confidence that her smile would make him forget any annoyance. Edward didn't need to know that she had spent the afternoon in the company of Mr. Warden, an elderly gentleman who sported a diamond tiepin as big as her pinky nail. A diamond that Linda imagined would look better, far better indeed, set into a ring for her finger. That little trinket, along with a few others she had "earned" during this voyage, rested very nicely at the bottom of her trunk.

Her look was pure seduction. She knew Edward was perfectly willing to succumb. "Did you want something in particular?" she asked.

Edward shrugged. "The captain said he expected to reach port by this evening. I thought we might finish that bottle of brandy before docking."

"That sounds lovely," she readily agreed, for Edward had proven himself a most expert and generous lover. She remembered the way they had begun the bottle, their positions, their state of undress, and thought they might finish it in much the same fashion. "Were you thinking about sharing the bottle in your cabin?"

"I was."

The afternoon's activities should have exhausted her. Despite the fact that she'd damned near worked her ass off, trying to get the old man to finish what he'd been so eager to begin, she was more than ready for a delightful diversion.

Poor Mr. Warden. Despite her efforts and expertise, the old man almost hadn't managed it. And when at last he had, he'd fallen into a deep sleep, no doubt aided by the sleeping draught she'd wisely added to his wine. Mr. Warden was asleep even yet and would no doubt stay that way until long after the ship had docked. Long enough for her to make herself scarce.

Linda smiled at the idea and, remembering the diamond she now possessed, thought that Mr. Warden had probably never spent a more expensive afternoon.

Edward's casual offer to wile away the evening sounded intriguing, especially since she'd already sampled the available men aboard ship, as well as a few who weren't so available, and found Edward to be the best of the lot. The man was generously proportioned exactly where a man should be, and knew how to use his gifts to heighten a lady's pleasure. She'd be a fool to decline his offer. "I'd enjoy that very much, Mr. Stacey."

Linda's morals might have been only slightly above those of a bitch in heat, but she knew the value of decorum. She'd practiced the ways of a lady until they had become second nature. And no lady would be seen entering a man's cabin on his arm. "Is your door unlocked?"

"Here's the key." He pressed it to her palm.

"Good. Why don't you meet me in say five minutes?"

Linda left Edward at the railing. Moments later she was in his cabin stripping away her clothes. She was anxious—more than anxious if the truth be told, after having spent an afternoon coaxing a limp member into action—to feel a healthy male thick and hungry inside her. Anxious enough to put aside her usual subtleties. By the time Edward joined her she was positioned in a seductive pose upon his bed, quite naked, quite ready to enjoy their last few hours on board.

Sometime later, taking a short breather, they lay facing each other, their bodies damp with perspiration, relaxed and sated for the moment. "Where are you going once we reach Williamsburg?" he asked.

Linda shrugged. Where she was going was, in fact, none of his business. Linda didn't much like a man pushing his nose into her affairs. The truth was, she didn't much like men at all, at least not outside of bed. "I thought I'd do some traveling." She'd have to do quite a bit of traveling in fact, once Mr. Warden realized his diamond was gone. She shouldn't have taken it, she supposed, for in the taking she'd put more than herself in danger. Still, Mr. Warden was heading north. He wouldn't think to look west. "New York, perhaps," she lied. "I know some people there."

"Men?"

"Of course." Linda laughed, thinking the last was probably true, for she knew countless men and hadn't a doubt, had she made inquiries, she would find a few in New York. "Why?"

"Well, I'm off to Charlottesville. I thought if you weren't doing anything terribly important, you might come along."

"What's in Charlottesville?" she asked softly, suddenly on guard.

"A very wealthy grandmother. She doesn't know it yet, but she's about to give me my inheritance."

Linda relaxed. For a minute she had thought . . . She gave a mental shrug, knowing it didn't matter what she thought. There had been other times when a backup had been sent to make sure she got the job done. Occasionally a client doubted a woman had the expertise of a man. She hadn't as yet had a problem proving them wrong. "And how will you manage that?" she asked.

"I don't know yet, but I will."

"She must be old."

"Close to eighty, I think."

Linda shrugged. "So why not wait for her to die?"

Edward felt some shock at the cold, heartless words. Granted, he might take what he pleased from the old lady and never give his thievery a moment's thought, for it would all be his one day. Still he did, in his own way, care for the old woman and never thought to see her dead. "She won't die. She's too ornery for that," he said almost fondly. "Trouble is, I need the money now," he said as his hand reached for Linda's breast. "Will you come with me?"

She knew, of course, that she would. By a lucky coincidence, Charlottesville was her own destination. She smiled mysteriously and murmured, "Perhaps."

His hand moved lower, and then lower still, and she sighed eagerly as she parted her thighs to his extremely talented fingers. "Yes, now that you've asked so prettily, I think I will go with you."

Zachary sat in bed, propped up by pillows as he finished the last of a thick, delicious roast, carrots and potatoes and onions, smothered in gravy.

Melanie sat at the table, Caroline in her arms. She was feeding the baby mashed potatoes and gravy. "What a good girl," she said and then, to the child's father, remarked proudly, "Caroline ate a whole potato."

Zachary watched his daughter swallow the last spoonful and smiled. It had been days since he'd touched her and he greatly missed her sweetness. "Bring her over here for a minute, will you?"

"As soon as I get her cleaned up. Looks to me like her dress enjoyed the gravy even more than she did."

"It doesn't matter. I'm lonely over here."

With a wet towel Melanie quickly washed away the worst of the mess and handed the child to her father. "You're about ten feet away from the table. How can you be lonely?"

"You only pay attention to Caroline," came his decidedly childish whine. "It's easy to be lonely when you're ignored."

Melanie frowned. "You're being ridiculous again. Caroline needs my attention. She's a baby."

"I need it too."

"Why? Are you feeling poorly?" Melanie reached a hand to his forehead, checking for a fever. He was cool to the touch.

"As a matter of fact I am."

"How?"

"I've been lying here alone all evening. You haven't even spoken to me once."

"Of course I have." She sighed. "Zachary, you're acting like a child."

"I'm acting like a man who needs his woman in bed with him."

"Oh," she said softly.

"My offer still stands, you know."

"What offer . . . " Melanie didn't finish. She knew by the wicked look in his eyes exactly the offer to which he referred. "Perhaps after Caroline is in bed for the night."

"Perhaps?"

Apparently the man wanted something more definite. Melanie chuckled as she left him with his daughter and went about straightening the kitchen. "I need something heavy for the top of this." Melanie was spooning the last of the sliced roast into a wide-mouthed jug. She put it outside in the cold again, but with more preparation this time. An animal had helped himself to the chicken soup she'd left there last night. She wouldn't be pleased to see that happen again.

"There's a rope hanging from the porch roof. Tie it to the handle."

Melanie washed the dishes, added wood to the fire, and warmed water for Caroline's bath, all the time listening as Zachary gently conversed with his daughter.

He spoke in a low tender tone, but in words one might use while addressing an adult. And he did it as if the baby were fully capable of understanding. If he continued along on this vein, perhaps she soon would.

Melanie smiled, for if Zachary's sudden cries and Caroline's giggles meant anything, the baby was having a delightful time pulling her father's chest hairs.

"Stop! No! Help!" he cried in a voice filled with supposed terror, to the baby's absolute delight. "Stop her! Save me!"

He raised the blanket, pretending to hide. "What are you doing?" he asked, his voice suddenly normal again, as Melanie lifted Caroline to her hip.

"Saving you, of course."

Zachary grinned.

"It's time for her bath. And if you get her too excited before bedtime, I'll never get her to sleep."

Melanie quickly stripped the baby and placed her in a bucket of carefully tested soapy, warm water on the table. But Caroline, excited from her father's playing, wasn't ready to calm down. She splashed the water, laughed in delight at the results, and splashed again.

"Oh, Lord," Melanie said. "Caroline, stop it, you'll get soap in my—" Melanie gasped. "Zachary, get over here!"

"What?" came his almost instant response from behind her.

"Watch the baby, I can't see a thing. I've got soap in my eyes."

Zachary handed her a towel and laughed as his daughter poked her finger into the floating soap suds. "That's soap, Caroline. Say soap."

Melanie squeezed her eyes against the stinging and spoke into the towel. "She can't say *soap*. She can't say anything yet."

"She says *da da*," he returned proudly.

"Only because you keep saying it. She doesn't know what it means."

"Of course she knows what it means."

Melanie sighed, pulling the towel from her face the moment the stinging began to lessen a bit. It was then that she realized Zachary had come from the bed naked. She averted her gaze. "You're being ridiculous again."

Zachary frowned. "Are you telling me she's not brilliant?"

"I'm telling you she's a baby."

"She can say *soap*. Listen," he said to Melanie and turned his attention to his daughter. "Say *soap*, Caroline."

The baby returned a very clear, "Ine."

Zachary's eyes rounded in astonishment. "Did you hear that? She said her name. God, she *is* brilliant. Have you ever seen a baby so clever?"

Melanie smiled. "I'm sure I haven't. And I'm equally sure the next thing she'll say is 'Daddy's naked again'."

For the first time Zachary seemed to realize he was standing in his kitchen without a stitch on. "Oh. Do you think she notices that sort of thing already?"

Melanie knew the baby did not. But *she* did and noticing his state of undress left her oddly shaken. "It might be better if you went back to bed or put something on."

Zachary moved toward the shelves above the dry sink and took down a towel. He wrapped it around his hips and tucked in one corner.

Well, at least he was covered, Melanie thought. No sooner had the thought made itself known than she realized it didn't matter. The material lay low on his hips, just below his flat stomach. Just above an enticing bulge. Lord, that just might be worse than wearing nothing at all. All it seemed to do was accentuate the covered portion of his body and exaggerate her need to see more.

"Better?" he asked, having no notion of the trauma he was causing to her senses.

Melanie had to clear her throat twice before she could manage, "Fine."

She finished bathing the baby and had her dressed for the night and wrapped in a warm blanket, cuddled upon her lap before the crackling fire, when Zachary opened the door to a blast of freezing air and pulled the large brass tub inside.

"What are you doing?"

"I need a bath."

"So you stepped outside barefoot and almost naked?"

"Only for a second."

"Obviously Caroline did not inherit her brilliance from her father."

Zachary chuckled as he hung a huge pot of water over the flames and then tore the quilt from his bed, wrapping it tightly around his shoulders as he took the seat opposite her.

He couldn't hide his shivers. Melanie's gaze silently questioned his common sense. "Of course, you couldn't have done that first."

"Don't nag at me, Melanie, I'm feeling weak and in real need of some of that tenderness you're giving Caroline."

Melanie grinned. "Well, I'd give it to you, but I can't fit you on my lap."

"Later in bed. Hold me then." His words didn't hold a question, but his eyes did.

Melanie watched him for a long moment before she smiled. Zachary took that smile for agreement and leaned back, closing his eyes as he waited for the water to warm.

They sat in silence until Caroline slept. And as she cuddled the baby to her warmth Melanie watched the man across from her. It suddenly dawned on her, to her surprise, that despite his size, despite his strength and manliness, he needed tenderness as much as the smallest creature on earth. Odd that she hadn't realized that before. Odd that she hadn't thought of him as anything but the strongest, most handsome and powerful man she'd ever known. How silly of her. The man was a human being, after all, possessing all the fears and hopes of the rest of mankind. By simply being alive he knew happiness, sorrow, laughter, tears, weakness, and strength. Lord, what could she have been thinking? Of course he needed tenderness upon occasion.

Caroline was asleep. Melanie brought her to her crib and tucked her in. Next she ladled water into the tub and gathered soap and towels for Zachary's bath.

"Zachary," she said gently, touching his shoulder. "Your bath is ready. Wake up."

"Sorry," he said as he rose on unsteady legs and with trembling hands stripped away the towel and quilt. A moment later he was sitting in the tub.

Melanie couldn't help but notice his trembling. "Are you all right?"

"I'm fine. I should have slept more this afternoon, is all."

"I knew it. Did I not tell you as much? I knew you had no business . . . " Melanie gasped as she was suddenly tugged fully clothed into the tub. Water splashed everywhere. She gasped again while wiping the water from her face, and she was just about to give this fool a piece of her mind when he said, "I don't care if I die. Loving you was worth it."

There was no way she could resist him after that.

Zachary smiled and then his mouth was on hers. She didn't object as he pulled both dress and chemise over her head and flung them to the floor. She found herself helping, nearly as eager as he, as he reached for the tab of her petticoat and again as he pushed her drawers down her legs.

She knelt facing him, her knees on either side of his hips as his hands moved lovingly over silken, wet flesh. Melanie was obviously enjoying the lusciousness of wet skin rubbing together, her breasts against his chest, her belly against his, her legs along his thighs. "I can't tell you how good you feel."

Judging by the way he touched her and the low sounds that were slipping from his throat, Melanie thought she knew well enough. She smiled, and with suds-filled hands ran them over his chest, her mouth finding his shoulder irresistible. "I wish I could say the same. Too bad I'm not enjoying this at all."

"You're not? Are you sure?" he breathed as he leaned back, his eyes half closed, enjoying the sweet investigation of his neck, shoulders, and chest. She rinsed him and then her hands were at his belly and drifting steadily lower, her mouth at his collar bone and then at his chest.

He could hardly understand her words, what with the way she was dragging her mouth and tongue across his chest. "The truth is, I've never much enjoyed touching a man," she said.

She felt him stiffen and leaned back enough to watch his face. He opened one eye and looked very dangerous as he said, "If I'm not mistaken, you've never touched any other man but me."

Melanie sat back and grinned. "That's not true. It can't be true. I must have touched a man before."

"An offered arm?"

Melanie reached for his arm, finding it hard with muscle and slick with soapy water. "Yes, an arm, but never an arm like this one."

"A chest?"

"Well, now that I think of it, I have."

"But his clothes were on," Zachary offered hopefully.

"Of course his clothes were on. What do you think?"

"I think I never want to leave this tub, never want you to stop touching me."

"Never?" He moaned as her hand moved below his belly. "The water will get cold."

"I don't care."

"It seems to me you don't care about much as long as you have a naked lady on your lap or in your bed."

"Well, the truth is, a naked lady has the tendency to cause a man to forget some things."

"Some things? *Every* thing, I think."

He smiled.

Melanie touched him, feeling confident at his low moan. "It's very big, isn't it?" she asked as she measured his length and width with her fingers.

"You've felt it before." His chuckle was wicked. "You've seen it as well."

Melanie laughed, the sound deliciously happy, and hid her face against him for a second. "You can't blame me for being curious."

"Did you like what you saw?"

"Well, I'm not sure I'd say *like* exactly."

"You mean you more than liked it?"

"I mean, it's sort of strange looking."

Again he opened one eye and frowned. "Do you think so?"

"Well, I'm sure you wouldn't think so since you've had it with you for a bit."

Zachary grinned. "I haven't given it much thought, but yes, you might say that."

"I think your body is beautiful, except that this looks sort of angry."

She hadn't stopped touching him, measuring him, and for that Zachary was thankful. He sighed his pleasure. "Does it? It's not, you know. It's not the least bit angry. As a matter of fact, he's very nice once you get to know him."

Melanie grinned for she had not missed the sudden shift to a personal pronoun. "They say first impressions are usually inaccurate. I should probably get to know him better."

"I think that is a very good idea."

Melanie answered his grin with one of her own and then bit her bottom lip as her hand moved lower. She frowned just a little. "Where are his friends?"

Zachary's eyes widened before he laughed aloud. "His friends?"

"Yes, you know those two things that . . . What are you doing?"

"I'm getting up and so are you."

For a man who, only a few minutes ago, had professed weakness, Zachary seemed much recovered indeed as he swung her into his arms and allowed them both to drop naked and soaking wet across his bed. "Now," he said as he stretched upon his back, exposed for her pleasure. "Now you can get to know him and his friends at your leisure."

"I hope you know you just soaked the bed."

"I don't care."

"There you go again, not caring."

"Did you want to see his little friends or not?"

Melanie glanced at his body, most especially at the part of his body in question. "Well, actually . . . ah, I mean, now that you mention it . . . "

Sometime later Melanie lay against the propped-up pillows, her arms around a reclining Zachary. She cuddled him close to her breast. "It's getting better every time we do it," she said against his dark hair.

"I know."

"Is it supposed to?"

"I don't know. Nothing like this has ever happened to me before."

"What if it keeps getting better and better? What will happen then?"

"I suppose we'll find out," he said as his lips nuzzled the crest of her softness, bringing the tip to hardness once more.

"We really can't do it again, Zachary."

"Why not?"

"Because we've done it twice already and you're exhausted. You haven't recovered from your wounds yet."

"All right. We'll wait a few minutes."

"I'm getting cold. Which of us is going to get the quilt?"

"I don't know. Who do you think?"

"I think if you were a gentleman, you wouldn't have to ask that question."

"But I'm weak, remember?"

"It's convenient, don't you think, that you remember your weakness only upon occasion?"

Zachary chuckled as she moved out from beneath him. He dozed and awakened as she swung the quilt over them as she returned to the bed. "Move over, you're hogging the whole bed."

"What took you so long?" he asked, his voice low and sleepy as his arms pulled her close against him.

Melanie shivered against the chill and snuggled closer, pressing her rump to Zachary's middle. "A man I know tore my clothes off and—"

"That was smart of him, don't you think?"

"And left them in a wet pile upon the floor. I had to wring them out and spread them before the fire."

"You wear too many clothes."

"Something you could never be accused of, I'm sure."

"Turn around."

"Go to sleep."

"I will, just turn around so I can feel you against me."

Their time together was almost over, Zachary knew. Spring would come and she'd leave soon afterward. But in the meantime she was here, his to enjoy, his to touch, his to love until they were both lost to the madness. He couldn't get enough of her and his lusty need surprised even him, for it took only a look, a smile, and sometimes not even that to make him hungry for her again. And never once did he take her without remembering that the clock was ticking, that their time was growing short. That soon the agony of her leaving would be upon him and his life would never be the same again.

Douglas Hamilton would soon marry the prettiest girl in town. He owned his farm outright and had put enough money aside to ensure his bride a happy, secure future. Douglas could have invited his brother in a letter, but because Zachary only lived in the next county, he preferred to do it in person. It wouldn't take but a day or two to ride there and back. What with working his farm, harvesting his crop, and then planning a wedding, Douglas hadn't seen his brother in almost a year.

If the weather held, he'd visit Zachary next week, Douglas decided. Yes, that should give him plenty of time for a little visit before the wedding.

The side of the ship hit gently against the rope-cushioned wooden dock. At last. Land had been sighted last night, but it had taken hours longer before the ship had traveled the river to finally moor in Williamsburg. The journey had taken far longer than Edward would have liked, far longer than he could afford, and it wasn't over yet.

Edward and Linda watched as the blanket-wrapped corpse was taken from the ship. Mr. Warden had died in his sleep last night. Linda felt not the slightest flicker of remorse, even though his death lay most assuredly at her hands. The truth of the matter was, she had not set out to purposely do the man in It had been an accident. No doubt she had given him a tad too much of the sleeping draught, and apparently his heart hadn't been able to handle the excess. Either that or his heart hadn't been able to handle the afternoon he'd spent with her. She almost smiled at the thought. At least he had gone the way most men wanted to go.

Edward and Linda hired a coach and four and after their trunks and bags were secured to the rear, soon settled themselves inside.

Despite the powerful team, it would take several days to reach Charlottesville. Posts along the way would supply changes of horses as well as meals and drink for a nominal fee. Considering they had all the privacy they needed, both Edward and Linda thought to relax and enjoy the trip as best they could.

Still, the moment they left the city behind, Edward grew oddly morose and paid little attention to Linda, who sat across from him. His gaze was directed to the dark green scenery, remembering what it had been like when he'd been a boy. The beatings, the endless hours of hard work, the hatred he'd felt for his abusive father and his mother who sought her own comfort in jugs of hard cider. Edward never noticed as Linda removed her jacket and opened the buttons of her high-neck blouse.

Linda smiled as she moved from her seat and settled comfortably between Edward's thighs. Her hand moved over the soft bulge she found there as she asked, "What are you looking at?"

"Nothing. That's the problem, isn't it? I've never seen a place with so much nothing."

He eyed the landscape, which appeared to grow more dense with forest with every passing mile. Edward didn't like the country, not even the civilized country in England, and took no delight in what was to his way of thinking only bleak wilderness. He hated the color green. Hated anything and everything that reminded him of his childhood and this godforsaken place. He'd left the moment he was able and had never once regretted his decision.

What the hell had ever possessed his grandmother to settle just outside of the small town of Charlottesville, when cities like London or Paris enticed? She might as well have settled on the moon, for all the excitement this country afforded.

Edward pulled his thoughts from the past, finally noticing what his traveling companion was about. He watched as her fingers ran over his trousers and thought he'd never met a woman with so great an appetite for sex. He was fortunate indeed to have come across her. Because of her, a dull journey had become palatable.

"It's too bad we couldn't have stayed a few days in the city," Edward said, preferring the comfort of a bed to this cramped, rocking coach. But as the lady disposed of the securing tabs of his trousers, and began to bring his member to a decidedly more robust state, Edward thought the coach might be spacious and comfortable enough after all.

"Why didn't we stay a few days?" Linda asked.

"Truth is, I'm down to just about my last shilling." That was a lie, of course. Edward had a goodly sum gained after a few evenings spent in friendly games of chance on board ship. No one had realized he was a gambler by profession, and he had easily picked the unsuspecting travelers clean. Granted, the money he'd won was nothing compared to the fortune he was about to claim. But the reason he hadn't given in to the temptation was twofold. One was he hated the colonies and couldn't leave them soon enough. The other was that he had to get his hands on a substantial sum of money and return to England before it was too late.

Linda laughed. Having had no need to make herself scarce since Mr. Warden had nicely obliged by dropping dead, she felt no particular hurry to travel inland, although she would have in due time. A stay in one of Williamsburg's inns might have been just the thing. "And you are in a hurry to see your grandmother," she reminded Edward.

"That I am." *Anxious* was closer to the truth.

"After your business is done then? We could have a pleasant little stay. I think I'd like to see New York then." It would have to be a quick stay, she thought, for she had pressing business back in England.

Edward knew he wouldn't give in to her wants.

Still, watching her work her sorcery over his helplessly growing organ, he thought he might promise her anything. For a short time he forgot even his hatred for this ugly country.

The *Charity*, having picked up a particularly good wind, carried Mr. Harry Stone at last to the colonies. The journey had taken weeks longer than it should have, but he was finally here, finally within reach of his daughter. Mr. Stone immediately hired a horse and, taking directions and advice from Mr. Joseph, the livery owner, set out for Charlottesville. Taking only the bare necessities with him, he ordered his bags to be sent on later.

Linda checked the ivory buttons of her blue traveling suit jacket and smoothed her skirt into place as the coach slowed to a stop. She smiled as her gaze lingered on the source of Edward's obvious discomfort. That he wasn't the least bit finished with their second go around was obvious. The truth of the matter was, she wasn't finished herself. Still, neither of them had a choice in the matter. The coach was pulling to a stop. They had been traveling the greater part of the day and it was time to change horses. Time to put aside their entertainment and satisfy other, less base appetites.

The station boasted of a small house that had been converted into an inn, a corral, and out buildings. Linda made a face, knowing she'd find no luxuries here.

Chapter 13

The constant jarring had seemed endless and Linda felt greatly relieved when the coach turned into a long drive at last. She'd enjoy a clean soft bed tonight, she thought. Best of all, she wouldn't have to sleep alone. Not that she'd slept alone last night. Not that she'd slept at all, in fact.

The last inn had been the smallest of all, affording travelers only two rooms on the second floor. The one for men had two beds, where more than five were forced to sleep together.

Linda supposed the women managed a bit more comfortably, having three beds in their room. She might have been reasonably comfortable had there not been five women and four children assigned to those beds.

Linda was meticulous in her personal hygiene. She bathed daily, if possible, and washed her hands at every opportunity.

She hated dirt, for dirt reminded her of London's streets, the hovel she'd lived in as a girl, and a mother who always smelled of men, their perspiration and sex.

She was not happy at being forced to share the room, but mostly she was not happy about the children. Linda did not like children. In truth they disgusted her. Dirty hands and faces, snotty little noses—she couldn't imagine being touched by one and refused to sleep in a bed where one might lay.

Because of the little beggars, she had sat all night in a chair waiting for dawn to break and her journey to continue. She'd dozed a bit early this morning, but the uneven dirt road had allowed for little real rest.

Edward's grandmother owned a large plantation that stretched far into Virginia's Blue Ridge Mountains. The house was huge and very comfortable indeed. Best of all there were servants, mostly indentured and a few slaves, to do her bidding. As soon as the coach came to a stop, and Linda was shown her room, she ordered a bath. Then she slept for two hours.

Edward's grandmother proved to be indisposed. She sent a message saying that her grandson and his friend should make themselves comfortable and she would see them in the morning.

That evening a huge platter of chicken, sweet potatoes, and creamed corn, along with hot crusty bread, were provided them. They ate in a dinning room that held chairs enough to accommodate thirty. Linda had seen nothing but woodland during her trip and wondered if thirty people existed in these parts. After eating, they retired to the back terrace where Edward smoked a cigar and Linda one of the few cigarettes she allowed herself each day. Each sipped from snifters of brandy.

Linda eyed the crystal glass. There wasn't a doubt that the old woman had money, for if nothing else the china, flatware, and furnishings boasted of the fact. What she couldn't understand was why Edward seemed satisfied with a portion when it would have been so easy to have it all. Still, that was Edward's business, she supposed. "What do you imagine we might do with ourselves tonight?" she asked.

Edward knew, of course, what she wanted. What she always wanted. The trouble was nothing happened in this house that his grandmother wasn't aware of. And he wasn't about to upset her by flaunting his indiscretions, when he was in such desperate need.

His intention was to ask the old lady for the money. He'd steal it only if she refused.

"The trouble is, there's nothing to do," he replied.

Linda frowned. Apparently he didn't understand what she was about. And not being one prone to subtle hints, she thought to make herself perfectly clear. "Which room is yours?"

"I'm afraid there won't be any of that while we're here." He took a deep drag on his cigar and slowly released a thin stream of smoke. "My grandmother would have apoplexy."

Linda laughed. "Would she? And is that supposed to stop us?"

Edward emptied his glass before saying, "It's important that she should not be annoyed."

"You're afraid of her." It wasn't so much a question as a statement of fact. Linda was surprised that a man like Edward should be afraid of some little old lady. She didn't much like fear in a man and decided he had a problem that needed settling forthwith.

The fact of the matter was, Linda liked it here. Certainly it was far better than some country inn. She might use this place as a base while going about her business. And while here, it would be ridiculous to deny herself, when a man was so obviously and easily available. No, she thought, any obstacles to her pleasure should be easy enough to overcome.

Early the next morning, Linda asked one of the

grooms to take her to town. In Charlottesville she shopped and made discreet inquiries. She was not at all happy to note yet another impediment in what should have been the most simple task.

She returned to the plantation already annoyed, only to find Mrs. Henrietta Stacey up and about. Linda had imagined her as a little old lady. Well, she was old, but hardly little, and as far as Linda could tell, miles from being a lady.

The woman looked and acted like a warhorse. Granted she might have shown her grandson a flicker of tender regard here and there, but the woman saved none of that emotion for her female guest. Indeed, Linda was quickly and in no uncertain terms told that no lady of quality traveled alone with a man. Obviously Linda could not be such a lady and therefore she was not welcomed here.

Linda had been the recipient of insults before, some far worse than this. She didn't much care what the woman thought of her. Indeed, what she did and how she lived were her own business and no horse-faced bitch was going to say otherwise.

Linda shot a helpless, obviously uncomfortable Edward a quick look of disgust, smiled at the old lady and retired to her room, promising she would of course take her leave in the morning.

She waited until late that night, sitting alone in her room, silently cursing the weakling Edward who had brought her here. The clock ticked upon the mantel and she watched with growing anticipation as the hands moved at last to three.

Tonight she intended to do something she'd never done before—kill for her own pleasure. By and large, she considered herself a professional who acted on behalf of others for money. Of course she could have gained at least as much money and status to boot had she married some wealthy man. She could have, she supposed, taken to the life of a thief. But neither interested her, for after the first time she killed she knew money wasn't the whole of it. Money couldn't compare to the rush, the thrill of excitement when holding in her hands the power of life or death. It was better than sex, better than anything she'd ever known. Those were the only times when she felt truly alive.

She was about to kill again, but for the first time, Linda wondered if tonight she would feel more than a rush of excitement. Tonight she might feel satisfaction.

The hallway, dimly illuminated by two candles, one at each end, was filled with shadows. Silently she made her way to the old woman's door and slipped inside. It took a few seconds for her eyes to adjust to the darkness. It was then that she saw the canopy bed and the lone figure asleep at its center.

Moments later, Linda smiled as she moved away from the bed. Smiled because the exhilaration had been magnified a hundredfold. There had been immense satisfaction in covering the bitch's face with a pillow, in pressing down hard until the body beneath hers ceased to move.

She breathed heavily. She always did after watching a victim struggle to live. Her blood raced and she knew she wouldn't calm down for an hour or more.

She moved silently to Edward's room. A moment later she was in his bed, her hand reaching for what she wanted.

Linda felt only mild amusement when the body she encountered turned out to be female. She understood then why he hadn't come to her room since their arrival. The woman was naked. She stirred at her touch, bringing Edward awake.

It didn't upset Linda that Edward shared his bed with another. What annoyed her was that she'd been made to do without. "What are you doing?" he whispered, suddenly awake. "My grandmother . . . "

"Is asleep. You might have invited me to join you in your diversions, Edward."

He invited her then and thought he couldn't have enjoyed himself more. It was a struggle indeed to muffle his grunts and groans. Not until morning did he learn that there had been no need.

Two days later, Mr. Stone pulled his horse to a stop outside Charlottesville's general store. He was hungry and tired, but most of all anxious, knowing he was within hours of seeing his Melanie again. He'd contacted Ellen first at Mr. Martin's place some fifty miles east of here. There he'd learned Melanie's exact whereabouts. Mr. Stone could not contain the happiness in his breast, nor the smile that curved his handsome mouth.

Douglas Hamilton's horse picked his way through the dense evergreens that grew two days north and west of Charlottesville. The mountain paths were passable, for winter had finally been laid to rest. Now only mud impeded his journey, for the melted snow had left the ground soft and Douglas's horse sank deep into the muck with every step he took.

Douglas never realized he was traveling in the wrong direction, for he'd come upon the road after the fork that would have led south. He wouldn't realize his error for another day.

Winter was over, and signs of spring dotted the forest that surrounded the small farm. Birds chirped more loudly every day. Rabbits darted from shadowy bowers to enjoy brief moments of sunshine. Squirrels devoured the last of their supplies before setting out to enjoy the fresh crop spring and summer would offer.

And with the coming spring, Zachary and Melanie both grew aware that their time together was almost at an end. And because of the awareness, their love-making grew more frequent and intense.

The touch and feel of her was etched into his heart. Her scent, her soft sweet laughter were more necessary to his life than breathing. The sparkling darkness of her eyes was his torment. There was nothing about her he didn't want, didn't love, and Zachary knew the years ahead offered only aching memories, beginning the day she walked away.

Melanie never mentioned leaving, but the word hung between them as clearly as if it had been shouted. He hadn't asked her to stay. Clearly he didn't want her to stay. Melanie thought for a time to hold back her favors, imagining that withholding them would force him to offer promises, but she knew she could not.

Yes, he felt a touch of tenderness for her, but tenderness wasn't love. Tenderness wasn't longing. And whether she took with her the memories of their loving, or not, she would leave.

Melanie fought against melancholy. She wouldn't leave him with memories of her tears, her sorrow. She'd be happy, or at least pretend she was, until the last.

Melanie put away the last dish and wiped the table free of crumbs. It was then that she felt his arms encircle her waist. "Is she asleep?"

"Sound asleep."

"You're getting very good at putting her down for the night."

"I'm good at other things as well," he murmured, his voice low and husky as he brushed his body against hers.

"Would you like some tea?"

"Coffee, if you don't mind. How much tea have you left?"

"Not much, I think."

Without thinking he said, "I'll get some the next time . . . " Zachary didn't finish and Melanie didn't question him. He'd stopped because he knew he wouldn't be bringing back tea from town. Zachary didn't like tea all that much and she wouldn't be here to drink it.

Melanie gathered her courage and forced the words, steeling her heart to the pain that would surely come. "When are we going to town?"

Zachary didn't pretend to misunderstand. "It might be dangerous yet for you to go to Charlottesville. The authorities there might still be looking for you. A trip to Williamsburg would be better. You could find a ship there and book passage home. I'll stay with you until you sail."

Melanie took a deep breath. Her life was falling apart. She'd missed her monthly time. Was she pregnant with his baby? She *could* tell him. He'd let her stay if he knew she was going to have his child. But, no, he had to want her for herself.

She'd have a hard time of it, she knew. Unmarried mothers—and she would be unmarried soon enough—were shunned by polite society. Friends and acquaintances would snub her. She'd been missing for so long, everyone would know Townsend could not be the father.

Her father was a prominent man, wealthy, influential. Even so, there would be a scandal. And even if she cared not at all, her father and sister would still suffer for it.

Still, there was no help for it, for she'd never give up this child. Somehow, someway she'd bear up under the disgrace of an annulment and a child that could not be her husband's. She wouldn't stay in London, she thought. She'd retire to the country, to her father's farm, perhaps never to leave it again. It wouldn't matter. After she left this man she wasn't likely to experience true happiness ever again.

"I haven't the money," she said lamely, as if money were all that was needed here.

"I'll give it to you."

She nodded. "When?"

"The roads are muddy from the melting snow. Next week they should be better."

"And if it rains?"

"If it rains we could wait a few more days."

And drag out the torture? Melanie came to a sudden decision. She would not stay any longer. If he was set on seeing her gone, there was no sense in dragging out the inevitable. "Do we have to wait?" She forced the trembling from her voice. She wouldn't cry. She absolutely would not cry.

"I'd rather not take Caroline into the rain and with the mud already so deep, the horse might get hurt," she said.

Zachary turned her to face him. "Are you so anxious to be gone, Melanie?"

She forced a weak smile, her dark eyes begging for an answer to a question she dared not voice. "Not anxious, but I think it's time, don't you? There isn't anything here for me, is there Zachary?"

He watched her for a long moment. He knew what she wanted, what she needed to hear, but he couldn't say it. He hadn't the right to keep her from her old life. She'd never be happy if he did. She might appear happy for a time, but soon her expression would grow vacant, her smile forced, as the yearning for a better way of life took hold. And he couldn't join her. A man wasn't a man unless he could care for his own. Her money would ruin him, would ruin them. He had nothing but himself to offer and it wasn't enough.

There was no sense in furthering the misery, nothing to do but to bring this ill-fated love affair to a quick end. He wondered how many years would pass before the pain faded. "No, I suppose there isn't anything here for you."

Melanie tried another smile. "Besides, I miss my family. I can only imagine what Father must think, how he has suffered."

She missed more than her family, Zachary guessed. She missed her home and the luxury of servants waiting to do her bidding. She missed fancy clothes, friends, and parties. She missed a life he could never give her.

"I'll get you to Williamsburg as soon as I can," Zachary promised as his hands dropped from her waist.

They lay in bed that night, together but apart for neither slept, both caught up in the pain of parting.

Would she stay if he asked? Zachary thought she might, but he wouldn't ask. And he couldn't leave. He didn't fit anywhere but here. Certainly not as her escort, certainly not among the elite of London.

Melanie kept her gaze on the ceiling, watching the flickering shadows caused by the fire. Soon she'd be home, safe within the protection of her family, staring at yet another ceiling. But Zachary and Caroline had become her family, and this little house her home. She loved it here. Despite the hard work, she had come to love it because the man she wanted and the child she wanted were here.

Should she beg to stay? *No.* Melanie sighed, knowing the truth of it. She couldn't plead for a man's love, especially not a man like Zachary. He either had it to give, or he did not.

Melanie sighed again as she heard the first few drops of rain hit the cabin's window and knew she wouldn't be leaving anytime soon. The ground was already saturated from the melting snow.

The room's only light came from the fire in the grate. Still it was enough, more than enough, to see his eyes upon her, glittering with desire. He wanted her, she knew, and she had not the strength to refuse.

He touched her face, his fingertips moving over her forehead, her nose, her lips, her jaw, as if for the last time.

To her shame, it took only his touch to bring her to him. There was something lacking in her character, she was sure, for she hadn't the will to resist.

He groaned, his mouth against her throat. "Melanie, Melanie." But the softly spoken word offered no promise. And Melanie knew it never would.

Chapter 14

◇〜〜◇

It was still raining when Melanie awakened the next morning to the smell of a pipe and the sounds of someone moving about in the kitchen. It was Gray Cloud, she knew. Zachary never smoked this early in the morning. And Gray Cloud's tobacco was distinctly different, sweeter and yet stronger.

Melanie moaned as her stomach churned sickeningly. Most mornings she was able to control the nausea that occasionally attacked, but there were other days and some smells that were beyond bearing. She grabbed the quilt to her naked body and with a groan thrust herself from the bed on wobbly legs. With one hand holding the quilt around her, and the other pressed firmly to her mouth, she ran barefoot for the door.

Her stomach emptied itself the instant she reached the edge of the porch. Melanie leaned weakly over the thick wooden railing, helpless between breathless gasps and silent prayers. And then finally she moaned again, this time in relief, as the nausea began to pass.

The door opened and Gray Cloud pressed a cup into her hand. Melanie sipped gratefully of the hot minty liquid. Moments later she moved inside. Sitting on the bed, she finished the drink, her lurching

263

stomach soothed. She listened as a pan hit against the table.

Apparently Gray Cloud had invited herself for a short visit. No doubt she did that now and again, for she certainly seemed comfortable in Zachary's kitchen, and asked no one's permission as she prepared the morning meal. Melanie was grateful for the company.

The moment she was able to think clearly again, she knew it had been a mistake to have allowed Zachary to make love to her last night. Their problems—or perhaps it was only *her* problem—remained just as solidly in place. In truth her sorrow had only increased with the coupling. Where once they had talked and teased after loving, last night they had said nothing, their silence filled with promises that would never be spoken.

After last night, she could only feel awkward and ill-at-ease in his company. Melanie sighed softly. If only she had not given her heart to this complicated man. She prayed for the rain to stop, for she'd suffered this torment of wanting and yearning long enough. She wanted to go home.

Thanks to Gray Cloud's potion, Melanie felt much her old self. She cleaned and dressed the baby before preparing her a small pot of porridge. Caroline played on a blanket on the floor as Melanie sat at the table.

Melanie watched as Gray Cloud cut thick slices of ham from a bone and dropped each into a large black frying pan. "Your man is pleased," she said.

There was no sense denying her pregnancy to this astute woman. "Zachary doesn't know."

Gray Cloud raised a puzzled gaze from her chore.

Melanie didn't wait for the question. "And no, I won't be telling him."

Gray Cloud's expression became amused. "You won't hide it for long."

"I'll be leaving soon."

Gray Cloud couldn't seem to fathom the possibility. "Leaving?" she asked. "With a man's baby in your belly?"

Melanie shook her head. "You don't understand. Zachary wants me to go."

"Because he doesn't know."

There was a long moment before Melanie finally said, "He won't ever know."

Gray Cloud's black gaze narrowed thoughtfully. "You think he would want you only because of the child."

"I know it," Melanie said with absolute conviction.

"He cares for you."

Melanie shrugged. "Perhaps. But not enough."

Upon Zachary's return from the barn, Gray Cloud was more abrupt than usual and responded with only a grunt when he spoke. Zachary didn't seem to notice until later that night, when Gray Cloud ladled stew over cornbread and spilled a good portion into his lap. Zachary jumped from the table, brushing away spilled potatoes, meat, and burning gravy. He glared at the old woman. She said nothing. Puzzled, he looked to Melanie for an answer. "What the hell is the matter with her?"

"I don't know what you mean."

"She hasn't said two words to me all day. And she just threw my dinner in my lap."

"It was an accident. And stop yelling, you're frightening the baby."

Zachary grumbled a low curse and sat down again, eyeing Gray Cloud closely. "Something is the matter. I know it."

Melanie held her breath and gave a silent prayer

that the woman would not divulge her secret as she looked knowingly first at Melanie and then at Zachary.

"You are in need of one of my potions, I think," Gray Cloud finally said. "It will soothe your stress and cause you to make the right decisions."

Zachary frowned at her cryptic words, baffled as to their meaning. "I don't need anything but a little conversation. And what the heck did that look mean?" He addressed the question to Melanie.

She breathed a silent sigh of relief. If Gray Cloud was going to say anything, she would have done it. Her secret was safe, she was sure.

Melanie couldn't help but marvel at the changes in Zachary. When she'd first come here, his habit had been to converse mostly in grunts, and not even that while eating. Now he wanted conversation with his meals and grew annoyed when faced with stony silence. Melanie wondered if he realized how much he had changed.

"What look?" Melanie asked, in response to his earlier question.

"The one she gave you and the one she gave me. What did you tell her?"

His confusion was obvious. Melanie shrugged. "I told her I was leaving."

He looked at Gray Cloud across the table. "Are you angry at me, because Melanie is leaving?"

"Some men are fools."

"There, I told you something was wrong," he said for Melanie's benefit, satisfied to have gotten to the truth at last. To Gray Cloud, he said, "For your information, old wise one, she's leaving because she wants to leave."

"Because you didn't ask her to stay."

Melanie stiffened and said quickly, "I don't think—"

"Mind your own damn business," Zachary interrupted in almost a shout.

Caroline's jaw trembled. Her big blue eyes filled with tears. She sucked in a jerky breath and Melanie went to her, comforting her with soft, soothing words, "Don't cry, sweetheart. Daddy didn't mean to yell."

His voice was decidedly lower when he spoke again. "I think I can answer for my own actions, Melanie. I don't need you to tell her what I meant."

Melanie glared at his back. "Fine. You may cry all you want, Caroline. Daddy meant to yell."

Zachary muttered a sound of disgust as he shoved aside his plate and left the table. A moment later the door slammed behind him. He hadn't a notion why Gray Cloud had suddenly gotten a tick up her ass, but it was a sad day when a man couldn't find peace in his own home.

It rained all the next day, and the next, and the one after that. Melanie's last night stretched into a week and then eight days. The rain looked as if it might never stop. The ground couldn't absorb it all and water rushed over the sides of shallow creeks to form rushing rivers. It dared anyone who ventured forth to be lost forever in bottomless sucking mud.

On the eighth day, Melanie sat on the porch wrapped in a blanket, holding Caroline in her arms as she rocked the baby to sleep. The steady drumming of rain on the porch roof was soothing. Melanie yawned and leaned her head back, her eyes closed.

She hadn't been sleeping well lately. She shared Zachary's bed, but no longer knew the luxury of his warmth, the feel of his arms holding her close, his hands touching her, bringing her awake in the night to the delicious pleasure of loving him.

Zachary never touched her now that the decision had been made that she would leave. No doubt the fact that Gray Cloud slept only a few feet from the bed contributed to his lack of ardor.

But Melanie didn't want to make love with him. To do so would only increase her sorrow, since she knew those precious moments meant nothing to him. How long would this rain last? How long before she could put the pain behind her and begin anew?

Zachary treated her kindly still, but now they ate in silence and shared a bed in silence soon after their evening meal.

Melanie watched as Zachary made his way through a half foot of mud from the barn to the porch. He stood in the rain for a long time, water pouring from his hat as he watched her holding his daughter.

The sight was indelibly etched into his heart, his soul. How could he survive without her? Without her smile. Without her laughter. Without her scent. Beneath her eyes soft shadows marred her perfect skin. She hadn't been sleeping well lately. Zachary knew that for a fact since he lay beside her every night equally sleepless.

The air was cool and damp. He wondered if she might not take a chill. "Are you warm enough out here?"

"Yes, thank you."

"Not too cold?"

"No."

That seemed to be all they had to say to each other. Apparently Zachary felt the same for he cleaned off his boots and entered the cabin.

* * *

Douglas mounted his horse with a groan. He knew he'd been going the wrong way, knew it before he'd stopped at the farm to ask directions. Damn, he had traveled a full day out of his way. Now he'd have to retrace his steps back to the old road. It would take him that much longer before he reached Zachary's place. Perhaps he should return home and send the wedding invitation by mail after all. But, no, he would go on. He'd come this far, after all.

"Come on Caroline, you can do it."

Melanie's face beamed with love as she watched the little girl let go of the chair and take one wobbling step toward her. "I'll catch you, sweetheart. Don't be afraid."

Zachary stood just inside the door, left open to the warm spring breeze. His gaze took in the fact that Gray Cloud was gone again. He frowned, wondering where the woman took herself off to every day. Not that he'd ask. What she did was her own business.

They had a strange relationship, he supposed, for it went far deeper than it appeared on the surface. He greatly respected her. Often he strove to please her. But of late his efforts seemed useless. She had said nothing when he'd offered her a large honeycomb, even though he'd suffered five bee stings in getting it. She'd said nothing when he'd added four beaver furs to her bedroll. The woman obviously was angry, probably because Melanie was going home.

Gray Cloud couldn't be expected to understand why Melanie could never stay. Gray Cloud had no notion of class distinction. Zachary thought he might explain someday, when the worst of his pain had eased. In the meantime, her silence was about to drive him mad. Still, for some inexplicable reason, he tolerated her company.

Zachary's eyes widened when he noticed his daughter standing bravely on her own. A moment later she moved toward Melanie. He hadn't realized until this very moment how fast she was growing. Melanie had been here a little over six months and Caroline had been almost five months old when she arrived. He couldn't believe she was already beginning to walk. She was still a baby, of course, but his baby was fast growing into a little girl.

Caroline took two more steps before falling forward into Melanie's waiting arms. Melanie laughed as she spun them both in a circle while giving soft shouts of cheer to the child and her accomplishment. Caroline screeched happily as she clung to her neck.

"Let's try that again," Melanie said, standing Caroline at the chair. "We'll surprise Daddy."

"Daddy's already seen it."

Melanie gave a small start as her gaze moved to his.

"Oh," she exclaimed softly.

Caroline began a chorus of, "Dad dee, dad dee, dad dee."

"Don't you think she's a little young for that?" Zachary asked.

"Not at all. She's eleven months old." Melanie backed a foot or so away. "Come on, Caroline, show Daddy you can walk."

Caroline complied by again taking three steps and falling into Melanie's arms with another shriek of laughter.

"She's bound to damage her legs. The bones can't be strong enough."

"Of course they're strong enough," Melanie replied. She turned her attention to the baby in her arms. "Your daddy is ridiculous."

Caroline dutifully and precisely said, "Dad dee

dickless." Her father laughed, a deliciously rich
sound of amusement, and Caroline, taking his laughter as praise, repeated, "Dad dee dickless."

Melanie handed the baby to her father, trying to
avoid the gleam in his eyes. Her cheeks were flushed
a lovely shade of pink as she headed for the kitchen
to prepare the evening meal.

It had stopped raining last night. Ignoring the pain
in her heart, she forced herself to ask, "Can we leave
tomorrow?"

"The ground will be soft yet."

"The next day then?"

Zachary sighed as he watched her back, stiff and
unyielding. There was no use delaying the inevitable.
The longer she stayed, the more pain he'd suffer
upon her departure.

"The next day," he agreed.

Linda knew she was lost.

Every day she had ridden out from the plantation,
and in an ever-widening circle, had discreetly inquired of all she met, if they knew Mistress Melanie
Townsend. Only this time she had ventured a bit farther than usual. It was late, almost dark in fact, and
nothing, not a tree, rock, or the trail she traveled appeared familiar.

She cursed the fact that she'd been forced into
making this search. Usually finding her prey was the
least of her problems, but this woman appeared to
have vanished into thin air.

Linda's instincts were good. One couldn't manage
in her chosen career without good instincts. And
she logically assumed that Melanie Townsend was
nearby. She'd left without a horse, without coin.
Someone must have taken her in.

She might have missed the cabin had the scent of

smoke not alerted her. A soft light shown from one window like a beacon summoning her from out of the darkness. With a sigh of relief she urged the horse down a gentle slope into a shallow valley. She'd found shelter for the night. Tomorrow, after getting directions, she'd return to the plantation house to being her search again.

Zachary heard the approaching rider long before Rusty growled or Melanie stirred. In a second he came from the bed. After shoving his legs into his trousers, he ran to the door. Zachary slipped outside, gun in hand, before Melanie could say a word.

He stood on the porch, his back pressed to the wall. No one moved through the mountains at night. No one unless they were lost or up to no good. After what had happened with Black Bear, Zachary was taking no chances. He stood in the corner of the porch, unseen, ever alert as the horse came closer.

"Hello," called a woman's voice from out of the dark. "Is anyone there?"

Zachary did not relax. Women did not travel these mountains alone. No doubt there was a man with her. A man who might even now be waiting for the first opportunity to make his presence known.

"What's your problem, ma'am?" Zachary called from the shadows.

"I've become lost. I went riding and can't find my way back. Can you help me?"

Zachary stepped forward. "Where are you from?"

"The Stacey place, near Charlottesville."

Zachary was familiar with the Stacey plantation, which was a good six hours north and east of his place. Still she might lying; he was taking no chances. Not when he couldn't see if others might be with her. "You can use the barn. It's out back." He nodded his head. "There's a water pump behind you, if you or the horse is in need."

At Zachary's less than neighborly offer, Melanie, wrapped in a blanket, stepped onto the porch. "Oh please, come in. Are you all right?"

Zachary glared at Melanie. She failed to notice in the darkness. What the hell did she think she was doing, inviting strangers into his house? Granted this one appeared to be alone, but he wasn't so naive as to believe every story she'd said.

When Zachary followed the woman inside a few minutes later, Melanie had dressed and set a pot of coffee on the fire to heat. Almost immediately he returned to his porch, watching, waiting, moving around the house, listening for the sounds of another visitor.

Zachary shrugged as he returned to the cabin. Perhaps he was being overly cautious. The woman appeared to be alone.

"I can't begin to thank you for your hospitality," she said, accepting Melanie's offer of a seat at the table. "Lord, I thought I'd never find you."

"You were looking for us?" Zachary asked, surprised. Melanie's hands shook as she poured coffee. Over the woman's head their eyes met. Zachary moved closer and slipped his arm around her waist, hugging her against his hip in a comforting gesture.

Their visitor drank thirstily of the lukewarm coffee. "No, but I smelled your fire. I knew someone had to live around here."

Melanie visibly relaxed and moved to the larder. She cut off a chunk of bread and placed two slices as well as butter and jam before the lady.

The food disappeared almost as soon as it was served. Melanie cut more bread. "How long were you lost?"

"Hours," Linda said, without looking up from her meal. "I rode out from the plantation early this morning and couldn't find my way back." She finished off another chunk of buttered bread and downed her third cup of coffee.

Once her stomach was full, the stranger grew obviously tired. Zachary watched as she tried to hide a yawn and reconsidered his intention to put her up in the barn. After all, a woman alone could hardly pose his family any danger. And his home was large enough to accommodate one more.

"You can bed down before the fire, if you like."

Linda could barely control her grin as, thirst and hunger finally appeased, she took her first good look at the lady of the house. She knew who she was, of course, for she'd once studied her portrait quite carefully. There could be no mistaking the Duchess of Elderbury's dark eyes. The soon-to-be late Duchess of Elderbury, she silently corrected.

Damn, but she was better than most. She had known that the duchess, if still alive, would be found in these parts.

Her mind was suddenly filled with possible plans as she watched Melanie create for her a bed of furs and blankets. She considered the possibilities and then reconsidered.

An old woman slept before the fire. Linda dismissed her as insignificant. Her problem was that the duchess and the man who owned this place were sleeping together. Obviously what had to be done could not be done tonight. No, the Duchess would die, but not right now.

Linda wondered if she should stay on or return to the plantation tomorrow. After some thought she decided to leave. In a day or so she'd return, this time with supplies. Then she'd lie in wait and kill the woman at the first opportunity. Perhaps on a morning visit to the privy. Linda smiled. She'd know when the time was right.

She settled herself near the old lady, her mind so filled with plans that she didn't hear or answer Melanie's soft good night.

On the opposite side of the hanging blanket, Zachary and Melanie lay down on opposite sides of the bed.

Zachary slept lightly, just in case . . .

By the time the first glimmer of sun showed itself the next morning, Zachary had left his bed, just as he did every morning, careful not to give into the temptation to linger at Melanie's side. He thought to hurry their visitor on her way.

Zachary felt a wave of disappointment as he checked the lady's horse. A shoe was cracked. It would have to be replaced or the horse would grow lame. Zachary started the fire in the small lean-to beside the barn. The fire was soon as hot as blazes. Zachary hated this part of farming more than anything. He wore a heavy apron over a naked chest, his body sweltering and black with sweat and soot as he shaped a piece of iron into a horseshoe.

Inside the house, Gray Cloud prepared the morning meal. Linda sat in the rocker and watched the woman. The duchess played with the baby, if one could actually call it that. The child sneezed and Linda cringed, wondering how anyone could bring themselves to wipe such a creature's nose. Still the duchess seemed to think nothing of it as she cleaned the baby's face and then returned the soiled handkerchief to its place inside her sleeve.

"Would you like to hold her?" Melanie asked, as

any proud mother might, believing anyone would jump at the chance.

"I'm not very good with children. As a rule they don't like me much."

"Nonsense," Melanie said as she handed the baby over, "Caroline likes everyone."

The baby cried, of course, just as Linda knew she would, and was quickly taken again into her mother's arms. Moment's later, the baby played on the floor while porridge was prepared. Linda contemplated how she'd go about seeing to this woman's demise. She could have easily done it right now, had the old Indian woman not been there. Still, Linda had found that planning was half the pleasure, and she didn't mind in the least that the job would be delayed. She chuckled softly, pretending to be amused by the baby playing at her feet. In truth she was imagining something quite different . . .

Linda eyed her intended victim coolly. She was a pretty little thing, she supposed, but Linda had disposed of others at least as lovely. One woman, whose husband had paid a huge sum to see her dead, had been particularly beautiful. Linda might not have remembered her at all, for there had been many over the years, if she hadn't proven to be stronger than she looked; she had nearly escaped her death, almost killing Linda instead.

Linda's thoughts were interrupted as Zachary entered the house, wiping briefly at his soot-covered hands and chest—a chest Linda couldn't help but admire. She felt a familiar stirring at the sight and thought perhaps, just perhaps . . . And then she forgot her thoughts as Zachary reached for his daughter and smiled as the baby planted a wet sloppy and, to Linda's way of thinking, disgusting kiss upon his cheek.

"Ma'am," he began, "your horse has a cracked shoe. I've made another. I'll have to replace it, or he'll never get you back."

"This is the Countess Vatalti, Zachary," Melanie said, realizing as he spoke that he still didn't know his guest's name. "Linda Farrell."

A countess? Zachary frowned at the improbability that another of high birth should have come upon his small home.

Linda left just before the noon meal, with a gift of bread and a small chunk of cheese.

Gray Cloud stood beside Melanie as the woman disappeared over the first hill. "She's evil, that one," she bluntly accused.

Melanie frowned. "How could you know?"

"The baby knows." Gray Cloud nodded mysteriously. "I know."

Melanie silently waved aside the old woman's words, attributing them to pure imagination. Certainly the Countess seemed pleasant enough and had given them no reason to suspect her of anything evil. No, she was simply what she claimed, a woman who had lost her way.

As she followed Zachary's directions back to the plantation, Linda considered her problem. How to do what she must with the man about? Obviously he cared for the Duchess. It was easy to see it in his every look and touch. Far too protective, he rarely left her alone for more than a few minutes at a time. Still, she'd find a way. She always did. What she needed was a little time. If no opportunity presented itself, she supposed she might, despite the man's appeal, and her vague plans to enjoy his body for a short time, take care of both at the same time. A fire perhaps. Linda shrugged at the thought, knowing she'd do what she must.

It was well after the noon hour that same day when Melanie answered a knock on the door. She no longer took pains to hide her presence there. She would be leaving in the morning. By the time word reached authorities, she'd be long gone.

"Yes?" she asked of the man standing in the doorway.

Douglas Hamilton frowned, for the woman who answered the door was a stranger. He knew this was his brother's farm. It hadn't been so long since his last visit that he could have mistaken one place for another. Could Zachary have sold out? Could he have moved without letting him know? "Does Zachary Pitt still live here? Do I have the right place?"

"You do. He's in the barn."

The man touched the brim of his hat, offered his thanks and followed her directions.

Zachary was cleaning out a stall when he heard a familiar voice ask, "Where's Margaret?"

He turned and dropped his rake as a grin split his mouth. The two men hugged, a bit stiffly perhaps, but with feeling. "Doug, damn, what are you doing here?"

"I came to invite you to my wedding. Who is the woman who answered your door?"

"Her name is Melanie. Is it Megan? Has she waited all this time?"

Douglas grinned and said cockily, "The woman knows a prize when she sees one."

Zachary laughed. "So you're finally getting married? I wondered when you'd get around to it."

Douglas grinned. "It took me a while. I wanted everything to be perfect."

"Meaning, you paid off your debt on the land already?"

"Tobacco has brought in a good price these last few years," he said. "What's she doing here and where is Margaret?"

"Margaret's dead."

Douglas seemed to stagger slightly. "Jesus! And you never let me know?"

"I didn't know myself for a long time. She left about eight or nine months ago."

Douglas frowned, still shaken by the news. "She left? Just like that?"

"I don't have to tell you she wasn't happy here."

"Yes, but you're buying the Simmons place, aren't you?"

"I am but she couldn't wait. Or maybe she really fell in love with young Armstrong."

"What? She left with another man?"

Zachary sighed, feeling not a trace of the anger he once had. He nodded.

"Damn that must have been hard on you."

"If you mean, did I miss her, I promise I did not. Margaret made my life miserable. You must have known that. She didn't keep her complaints to herself, even during your visits. But it was hard caring for Caroline while working this place."

Douglas grinned. "Caroline? I take it I have a niece, then?"

"You have," Zachary said, as only a proud father could. "Let's go to the house and you can meet her."

Just then Melanie appeared with the baby in her arms.

"Melanie, have you met my brother, Douglas Hamilton?" Zachary inquired as he took Caroline into his arms. "And this, of course, is Caroline," he said, his voice softening with love.

Melanie took Douglas's offered hand. "How do you do, sir?"

"Mistress," Douglas returned, still unsure of this woman and her reason for being here. Was she perhaps Zachary's new wife? A neighbor? A bond slave? He couldn't know since neither seemed to think it important enough to say.

"I knew you looked familiar," Melanie said. Douglas was almost as tall as Zachary, younger perhaps but just as handsome in a decidedly more polished and urbane fashion. He had a friendly look to him, and Melanie thought him an agreeable sort.

"Where's Gray Cloud?" Zachary asked.

"Gone again."

Zachary nodded and glanced at his brother's confused expression. "Come into the house. I'll explain."

After they moved into the house, Melanie put Caroline to bed. Zachary heaved a heavy jug to the table and took down two cups from the shelf. "Caroline will sleep for a bit," Melanie told them. "Call me when she awakens. I'll be outside."

The two men talked for hours, then continued to catch up on news when Gray Cloud appeared again and she and Melanie began to prepare dinner.

Douglas slept where Linda had the night before.

Melanie lay beside Zachary that night, her voice low so as to not disturb their guests. "If he's your brother, why does he have a different last name?"

"Because as a boy, he was adopted by another family. Eventually his adopted family moved from England and settled about fifty miles from where I lived." Zachary smiled. "It didn't take long before we came to know each other. Everyone kept saying, 'You've got to see this young boy at the Hamiltons' place. He looks just like you.' And then one day, about six or seven years ago, he rode into town and we both knew."

"There's a resemblance, but he doesn't look *just* like you."

"He looked more like me when we were younger."

Melanie smiled and allowed her hand to touch her stomach. She couldn't help but wonder how this child would look. He'd have dark hair, she thought, but would his eyes be blue? Would his features be large like his father's? Would he be a big man, or more slight like his uncle? For just a second she felt guilty because he and his father would never know each other. Had she the right, she wondered, to keep them apart forever? But then she forced the guilt aside. Perhaps it was selfish, but she needed more than the love Zachary would feel for this baby. She needed him to love her first.

The next morning Melanie awakened to Zachary and Douglas shouting at each other outside. "I know what I'm doing!"

"The hell you do."

Melanie hurried into her dress. Quickly she opened and then closed the door behind her. "Why are you shouting?" She smoothed her dress into place and brushed a lock of black hair from her face, even as she glared at both men. The sun showed barely a glimmer of its promised light, not yet having edged over the mountains. "What's the matter? Why are you fighting?"

Zachary had no intention of explaining the argument to Melanie, especially since it involved money, a touchy subject where she was concerned. "What are you doing up?" he demanded.

"Lower your voices or you'll have Caroline joining the two of you."

Obviously angry, Douglas turned to Melanie. "My brother is a damned fool."

"Shut up, Douglas."

Melanie's gaze moved from one brother to the other. "Why are you angry?"

"I don't take to anyone telling me my business, is all," said Zachary.

"I want to loan him money."

"And I don't need it." The truth was, he could buy the Simmons place today if he wanted. Only he wouldn't. He needed the money to operate, money to fall back on if his crop failed. To buy the land now would take just about all he had saved and greatly increase his chances of losing everything. "I appreciate the offer, Douglas, but I don't need it."

"Why the bloody hell not?" came an obviously exasperated response. "You can't be happy here."

"I've already told you, I don't mind waiting a bit."

"But you don't have to wait."

Melanie was beginning to think she understood. Zachary did not want to better himself. There could be only one reason, of course. He preferred to keep the class differences between them as deep and wide as possible. Surely he was making his disinterest in her plain to see.

"Never fear, Zachary," Melanie said, thankful that her voice did not waver. "I shan't be bothering you no matter what you decide. You might as well take the loan."

Douglas frowned, wondering what the woman was about? She wouldn't bother him? Zachary had told him she was leaving, going home to England. Her words made no sense at all. Then again, nothing about this entire conversation made sense.

Zachary did not respond to Melanie's softly spoken accusation, for the words were clear enough to him. She thought he was refusing because of her. He wasn't. He wished to God the differences between them could be solved as easily as she imagined. That he could buy a plantation and all their problems would evaporate. That in the buying he would suddenly become a gentleman worthy of a lady like her.

Melanie's dark gaze appeared fathomless as she turned to Douglas. "Will you be staying long, Douglas?"

"I must leave today, I think. The weather delayed my arrival. If I stay any longer, Megan will worry."

"Will you wait for me then? I'll come with you, if you don't mind. Perhaps you could drop me near a stagecoach."

"Of course," Douglas said as he watched the silent communication between her and his brother. Something was happening here. Something he didn't understand. Still, it was a moment so private and intimate that he felt embarrassed to watch. He cleared his throat and said uneasily, "Well, if you'll excuse me for a minute."

Neither responded as he walked away. Their gazes clung, their hearts open, ready to say, ready to hear.

Forever and a minute, they stood there: Zachary memorizing her face, wondering how he was going to live once she had gone; Melanie silently begging that he ask her to stay. And when, as the ticking seconds grew into long silent moments, she realized he would not, she turned. Her hand was on the door handle when she said, "I'll have coffee ready in a few minutes."

"Melanie, I . . . "

She turned back, hope alive in her eyes. "What?"

He cared for her. She knew he did, but did he care enough? He had to say it.

But he didn't. "Nothing." Zachary shook his head. "Nothing."

Melanie nodded and walked into the house.

Chapter 15

It was a six hour ride back to the plantation. Linda was on the road almost three hours before she understood the vaguely unsettling feeling gnawing at her gut. Nothing had been said and yet there was something, something she couldn't quite name. She stiffened as she remembered the little carpet bag and the dress that had been folded into it. It was then that she knew the Duchess wouldn't be there when she returned.

Linda cursed, knowing she had made a serious mistake. She didn't often make them, but when she did, she wasted no time in correcting them.

Of course she could return and lie in wait for the duchess, allow her to leave and then follow. Linda knew that if the duchess left the farm it could only be for a ship that would take her home. And a ship, after all, was a perfect place in which to do what needed to be done. The problem was she couldn't be sure she wouldn't somehow miss her. There was always a chance they might become separated. A chance the Duchess of Elderbury might evade her fate for a time. Perhaps for too long a time.

No. She had to go back. There was no other way.

Hours later, Linda urged her tired horse over the hill's crest, just as night covered the valley. She was exhausted, but instead of heading for the barn she rode instead toward the woods that bordered the property. She tied the horse there, out of sight, and headed for the barn on foot, happy to find a small measure of comfort in the hay-filled loft.

Before returning home, Douglas rode with Zachary over his fields. Zachary thought he might try tobacco this year. If the crops brought in half of what Douglas promised, he wouldn't have to wait much longer before he had enough money to buy the plantation.

While he and Douglas were gone, Melanie realized there was no more milk. She left Caroline with Gray Cloud and hurried toward the barn. Her time was short. She didn't want to leave Caroline even for a minute, and had thought to hold her during her morning nap. But the baby whined, wanting milk. In a hurry, Melanie decided she wouldn't milk the cow thoroughly, just take a cup or so for the baby.

Perhaps because the cow was an ornery sort and knew she could, she often gave Melanie a hard time of it. "I don't want you to get excited this time, Jess," Melanie said. "Just let me take a little and I'll be on my way."

Melanie brought a short stool into the stall and sat at the cow's side. The moment she reached for the udders, the cow began to lean toward her. Melanie jumped to her feet and shoved Jess back into place. "We'll have none of that today, thank you."

Again she sat, muttering, "I've no time for nonsense." She slapped her side. "Stay still." And to her amazement the cow obeyed.

"You take easily to the farming life."

Melanie gave a start at the sound of Linda's voice, for she had thought herself to be quite alone and hadn't expected to see this particular lady again. And with her surprise came a niggling fear.

"Not as easily as I might have liked, I'm afraid," Melanie said. "What happened? Did your horse grow lame after all?"

Linda shrugged. "I never could follow directions. I got lost again and returned last night. I didn't want to bother you, so I slept in the loft."

"Oh dear, that couldn't have been comfortable. After I'm finished here, come with me to the house and I'll make you something to eat. You must be starving."

"Where is Zachary? I mean, Mr. Pitt?"

"He's with his brother. They're looking over the fields. Zachary is thinking he might plant tobacco."

Linda had heard the two men talking earlier as they saddled their horses. She had smiled then, congratulating herself that she'd thought ahead and tied her horse in the woods.

She smiled, realizing that Zachary would be gone for a bit and she was finally alone with her prey. She might never get a better opportunity.

"I had the feeling you were leaving soon," she said.

"I am. Today, in fact. How could you know?"

Linda grinned, please with her own cleverness. She moved into the stall.

The cow moved nervously, and mooed loudly as she swung her head and backed up, almost knocking over the pail. "You shouldn't come in," Melanie warned. "This cow tends to get a bit fidgety. You might get hurt."

Linda did not enjoy cows, but she wasn't afraid of them either. "I don't think so, Duchess."

It took a moment before Melanie realized the

woman had called her by her title. She raised puzzled eyes from her chore. "How did you know?"

Linda laughed, but didn't bother to respond. Instead she asked, "Will you be happy to see England again, Duchess?" As she spoke she took the knife from her pocket and held it within the folds of her skirt.

"I will. I miss my father and sister terribly." Melanie frowned as Linda moved closer. "But how did you know I was a . . . ?"

Linda's smile grew suddenly hard, devoid of humor. "Because your husband sent me to find you."

"Did he?" Melanie felt some surprise at that. She wouldn't have expected that Townsend would care where she was, or what had happened to her. In fact, she still wondered if Waverly Townsend had been responsible for her kidnapping. "Well, he should have known better. I won't be coming back to him. Not ever."

"He wants to make sure of that, I think."

Melanie felt a jolt of fear. Something was amiss. She stood and took a step back. "What do you mean, he wants to make sure?"

"I mean, he sent me to kill you."

Melanie laughed uneasily. "You're having a bit of fun, I'm sure."

"I'm afraid not. You see, I've hired out my skills before."

A chill raced down Melanie's spine at the sudden fire in this woman's eyes. She appeared to be filled with nervous energy. Melanie could almost feel the air around them crackle with it. "And you mean to kill me?" she asked.

"I do."

"Just like that?" Melanie couldn't believe anyone could simply murder another, not unless caught in the throes of anger or insane with a need for revenge. There had to be a mistake.

"Of course, dear. See?" she asked, showing Melanie the knife. "Your husband said you hated this knife. He thought that using it would be a nice touch."

Melanie knew then the truth of the situation. The knife belonged to her husband, there could be no doubt. Obviously she had been right to suspect his role in her kidnapping. But because she hadn't died, he had sent another person to finish the job. She took a step to her right. "Zachary will . . ."

Linda shook her head. "He won't find your body for a bit." An oddly pleasant smile curved her lips. "It will go easier on you if you don't resist."

Melanie shuddered. She watched as an eager, almost playful light shown in Linda's eyes.

Without another word Linda suddenly lunged forward, the knife held high above her head. She swung downward with deadly intent, missing her target as Melanie screamed and dashed to her right.

Melanie screamed again and slammed into a wall. The cow blocked her path and there was nowhere else to go.

And then Jess mooed again, louder this time, and kicked her hind leg. The movement brought her body hard to her right and hundreds of pounds of bovine flesh crashed against both women, just as Linda thrust the knife forward again.

Melanie hardly realized the air was knocked from her lungs as she watched in breathless horror as the cow took the blow intended for her. The knife slid easily and deeply into the animal's back. Jess shuddered and bellowed in pain as Linda shoved her aside.

Melanie was driven by the need to escape. The instant the cow moved, she slid along the wall, keeping the cow between her and the madwoman.

Linda released an eerie sound of elation as she lunged, trying to reach Melanie over the back of the cow. The knife sliced into Melanie's shoulder and arm, producing a thin trail of blood.

She hardly felt the grazing knife blade in her desperation to get away. She screamed for Zachary. Somewhere in the back of her mind she knew there was no chance that he could hear, for the fields he rode were far from the barn. Still she could not stop her screams.

And above the screams, above the thunder of blood pounding in her temples, Melanie heard Linda's inhuman laughter.

Linda was aware that the knife had only grazed Melanie. Still, caught up in the moment she never thought to hold back yet another deadly thrust. Again Melanie evaded the blade, which again cut into the cow instead.

Linda cursed, growing impatient. Had she come upon the woman unaware, the deed would already be done. Still she rarely killed quickly, for the best part was feeling her victim's fear, sensing the power she held over life and death.

In the stall beside them, Gray Cloud's stallion whinnied in agitation and reared up on his hind legs. His hoof hit hard against the stall. He reared again, this time grazing Linda's shoulder. She groaned, feeling the blow but not the pain. She was possessed by the kill, and like an animal scenting blood, she laughed madly and slashed forward again.

Melanie knew she had only seconds to live. "Zachary!" she screamed again. Trying to keep as much distance as possible between herself and this madwoman, she edged toward the door.

And then she lunged, but it was too late. Linda was on her, grabbing her from behind. One arm went around her throat. The other held the knife against her jaw.

Linda laughed triumphantly. In another second it would all be over. She shuddered, lost in the thrill of it.

Melanie was a small woman, but stronger than she looked. Even filled with the strength of madness, Linda realized almost instantly that this wasn't going to be half as easy as she'd first supposed.

Melanie caught Linda's wrist and forced it down and under, turning the blade toward the attacker.

Linda wondered if her wrist would break from the pressure. She tried to free her hand, tried to tear herself away, but Melanie was the stronger of the two. Linda took a step back.

And then, still struggling, they were pressed against the cow's bloodied side, their clothes, their faces, their hair wet from the still bleeding wounds.

Suddenly Melanie's foot slipped and she dropped to the floor. Linda smiled. Luck had not failed her after all. Melanie's fall had assured her victory. She laughed again, knowing there was no way she would fail to win. Not now.

Then she felt a sudden, hard jolt to her midsection. There was no pain, merely a slight discomfort that restricted her ability to breathe. Linda ignored the sudden breathlessness, too engrossed in the kill to imagine what it could mean. She never noticed that her laughter had turned into an odd, breathless wheezing.

She slashed forward with the knife for the final kill and then narrowed her gaze, puzzled. How could she have missed? Something was wrong. Why was it suddenly so hard to breathe?

Melanie scrambled toward the door, desperate to escape. And then she was outside, covered with blood, rolling over the dirt ground, but alive, without knowing how that could be.

She came to a stop, fully expecting to find Linda behind her ready to finish her off with one final plunge of the knife. Melanie turned, anticipating the attack, only to find Linda staring blankly at the handle of a knife imbedded in her chest. A handle decorated with one feather and Indian beadwork.

Linda released a scream of hatred and rage. And then, her eyes still open, she fell forward, raising a small cloud of dust upon the barn's hay-covered floor.

Melanie shuddered, hardly able to rise to her feet. She trembled as if palsied. Gray Cloud, miraculously beside her, helped her to the door and leaned her against the barn wall. One side of Melanie's face and neck was covered with blood. Quickly Gray Cloud's hands moved over her, searching for wounds. Gray Cloud saw the cut in her arm, but by then knew the blood had not come from Melanie. She breathed a sigh of relief.

Melanie leaned her head back against the wall and closed her eyes. In an instant they were open again. "She's dead, isn't she?"

Gray Cloud nodded.

"Are you sure?"

"She is," Gray Cloud returned and Melanie knew she was.

"From now on, I'm going to believe everything you say. I don't care if it sounds crazy or not."

Gray Cloud grinned.

They heard the sound of galloping horses. "He comes," Gray Cloud said.

Melanie nodded, but above the pounding hooves

came Caroline's cries from inside the house. "Bring Caroline outside, please? I can't go in like this. She'll be afraid."

Gray Cloud nodded and left her.

Zachary pushed his horse to the limit, but Douglas's horse was faster. He got there first.

"Good God, what happened?" he asked as he tried to bring his horse under control.

Melanie was afraid to move, for her knees were threatening to give out under her. "I'm all right," she said just as Zachary pulled his horse to a stop.

But all Zachary could see was blood. It covered one side of her face and neck; it soaked into her dress. He stood before her in an instant. "Are you all right?" She wasn't, of course. She was hurt, badly hurt, he thought. No one could bleed like that and not be badly hurt.

He couldn't breathe for the fear that stole his own soul. There wasn't a part of him that didn't tremble as he waited endless moments for her answer.

"There's a woman dead in the barn," Douglas said.

Zachary glanced into the dim interior and frowned at the sight of the Countess lying on the barn floor, Gray Cloud's knife embedded in her chest.

"What happened? Are you all right?" Finally he found the courage to touch her face, her neck, searching for the wound as Gray Cloud had. He couldn't find anything and yet he couldn't let the terror go.

He picked her up in his arms. "Stay with her," he said, nodding over his shoulder toward the woman, not knowing if she were dead or not. He moved toward the house.

"Wait. Caroline will be afraid." Melanie no sooner said the words than Gray Cloud appeared at the door, Caroline in her arms. She moved quickly from the house.

A moment later Zachary came to a stop just inside the door. He put Melanie down but refused to release her completely. He couldn't bear the thought of not touching her as he said, "Tell me you're all right, Melanie."

She wasn't sure of anything but the safety she felt in this man's arms. She pressed herself to his chest.

He cupped her face and forced her gaze to his. "Tell me what happened."

Reaction set in then, trembling, tears. She swallowed, shuddered, and tried to respond with a shaken, "She almost . . . "

Zachary pulled her tightly against him, wrapping his arms around her small frame. He wanted to know all that had happened, but Melanie was in no shape to tell him. Not now. "All right, don't think about it. Just tell me you're all right."

"I am."

"Let me see your arm."

Melanie showed him the shallow cut. It had already stopped bleeding. "I'll clean it in a minute." And he would, he promised, as soon as he could tear himself away from her, as soon as he could stop shaking.

They stood there for a long moment, neither willing nor able to part from the other. Melanie buried her face in his shoulder, breathing deeply of his scent, knowing his touch was bringing a calmness she could never have found otherwise. And then her voice broke as she whispered his name.

She was crushed in his arms, held tightly enough to steal her breath, and still she tried to get even closer, knowing he couldn't ever hold her tightly enough. He tore the blood-splattered cap from her head, his fingers sinking into her thick black hair, pulling her face up.

His breath came in rapid gusts across her face. The smell of his skin, the feel of his body, hard and wanting, were more than she could bear. She whimpered a small sound of pleading, of desperate longing.

And then his mouth was on hers, almost vicious in its need, pushing her lips apart, his tongue thrusting deep into her warmth, demanding that she give over this one last time.

She was his. He marked her as such with every kiss, with every touch, and Melanie knew she could never call her heart, her soul her own again.

"I heard the scream. I thought . . . " He couldn't finish as a powerful shudder tore through his body. He pressed her against the closed door, his body hard against her. His need for her so raw, so urgent, he never thought to bring them to the bed. "I thought, God, Melanie, I thought . . . "

And then he was kissing her again. Kissing her as if he'd never stop.

Their two souls cried out for love as she tore at his shirt, searching for the warmth, the texture, the taste of him.

She bit his lip and then moaned in ecstasy as he did the same in return. His hands were under her dress, pushing aside the obstacles that kept his body from hers. She pressed her mouth to his shoulder, his neck. Her tongue touched his salty skin and Melanie thought nothing had ever tasted so good.

"Promise me you'll never die." He kissed her again, kissed her until she couldn't think beyond the sensation of this man's mouth. And then amid desperate kisses came desperate urgings, "Promise me. Promise me."

It was an impossible request and yet Melanie never hesitated in her response. Her head fell back, her eyes closed, and she moaned as his hands touched her body. "I won't. I swear I won't."

Their bodies pressed tightly together and it wasn't enough, not nearly enough. His hands found her warm and ready. There was no way he could stop. She pulled at his trousers, until the tabs came free and the material fell aside. She'd never felt him so hard, so thick, so hot.

He gathered her up against him, her legs around his hips, her arms clinging to his neck. He yanked her chemise down, exposing her breasts, for the pleasure of his mouth, for his whiskered cheeks.

And then, with his mouth still on her breast, he surged into her. She cried out at the tremendous force of their coming together.

Hot searing flame, burning heat. Zachary knew only delicious sensation and in the knowing almost missed her cry. Beyond the thunder of his heart, he cursed his roughness. "Did I hurt you?" He prayed that he hadn't. He'd stop if he had. He swore he would, only he didn't know how he could bring himself from this luscious heat.

"No," she gasped as he pressed deep into her body, joining them forever as one. "No," she said again, and then groaned as his body moved back and then forward with devastating force.

They were desperate for each other, desperate to experience again the magic that had almost been lost forever. It took only a few strokes and her body almost instantly stiffened with convulsing waves of pleasure. It had never happened like this before. It had never come so fast, so hard, with such mindless urgency.

And as the waves of her pleasure squeezed around his sex, pulling him deeper into the madness, Zachary gasped, "Not yet!" His eyes closed as he threw his head back, grimacing, even as his body moved helplessly forward. "I want to feel more," he choked, as his body drove deep into her and then convulsed, filling her with his sweet warmth.

"Too fast. Melanie, it was too fast," he groaned breathlessly against her breast, loath to leave her so soon.

Zachary came slowly from the fog of passion. He couldn't be sorry for what he'd done. No doubt it shouldn't have happened, but he couldn't let her go.

And then he saw her eyes, filled with boundless love, and Zachary steeled himself against the temptation of giving into that love.

Her legs slid to the floor as he pulled back a bit and adjusted his still aching sex into his trousers. He said nothing and his silence was the loudest sound she'd ever heard.

She knew he loved her. For the first time she was certain that he did. He couldn't have touched her, kissed her, made love as he just had if he didn't love her. He couldn't have bared his soul if he hadn't felt as she did. But sometimes love wasn't enough.

Nothing had changed, despite this wild coming together. He was stubborn and proud. They'd had this moment, this one moment. It was all they'd ever have.

Melanie's dark eyes bore into his soul while she prayed for control lest she burst into tears and embarrass them both.

Melanie watched him for a long moment before she was finally able to say, "Would you tell Douglas I'll be ready to leave in a few minutes?"

She moved away from him to the soap and pitcher of water on the table. "I have to change. Could you ask Gray Cloud to look at my cut?"

* * *

Harry Stone had finally found his daughter's servant Ellen, only to learn that Melanie had gone, no one knew where.

Ellen had said Mr. Moody had bought Melanie's service, but she had run off. Talk had it, she might have been involved in a young man's death. Harry didn't believe it, of course. Melanie could never kill someone. He doubted she was capable of the feat if her very life depended on it.

He'd come all this way only to find her gone, perhaps forever lost in the colonies, perhaps already dead in the wilderness.

Harry glared at the tall, thin, unattractive Blanche Moody. "It does not matter how you rave, madam, my daughter did not kill your son. Think for a minute. She was a grown woman. What interest would she find in a boy ten and six?"

"Her interest was plain enough, sir. Her aim was to seduce him."

Harry sighed at the nonsensical response.

"I see you cannot bring yourself to believe it. But ask yourself this, 'Why then did she run?' "

"Perhaps you should ask yourself madam, 'What did your son do to her to cause her to run?' "

Blanche made as if to slam the door in his face. But Harry Stone shoved it back, uncaring when it banged against the woman's leg. "She was very much like you, I think," Blanche said. "Thick-headed and determined. A most disagreeable girl to be sure."

Harry grinned at the thought, for his daughter was indeed very much like him. Not in the least disagreeable, but very determined. Many had been the battles between father and daughter. If only she were here now to engage him in a contest of wills.

"Where did it happen?" he asked.

Blanche pointed toward the road. "Three miles

west about a hundred feet into the woods. We found
my son's body there."

Harry Stone might have offered his condolences at
the woman's loss, but as he turned to look at the
road, the door slammed behind him. He sighed. A
moment later he was again astride his horse and riding off.

Harry brought the horse to a stop some distance
down the road. Three miles, the woman had said.
This might be the very place. *And if it is, what
then?* came a voice from deep inside. What then indeed? Harry wondered as he breathed a deep sigh.
What did he think to find in these woods, upon this
road, more than six months after Melanie had disappeared?

He could search from now until forever without
finding her in this wilderness. There was a good
chance, more than a good chance in fact, that Melanie
was already dead. In truth, there were a dozen ways
that a woman alone in these woods could have
found her end. Hunger, thirst, and exposure to the elements could have easily done the job. Snakes, wild
animals, especially bears or a mountain lion ... Indians ...

Harry shook aside his gruesome thoughts. He was
probably the worst of fools, but he wouldn't believe
her dead. Not until the day he saw her body.

Chapter 16

Melanie held the baby tightly to her as she watched Zachary and Douglas bury Linda's body in an unmarked grave just beyond the edge of the woods.

Caroline was a talker, learning more words every day. Still much of what she said was largely unintelligible. "Tree, honey? Are you trying to say tree?"

"Fee," the little girl responded enthusiastically and suddenly kissed the only mother she remembered with a loud, smacking, deliciously wet, "Awwah!"

The ache in Melanie's chest grew. She loved Caroline as much as if she'd given birth to the child herself, and she was tormented by the thought that they would soon be parted.

Douglas brought the shovels back to the barn as Zachary and Melanie made their way to the waiting horses. "Could you do something for me?" she asked.

Zachary waited for her to go on.

"Could you talk about me once in a while, so she might not forget? Could you tell her that I'll love her always?"

Zachary nodded, but did not look at her. He

couldn't without begging her to stay with him forever.

"Perhaps someday she could come to England for a visit. Would you allow her that?"

Zachary shrugged and looked off into the distance. "When she's old enough, perhaps."

Melanie nodded, knowing he would not, knowing this was the last time she'd ever see them. She swallowed back her tears, and after one last kiss and hug handed the baby to her father.

"Good-bye, Zachary." Melanie took a deep, steadying breath. She tried for a smile, failing miserably. Still she would not leave without saying something of what was in her heart. "Had I some strength of character, I should wish you a happy life, but I won't. I wish you instead . . ." The words choked in her throat, for no matter how he had hurt her, she could wish no harm to befall him. She struggled for control, and took another deep breath before forcing herself to go on. "That's not true. I do wish you happiness." A moment later she mounted Linda's horse. It had been decided that she would take the animal all the way to Williamsburg and leave orders there for its return to the Stacey plantation.

In a barely audible voice she said, "Good-bye, Caroline."

Melanie turned toward the house and smiled at Gray Cloud. They had already said their good-byes. She rode to the crest of the hill and waited. Now that Zachary could no longer see her, she let the tears stream down her face.

By the time Douglas said good-bye to his brother and joined her there, she was ready to go on.

Harry Stone turned his horse back toward Charlottesville, a plan already forming in his mind.

Once in the city, he'd set up a command of sorts. He'd offer a great reward and hire the best men money could buy. They would find his daughter. If she lived still, they'd find her and bring her to him.

Harry had left Ellen in a small inn, after buying her freedom from Mr. Martin. There he collected both Ellen and his trunks that had arrived from the ship. Next he booked passage on the stage that ran between Charlottesville and Williamsburg. Riding beside the stagecoach with Ellen and few others comfortably inside, Harry felt his hopes rise for the first time in days.

Three days later, the stage pulled into the courtyard of a rural inn. They were a day, perhaps a day and a half, from the city. Harry could hardly wait to set his feet upon the cobblestoned streets and walkways. He could hardly wait to begin the business of finding his daughter.

"How is Jess?" Zachary asked, knowing Gray Cloud had seen to the cow's wounds.

"I told you she'd be all right, and she is."

Zachary sat at the table, acutely aware of the tense, accusing silence. From the moment Melanie had ridden away, Gray Cloud had set out to annoy him. First she'd burned the stew left over from last night. Then she'd served it for his noonday meal with coffee as weak as water. Zachary knew this woman never burned anything and she was well aware of how he liked his coffee. She'd done it on purpose all right.

Now for dinner she had served some kind of meat he couldn't swallow. Considering her present mood, it was probably rat.

After chewing a piece of it for close to five minutes before he thought it safe to swallow, Zachary followed it with a swig of whiskey, only to gasp as the fire spread all the way from his lips to his stomach. It was a long time before he could breathe. He wiped his mouth with his sleeve and glared at the silent woman sitting calmly before him. "What did you put in it?"

"In what?" she asked coolly.

Zachary knew she had tampered with his whiskey, but he was sure she didn't hate him enough to have poisoned him. No, she was angry and obviously wanted to see him suffer. Zachary figured the best thing would be to get this business out in the open. Maybe then he could find a little peace. "All right, tell me why you're trying to kill me."

Gray Cloud lifted one eyebrow and said in all confidence, "If I tried, you'd be dead."

Zachary figured she was right about that, for no one knew more about potions, good and bad. "All right, tell me why you're making me suffer then."

"Because stupid men should suffer."

Zachary sighed "Gray Cloud, you don't understand."

"You're right about that. I don't understand why a man would let the woman he loves go away. Especially when that woman loves him and his baby."

"You're right." Zachary's voice broke. He cleared it and tried again, wondering if he had the strength. Melanie had been gone only a few hours and he was hurting so bad he could hardly stand it. It was almost impossible to talk about her. "You're right that we love each other. But sometimes love isn't enough."

Gray Cloud gave him a look that clearly expressed what she thought of his logic.

"She comes from a different world. She's had servants, money, everything she's ever wanted."

"She wanted you."

Zachary sighed. It was obvious he wasn't making himself understood. "Gray Cloud, listen to me. She wouldn't be happy if she stayed. She would miss her family, her friends, the luxuries she's always known."

"She was happy," Gray Cloud said flatly. "And you took the happiness away."

"Damnit! I know what's best for her."

Gray Cloud leaned back in the chair and eyed him thoughtfully. "Maybe you do. Maybe she was just a stupid woman who couldn't know what she really wanted."

Zachary refused to reply to her sarcasm.

"I should tell you a story," Gray Cloud finally said.

Zachary often listened to her stories, but he wasn't in the mood for one tonight. Still a story was preferable to her nagging or the silence that only increased his misery.

"A long time ago a great warrior fell in love with a young girl."

"Gray Cloud," he said threateningly.

"Don't interrupt."

He sighed, knowing he didn't have much choice. The woman was determined to say her piece. He rolled his eyes toward the ceiling and waited for her to go on.

"They married and had many children. The oldest was a boy who thought himself far above everyone. You see, the gods had blessed him with a face more beautiful than any ever before created. Young girls wept simply because he didn't smile their way.

"One day he fell while climbing a mountain. He almost died, but a maiden who lived nearby nursed him back to life. His face was scarred. He was no longer beautiful, but he didn't know it. The maiden loved him despite his ugliness, but he thought he was too good for her. When he was well again, he went back to his village. His mother loved him despite his scars. His father cared little for looks and treated him the same. His brothers and sister felt too bad to say anything. And the young man thought he was still beautiful.

"Years later he came upon a lake. The water was very still. For the first time since he was a young man he could see himself. He understood then why women no longer stared at him with admiration.

"In the end he died an old man, alone."

"Meaning what?" Zachary demanded. "I'm ugly and should take what I can get?"

Gray Cloud laughed.

"What the hell does the story mean?"

"It means he was blessed and never knew it, because his blessing wasn't his beauty. His blessing was the one young maiden who loved him. He lost her because he was so filled with pride."

Zachary scratched his chin. "I suppose you mean *my* pride."

"I mean, we haven't the right to question God," Gray Cloud said. "He gives us gifts and we're bound to take them simply because it is his wish. In the story the boy threw his gift away, but a wise man would take every blessing offered."

"And I'm wise, right?"

"I always thought you were."

Zachary wondered if she could be right. Could it have been his pride and not Melanie's money that had stood between them? Could it be that he had held himself above her, believing her rich and therefore somehow lacking? Zachary wasn't sure. All he knew was that she had been happy here. Margaret had never been happy, not from the first day. Didn't that mean something? Didn't that mean that Melanie was the kind of woman who could manage without luxuries? Didn't it mean that she loved *him* more than she loved perfumed soap and silk clothes? God, hadn't he seen exactly that in her eyes this very morning?

All he knew for sure was that Melanie was gone and his pain was so great he couldn't think.

Caroline had needed him today. He'd tried to play with her this afternoon, but he couldn't shake aside the pain, not even for an hour. The pain would be there tomorrow, he knew. Tomorrow and all the to-morrows after.

And what exactly had he proven? That he knew how to suffer? That he could manage the pain as he ate, as he worked, as he held his daughter? That he faced the rest of his life with misery as his closest companion? There had to be more to life than that.

He might be a stubborn man, a prideful man, but he hoped he was a smart one. He came to a decision. Money and pride didn't matter. All that truly mattered was Melanie and the fact that they loved each other.

He was going after her.

A great weight lifted suddenly from his shoulders and Zachary's slow grin brought an answering smile to Gray Cloud's face. "I need you to do me a favor," Zachary said.

"Just go. I'll be here when you get back."

"I won't return for a long time. She has to go back to England. There are many matters that need to be settled. And I'll go with her."

"Make sure you do."

Zachary grinned. The woman surely loved order-ing people around. "Can you pack Caroline's clothes?"

"I already have." She nodded toward a bag on the

floor near his bed. "The clothes you wear to town are in there too."

Zachary laughed as he lifted her from the chair, swung her to her feet, and nearly crushed her in a quick hug. He dropped a kiss on top of the wise woman's head, even as he wondered how long he might have gone on suffering, if it hadn't been for her.

The trip to Williamsburg proved long but uneventful and except for feeling a bit tired, Melanie fared well. The weather was good, the road dry, which enabled them to move along at a brisk pace. By tomorrow they would reach the city, and she would book passage on the first ship leaving for England. Douglas would leave her then, having already been kind enough to accompany her farther than they'd originally planned. He was anxious to get back to his fiancée. Williamsburg wasn't so very far out of his way, since he lived to the north, midway between Charlottesville and the city.

It was growing dark and Melanie thought an inn shouldn't be too far off. A few such establishments dotted the miles that stretched between Charlottesville and Williamsburg, offering the opportunity to change horses and giving the passengers a chance to stretch their legs and down warm meals. Travelers such as Douglas and herself also took advantage of the sometimes meager overnight accommodations.

Melanie hoped this inn would boast of clean bedding. Last night, despite the costly room, she'd spent the entire night on the floor, her only cover her jacket, for both mattress and bedding appeared to be otherwise occupied with tiny creatures she was loath to disturb.

Moment's later, she and Douglas pulled their horses to a stop in a wide courtyard that separated barn from inn. Chickens roamed freely, dodging the wheels of a coach only now rolling to a stop.

Preoccupied, Melanie didn't notice the man riding beside the coach, nor did she glance at the passengers disembarking. She dismounted and tied her horse to a hitching post. After gaining direction from a yard hand, she found the privy behind the barn.

Moments later, she opened the inn door to find Ellen standing first in line, patiently awaiting her turn to be served a meal. The two women gasped and then stared as if each had seen a ghost.

"Ellen? Is it you?"

"Lord have mercy, I can't believe it." The older woman grew white to her lips and wobbled a bit, obviously stunned.

"It *is* you," Melanie said, reaching for her longtime companion and friend. She hugged her tightly against her. "Oh, Ellen, I've missed you terribly."

Melanie took a step back, holding the woman's shoulders. "Are you all right? Has Mrs. Martin treated you kindly? Where is she? What are you doing here?"

"If you let me get a word in, I'll tell you."

"Have you run away? Did she hurt you? Oh, just wait till we get home. Father will fix those people. I'll make sure of it."

"And how will you make sure of it, missy?"

No one called her *missy*. No one but her father. Melanie knew at once that he was standing behind her.

A moment later she was in her father's arms, crying like a child, hugging him so tightly he was amazed at her newfound strength. "Oh, Father, it's been so . . . " She wanted to saw *awful*, and she wanted to say *wonderful*, for her adventure had been both. She said instead, "Long."

"Let's go inside," Harry Stone said, realizing they were suddenly the center of attention. Every bit an Englishman, he despised public displays of emotion. "We'll get rooms, have dinner. You can change out of those rags and we'll talk."

Melanie sat in a tub of warm sudsy water, which she was ever so much enjoying because this time she hadn't had to fetch it. Ellen fussed over her, sitting in a chair at her side. First she shampooed her long hair and then set out to undo the damage that months of hard work had done to Melanie's hands.

"Lord have mercy, what have you been doing, pushing a plow?"

Melanie laughed as she glanced at her split and cracked nails surrounding by roughened skin. "I might have been, had I stayed any longer."

"Where were you? I was so worried when I heard you ran away."

"A farmer took me in," Melanie replied. "As a matter of fact, his brother and I are ... " Melanie gasped. "Oh dear, Mr. Hamilton! With all the excitement I quite forgot about him. Go to the desk, Ellen, and leave word that Mr. Hamilton should meet me in the taproom in half an hour."

"But ... " Ellen's gaze was filled with doubt.

"All right, an hour. Just hurry, before he begins to think I've disappeared."

Moments later, wrapped in a robe, Melanie dried her hair before the fire. She was attempting to brush out the tangles when Ellen returned. "Here, let me do that."

Melanie sat in a chair and sighed as her friend began to smooth out her long hair. "That feels good. I've forgotten these little luxuries."

"How far along are you?"

Melanie said nothing for a long moment. She should have known better than to think Ellen wouldn't notice her pregnancy. She was still slender, but her belly which had always been flat, was now softly rounded, and her breasts, which had always been large, had grown enormous. "Don't tell Father."

"It won't be long before no one will need to tell him."

"I'll do it. I just have to find the right time."

"And distance? You don't want to marry the father?"

"There will be no marriage," Melanie said, her tone brooking no argument.

"Does he know?"

"He's never going to know."

"Why not? Hasn't he the right to—"

"No, he hasn't. He has no rights at all."

"Melanie."

"You needn't reprimand me, Ellen. The man does not want me. I'm mortified to think how close I came to begging him to let me stay. I have no doubt that he would have refused me outright." She took a deep, steadying breath, forcing aside the pain that sliced into her chest. "I know what I'm doing."

"You're best off without him, then. Any man who could reject you is no man in my eyes."

"That's all I seem to find."

At Ellen's puzzled gaze, Melanie clarified. "Men who reject me."

Ellen, not being privy to the intimacies of Melanie's marriage, had been under the impression that it was Melanie who had done the rejecting. After all, it had been she who had left her husband, not the other way around. Even though she was just burning with curiosity to know the truth of the matter, Ellen asked no questions. She figured all would come out eventually. *It always did.* She needed only patience.

Ellen finished Melanie's hair and helped her dress. Melanie couldn't deny that the silk underthings felt wonderful against her skin. She'd forgotten just how wonderful.

Douglas Hamilton sat at a table waiting for Melanie and checked his pocket watch, noting that he had five minutes before she was due to appear. He sighed as he finished the last of his tankard and then frowned as a fine lady stopped beside him.

He looked at her, "Ma'am?"

"You mean to say I look that different?"

"Excuse . . . " Douglas gasped and surged to his feet, almost toppling the chair in his haste. "Melanie, what are you doing? Where did you get these clothes?"

"They're mine. My father brought them along. He thought I'd need a change of clothes. They were left behind when I was kidnapped, you see."

"What are you talking about?"

Melanie laughed and sat down. "Buy me a tankard, sir, if you will. I'm thirsty. All this explaining is drying out my throat."

Douglas sat and did as he was asked. It took a long time before the dazed look left his eyes.

Harry Stone found his daughter in the taproom talking to a handsome man. He soon learned that they were friends and traveling companions.

"And his brother saved your life?"

Melanie smiled, without correcting her father's misunderstanding. "I have a lot to thank him for," he said.

More than you know, she added silently. *And the sooner we leave this country, the better off both of you will be.*

Melanie suffered under no false illusion that her father would treat Zachary Pitt with kindness once he learned of her condition. In fact she didn't doubt but what he might become violent. And, if truth be told, she wouldn't mind delivering her own blow to the stupid clod of a colonist who would not admit to loving her.

Melanie tore her mind from the one man she couldn't seem to stop thinking about and swore she wouldn't think about him again. She wouldn't. The beast wasn't worthy of even a moment of her consideration.

"What's the matter?"

"What?" Melanie returned, glancing toward her father with a stab of guilt.

"You look as if you're about to cry."

Melanie shook her head and smiled. "I'm tired, is all."

"We will stay here a few days. You need to rest."

"I'd rather not, if you don't mind. I'd rather get to Williamsburg as soon as possible."

"Why? Is it that mess about Joshua Moody? I assure you, you needn't worry on that score."

Melanie's eyes widened in surprise. "You know about Joshua?"

Her father shrugged. "Ellen directed me to Mrs. Moody, in my search for you."

Melanie sighed. "I don't know how you expect to straighten it out, Father. The boy is dead and no amount of influence will alter that fact."

Douglas choked on his ale and it took a few powerful slaps on the back to bring his breathing back to order.

Harry Stone seemed not to notice the interruption. He didn't care that a virtual stranger sat witness to this conversation. He knew his daughter well for the lady she was. She could not be at fault here. "Tell me what happened."

Melanie told her story with little emotion. She kept mostly to the facts, hardly revealing a glimmer of the terror she had known.

Afterward, her father sighed, even as Douglas's eyes widened in admiration at her cool control and amazing fortitude. Zachary had lost himself a prize in this woman, Douglas thought. He had known within minutes that the two were in love, for such soft smiles and tender looks could mean no less. He wondered if his brother realized just how truly stupid he was being.

"Just as I thought. Before boarding our ship, we will seek out the magistrate and straighten out this entire matter." When Melanie's dark eyes clouded with apprehension, her father added, "Have no fear, missy. All will be well, I promise you."

Melanie knew he spoke the truth. He'd take care of everything. He always did. She sighed her relief and Harry took the sound for exhaustion. "Would you rather I sent your meal upstairs?"

"No, I'm fine." At her father's look of doubt she said, "Truly."

Melanie consumed a full plate of hot roast beef, potatoes, and carrots. She ate two portions of bread and butter and drank another full tankard of ale before sighing in contentment and leaning back in her chair.

Harry couldn't help but notice that his daughter had lost a great deal of weight since he'd last seen her. That combined with the shadows beneath her eyes gave her a delicate appearance. Yet her appetite was healthy. A moment later he dismissed the thought, imagining it had probably been some time since she'd eaten such tasty fare.

Chapter 17

By the time Zachary set out for Williamsburg, he was eight hours behind Melanie. She'd stop for the night, he was sure. He would not. He'd find her. No matter what it took, he'd find her.

Had he thought to be gone for only a few days he might have left his daughter behind. As it was, he expected to be away for several months, perhaps longer. For once he found Melanie, he would accompany her to England. He could not leave Caroline that long. And because he couldn't, both father and daughter suffered the trip in misery.

Caroline wanted to be put down and whined incessantly. Zachary was relieved from her fretting only at night when she slept. During the day she fussed because she was tired, because she wanted to play, to eat, to stand rather than be held securely in her father's arms on horseback.

Even though Zachary allowed himself only a few hours of rest each night, they were not able to travel as quickly as he'd anticipated.

Zachary longed to find Melanie before she boarded a ship. But Caroline's fussing grew worse as one day passed into the next. It was still light when he approached an inn one day outside of Williamsburg. Zachary thought he'd stop and allow Caroline a full day's rest. In truth both father and daughter needed a break from this grueling journey.

It was just past the dinner hour when Zachary, after seeing to Caroline's care for most of the afternoon, watched her fall into a peaceful sleep. He summoned a maid to watch over her for an hour or so and headed for the taproom.

Had he not noticed his brother, Zachary would never have recognized Melanie as the woman sitting across from Douglas, so finely was she dressed. For just a second Zachary fell prey to doubt. Did he truly belong with this woman, or she with him? He took a deep breath. The time for hesitating had passed. He'd made his decision and had come for only one purpose, to claim this woman.

Zachary knew she would be angry, knew as well that she had every right to be angry. He approached the table and said her name.

Melanie glanced in his direction, instantly assaulted by emotion. The first, of course, was happiness. No, more than happiness, she was euphoric that he had followed her. There could be only one reason why. He loved her. No doubt the bloody fool had realized the fact only after she had gone. And then came anger that he had caused her to suffer when there had been no need. She almost shook with fury that this man dared to come upon her with an innocent smile and calm manner, after his pride had torn them apart.

Obviously he was looking for forgiveness. She wouldn't give it easily.

"Excuse me, sir?" she said, forcing a blank look.

Zachary grinned. He knew he deserved her fury and was perfectly willing to take his due. Still, her little act wasn't about to deter him. "We have unfinished business, I think."

"Have we?" Melanie frowned and Zachary thought her a skillful actress. If he didn't know better, he would have sworn that she didn't know him. "I beg your pardon, sir, but I can't seem to remember who you are."

Zachary was finding it difficult to keep from laughing. In another minute he just might grab her and kiss her right here, in front of everyone. "I think you do."

Harry Stone stood and eyed the man standing at his table, addressing his daughter in the oddest fashion. A man dressed as a laborer. Who the hell was he? "Do you know this man, Melanie?" he asked.

"No!" she said, too emphatically and then to Douglas, as if her response had settled the matter, "I'm sorry I will miss your wedding. Please tell Megan I wish I could have been there."

Douglas grinned. It was obvious what she was about. "Perhaps you will visit if you ever return."

"I won't be returning."

"I think you will," Zachary said, with all confidence.

"And have you taken to thinking now?" Melanie asked sarcastically, goaded into acknowledging their acquaintance when she should have continued to ignore it.

Harry Stone, still standing, addressed the stranger. "Do you know my daughter, sir?"

Until that minute Zachary hadn't realized the man with them was her father. He was amazed. Apparently Melanie's father had tracked her down, despite the fact that she had never posted her letter to him.

Before Zachary could answer, Melanie said, "Father, the man hasn't all his senses. We'd do well, I think, to ignore him as best we can."

Harry hadn't missed the fact that his daughter

seemed to know the man, despite the fact that she'd only just said otherwise. There was more here than met the eye.

"Why not join us, sir. Perhaps we can straighten out this—"

"If he sits, I'm leaving," Melanie announced.

"Why?" her father asked. "You said you don't know him."

"I don't sit with strangers."

"Melanie," her father warned, wanting the truth.

"All right, I know him. I just don't *want* to know him."

"I'm afraid she's upset with me, sir," Zachary explained, moving to the only available chair.

"Sit down and tell me why."

Zachary sat. "*Why* is probably not important. The fact is, sir, I want to marry your daughter."

All three of them stared at him, in total shock, for a proposal of marriage was perhaps the last thing any of them had expected. Douglas was the first to break the silence. He slapped his brother on the back and grinned. "Congratulations!"

Melanie came abruptly to her feet and glared at the grinning fools. "I'll be in my room."

"I'll be right back," Zachary said as he made to follow her, leaving her father and his brother behind.

"I should—" Harry murmured, trying to understand what had just happened.

"You needn't worry, Mr. Stone. My brother is harmless."

"Your *brother?*" Had the entire world gone mad?

Douglas smiled. "Zachary Pitt is my brother. He and Melanie are in love."

Instead of bringing a calming effect, his words further upset Harry Stone. "You're mistaken there, sir.

My daughter, the Duchess of Elderbury, is already a married woman."

Douglas felt suddenly more than a little uncomfortable, for until this minute no one had mentioned that she had a husband. When Mr. Stone stood and said, "I must see to my daughter. Good night to you, sir," Douglas didn't try to stop the man again.

Zachary caught up with Melanie at the first landing. "Wait a minute," he called. She began to run. "Melanie, damnit!" he growled, hot on her heels.

"Don't do that," she said, coming to an abrupt stop and spinning to face him.

"Don't do what?"

"Don't chase me. I hate it."

Zachary grinned at the little shiver she couldn't hide. "We need to talk."

"I don't think so."

"Melanie, you might as well listen. I'm not about to give up until you do."

"Fine. Go ahead then."

Zachary looked around the hall. Hardly private, even though it was empty for the moment. "This isn't exactly where I planned—"

"You had no trouble proposing marriage in front of my father. I think it can't be so hard to talk to me now, while we are alone."

Zachary sighed. "I probably shouldn't have said that, what with you still being married and your father there and all."

"Go away, Zachary. I don't want to talk to you."

And then her father was there, asking his daughter if she was all right.

Melanie smiled, set on ignoring Zachary completely. "I'm fine, Father. Just a little tired."

"You should go to bed, I think."

"Yes, I was about to. Good night, Father." A moment later she disappeared behind a bedroom door.

"Lock the door," Harry told her, and nodded in satisfaction as the bolt shot home.

Harry Stone glared at the man who had dared to annoy his daughter. "My daughter has made herself perfectly clear, sir. She does not want to talk to you."

Zachary would have liked to break the door down. He had to get her to listen. But now wasn't the time. He hadn't a doubt there would be others.

"Good night, Mr. Stone."

"Good-bye, sir," Harry returned.

In Williamsburg, before booking passage, Melanie and her father stopped first at the magistrate's office. With her father at her side, she again told her story. The fact that she was the Duchess of Elderbury and her father knew some very important people in London went far toward convincing the man of her innocence in Joshua Moody's death. The magistrate dismissed all charges.

The *Bristol* was tied to its moorings, due to depart in two days time. Zachary checked the passenger list before buying his ticket. Melanie and her small party were aboard, or soon would be, for their names appeared on the list. He felt vast relief. She might have ignored him at the inn, and disappeared before he could find her again, but the woman loved him, he was sure. She was furious and needed time, but Zachary was sure he could convince her to forgive him. And a long journey might provide just the time she needed.

After buying his ticket, Zachary headed for the magistrate. If things worked out as he imagined, and he thought they most likely would, they'd be returning to the colonies within the year. And before they did, he meant to ensure that Melanie wouldn't flinch every time there was a knock on the door. Zachary was going to lie through his teeth, but Melanie would not suffer another moment of fear due to the uncontrolled lust of a young lad. Not if he could do something about it.

Two hours after Melanie and her father had left, Zachary gained an interview with the same elderly magistrate. Zachary began his story in his finest, most cultivated voice and manner, and thought Mrs. Morrison should be proud of his efforts. "I thought I should report a crime, sir. The report should have been made a sight sooner, I'm sure, but my baby wasn't well at the time."

The magistrate frowned. "What crime?"

"Last fall, well actually at the end of last summer, in fact, I was traveling home, having gone to Charlottesville for supplies, when I heard a woman cry out for help.

"I stopped my wagon, hoping to be of some assistance. I entered the woods, following her screams, and found a young woman being sadly abused by a gangly looking boy. He was naked and obviously trying to force his attentions on her."

The magistrate studied Zachary's unwavering expression, then nodded. "Go on."

"I was about to interfere when the woman managed to escape the boy's hold. She ran, but not before throwing his clothes into a creek. The boy ran after his clothes, slipped and fell. Apparently he hit his head, for he did not get up."

"And you saw no reason to come to his aid?"

"I believe he was already dead sir."

"Did you make yourself known to the woman?"

"I did not. I felt to do so would only add to her distress, for she was beside herself with terror."

"And you couldn't have calmed her?"

"Her dress was torn. She would have been doubly distressed if she knew a stranger had witnessed her nakedness."

"I see. What happened then?"

"There was a horse nearby. The woman was still crying when she mounted the animal and galloped away. I checked the boy then. It was as I thought. He was dead."

"Do you know who the boy was?"

"I do not."

"Where do you live?"

"About five days west and south of the city. I'm afraid little news reaches me there."

The magistrate's wise gaze moved toward Caroline and back to her father. "Your little girl appears recovered."

Zachary knew the magistrate had some doubts, especially since he'd reported the event seven months too late. Still for Melanie's sake he'd swear his story on a Bible if need be. She wouldn't suffer because of another's depravity. "She is recovered. Was, in fact, for most of the winter. The snows came early this year. Once they started, I couldn't get out."

The interview was soon over. Zachary left breathing a sigh of relief, without learning that all charges had already been dropped.

Zachary stopped at a hawker to buy two meat pies. He had no notion of when they'd next eat and thought Caroline should have something before settling down for a nap.

At the ship he showed his ticket and was directed to a cabin.

Tired from days of hard riding, Zachary and Caroline slept almost immediately.

The gentle dipping of a ship heading out to sea only deepened their slumber. It was early the next morning when Zachary awakened to the clatter of dishes being brought to the cabin beside his. Apparently someone was being delivered their first meal of the day. Zachary thought he could do nicely with equal service and stopped the steward with an order.

While he waited, he washed and shaved. Next he awakened Caroline and spent some delightful time with her. She was much happier in the cabin than she had been on horseback. Still there was another person's company he greatly desired.

The porter returned with a tray and Zachary inquired of the duchess. Yes, she was traveling with them. In fact her cabin was only four doors from his.

After their meal, Zachary changed into his town clothes and dressed Caroline in her prettiest dress. He smoothed back his dark hair and after one last nervous glance in the mirror, left his cabin for the one four doors down.

Zachary stood Caroline before the door. Now that their meeting was at hand, he found himself not half so brave as he'd first imagined. Melanie had been far more angry than he'd supposed. It wouldn't hurt, he thought, if Caroline first broke down the lady's defenses. He knocked and moved to the side.

The door opened and an older woman smiled at the sight of his daughter standing there apparently alone. "Oh dear, what have we here?" she said as she guided his daughter inside and shut the door.

"What?" Melanie asked as she lifted her teacup to her lips. An instant later the cup clattered to the table. "Caroline!" Melanie gasped, as she rushed to the child and hungrily brought her into her arms. "Oh

Caroline, I missed you so much," Melanie said, hugging her tightly and depositing a dozen kisses over the child's face.

Caroline was a loving little girl, but even she thought this show of affection a bit much. She squirmed, whined her displeasure, and turned her face away.

Only then did Melanie ask, "How did you get here?" And then, "Watch her," she said as she nearly wrenched the door from its hinges and dashed from the room, her gaze wildly searching the companionway. In an instant she found him.

She was gorgeous, Zachary thought. She wore a white silk robe, tied at the waist, her black hair curling wildly down her back and over one shoulder. Her cheeks were flushed with emotion. Zachary wondered if there was a woman alive to compare with her. He'd seen her more agreeable perhaps, but never more beautiful. He'd seen her dark eyes half closed in passion, where now there was anger; her skin flushed with the heat of passion, now was red with anger. He'd seen her naked and yearning, and now he saw only stiff fury. And still, she quite stole his breath.

Melanie had prayed for just this scenario, or one like it, a hundred times and thought that she might have flung herself into his arms, upon seeing him again.

Zachary suffered under the hopeful delusion himself.

But Melanie was still furious that he had dared to propose marriage to her last night, while her father watched in astonishment. And for not telling her he was taking the same ship and for standing here with a confident grin curving his mouth, his arms folded casually across his chest as he leaned against a wall. The sight of him was almost her undoing.

"You beast. Tell me you planned this all along and I'll box your ears."

Zachary hadn't expected a loving greeting. No, the loving part would come later. Still, he saw a good deal of humor in her threat. It wouldn't be boasting to imagine he was a bit stronger than the lady. Still he would have enjoyed seeing how she might carry through on her threat. Indeed, he could imagine himself enjoying that and quite a bit more.

"If you join me in my cabin, you could try."

Melanie was enraged that he should dare see anything amusing in this situation.

"We should talk."

"I have nothing to say to you," Melanie said and calmly returned to her room, closing the door firmly behind her. He heard the lock fall into place.

Zachary knocked.

No response.

He knocked again. "Melanie, open this door."

"I don't want to see you."

"Well, that's too bad, isn't it? You have Caroline in there."

"Tell me your cabin number and I'll have Ellen bring Caroline back in a few minutes."

Zachary considered knocking the door down. He didn't care about making a scene. Not for himself. He cared only that Melanie shouldn't be further angered. Clearly it was going to take a bit of work on his part to win her over. So he gave in to her demand and returned to his room. He waited for almost an hour before he heard a soft knock.

The woman holding his daughter looked to be an agreeable sort. He supposed she was Ellen, Melanie's companion. Perhaps he could solicit her help.

He reached out a hand in greeting. "It's Ellen, isn't it?"

The woman nodded. "Mr. Pitt?"

"Ellen, I wonder if you wouldn't do me a great favor."

"I can't talk to her. She just about bit my head off when I tried."

Zachary sighed. "If I could have a minute alone with her, I might be able to—"

"She won't make it easy for you."

"No, I expect she won't. Will you watch the baby for me?"

Ellen smiled at Caroline, who had climbed aboard the bunk. She sat at the edge swinging her legs over the side as she looked about the room. A moment later the ship dipped and Caroline lost her balance and fell off the bunk. She cried, the sound loud and piercing. Melanie was instantly in the cabin, taking the baby from Zachary's arms as the baby sobbed out, "Nee, Nee."

"What did you do to her?" Melanie demanded, snuggling the baby closer, delighting in the small arms that wrapped tightly around her neck, never seeing Zachary's annoyed glare.

Melanie spoke to the child in a soft, soothing tone and kissed the red mark on her forehead. "Is it better now, sweetheart? All gone?"

Moments later the child was calm, but no amount of persuading could bring her from Melanie's arms.

"She's afraid you'll leave her again," Zachary informed her.

"Did she cry when I left?"

Zachary nodded.

Melanie glared at him, for his daughter's tears were solely his doing.

"She looks like she's ready for a nap," Ellen said. "Do you want me to hold her?"

"No, I'll stay with her until she falls asleep."

Ellen closed the door behind her as she left.

Melanie rocked the baby in her arms. "You don't have to stay," she told Zachary. "She'll be asleep soon."

"This is my cabin. Where would you like me to go?"

Melanie shot him an angry look. "You should know better than to ask a lady a question like that, Mr. Pitt. I just might tell you the truth."

Zachary grinned. Melanie looked away from his smile.

"If I went to hell, Melanie, would you keep Caroline and raise her as your own?"

"That's an idiotic question. I love her. Of course I would." A moment later she asked almost conversationally, "Can I hope for your death anytime soon?"

Zachary laughed softly. The sound cut into her heart. "One doesn't have to die to go to hell, Melanie. The truth is, I've just come from there."

She refused to look in his direction, refused to respond as well.

"Do you want to know where it is?"

Again she did not reply.

"Hell is anywhere you're not."

"Amazing, isn't it, Mr. Pitt, how you can turn your emotions on and off."

"I've never turned off what I felt for you, Melanie. I only forced myself not to show it."

"It's the same thing, isn't it?"

"Do you think so? Right now, you're angry with me. Does that mean you don't love me?"

She was *not* going to admit to loving this man. Not

after what he'd done. Not after the suffering he'd caused her. "I don't want to talk about it."

"Fine. You don't have to say a thing. I'll do all the talking."

"There's nothing you can say that will change my mind. It's too late."

"I could tell you that I love you, only that wouldn't be entirely true."

Melanie glanced up from the baby and sighed. "I'm sure it wouldn't be."

"Love couldn't feel like this. It couldn't push me into the depths of despair at the thought of never seeing you again. It couldn't make my heart melt while watching you with Caroline, holding her, touching her, having her turn to you when she's hurt. Loving you couldn't be my reason for living, for getting up each morning, with the simple hope to see you smile, a smile that fills my heart. Love can't bring sunshine where there was once only darkness. No, this can't be just love. It has to be more than that."

Melanie's gaze narrowed. She'd never heard him speak like this before, never thought him capable of such poetry. "Did you read that somewhere?"

A smile curved his handsome mouth and Melanie's stomach twisted uncomfortably. "It was on one of the potato sacks."

She ignored his teasing. "I hate you for what you did."

"No, you don't. You're angry with me for what I did. You love me."

"Perhaps, but I don't trust you. Why, tomorrow you might take it into your head that you don't love me again. Then what?"

"That won't happen."

"How do I know it won't? It's happened before."

"Listen to me. I've always loved you. I just never told you."

"Why the bloody hell not!" Melanie winced as Caroline stirred. "I'm sorry sweetheart. I forgot you were sleeping."

"You know why. I have nothing. How the hell could we ever—?"

"Have you somehow come into money since last week, Mr. Pitt? Have you discovered a diamond mine, or perhaps gold on your property?"

"I hope to hell not. It's not my property."

"Why are you here?"

"Because I'm going with you to England, just as you asked. At least until you get the annulment."

"I never asked."

"Your eyes did."

"I'm taking back my offer."

"All right, forget about me. What about Caroline? Do you want to leave her?"

"Are there no depths to which you will not sink?"

"None. Not when the prize is you."

"So now you want me. But you're just as poor as ever?"

"I am."

"What changed your mind then? What are you doing here?"

"Ellen was right. You're not making this easy." Zachary took the sleeping baby from her arms and placed her on the bed. He then brought Melanie to her feet, but she refused to allow him to get too close, refused to step into his arms.

"You don't deserve it to be easy, Mr. Pitt."

"I'm here because I realized living without you isn't living at all. So I swallowed my pride and came for you."

"Then cough it back up again. I don't want you."

"You're lying. Shall I prove it to you?"

Melanie knew what that look meant. "Prove what? That I forget how to think once I'm in your bed? I expect the day will come when I'll do as much with others. It means nothing."

Zachary ignored her reference to other men. Ignored as well the murder he felt in his heart at the very thought.

"All right. Tell me what you want. What will it take to bring us back together again? I'll do anything. Just name it."

She shook her head, refusing to lift her gaze from the floor. "I think it's too late." Melanie wondered if she spoke the truth, if it wasn't her own pride stopping her from falling into this man's arms.

"We'll see. We have weeks to work this out before reaching England. Will you have dinner with me?"

"I'll be dining with my father."

Zachary nodded. "How did he find you? How did he know where to look?"

"Ellen posted a letter. He was searching for me when we found each other at the inn just before reaching Williamsburg."

Zachary nodded, wondering for the first time if he wasn't fooling himself. She was with her father again. Surely that had to have influenced her some. "I see," he said, feeling despair at the thought of the richness of her dress, the diamonds in her ears. Why, the cost of this one dress could keep both him and Caroline for a year. What the hell did he think he was doing? Why had he come after her? Was he out of his mind?

"You see what?" she asked.

"What?"

"What is it you see?"

"I see your clothes. You look beautiful."

"Thank you. But what does that mean, you see my clothes?"

"Nothing."

"On the contrary, Mr. Pitt, it means something. A man doesn't go around saying, 'I see,' when he doesn't. What exactly do you see? A fancy dress? Are we back to money again? My money versus your pride?"

"I didn't realize . . ."

"What? That I had so much? Has your pride taken a mortal blow?" Zachary looked at first stunned and then trapped. A blind man could have read his thoughts. "Coward," she murmured, her voice tinged with disgust.

"Do you think so?"

"I'm afraid you leave me to think nothing else. Right now you're wondering what you can do to escape this situation, are you not? I can almost hear your thoughts. 'How can I tell her I really don't love her when I just said I did'?" she sneered. "You're thinking that, aren't you?"

"I'm not. I just never realized . . ."

Melanie sighed. "It's hopeless. I'm not giving up everything just because money makes you uncomfortable. If you can't accept it, then that's just too bad."

"Melanie, you'll have to give me a chance. I didn't realize you were so rich."

She counted to ten and then asked, "Are you used to it yet?"

He smiled, knowing it would take a bit longer than a few seconds to do the trick. Still he said, "Yes, I think so." And then, "All right."

"All right? What do you mean, all right?"

"I mean, it's all right with me if you keep your money."

"Thank you very much," she said with more than a touch of sarcasm, for she had every intention of keeping it. "I shall."

"Are all your clothes like this?"

Melanie glanced down at her gown. It was indeed a lovely concoction of soft lavender silk, the skirt gathered at the hip to reveal a petticoat three shades darker underneath. The gown was far too elegant for day wear, but her father had brought along a trunk filled with the best she owned and this one was the least elaborate of all. Still, Melanie would not soften the blow. Zachary should know the worst of it.

"Most of my clothes are like this, yes," she said.

"How much exactly are you worth?"

Melanie laughed. "If one has to count it, Mr. Pitt, surely it's not enough."

He frowned and shook his head. "Why do you want me then? A woman like you could have—"

"Because I love you, you idiot," she said a bit too loudly.

Zachary grinned. He'd won. It wouldn't be long now before he held her in his arms. "Do you? Do you truly?"

Melanie looked everywhere except at the man standing before her. "I didn't mean to say that. What I meant to say was, I hate you."

Zachary ignored her. "You don't just love what I do to you in bed? You really love *me?*"

"I said—"

Again he ignored the attempted amendment. "You know what I think?"

Her hands moved to her hips and she glared at him.

"I think we would be a lot more equal if you took off that dress."

Melanie swallowed at the thought, her skin growing warm. Her entire body tingled in response to his less-than-romantic words. God, there was no hope for it. She did love him. Loved him beyond all reason. She'd thought to give him a bit more trouble than this, quite a bit more trouble before falling into his arms. "I don't think so," came her weak response.

"Why?"

"Because what I'm wearing under it is just as lavish."

"You could take that off as well."

Melanie almost groaned at the longing she felt and wondered how she managed to keep her hands from tearing away the dress. "And that would make us equal?"

"In all things that are important."

He'd hit upon the truth. In all things that were important, money being the least important of all. She'd known that for some time. It had taken Zachary quite a bit longer to come to the same conclusion.

There was no sense in denying it. She loved him, stubborn fool that he was.

Melanie said nothing as she turned and opened the door. At first Zachary thought she was running away. He almost reached out for her when he heard her say, "I'll get Ellen to watch the baby."

Hardly a minute went by before Zachary heard Ellen's soft knock. "She should stay asleep for about an hour. Is that all right?" he asked.

"Don't worry about us, we'll be fine. You two just have your little talk."

Zachary smiled at Ellen. His smile turned into a grin as he stepped into the hall and approached Melanie's cabin. He was disappointed to find it empty, but sighed in relief seconds later when Melanie returned.

"Where were you?"

"Telling Father I won't be taking a walk on deck with him after all."

Zachary nodded and watched her intently, almost afraid to say or do anything that might ruin this moment. "Are we about to have our little talk now?" he asked.

Melanie looked puzzled and then laughed. "I could have told her what we're really going to do, but she would have fainted, I think."

Zachary chuckled, a low rumbling sound.

Melanie shrugged her shoulders and arms out of the silk dress and twisted the fabric around her to undo the buttons down the back. Zachary took off his coat and shirt.

She stepped out of the dress and placed it neatly over a chair. Zachary watched in amazement as she flung aside one layer of petticoat after another. He'd imagined women only wore this elaborate nonsense when going to court.

And then his mind touched upon a horrifying thought. Did Melanie regularly go to court? Would he be expected to accompany her? Zachary found himself asking, "I hope to hell you don't go to court."

"I did once. I didn't like it much and probably won't go again. Why?"

He breathed a sigh of relief. "Because I'll never learn to curtsy."

"Men don't curtsy; they bow."

"Of course. Hurry up," he said as he flung his boots aside. She finished with her petticoats at last. A tight corset squeezed her waist and thrust her breasts forward and up. He hardly noticed the frilly drawers and black silk stockings, held up by black lace garters. The sight of her just about took his breath away.

"Lord," came a low desperate sounding husk, "I

hope it won't always take this long to get you naked."

Melanie bit her bottom lip, unable to hide her smile at the almost stunned look in Zachary's eyes.

"Your father's going to hate me."

"My father's going to love you."

Zachary cursed, knowing there was trouble ahead. Her father wouldn't be happy to see his daughter involved with him, a man who had nothing. He'd surely think that Zachary was after her money.

She struggled with the ties at her back.

"You know what he's going to think, don't you?" he said.

"I only care what *you* think."

Zachary sighed, knowing now wasn't the time to go into it. He had better plans for the next hour. "What excuse did you give your father?"

"That I was tired." She grunted as the ties grew tangled. "I can't get this thing off."

"Leave it. We'll take it off later. You aren't really tired, are you?"

"No." She shoved her drawers down her legs and kicked them aside. "But I fully expect to be."

Chapter 18

Much later, as the pleasure began to ease, Zachary was able to think again.

Melanie smiled as she leaned forward, her breasts swaying deliciously above his face, her legs still straddling his thighs. She rotated her hips, bringing a soft moan to Zachary's lips. "I'll do the stockings, if you help me out of this corset," she whispered. Zachary rolled her onto her stomach. He worked the ties free.

Melanie took a huge breath in relief as the corset came free at last. "God, that feels good."

He frowned at the marks made by the whalebone on her skin. "Why do you wear this thing? Look at the marks." His mood turned pensive. "And what are we going to do about us?"

She rolled to her back; the corset dropped to the floor. "I wear the corset because a tiny waist is the style and I can't fit into my clothes without it. And, the first thing we're going to do about us is to tell Father that I left my husband shortly before he had me kidnapped."

Zachary began kissing the red marks that ran the length of her midriff. "What?" He was up on his elbows, his eyes wide with surprise, and his voice grew appreciatively louder as he exclaimed, "You haven't told him even that?"

"There hasn't been time."

"He thinks you and your husband are still—"

"I won't have to tell him a thing if you keep shouting. He'll hear it for himself."

"Oh God," came Zachary's morose reply as he dropped his head to her stomach and sighed, "No wonder he looked so shocked the other night. Tell me what he does know."

"He knows I was kidnapped. He knows I was sent to the colonies and sold as an indentured servant. He knows you took me in when I ran from the Moodys."

Zachary rolled to the edge of the bed and sat up. He dropped his head into his hands and rubbed his face. "Wonderful. I asked to marry you and he still thinks—"

"I'll talk to him. Don't worry."

"He'll have me shot."

Melanie chuckled at the bleakness in his tone. "You might have thought of that before you seduced me."

Zachary glanced behind him and grinned at the sight of her lying all warm, pink, and naked for his pleasure. "I wasn't thinking very clearly at the time."

"I remember. You said a naked lady makes a man forget certain things."

Zachary nodded and moved again to her side, unable to resist her sweet allure, knowing they had somehow switched roles and she had become the seducer. He couldn't have loved it more. He pulled her against his body as his mouth nibbled her softness. "Besides, I didn't love you then. At least I wasn't aware of loving you."

"No?" she asked, as she ran her fingers through

his long black hair. "What did you think at the time?"

"That I shouldn't let the chance go by to sample this sweet ass."

Melanie hit him. He laughed and she hit him again. "Villain."

Zachary grabbed her hands and held them to her sides. Leaning over her, he dared, "Tell me you were madly in love with me then."

"I was."

He nuzzled her breast, licking the tips into hardness and then burying his face against her softness. "Now tell me the truth."

"All right," she said with some reluctance, "perhaps not madly."

"Not in love at all, am I right?'

"I don't know. The seduction and the love came together. They snuck up on me." She shot him a scowling glance and finished with, "You planned it all, I'm sure."

"I planned the seduction."

She would have hit him again had her hands been free. "Beast. I'm going to tell the baby all of it. He should know what kind of a father . . . "

Zachary chuckled, released her hands and came to rest on his elbows, the upper part of his body suspended slightly above hers. He cupped her face, brushing back wisps of hair. "Even if you told her, Caroline wouldn't have a notion . . . " His words faltered as his blue eyes narrowed in thought. Melanie had said *he*, not *she*. A frown creased his forehead. "What baby?"

She smiled, a deliciously sweet, secret smile. "Well, that's another thing I haven't told Father."

"You're going to have my baby." His blue eyes darkened with emotion. He'd almost lost her, almost

lost her and his baby because of pride. Zachary realized then that he didn't care about anything except
seeing this woman grow round with his child and
loving both her and his baby forever. "You haven't
told *me* yet either."

"Haven't I?" She smiled again as she reached between their bodies. "Well, I've been busy."

"Have you?" he asked, shifting his hips so she
could reach all of him. "Busy how?"

"Well first, if you remember correctly, we were ar-
guing."

Zachary nodded and, finding her top lip particularly irresistible, began to kiss it, suck it, and caress it
with his tongue. "All right. What about later?"

"This is later."

"I mean between the argument and later."

"Are you trying to fight with me?"

Zachary laughed, his eyes warm with happiness. "I
should wring your neck. You were leaving with my
baby."

"*My* baby," she corrected. "And leaving was your
idea."

"I was a fool."

"I'll remember you said that."

Zachary's chuckle contained both delight and res-
ignation. "I know you will. I hope you remember this
as well."

Melanie moaned as his mouth moved down her
body, her entire being anticipating every movement.
And when he reached his goal at last, she could only
breathe out on a sigh, "Lord, I think I'm not likely to
forget it."

They sat at a small table in the ship's dining room
as Melanie told her father everything, beginning with
the night she had discovered Townsend with his

lover, and continuing with the sure knowledge that her husband had been behind not only the kidnapping, but also the murder attempt.

Melanie watched her father's face turn nearly purple with rage and pushed the glass of brandy closer to his hand. "That son of a bitch," he said almost in a whisper. "I'll kill him!"

"You won't, Father."

"I'll have Townsend brought up on charges. I'll ruin him. He won't be able to show his face . . ."

Melanie shook her head, knowing the impossibility of her father's threats. "There is no proof."

"What about the knife? That's proof, isn't it?"

"He would, I'm sure, swear no knowledge of it, or claim it had been stolen or lost. He's a lord of the realm. In the end, his word would be believed. No, the best thing is a quick annulment. He'll have nothing to gain from my death then."

Harry Stone sighed. "My God, I can't believe I forced you into this marriage. You could be dead now, all because I wanted you to be a duchess."

"It wasn't your fault. Townsend treated me kindly always." That was partly true. Melanie simply did not mention the things he had done to her in bed. "The title of 'Duchess' is very appealing to a young woman. And who could have guessed his true nature? There were rumors, but I never thought them true."

"Nor did I."

"Drink the brandy. There's more, you should know."

An almost terrified look entered his eyes just before he downed the amber liquid. "What else?"

"I've fallen in love with someone else."

"You didn't have an affair before you left Townsend?"

"No, it was nothing like that."

Harry sighed. "But it's something almost as bad. I'm not going to like him, am I?"

"I have no doubt that you will love him, eventually."

"Melanie . . . "

"Hear me out, Father."

Harry poured himself another drink. "Go ahead."

"Well, you'll remember I told you about the farmer who took me in?"

His eyes narrowed and he wiped his forehead with his handkerchief. "I know for a fact I'm not going to like this."

"Perhaps, but considering my delicate condition, you have no choice in the matter."

Harry moaned again. "Are you trying to kill me?"

Melanie smiled and tapped her father's hand. "You'll love him, just wait and see."

"When will I meet him?"

"Actually, you've already met."

Harry Stone hadn't met many people since his arrival in the colonies. It didn't take five seconds for him to realize the man in question, especially since the bizarre young man who had approached them the other night at the inn was obviously a farmer. "Good God, not that madman!"

"Father, I know his actions were a bit peculiar, but he was under the impression that you already knew about Townsend and the fact that I would be seeking an annulment."

"Am I correct in assuming he's on board ship even now?"

Melanie thought she'd never heard a question asked in so dismal a tone. Still, she had every confidence that all would work out in the end. "You are."

"And next you're going to tell me he doesn't want you for your money. Am I right?"

"Father," she gently reminded him, "Townsend married me for my money."

"He had a title to offer you in return. What does your farmer have?"

Melanie knew she couldn't allow this most important relationship between her father and her future husband to begin on the wrong foot. Her father had to know just how vehemently Zachary had objected to the very thought of her money. And yet if she said as much, would her father believe it? She wasn't about to take the chance.

For the first time in her life, she was going to lie to her father. The thought did not instill happiness, but considering the fact that her father was already suspicious, she knew nothing less than a slight varying of the truth could bring peace to her family. "The truth is, he didn't know I had money until he found me at the inn, dressed in fancy clothes." Thankfully, she could say the rest as gospel. "And I don't mind telling you that it does not sit well with him."

Harry sighed. To say he was less than satisfied with his daughter's actions over these last months would have been a gross understatement. Still the past was past and her pregnancy certainly limited their choices. "Are you sure you love him?"

Melanie nodded. Her eyes shone with love, leaving her father with no doubt.

"Then why did you leave him in the first place?"

"We had an argument. I left in anger."

"And how far along are you?"

"Three months."

"Three months? You were only gone a little more than a year."

Melanie laughed. "Are you asking for the particulars?"

"No. I imagine a farmer's life to be a lonely one. The man was no doubt randy, ready for a go at the first female to cross his threshold."

"Father," she said, her voice carrying a clear warning. "You will like him. I'm afraid I shall have to insist upon it."

Harry laughed. "I hope you know you're becoming more like me every day."

Melanie smiled into his laughing eyes. "Besides loving you, I happen to like you very much. So if you don't mind, I shall take that as a compliment." She stood, leaned down, and kissed him on the cheek. "I think I'll rest before dinner."

"You were resting all day. Are you feeling . . . " Harry was more than a little surprised at his daughter's guilty flush. That was all it took for him to know the truth of it. "Damn. Well, we'll have no more of that nonsense. I can't have my daughter's reputation sullied."

"I'm afraid it's too late for that. The baby won't wait the full nine months after the wedding."

"It will according to the legal papers I'll have drawn up, and I don't care what the cost." Melanie might have been a married woman about to seek an annulment, but she was Harry Stone's daughter first, and Harry Stone would never permit a hint of scandal to touch his family. She had been gone for more than a year and could not claim Townsend as the child's father. The pregnancy would proceed in seclusion, of that there was no doubt. "In the meantime, I suggest a trip to the Continent, or perhaps a stay in the country."

"I think the country," she returned without hesitation.

"I see you've thought about this at length."

"As you say, Father, we are much alike. I'll see you at dinner."

Harry delayed her leaving by reaching for her hand. "I'll be in my cabin. I expect to see your man there in fifteen minutes."

"Yes, Father."

"What the bloody hell am I supposed to say? I'm sorry, sir, for bedding your daughter?"

"Are you?" she asked, unable to suppress her laughter.

Zachary stood almost at attention while Melanie brushed a piece of lint from his jacket. At her question he shot her a sideways glare. "Melanie, don't aggravate me more than necessary, all right?"

"I take it then that you're not sorry."

"This is not the least bit amusing. Stop laughing."

She ignored his grumpy words. "Then you'd best not say you are. Father appreciates honesty."

Zachary breathed, "Oh God," while casting his gaze toward the ceiling. "Why do I feel like I'm walking toward the gallows?"

Melanie giggled and Zachary grabbed her for a long, fortifying kiss. He felt decidedly better afterward. Better until she said, "Oh, I forgot to tell you. Father said there will be no more of this nonsense."

"What nonsense?"

"The two of us spending the afternoon in bed."

Zachary pulled back, his eyes wide, his features frozen in shock. "You told him?"

"He figured out that I wasn't resting this afternoon."

"Thank you." He nodded his head. "Thank you very much." A moment later she was standing alone in her cabin, unable to control her soft laughter.

* * *

"I'm afraid I was unaware of the situation when we met at the inn. My daughter has enlightened me since then. I hope you will accept my apology."

Zachary hadn't known what to expect during this interview, but it certainly wasn't an apology. He felt a fraction of the stiffness leave his spine, for the opening comment seemed to have put them on equal footing. Almost.

"I understand you want to marry my daughter."

"Yes, sir." Zachary downed the offered brandy in one nervous gulp.

"You don't mind my asking what it is you have to offer her?"

"Not nearly as much as you'd like, I'm sure, sir. The fact is, I'm about to buy a plantation near Williamsburg, on the James River." Zachary knew as he said the words that he wouldn't wait any longer. He would borrow the money from his brother. He didn't care that he'd be starting off in debt. He was going to marry the woman he loved, and it didn't matter what it took. "The house is large, sir. Quite large indeed. I'm sure Melanie will be happy there."

"A gentleman farmer." Harry thought he could live with that. More importantly, he thought Melanie could, although he'd be loath to see her live an ocean away. "I see."

Zachary said nothing.

"And with a plantation you hope to provide for her?"

"It would be my honor to provide for her, sir. With a bit of luck, we should manage very well."

Harry Stone nodded. The man appeared to be a decent sort. Fairly well-educated. Far from sophisticated, but his steady gaze suggested honesty and a certain strength of character. He sported none of the lace, ruffles, and plumes of a man of fashion; his attire was somber and unadorned. He was nervous, but Harry thought he had every right to be nervous after what he'd done to his daughter. Zachary Pitt wouldn't have been his choice, of course, but it was a bit late for choices, he supposed.

"The annulment proceedings will begin the moment I arrive in England. Until it is final, Melanie will be staying in the country."

"Yes, sir."

"I hope I don't have to tell you that no scandal can be attached to her name."

"I quite understand."

Without knocking, Melanie opened the door to the cabin. Exhibiting not a shred of embarrassment at having obviously listened to the entire conversation from the companionway, she asked, "Are you suggesting that we not see each other for the next six months?"

Harry glared at his daughter. "I was under the impression that this was a private conversation. And the next time you eavesdrop, do it more discreetly."

"What is this nonsense about scandal? Do you expect that I will parade about the place naked?"

Zachary cleared his throat and pushed his finger between his throat and the cravat Melanie had insisted he wear, while wishing to hell he could think of a way to shut her up. Her flippant comment was not exactly going over well with her father, if the narrowing of his eyes meant anything. "The thought hadn't crossed my mind until now."

Oh Lord, he was going to wring her neck.

"I'll act the perfect lady, I assure you."

"I have no doubt that you will."

"Meaning you will make sure of it?" Melanie didn't wait for her father to respond, but added, "All right, if it's a chaperon you want, Aunt Matilda can come live with me."

Harry laughed. "Good choice, considering she's almost totally blind and half deaf."

"Aunt Matilda and Ellen."

"Ellen wouldn't think you scandalous if she sat by the damned bed and watched the goings on."

Melanie ignored her father's revealing remark while Zachary moaned. "I will not go six months without seeing him," Melanie insisted.

"And I don't expect it of you. There's no reason why Mr. Pitt cannot stay with us."

Melanie grinned, for she hadn't until this minute understood her father's intentions. He would be staying in the country with her. She wasn't at all sorry, for she loved her father dearly and knew she would miss him terribly when she returned to the colonies.

Harry turned to Zachary. "Are you sure you want to marry her? She's incorrigibly willful, you know."

"I know. She needs a strong man to rein her in."

Even though she'd just done as much to Zachary, Melanie hardly appreciated being spoken about as if she were no longer present. She shot both men evil glares as she flounced from the room.

Melanie stepped silently into Zachary's cabin. Caroline was asleep on the narrow bunk. The room was dark except for the small lantern hanging from the ceiling above a tiny table. Beside the table, Zachary sat half asleep. She closed the door behind her. "Excuse me, sir, but I'm looking for a strong man to rein me in."

Zachary was no fool. He heard the edge in her voice and knew it was time to apologize. He came to stand before her. "I'm sorry I said that, but I had to say something to win your father's favor."

"Are you very sorry?"

"Very."

She grinned. "Perhaps I'll let you make it up to me."

"Will you? How shall I?"

"I'm sure you'll think of something."

Zachary chuckled softly as he lowered his head, his mouth coming even with hers. He kissed her long and hard, wishing he'd never have to stop, wishing she could stay with him for the night. "I feel like a schoolboy about to get caught with his hand in a cookie jar."

"Well, now that you mention it, I do have a cookie or two on me."

Zachary ran his hands over the silk robe she wore. "Do you? You've hidden them well then."

"I could show you where they are."

Zachary sighed and rested his chin upon her head. "I can almost feel your father watching us. He's sure to ask Ellen where you are."

Melanie chuckled as she reached for him. They stood just inside his room, Melanie's back pressed against the door. "Ellen is asleep. Father is asleep. No one knows I'm here."

"Suppose someone sees you going back to your room?"

"The companionway is dark. There's only one candle at the far end. Are you ready to find a cookie yet?"

"You are a greedy creature," Zachary said as she pushed his trousers and long johns down his legs.

"You've no one to blame but yourself. Melanie Stone was once a demure lady who would have had the vapors if a man had suggested that she come to his room at night. Not that she would have known what to do once she got there."

"But *you* do."

Melanie untied her robe and rubbed her naked body against his. She chuckled softly at the surprise in his eyes, knowing he hadn't suspected she was naked beneath it.

"You're very wicked." Zachary gasped, unable to tell her the extent of his delight.

"I suppose I am." Melanie said, obviously enjoying the thought. She ran both hands down his body, stopping only when her fingers curved around his sex. Her mouth smoothed over his shoulder and down his chest as she murmured, "Shall I show you the extent of my wickedness?"

Zachary groaned as she did just that.

Zachary absorbed the soft sounds of her release into his mouth and then, breathing heavily, leaned against her, forcing his trembling legs to support his weight. "I want to sleep with you. I want to hold you all night."

"I know."

"Stay with me for a while."

"If I stay any longer, it will be light before I leave."

"So you came only to use my body and discard me afterward?"

Melanie laughed. "I hadn't thought about it like that, but the truth is, you aren't far off the mark."

Zachary couldn't honestly say he minded. "What are we going to do when we get to England?"

"Father's lawyers will begin the annulment proceedings, and we'll go directly to our country estate. It might be months before the papers are ready, before I can sign them and return to America with you."

"I don't care, as long as we're together."

"What about your farm?"

"Gray Cloud will stay there until I get back."

"I heard you tell Father that you're buying the Simmons plantation."

Zachary nodded. "I have enough money, but I'll borrow more from Douglas, just to carry us over."

"There's no need for that. You will have my dowry."

The words *dowry* and *farmer* hardly being synonymous, Zachary hadn't realized until this minute that this woman would come to him with a great deal of money. He grinned. "A dowry, huh? Yes, now that you mention it, I can see why your father would pay me to take you off his hands."

"We're not married yet, Mr. Pitt. I could change my mind at any time," she warned.

He ran his hands down her body, inside her open robe. "We're as good as married, and you won't change your mind."

"I think you're a little too sure of yourself."

"If I am, it's only because a very wicked woman seduced me tonight."

Melanie sighed as his hands slid down and then up her thighs, lingering where she wanted them most. "I should probably have a word with her."

Zachary chuckled softly. "I wouldn't."

"No? You mean you weren't shocked by her actions?"

"Perhaps I was, a little, but I think she hoped I'd enjoy being shocked."

"And did you?"

His mouth brushed gently over hers as he whispered, "The truth is, I can't think of anything I would have enjoyed more."

Chapter 19

Melanie chuckled happily as Caroline let go of her father's hand and ran into the room, almost falling into her arms. She was in the sitting room of her family's country estate, on the floor holding her new nephew, Tommy, against her. Upon spying her mother and the baby, Caroline jealously hugged her and tried to climb over the baby to get closer. "Careful, darling, you'll hurt the baby."

Melanie placed Caroline on her lap and together they inspected the baby. "Isn't he pretty?"

"Pweedy."

"Can you say baby?"

"Baby," Caroline responded dutifully.

Melanie grinned as Zachary poured himself a glass of water, sat in one of the room's many chairs, and contented himself by watching the goings-on. "She's so clever." Melanie accentuated the word with a grunting hug. "Only one year old and yet she can say so many words."

"She's *too* clever, if the truth be told."

Melanie smiled. "What do you mean?"

"It means, I'll have to watch my language. While I was looking at your father's horses, I said, *d-a-m-n*." Zachary spelled the word. "And this little one," he nodded toward his daughter, "felt the need to repeat it at least a dozen times."

Melanie laughed. "If you keep it up, she'll have a lot to teach Tommy one day." Directing her comment to Caroline, she added, "Daddy will have to watch what he says, won't he sweetheart?"

"Daddy," Caroline said as she tried to lift Tommy's closed eyelids.

Mary, the baby's nurse, came into the room. "It's time for Tommy's feeding, ma'am."

Melanie allowed the woman to take the baby. "If you like, I could take Caroline upstairs. She could play in the nursery for a bit."

Melanie nodded and Mary took the children upstairs. With Zachary's help, she rose from the floor. They sat together on the settee. "Why didn't you wait for me? I wanted to show you the property."

Zachary knew what that meant. They'd been here five days and she'd claimed to want to show him the property every day, but in all that time, they had yet to see more than a certain copse of trees about a mile from the house. "I couldn't wait all morning for you to get up," he said. I have to go to London this afternoon."

"All morning? You call sleeping until nine o'clock 'all morning'?"

"Farmers get up with the sun. Have you forgotten?"

Melanie's eyes were filled with laughter as she replied, "I too could have awakened with the sun had not a certain man kept me up for most of the night."

Since he'd promised her father that no scandal would touch upon her, it had taken some bold persuasion on Melanie's part to convince him to meet with her, outside the house, after everyone had gone to bed.

"When a lady wears only a silk robe and carries a blanket, she shouldn't be surprised, I think, to find herself very late in returning to her room."

Melanie grinned at her own wickedness. "I never made love outside before."

"I know." A moment passed before he asked, "What did you think of it?"

Barely able to contain a grin, she shrugged. "It was enjoyable, I suppose."

Zachary chuckled. "You suppose that, do you? One might get the impression that it was more than enjoyable, what with all that moaning and then later . . . well, it's just lucky the gardener didn't awaken at your cries."

"I only moaned because a stick poked me in my back."

Zachary's gaze grew suspiciously innocent. "Did you cry out then because something else began to poke at you?"

Melanie laughed. And then, turning in her seat, anticipation showing clearly in her dark eyes, she said, "I have wonderful news."

"What kind?"

"Susan told me this morning that she and William are thinking of moving to the colonies. William already has a few investments there and thinks the opportunity to make money is boundless."

"That sounds nice."

Melanie pulled back a little, her eyes narrowing. "Don't get too excited," she said dryly. "You might have a fainting spell."

Zachary grinned at her sarcasm. He grabbed her and brought her to sit on his lap. "All right, it's wonderful."

"It's better than wonderful. It will be perfect," she insisted. "Especially if they live close to us."

"Are they thinking of settling in Williamsburg?"

"Susan said William isn't sure yet."

"If she's anything like you, she'll convince him to buy the property next to ours."

Melanie laughed at his easy acknowledgment of the power she held over him. "Wouldn't that be wonderful? I could see her every day and the children would grow up together. But best of all, Father would not stay here alone."

"No," Zachary agreed. "If both his daughters are settled in the colonies, he won't be far behind."

Zachary had met Susan and her baby upon his arrival there. She was a pleasant woman, more sophisticated than Melanie perhaps, but obviously every bit as uncaring in regards to Zachary's inferior social rank. Because Melanie loved him, Susan accepted him. Zachary only hoped her husband would do the same. William had yet to arrive at the house, business affairs having kept him in London. Zachary prayed for Melanie's sake that the two of them would get along.

"Susan is planning a weeklong house party. She knows such fascinating people."

Melanie felt Zachary stiffen. She leaned back and frowned. If she wasn't mistaken, Zachary's complexion had grown gray. "What's the matter?"

"You mean she has parties that last an entire week?"

"Of course. Why?"

"Melanie, you might as well know, I'm not much at socializing."

"Really?" she said with some exaggeration. "I never would have imagined."

"I'll probably disgrace you."

"You'll probably have all the women hanging on your every word and I'll be furious."

"My every word? You mean when I talk about planting?"

"I don't think it will matter much what you talk about." She narrowed her gaze. "As a matter of fact, I think it wouldn't hurt if we spent a few days in the city instead. I'm supposed to be in seclusion, after all."

Zachary couldn't have been more delighted at the thought that Melanie might be jealous. Still he was wise enough not to share his thoughts. Instead he hugged her tightly against him.

The fact was, he was more than willing to forgo the party. Still he found himself saying, "We'll be married in a few months. It's nonsense for you to remain in seclusion, especially since we'll probably be on our way back to Virginia before anyone realizes you are having a baby."

"Zachary, Father is very old-fashioned. It won't hurt to allow him his way, just this once."

Zachary agreed that Melanie should stay in the country, but not because she was going to have a baby. She should stay because her soon-to-be-former husband had tried to kill her a number of times. Zachary hoped the man wasn't even aware that she was back in England.

Because business had brought Harry Stone to the city early this morning, it had been arranged that Zachary would join him there. They were to settle particulars about the coming wedding. Zachary assumed that meant Melanie's dowry. Zachary thought he just might mention the coming house party and suggest that the fewer people who knew about Melanie's presence, the better.

He and Melanie were silent for a long moment before he said, "I like you in pink."

"So far you've liked me in everything."

"And most especially in nothing."

Melanie ran her hand over his chest. "I've been thinking."

"About what?"

"That you might like to take the horses for a ride. I could have a picnic packed and we could spend the day exploring."

Zachary knew exactly what kind of exploration she had in mind. He sighed in disappointment. "Tomorrow. I have to see your father today, remember?"

"When will you be back?"

"Late, I expect."

She sighed. "And Father will be with you."

Zachary moaned as her hand slid to his lap. It was impossible to resist this woman. "I'll step outside for a smoke. Leave the doors to the balcony open."

Waverly Townsend sat at his desk in his London town house, his mind on Duncan upstairs waiting for him. A fire took the dampness from the room, burning cheerily in the grate as he opened the small packet of papers that had just been delivered and scanned the cover letter. His face went suddenly white with shock.

Melanie was back. Alive and in England. Was the bloody woman a damn cat? How many times must he send someone to kill the bitch?

He dropped the letter from Harry Stone on his desk, his gaze taking in the legal document wanting only his signature for a quick and final demise of his marriage. He almost laughed at the thought. It was impossible. He'd never sign it now. He didn't care about Stone's barely veiled threats. He'd simply deny every accusation the man made.

He would refuse her an annulment, even knowing there would be a scandal. He'd survive the scandal.

It would be only her word against his. She had no real proof of his sexual preferences . . . or that he had tried to kill her.

What he couldn't survive without was her money.

He poured himself a drink. He had to think. There had to be a way. There always was. All he had to do was find it.

The letter suggested he make an appointment with her father, later this afternoon. Townsend thought it a good idea. She wanted an annulment. He wanted her money. Perhaps he could pretend to agree with her desires, if his desires also were met.

He smiled at the thought. Yes, that might work out very well.

Then he'd be completely free of suspicion when his wife died. And she would die, of course.

The problem was how? Obviously he couldn't trust anyone else to do the job right. And this might be his last chance.

He'd have to do it himself.

First thing was to find out where she was staying. She wasn't in London, he was sure, or word of her return would have reached him earlier. That meant, unless she was actually in hiding, she was at Stone's country house.

He called his manservant into his study.

Hunt was a quiet man, infallibly discreet. His young wife had already given him two children and was growing heavy with another. Because of his need to provide for them, he'd learned early on to close an eye to the goings-on when the duke was in residence. Hunt supposed the aristocracy were all alike; they all had a secret or two. And it was a manservant's job to keep those secrets.

Hunt asked no questions, but followed orders as any well-trained servant might. It took only a few hours to travel the forty miles to the Stone country home and then back.

His mission was to see if the house was in use. It took but a glance for him to realize it was.

"The Duke of Elderbury is here to see you, sir," Harry Stone's assistant announced.

Harry checked his watch. "He's early. Zachary, would you like to stay?"

Zachary almost jumped at the chance. The truth was, he'd like to kill the bastard who had so abused Melanie. He nodded.

"Show him in, James."

The duke entered Harry's office with a flourish. His cloak was lined in scarlet satin, his clothes impeccable. Everything about the man looked perfect, from his hair and pure white gloves to the soft sheen of his Italian leather boots. There was no denying his station, for his bearing and confidence exclaimed them loudly. And yet Harry was very well aware that the man's clothing and manners hid the most vile of natures. It took quite a bit of control for him to stay seated, for he itched to put his hands around the bastard's neck.

Townsend hardly noticed the man sitting near the desk. He supposed he was another assistant and instantly dismissed him as irrelevant. Waverly Townsend had no idea how dangerous the man was to him.

The duke smiled and sat uninvited opposite his father-in-law. "Shall we get right down to business?"

Harry wondered what business Townsend meant. As far as he was concerned, the duke would sign the papers and be done with it. "Of course."

"I take it the duchess is unhappy and wants to end our union."

"To put it bluntly, sir, at the moment I'm short of funds."

Harry's voice was ominously low. "You tried to kill my daughter, sir. Do you think I care about your finances?"

The duke looked stunned. "Mr. Stone, I swear—"

"You might swear on a stack of Bibles, but it will do you no good."

"I promise you, I haven't a clue as to why you would think such a thing."

"I think it because the woman who tried to kill Melanie told her you sent her."

"What woman? Whoever she was, she was lying."

"Is Melanie lying as well when she says you preferred men to her?"

"You'll never prove it. It's her word against mine."

Harry knew the swine was right. They could never

"I thought an amount equal to her dowry might do nicely."

"Did you?" Harry would have paid twice that to secure his daughter's freedom. Still he hated this man as he'd never hated another, and it galled him to hand over one shiny penny. There was a long moment of silence before Harry managed to put aside his hatred long enough for sanity to regain control. He breathed a deep sigh, "I'll have the money deposited in your bank today, before closing."

"And tomorrow you'll have the papers, all, as they say, signed, sealed, and delivered." Townsend smiled again, "Now that we've settled our little business, I wish you a good day, sir."

"Get out of my office Townsend, before I kill you on the spot."

Zachary watched the man leave Mr. Stone's office with all the ceremony and splendor with which he had arrived. He frowned. "You're going to pay him off?"

"I have little choice, I think."

Zachary knew he was right. "The man is dirt, but dangerous. Melanie can't breathe easy until he has nothing to gain by her death." The papers couldn't be signed soon enough to suit him. "Will you be ready to leave soon?"

Harry shook his head. "I might stay in the city tonight. I have a number of appointments this afternoon. Besides, I want to be here tomorrow when the papers arrive. You can stay at the town house, if you like."

Zachary shook his head. "I don't want to leave Melanie alone that long." He rose to his feet. "I don't trust him." He nodded toward the door. "There's no telling what he might do."

"He doesn't know where she is."

"Suppose he finds out?"

Zachary left the office and stopped for a quick dinner. An hour later he was on his way home to her.

The Duke was informed of the results of his servant's errand an hour after he returned from his meeting with Stone. "Thank you, Hunt," he said, his tone revealing none of his excitement. "I'll be leaving for the Continent early tomorrow morning. I expect to be staying on a bit. You can see to my packing as soon as you're able."

"Yes, sir. I'll start now."

Townsend nodded as the man gave a small bow and moved toward the stairs. It never occurred to Townsend to elicit his servant's silence. He took for granted that word of the ride to the country would be held in strictest confidence. And, of course, it was.

Zachary reined his horse to a stop at the driveway entrance and walked the animal the rest of the way to the barn. There a servant saw that the horse was unsaddled, rubbed down, and then left in his stall as Zachary headed for the house.

It was late, the house was dark, and everyone was asleep. Zachary decided to enter by way of Melanie's balcony, rather than awaken a servant, for he knew all the doors would be locked.

A trellis stood a few feet to the right. He climbed it easily. A moment later he was inside her room.

It took only a moment for his eyes to adjust to the darkness. Zachary quickly stripped away his clothes and was soon beside her, listening to her sleepy sigh as she unconsciously made room for him in the bed.

His mouth touched her warm flesh; his hands reached beneath her night dress. Melanie awakened with a smile of delight. "That feels lovely."

"Mmm," Zachary murmured against her throat. "It does."

"Who are you?"

Zachary pulled back and laughed quietly at the question. "I'm the cookie man, remember?"

"Oh yes, the cookies. Can you find them?"

Zachary's hand moved up her thighs, coming to rest at the beckoning warmth. "I think I have."

Later, lying replete and satisfied in each others arms, they spoke of the future, of the home they would share, of their child on the way and the children that would follow.

"*How* many?" Melanie asked, her voice rising.

He made a shushing sound. "Lower your voice. No one is supposed to know I'm here, remember."

Melanie made a conscious effort. "I thought you said six."

"I did."

"Zachary, I think we should have spoken about this before. Don't you think six is an awful lot?"

"Spoken before when?"

"I don't know."

He cuddled her against him and ran his hand down her back, cupping her backside and squeezing it delightfully. "Stop that, we're having a conversation," she protested.

"I know. And if I want to win, I'd best take every advantage."

Melanie giggled softly.

"It might not be six. We can't know what the future might bring."

"You're right about that, I suppose, but *six?*"

Zachary laughed and brought her closer against him. "We might have eight."

"Good Lord, eight babies," Melanie said, slightly stunned.

"Suppose we work on one at a time. That way you can get used to the idea."

His mouth drifted from her throat down her chest, working its way toward a prize of luscious softness.

Melanie's back arched and her voice grew husky as she murmured, "Zachary, we've already accomplished one."

He smiled at her teasing. "Practice. We've got to keep in practice."

"Oh, I see. Lest we forget how?"

"Exactly."

The next morning, Townsend sent his trunks to the docks. An hour later, he and Duncan bought their tickets and made sure they were seen boarding the ship. Arrangements were made with a porter for their luggage to be stored until Townsend sent a convenience from the winery. Also mentioned was the fact that the duke was feeling poorly and it would be appreciated if he were not disturbed during the short trip to France.

No one saw them disembark hours later. Seconds before the ship took sail, Townsend and Duncan walked down the gangplank, black capes covering their clothes. The two men went immediately to the first livery and hired horses.

It was imperative that everyone believe he had left England a day before the terrible tragedy that was soon to occur. He'd leave, in fact, soon after, under another name of course. He had every intention of being at his French vineyard when the terrible news came. He'd have to return to England for the funeral, but he imagined he could manage the inconvenience.

There was no need to hurry. Mistakes could easily be made by hurrying. Tonight would be soon enough to see his plan come to fruition. And after tonight he'd be free at last, free and rich.

Harry Stone waited impatiently for the papers to arrive. When the noon hour approached and they still had not, he left his office and went directly to the duke's residence. Harry left moments later, after being informed that the duke had left for the Continent early that morning.

At first Harry imagined that the man had merely cheated him out of a great deal of money. It wasn't until later that he remembered Zachary's comments. It wasn't until then that fear stole his breath away.

He raced his horse out of London.

Two hours later, Melanie was descending the stairs, dressed for dinner, when her father almost stormed through the front door. "What's the matter?" she asked.

"It's probably nothing. I just wanted to make sure you were all right."

Zachary arrived on the landing just then. "What does that mean, probably nothing?"

"The papers never came. And I need a drink." Harry entered the sitting room and poured a neat glass of whiskey.

Melanie followed him and sat down. She watched her father swallow his drink, only to refill the glass. She shot Zachary a worried glance. "Something is the matter," she said.

"I went to his place. His man said he left for the Continent early this morning. I had a bad feeling about the whole business so I hurried here." He tried to produce a smile of reassurance and didn't quite succeed. "It's probably nothing."

It took only a second for Melanie to realize it probably *was* something. Townsend was clearly up to no good. Obviously he had a plan in mind. And judging by his past actions, Melanie had no doubt that the plan was of some sinister nature. Filled with sudden trepidation, she began to pace.

"I think you shouldn't ignore your instincts. He's up to something. We all know it," Zachary said.

They all silently agreed.

"Which means he's going to try to kill her again."

Melanie made a small sound and Zachary took her into his arms. "Don't be afraid. He won't hurt you. I swear it." He rocked her against him for a moment before he said, "From now on someone should stand guard at the door. At all the doors."

Harry nodded and left the room, to see the deed done. He returned moments later and made no mention of the fact that Zachary still held his daughter in his arms. "I think we should return to the city," Harry said. "I have more people at my disposal there. She'll be safer."

Zachary nodded. "Tomorrow. We might be playing into his hands if we travel at night."

Harry agreed. Both men were thinking of the last time Melanie had made a run for the city and the kidnappers who had stopped the coach.

"Bessie is about your size," Zachary said, mentioning one of the kitchen maids. "Borrow one of her dresses and we'll go on horseback. If he's watching, he'll think you're a servant." Zachary hesitated before adding, "Better yet, wear trousers. Samuel." He nodded toward the boy sitting at the front door. "He must have an extra pair. With your hair under a hat, everyone will think you're a boy."

"What about my face?"

"We'll wrap the lower half in a scarf."

Later at dinner, when Susan learned of their suspicions, she wanted to instantly quit the house. She was dissuaded of the notion, however, upon realizing how closely she resembled her sister. Both women were of about the same size. Both had black hair. Susan knew she could easily be mistaken for her sister. Almost immediately after dinner she went to her room, where she stayed with Tommy, waiting for the long night to end.

Zachary and Harry knew they'd find no rest this night. They sat in the drawing room, fully prepared to wait out the darkness, fully prepared for a confrontation should Townsend dare to show his face. It was nine o'clock. It would be nine or ten hours before they could leave for the city with any degree of safety.

Harry took two handguns from their place on his study wall. They lay primed and loaded on a nearby table. His hunting guns were also ready.

The hands on the grandfather clock seemed to stand still. Melanie had never known time to pass so slowly.

Zachary checked the upstairs, most particularly the nursery. Finding it empty he soon discovered Caroline with Ellen. He had just returned to the drawing room when the clock chimed ten. "On any normal night, we'd be retiring now," he said.

"Zachary, I couldn't possibly sleep," Melanie replied.

Fully understanding her anxiety, Zachary nodded. "Have the servants put out the candles. If he's out there, we don't want him to notice anything unusual."

"I'll do it," Harry said. To his daughter, he added, "You stay where you are."

While he was gone, the house servants and cook retired for the night in rooms on the third floor.

The minute her father came back, Melanie said, "I've been thinking. We might be imagining Townsend's evil intent."

"I don't think so," Zachary answered.

"What are you doing?" she asked her father.

"Closing the curtains," he replied.

"Don't. They're always left open," Zachary warned."

"And if he's out there?" Harry asked. "We're easy targets. Even with the candles out, the fire provides enough light for him to see the entire room."

"Not along this wall. Especially not in that corner behind the chair," Zachary said, nodding behind him.

"I think you should go upstairs." Harry directed the comment toward his daughter.

Melanie shook her head. "I'm not leaving Zachary."

Harry turned his attention toward his future son-in-law. "Talk some sense into her, will you?"

"Melanie's room is no safer, sir. The balcony can be easily reached by way of the trellis."

Harry hadn't a doubt the man knew that fact from personal experience. *Damn*, the sooner he got these two hot blooded young people married, the sooner he could stop worrying about the disgrace that constantly threatened her name.

"But your father is right about the danger." Zachary brought Melanie behind the chair in the corner. He threw a cushion to the floor. "You'll be comfortable enough here, I think." He sat himself directly under the window. With a handgun at his side and two muskets primed and ready, there was no way that anyone was going to get to her, not without killing him first.

"What about the other bedrooms?" Harry asked.

"Melanie's room is the only one that needs watching, I think."

"Well, since the upstairs is so easily reached, I'd best station myself there," Harry decided.

Melanie listened as he climbed the stairs, listened until his footsteps faded into silence. It was only then that she turned to Zachary with a smile. "Father knows you were in my room last night."

"He knows I was in your room. He doesn't know it was last night."

"Why can't I sit next to you?"

"You're safer over there."

"But you're not."

"I won't be able to see anything from behind the chair."

Zachary smiled as she looked around the chair and frowned. "When we get you back to London, we'll find out if Townsend has really left for the Continent. If he hasn't, I'm not leaving you and I don't care what your father says."

"That could be a problem."

"I know. I'd rather he didn't hate me."

"Will you hate the man Caroline takes up with?"

"Caroline will not be taking up with a man. I've been seriously considering sending her to a convent."

Melanie laughed softly. "Wouldn't want her to take up with a man like you, I take it."

"I'd have to kill the bastard."

"Should I be insulted?"

"Why?"

"The intimacies we share are all right for me, but not for your daughter?"

"I love you, so the intimacies we share are exactly right." He hesitated a second and then his voice lowered, "Did you hear that?"

"It's Susan. She's pacing again."

"She has Tommy with her. Caroline is with Ellen. I don't mind telling you I knew some terror when I saw Caroline's bed empty."

"I can imagine."

"We shouldn't talk for a bit. If he's close by, he might hear us."

Melanie shivered at the thought. She felt so helpless, like a tiny creature being sought out by a huge animal hungry for his next meal. "I'm afraid. Let me sit by you."

Zachary crawled to her side, dragging his weapons with him. His arm around her, he cuddled her close against him. "Better?"

"Yes, much."

"You might as well sleep for awhile. You didn't get much last night."

Melanie chuckled remembering last night and the reason why she had not slept. Still she said nothing. Zachary had said they'd best not talk, and she thought he was probably right. Moments later, with her head cushioned on his chest, her breathing grew deeper and more regular. Zachary knew she was asleep.

The clock had just chimed two when he placed his hand over her softly parted lips and whispered, "Don't make a sound. Are you awake?"

Melanie came immediately awake and nodded.

"They're here."

"They? What did he mean by 'they?' "

And as if he could read her thoughts, Zachary said, "There are two of them. One is climbing the trellis to your room. The other has just come in through the dining room window."

Melanie nodded again, her heart pounding with terror.

"Promise me you'll stay here."

She nodded, so frightened she couldn't trust her voice to tell him to be careful. Instead she took him in a desperate embrace. Zachary released himself and whispered, "Don't worry. I'll be careful."

The fire in the grate was out. The two men had lost their advantage by waiting so long. Now only the moon cast a small patch of light upon the floor as Zachary crawled from behind the chair.

A boot scraped on the floor opposite the sitting room. The man was moving about.

Having studied the room earlier, mentally preparing for just this moment, Zachary made his way to the doorway. He stood there waiting for the man to step into the hallway.

Zachary steadied his breathing, knowing surprise would carry the moment. He waited in absolute silence, ready at any moment to pounce, and then frowned as a light suddenly flashed. Zachary wondered why the man would be so foolish as to light a match. He hadn't long to think on the oddity before he heard the swooshing sound of fire running up the wall.

The man was setting fire to the house and all Zachary could think was his baby was sleeping upstairs. He fought back the urge to run for the stairs, knowing he couldn't show himself. Not yet.

He had a minute. He had at least that. And then almost before Zachary realized it, the man was in the hallway, heading directly for this room, no doubt set upon starting another fire.

"Hold it right there," Zachary said, the gun aimed at the man's heart. And then from the side of his eye, Zachary saw movement. Too late he realized it was Melanie. Too late because the man took the opportunity and threw the jug he held.

It hit Zachary's hand and his gun fell to the floor.

In the end all the intruder could do was cry out for pity and protect his face as best he could.

The boy guarding the front door was long gone, as was the one at the back. Women were running down the stairs, a few falling over the two struggling men in their attempt to exit the house.

The dining room was ablaze. Melanie picked up the gun Zachary had dropped and ordered in a cool, clear voice, "Get away from him. Do it *now!*"

The intruder staggered almost drunkenly to his feet. He might have run then. What with the fire licking at his heels he no doubt should have, but he didn't. Instead he reached into his waistband for a gun.

Zachary's chest heaved from exertion. He turned toward Melanie. She didn't see the fire behind her licking at the wallpaper. She never saw it jump to her skirt. In a second she'd be completely enveloped by flames. Zachary forgot about his assailant, forgot everything but his lady. He charged forward, his body slammed with some force against her, just as Melanie pulled the trigger.

The assailant was propelled backward. The side of his head hit the first step as he fell dead.

Zachary beat upon the hem of her smoldering skirt. And then taking Melanie against him, he half dragged, half carried her from the house.

At last the fire was out, thanks to the help of a score of servants jostling buckets of water and beating the flames with blankets. Luckily the blaze had been contained almost solely to the dining room and part of the hall. Although black soot covered almost everything, the country estate had fared fairly well.

The same couldn't be said for the Duke and his

friend, who were both dead. Melanie felt almost guilty, her happiness was so great.

They would all leave for a nearby inn in a few minutes. In the meantime Melanie and Zachary stood in the dark sitting room, holding each other, silently giving thanks that they and all they loved still lived.

"I love you."

"I know." She tightened her hold at his neck.

"I tell you that all the time. It wouldn't hurt for you to say as much back to me."

Melanie chuckled. "Don't I say it enough?"

"No."

"You know what they say about actions speaking louder than words."

Zachary suddenly pulled back, holding her at arms length. "And what the bloody hell did you think you were doing standing in the doorway of a room that was on fire?"

"What the bloody hell did you think you were doing, fighting with a madman?"

"Don't change the subject."

"If I hadn't stood there, you'd probably be dead now. And then what? I'd be a widow before I was a wife." Zachary grinned at the nonsensical remark. "And you're the one who changed the subject."

Zachary pulled her against him, squeezing her tight as he fought back the horror of seeing her dress aflame. "I never want to be that scared again."

"You won't be. I promise."

They held each other for a long time before he said, "Melanie, you might as well tell me now, so I'm prepared. Am I never going to get in the last word?"

"That depends, I think, on where you are and what we're doing when you say it." Melanie ran her hand boldly over his backside and grinned at his low laughter.

"Good God almighty, can the two of you not stop that for a minute?" Harry Stone exclaimed, coming over to them.

Melanie laughed. Zachary did not release her, but she did turn in his arms and lean her back comfortably against him. "I imagine I could manage to stop for a minute, Father."

Harry breathed a hopeless sigh. His daughter faced certain catastrophe unless ... "I'm afraid the two of you will have to get married tomorrow, the next day at the latest. I'll manage a special license."

Zachary's gaze grew warm with anticipation, but Melanie complained, "Tomorrow? But I haven't anything to wear. All I own is bound to smell of smoke."

Zachary whispered close to her ear. "Find something. You're not going to need it for more than an hour."

And perhaps for the first time, perhaps for the only time Melanie dutifully said, "I'll find something."

Epilogue

Virginia Colony
Eighteen months later

Melanie took a tiny dress from the box of baby clothes. "Isn't this pretty?" she asked.

Zachary stood behind his wife in their spacious bedroom and grinned broadly. "Yes, it is. Are you trying to tell me something?" His fingers reached for the ivory buttons that ran down her back.

Melanie gave him a sharp look. "No. Our little Zach is only a year old. I'm not ready for another one just yet." She sighed, enjoying the sensation of Zachary's rough cheek upon her bare shoulder. "The dress is for Susan's new baby. Gray Cloud said it would be a girl. William wasn't exactly thrilled to hear the news, but you were right. I think he's starting to like Gray Cloud."

"She has that effect on people."

"I'm so glad you convinced her to live near us for at least part of the year. I need her help almost every day."

"And especially her help to have babies."

"Yes, well, it might be a while before I need her for that again."

Melanie might not have known it, but Zachary was of a mind to speed that process along.

"I know it will be a girl, and absolutely gorgeous."

"Who's gorgeous?"

"Zachary, you're not listening to me again."

"That's because I'm busy doing something else," he said nibbling at her exposed shoulder, discarding the pins that held her hair in place.

"Father was here today."

"Was he?" he asked as he managed to get her arms out of her dress. It wasn't until her petticoats dropped to the floor that he asked, "What did he want?"

"He said the price of tobacco went up again."

Zachary laughed. He was already a rich man and had enough tobacco to fill two warehouses. The contents of both were to be auctioned off tomorrow, in fact. "Is that all he wanted?"

"Mostly." She glanced at the French doors that opened onto a terrace and the St. James River below. "We should close the curtains."

Zachary did as she asked. A moment later he was back at her side.

"Oh, Father did say something else."

"What?" Zachary asked, not really hearing, for he had finally managed to bring her chemise over her hips and added it to the growing pile at her feet. Zachary would never understand why his wife insisted on wearing so many clothes.

"He's getting married."

"That's nice," Zachary said as her drawers followed her chemise. "Stand over by the mirror. I want to see."

"And you can't without a mirror?"

"Not all of you at once."

"You didn't ask me who he was marrying."

Zachary stood behind her and watched his hands as they moved over her body. He frowned. "Who is who marrying?" he asked, wondering what she was talking about.

"My father."

"Your father is getting married?"

"Right away, as far as I can tell," she said as she turned to dispose of his clothes.

Zachary allowed her the pleasure and did his share to help as he said, "Go ahead, tell me he's gotten Mrs. What's-Her-Name in the family way."

Melanie laughed at the thought. "She's going to be my stepmother. I think it's time you got her name straight."

"Her name will be Mrs. Stone, if she's your stepmother. I'll call her Augusta."

"So what do you think?"

Naked, he turned her toward the mirror again. "I think you're gorgeous."

"I mean about Father getting married."

"It doesn't bother you, does it?"

"No, I rather like the idea. I hate to see him alone all the time."

Zachary could have told her that her father probably wasn't alone as often as she supposed. Twice, during his early morning rides to his office in town, Zachary had seen his father-in-law coming from the widow's drive. Both times it had been far too early for a respectable morning visit.

"Why don't we think about that later. I have something else in mind right now."

Melanie laughed, a low, soft, seductive sound. "I can't imagine what that could be," she said as he brought her into his arms and carried her to their bed.

"The fact is, Melanie, we're in desperate need of more children."

"Odd, but I hadn't noticed."

"Susan is on her second."

"We already have two."

"But Susan doesn't have a large plantation to run. I need every hand I can get."

"And that's why you want more children?"

"I know they'll be small at first, but they'll soon grow."

"Is that really the reason?"

Zachary laughed. "It's one of them, but I have another."

"What?"

"Just close your eyes and I'll show you."

"If I close my eyes, I won't be able to see."

"There are times when we can see best with our eyes closed."

Melanie did as he asked and then ran her hands down his body, lingering where he loved her to linger the most. "You mean like this?"

Zachary sighed his pleasure. "You're getting the idea."

Avon Romantic Treasures

Unforgettable, enthralling love stories,
sparkling with passion and adventure
from Romance's bestselling authors

CAPTIVES OF THE NIGHT *by Loretta Chase*
76648-5/$4.99 US/$5.99 Can

CHEYENNE'S SHADOW *by Deborah Camp*
76739-2/$4.99 US/$5.99 Can

FORTUNE'S BRIDE *by Judith E. French*
76866-6/$4.99 US/$5.99 Can

GABRIEL'S BRIDE *by Samantha James*
77547-6/$4.99 US/$5.99 Can

COMANCHE FLAME *by Genell Dellin*
77524-7/ $4.99 US/ $5.99 Can

WITH ONE LOOK *by Jennifer Horsman*
77596-4/ $4.99 US/ $5.99 Can

LORD OF THUNDER *by Emma Merritt*
77290-6/ $4.99 US/ $5.99 Can

RUNAWAY BRIDE *by Deborah Gordon*
77758-4/$4.99 US/$5.99 Can